DAMIEN TYSON

ZIP CODE
(IN)JUSTICE

A NOVEL BY
NANETTE M. BUCHANAN

Copyright 2024 by Nanette M. Buchanan

All rights reserved. This novel is a work of fiction. Any reference to actual events, establishments, organizations, locales or persons, living or dead, is intended only to give the fiction a sense of reality and authenticity. Other names, characters and incidents are either products of the author's imagination or used fictitiously. No part of this book may be reproduced, stored in a retrieval system, or transmitted by any means, electronic, mechanical, photocopying, recording, or otherwise, without written permission from the author.

ISBN: 978-1-962402-49-1

Type of Work: Literary Fiction, Women's Fiction
Creation Date: November 2023
First Edition: July 2024
Cover Design: I Pen Books/Fideli Publishing

Published by
I Pen Books
www.NanetteMBuchanan.com

ACKNOWLEDGMENTS

To those who have lost loved ones to a system that has fallen short of its promises to protect and serve, I send my sincere condolences. Looking for justice, a way to move on beyond the tears only to hear of it happening over and over… I pray for a solution. To heal we must reveal, make public, take the blinders off and be awaken. This is my attempt through this writing to give thought, relief and maybe closer, though fictional, I realize…the root of the problem is a daily reality.

To my family

Staying with me, my support, my voice when I have gone silent has meant the most to me. Understanding my need to vent as the characters and the storylines become a blur has kept me on this journey. I pray that you give yourself the credit and commitment you've given me, because this is so much more than a nod of acceptance or approval. You've proven once again that without you I wouldn't find comfort and the freedom to write. Thank you for allowing me to be who I am with my pen.

To my readers

This genre is what I love… a good mystery, suspense-filled and one you just can't seem to put down. Cold cases have always interested me. I've often wondered why, or when one decides to no longer look for the clues or the reasons for a crime. Does the inconclusive evidence ever weigh on the mind of the investigator? Do they ever wonder if they deeply missed something that could resolve the case? Is it just a systematic way of dismissing what needed to be said or done?

Thank you for your ongoing support… and if you love a good mystery, that story that brings you satisfaction… I'm sure this won't disappoint. After all, I had you in mind as I always do when I Pen.

FOREWORD

When choosing this topic for the second book in the Damien Tyson, Cold Case Series I thought of the blatant injustices that have been revealed throughout history. History is repeating itself or if we just tell the truth… nothing has changed. Although in a more sophisticated manner, it is the same. Prejudice, racism, bigotry, separatism, and yes that almighty privilege has boiled over. From the pages of history, a fire that was smoldering has caught and is setting flames across our nation. We can no longer blame it on the time… the misunderstanding of ancestors. The fears of losing the privileges, their rights, the need to suppress other races because they didn't want to be dominated as they had dominated others can no longer be an excuse. Yet here we are years, decades later and those fears govern our living.

So, as we look at the laws that govern us throughout these states that are no longer united… I have chosen this topic to explore. This cold case series was not chosen because of the injustices of the recent days. I questioned what our society's so-called justice is; what we have felt for years and what you will feel as you read this book. That is why I call my writing "reality" fiction. Though the characters don't exist, the story is a reality that is lived daily.

The title Zip Code Injustice … just the title defines the reality we are faced with today. If there had been zip codes or registered areas in history, I'm sure the injustice may have been tagged to the plantations, the homeless neighborhoods, the sections of town where immigrants lived, the lower income communities. There were those who opposed the system, those who fought injustice, and those who lost their homes and lives during the fight. Today we question which side another may stand on, and in many cases, we can't tell the difference. It's a hard divide but it's impossible not to see injustice is no longer smoldering. There's truth in this novel that we must face as a multi-cultural, multi-racial, multi-whatever society. My prayer is that we put out the fires before they consume us all.

CHAPTER 1

Damien reached for the alarm and pushed the snooze button off as he lifted his head from his pillow. It didn't matter how many times he hit snooze he wouldn't recoup the hours of sleep he missed. His new sleep pattern was now a habit. After dinner, reading and binging on missed movies, he often didn't turn off his thoughts or the television until after two in the morning. There was always something on the television that caught his attention.

"Damn cable." Damien spoke aloud as he sat up. The phone rang which reminded him it was no longer the weekend. No one called him early on the weekend. He shook his head as the phone rang again.

"What's up man?" Jeffrey Porter sounded as though he had been up for hours. Damien frowned wondering how late it was.

"Porter, hey am I missing something or am I late?"

"Listen, I just wanted to remind you that those numbers went in last week. Prepare yourself brother, I'm sure you're due for a sit-in with the 'untouchables' or even the higher-ups. I don't know the order of the meetings, but I'm sure there will be meetings."

"Funny. Yeah, I'm sure they'll be looking for a way to question the report."

"They gave it a six-month run. What if they decide the game is over and we're back on the unit where we should be? You know solving the cases before they become closed, or cold?"

"What? You don't love our Cold Case Unit?"

"Sir, this has become work. You may not have noticed but we've asked for help and got crickets. Me, Kai, and you for the first, what three months? Now I ain't knocking old girl, Ms. White or Montez, but neither of them is real investigators."

"Porter, wait what time is it?"

"Six-thirty man. Why, ain't you up?"

"Never mind all that. Listen, Ms. White is there for analytics, we need her. Montez is an Investigator, he's new but I'd rather have someone I can groom. You know what I mean?"

"Okay, he'll catch up, I guess. So, this is the first report Ms. White compiled for us. What are they looking for?"

"Us to skip steps, forget procedures, ignore protocol. You know what they're looking for, better than that what aren't they looking for? I believe the report will stir some emotions. Especially Sheers and his boys. I told Ms. White numbers only. They'll have to ask where we are with any other information. Montez is looking into the numbers and making notes of the connections. I'm sure it will dig up what they've covered with unsuspected dirt."

"What? Why? If they want a report to give justification as to why the minorities are stuck on a unit that never really existed before why give them more to feed on? Really man, the unit was just a storage unit that was managed poorly. We don't even have enough crime in our district for this nonsense."

"You'd be surprised. Moorestown ain't that far from the circle of crimes in the cities. Crime is up and I'm sure the rise will increase the number of cases that have been pushed to the side."

"I'm just wondering why they would give this task to us. I mean these reports go to the commissioner and the governor."

"Exactly, and the thought is we won't know how to cover the mistakes. Look, I don't think this Cold Case Unit was a punishment. You're right, it was a unit that was a part of the Records Division. I think someone higher than the 'untouchables' have set their sights on a few cases. For that reason alone, we've been sent to fix the errors found."

"Okay, so we set it up, get things going and just as it's time to bust the guilty parties, the unit is crushed? Man, that's bull. They got us out of the way so they could do their dirt?"

"No, I think it's to find the dirt."

"So, has the meeting been set?"

"No, I haven't heard anything yet. Look you grab the coffee today. Please don't forget Kai's latte."

"Look all this special ordering stuff. She needs a man."

"It's just us man. Stop whining. I'll see you in the office. Oh, and since you called me this early, I know you'll be on time."

"What? That's you, bro'. Oh, call Amir he's got a surprise for you."

Jeffrey hung up the phone before Damien could ask what the surprise was. The three were good friends but Jeffrey and Damien were reassigned to the Cold Case Unit and Detective Amir Stands was with the DEA.

They worked together in the past, but since the reassignments they saw each other more during personal gatherings than professional business.

Damien didn't give the call another thought. He jumped in the shower. He'd arrive at work as he had most mornings before eight and before any of the team. Early mornings gave him time to prepare mentally for the unnecessary calls and interruptions. It had been more than a week for either and he was sure as Jeffrey pointed out the report would cause the phone to ring.

Kai left a copy of the report Phyllis White had prepared on his desk. Kai was the secretary who worked with him on the Homicide Unit. When he asked would she transfer to the Cold Case Unit she was excited to leave. After working with Tyson and Porter, known as Batman and Robin for eight years, she couldn't see herself working with the remaining investigators.

Tyson asked for more staff after being informed by Porter and Kai the workload was impossible for the three of them. He decided he needed the data recorded and Phyllis White, an older African American woman was chosen. He didn't mind and neither did she. Her no nonsense attitude didn't bother the humor he nor Porter displayed and after three months she blended in with the trio. Javier Montez joined them just before they declared the unit made it a year. He was a level one Investigator and was eager to learn. Tyson told him his longevity with the unit depended on his loyalty.

Tyson requested more staff, a secretary for Porter, an assistant for Ms. White, and at least two more investigators. As Porter said, he got crickets for an answer. The small team worked hard for six months. The report though reflective of only the first quarter, was thoroughly prepared.

He thumbed through the pages again, smiling. The questions would vary, dates, times, and connections. They'd want the details which were compiled but not submitted. They'd ask for total cases, types, locations, and what arrests were made.

No questions were asked previously about the responses. The report didn't detail missing evidence or what officers were assigned to any of the cases. Porter held on to that information and if necessary, that's what was reinvestigated to guarantee all was done before the case was declared officially closed. The duo concluded that was why they couldn't get more investigators. No one wanted an investigation reopened or the initial team questioned about their evidence. The lack of thorough written reports, or the dismissal of follow-up procedures was undeniably the reason for more than half of the files they reviewed. The others were violations within the department, overlooked injustice, altered paperwork, and unexplained conclusions.

It didn't bother Damien as much as it had his partner. It was just another reason to keep them from any new cases. It also caused the "untouchables" to be careful. Any case with their names on it were suspect according to Tyson and Porter. Philip Sheers blew his promotion and possibly being the head of the Homicide Unit once he lost his second civil lawsuit. He remained on the force by a thread and his father's reputation. Once Tyson was reassigned and promoted, Sheers made known his dislike for many of the minorities who made rank before him. Tyson was at the top of his list.

Damien Tyson didn't have family that ranked high enough to give him a pass. His background in the military spoke louder than any of the positions held by his uncles and father. Captain Dennis Worthy and Chief Walter Michaels kept an eye on Tyson without anyone in the department knowing they were his guardian angels. They too had to overcome the department's racial divide before becoming top officials. They saw Tyson and possibly Porter following in their shadow. It was their secret and they kept it well hidden.

Tyson didn't speak often to either the Captain or the Chief nor did they have any personal connections. Tyson did what he was told and asked no questions, but he could read between the lines. Someone was watching them. The test, would he submit the report he requested Ms. White to compile? Now looking over the results, he knew it would turn heads.

The phone rang, bringing Damien out of his deep thought. "Hello?"

"Hey, man, good morning. How was your weekend?"

"I should be asking you that. How was that vacation? Did you and Ms. Wilson have a good time?"

"We're good. Listen, uh, we've got some news to share with you."

"You finally asked her to marry you?"

"C'mon Tyson. No, she's uh content with being Ms. Wilson for now."

"Wow. You okay with that?"

"No but listen that's not what I called for."

"Amir, you don't sound right. What's going on?"

"We've been transferred. Well, you know Leana has been asking to be in investigations and me…"

"What, where are you transferred to?"

"We both are on board with you. I don't know who pulled this off but no title changes yet just reassignments."

"What?"

"Yeah, I wasn't told to change my ID or badge. Neither was she. We were told to report to you, uh, this morning."

"What the hell?"

"I didn't think you knew about it. I know you would have said something. Listen, I guess we'll all find out together."

CHAPTER 2

The office door's buzzer sounded indicating someone was waiting to be let in just as the phone rang. It was still early, before eight, and Damien couldn't figure out why there was so much activity going on during his "*quiet time.*"

"Good morning," he said speaking in the receiver. He held his hand up signaling the two people who were on the opposite side of the large bay windowed entrance.

The spacious room was once filled with rows of filing cabinets and cold case evidence boxes. It took more than a month to have the cabinets and boxes moved to an adjacent storage area. Once they were moved the space was converted and separated into office space with cubicles. Cubicles made ready for Ms. White and Kai and other vacant cubicles that Damien told them would be filled with staff eventually. It was more than enough room, but it had been an unfulfilled vision for more than six months. Tyson and Porter had offices that were attached to the abandoned space on the opposite side of the main entrance. The two adjacent rooms that were once used for storage of both cold case and closed files, were immediately approved for renovations. The outdated policies and procedures, manuals and other outdated memorandums were on the burn list. After going through questionable files, Porter thought it would be a bad idea to throw out any of what they may need later. They sorted through the manuals, reorganized the dusty fragile memos and addendums, and sent it all in new boxes to the basement. The Cold Case Unit looked complete even if the workload was more than any of them expected. After receiving the message explained on the phone to report to the captain's office at eight-thirty Tyson tapped the button to release the door lock. He stood to greet the persons who he was certain had mistakenly stumbled into his unit.

"I'm sorry, good morning. How can I help you?"

Damien assumed the spokesperson, who introduced herself as Investigator Miller, had been given the information regarding the assignment for herself and the young man who just nodded in agreement. He couldn't tell if they had worked together long, however, Investigator Miller had no problem with the needed introduction and explanation for their presence.

"I'm pleased to meet you Detective Tyson, I'm Investigator Laneice Miller and this is Investigator Carlton Chambers. We were reassigned to the Cold Case Unit?" She paused after the awkward question but continued, realizing there may have been some confusion. "You seem to be unaware of our assignment here."

"Yes, surprised is more like it, but hey, this is the Cold Case Unit so, welcome."

Investigator Laneice Miller's name wasn't one Tyson recognized. Her appearance reminded him of the recruits he would teach at least once a year when he was invited to the training academy. She was polished, which he noted immediately, complete with the two-piece pant suit and black pump heeled shoes. Her hair was pulled back into a neatly braided bun. Although he thought he could detect an accent, he couldn't tell if she was from an island or had a well-practiced "interview" tone. Her cocoa brown tan led him to believe she may have been from an island, but she could have been a New York native. She was young and she'd have to be careful with many of the seasoned investigators. He'd be sure to check over her paperwork. He was curious why she was told to report to his unit.

Investigator Carlton Chambers' name was on a completely different list. He was one Tyson skipped over when asked did he want one of the new hires from the department. It wasn't a mark against the young Caucasian investigator. Tyson didn't trust Sheers giving him a list to choose from. The young man seemed nervous. His plaid shirt would cause Porter to question his mode of dress and suggest he remain in the office and not go in the field. After shaking the nervous investigator's hand, he understood why he stood silent as Miller explained their presence. They stood patiently as Tyson reviewed the paperwork Miller gave him confirming the introduction. He deliberately didn't rush reading through the paperwork. The two stood in silence waiting for his acknowledgement.

"Let me show you the conference area." Damien smiled trying to ease the apparent tension. "It's a kitchen area we're getting together. There's a refrigerator here if you decide to bring food or beverage. We share a lot of what we eat and drink. I'm sure you'll get the hang of everyone's likes and dislikes once you blend in. Also, if we need to have a round table discussion there's room, well, there was room for all the staff in this area. I guess I'll be ordering a larger table and chairs."

He led them to the next room which was closed off from the hall traffic and any other entries. "The bathroom and small lockers, if necessary, will be put here as well. Like the ones that are on the units you're from…which are?"

"Oh, I'm from the Records Division. I made Investigator about two months ago. I was hoping to go to the Fraud Unit but after doing the training rounds, I'm here. I guess this is the next training?" Miller looked at Chambers for his take on the transfer.

"I don't know. I just go where I'm told. I was at the front desk for a while and then I did a few months in the Evidence Unit. I didn't really do much." Chambers didn't look at Tyson or Miller as he spoke.

"When did you become an Investigator?" Tyson paused bracing himself for the answer.

"I've been, well, sir about a year. I wasn't assigned to any unit though. I've been floating between units."

"I see. Okay, well, you're here and that tells me the floating days, for the both of you is over. You'll train in this unit and be here if your work meets the standards. If you want to leave, believe it's not your fit, please let me know and I'll have you moved. As you probably know this is a working unit. More mental work than physical but it's work, nevertheless. I will introduce you to our Lead Investigator, Jeffrey Porter and he'll get you settled. I've been told there will be two other reassigned seasoned officers, Investigator Amir Stands and Investigator Leana Wilson who will be joining the unit as well. They will be your go to before asking me anything. You'll learn more from them, they do the hard work. I'm here if you need me, but they'll teach you. Kai Davis is our secretary and Ms. Phyllis White is our Data Analyst. Javier Montez works with Ms. White. He's an Investigator in training as well."

An overhead light flashed twice, and the buzzer sounded again.

"That light lets us know someone just came in the front office. Once you receive an entry code, you can open the door yourself. The buzzer sounds loudly. We use it when we're here alone." Tyson deliberately neglected to inform them of the locations of the cameras he requested be installed.

The two investigators followed Tyson to the front. Porter laughed when he saw Tyson and his new shadows.

"So, you didn't say we would be having company. Good morning. Forgive me for not having coffee for you. I guess there is now a real need for a coffeemaker."

"Yeah, listen, that meeting is at eight-thirty. This is Investigator Miller and Chambers; they've been assigned to us. Amir called. He and Wilson will be here in a minute. Introduce everyone, talk shop or whatever. I'll be back with what I know is the new game plan going forward. The reassignments confirm the game has officially begun."

Miller, Chambers, and Porter watched as Tyson went out the door. Porter wasn't much on hospitality and told them to pick one of the vacant cubicles and make it their home. He assured them they would feel better if they thought of themselves as team members and not spectators.

"Listen we all get to play on this team. Chambers, I'm sure you've missed a few sporting events that you would have loved to go to huh?"

"Yeah, I guess you're right?" Chambers seemed to be more comfortable with Porter.

"What about you Investigator Miller? Sports or Concert?"

"Well, who's playing?" she teased. "Then again, whose concert?"

"See Chambers, she's a team player and just like a woman, can't be direct."

They laughed, as the tension lost its presence. Porter gave them a pass as he watched them decide on their choice of office space. Miller pointed to where Chambers should set himself up and he willingly followed her suggestion. Porter listened as they lowered their voices to talk between them. He wondered if the unit was now being watched. He was sure one of them was in training to be an "untouchable."

CHAPTER 3

The halls were filling with fast-paced movement and chatter. Damien proceeded slowly to the elevators. He wasn't in a rush. The Cold Case Unit had been moved to the first floor in the rear of the building. There was no need to argue about the location. Tyson and Porter knew their newly assigned duties as well as the location was to get them out of the spotlight. The archived files and records were kept in the basement, away from the building's daily traffic and that satisfied them as well. The main floor had many of the offices for community access. Complaints, licenses, fingerprinting, and the main precinct all kept the floor buzzing.

Damien nodded and smiled as he greeted workers and visitors while waiting for the elevator. The second floor was for active cases, investigations, bookings, and releases. The third floor held the offices of the Captain and Chief. There were also large rooms for training, meetings, and press conferences. Tyson dreaded the hours ahead knowing he'd be sitting in one of the hard, wooden chairs that outlined one of the large conference tables. He joined a few investigators on the elevator. Everyone seemed to be heading to the same floor.

The elevator doors opened to the hall adorned with photographs of past and present top-ranking officials and department heads. The other investigators exchanged "good day" wishes as they parted and went their separate ways. Damien was the only one headed toward the conference room. The polished floors and woodwork glistened. It was as though the third floor had a different cleaning crew. It always reminded him of a museum, everything in place and ready for presentation. The gold handles on the door marked 'Grand Assembly' were on every door on the floor. It was an impressive appearance for those who visited. A show of excellence for the media broadcasts.

Tyson smiled as he entered the room. Captain Worthy and Chief Michaels were the only ones in the huge room. He was sure this meeting was pre-arranged so they would get a heads up on what to expect. They were standing with their cups of coffee that Tyson smelled the moment he opened the door. There was a table set with food, as it was for all meetings held in the conference room. There were muffins, doughnuts, and bagels, coffee, tea, lemons, all the morning temptations for those who were to be seated for the discussion. Tyson glanced at his watch wondering if he was too early.

Captain Worthy was the first to greet him. "Good morning, detective or should I call you by that nickname they've got floating around for you."

Worthy and Michaels approached him with their hands outreached. The men shook hands and smiled.

"Hey man, get you some coffee and anything else you want. There's plenty here on the table." Michaels stepped to the side allowing Tyson a full view of the breakfast table setting.

"No, thank you. I've had my morning cup."

"You may need a few before we leave here this morning," teased Chief Michaels.

Tyson hoped his expression didn't speak. He had no plan to be there all morning. The chief and captain had always been close. Their years of service in the department began as recruits together. Tyson was an officer they watched go through the ranks. He deliberately downplayed their fatherly mannerism toward him. They understood but catered to him from a distance. It was the relationship that caused friction with Porter, him, and the "untouchables." No one understood the relationship that developed over the years with a white chief, black captain, and a detective, who had what a few called the "Batman Syndrome."

The men took seats at the mahogany table. There were folders placed at the front of the table stacked between the three of them. Tyson's curiosity raised again. Before he could ask any questions, Captain Worthy spoke up as he placed his personal folder and pen on the table.

"As you know we received your quarterly reports. Your unit has had quite a year. I mean you started with file cabinets and boxes. I must say and I'm sure the Chief will agree, you did a hell of a job pulling it together. Look Damien, we wanted you to be here early to let you know or talk about what you already know. There are those who questioned my choice in promoting you to Lead Detective, hell they know what's next. Master Investigator Tyson."

"Damien, your captain is being nice. Listen I'm white and I've always been white. I can't attest to what you may have, had, or will have to go through with your new position in this department. You're a target with that group you labeled 'untouchables.' Others know that too. They call the captain here your black godfather."

"Yeah, and he's your white godfather." Worthy and Michaels laughed as Tyson took a slow deep breath.

"Now we try to stay away from any of your reports, paperwork, or implementations. The last thing you need to have is that group thinking we put you in a position to come down on them. You've set a wheel in motion with this data and I'm sure you've got reports to back the data you submitted. I don't believe you deliberately intended on this falling on any particular group, but it did."

Tyson waited, hoping he wouldn't have to argue with the two men he admired. The data had no names attached, but it was evident they knew those associated with the cases mentioned. The silence that fell between them was a bit uncomfortable.

"Are you waiting for me to agree with you?" Damien asked. "Listen, you know me and my work ethics. I do what is necessary to finalize cases. You assigned me to cold cases and closed cases that should, be closed or for the most part have no loose ends. The data we documented in these reports indicates that there are cases that were closed without some of the basic investigation requirements being met. We found cases where questions weren't asked of witnesses, victims, or family members. There were those that were missing evidence that was recorded as collected. Pictures of items that should have been boxed or bagged are just thrown in without any indication of how they fit into the investigation of any case. My investigators even found evidence tagged and labeled in the wrong boxes. We had to begin a data report as we were boxing up cases making room for office space. We needed to be sure to close cases that were without a doubt cold cases or trial requirements were met."

"Wait Damien," Chief Michaels interrupted. "Are you saying that this information was not from investigations you were currently looking into?"

"Yes sir. Over the past year we've handled the cases as they come into the unit as well as cases that were filed and recorded as closed. Once it was evident that there were more questions unanswered in certain areas I wanted to know why. We investigated a few and found what the report shows. Not only was it obvious that the cases shouldn't have been closed but each of them involved the communities of our struggling citizens. The cases in some areas, or zip codes are just not investigated according to the regulations. It was as though each of the cases were filled with information from the day of the crime and little to none afterward."

"Damien, is this report complete and if not, how many more files do you have to go through?"

"No, that's not the question Worthy. Damien, where is the rest of the report?"

The two men leaned in hoping to hear there would be no other cases or hidden surprises.

"The data you have is from the boxes we separated. You see, they were marked complete, inactive, or defined as dead end. Some were to simply be filed as court documents as they've been closed in the courts. I thought once we took over the unit, we would be working on new cases that were coming into the unit. A few, as expected linked to others in the files, but I never thought the cases would be linked or considered closed without thorough investigations for completeness. So, we separated them. There're more than one hundred cases that come from the same communities. They show the lack of the basics, evidence that was never disclosed in court appearances, DNA evidence that was reported but not filed, and yes it connects people. I just don't know why. I can speculate but that would only compound the crimes committed in most of the cases. Chief, I submitted the report without details, just numbers and pointing out that these areas are being targeted. If we delve deeper, my unit is prepared to submit the missing pieces, the names connected, and the measures to complete the investigations."

Damien sat back in his seat as the two men looked through the folders they had in hand. Chief Michaels pulled out his pen and began placing checkmarks on the pages. Captain Worthy pointed to a few lines he read and murmured a few words to the chief.

"Tyson, we've been told this report is in the Governor's office?" Michaels looked over his tortoise rimmed glasses awaiting the answer.

"Sir, yes sir. I was informed all reports that referred to court cases, arrests, or pending litigation should be copied to the Governor's office. I don't know who handles them or if they do. I mean some of these cases go back a few years. I don't know if anyone reviewed these reports prior to me taking over the unit."

"You're absolutely right. I have that question as well. Why haven't we been made aware of these cases before you were assigned to the unit? Where did this information hide?"

"Listen, what we don't want is to have the Governor's office questioning us about the past and what we're faced with. Did you find any old data reports like the one you have here?"

"Not to my knowledge Captain. Ms. White and Investigator Montez created the data and realized the patterns and the names associated. Nothing was hidden. In plain sight sir, however, it seems once the out box was marked cold, no one opened them. We couldn't properly index them for storage without being certain of the case and category each fell in. The report submitted to the Governor's Office followed the guidelines as requested, only numbers for each category. It was Porter and I that noticed there seemed to be a pattern. We decided that an incomplete report would reflect on the unit. We decided to keep the specifics for a latter report if you or the Chief requested it."

"The meeting here is at eleven this morning. We brought you in early to get a heads-up on what you and the members of your unit know. I told Michaels there was more to this mess. This has Sheers' name all over it. You don't have to say so, but they've been behind this kind of shit for years. Chief we've got to stay on top of this or our boy here won't become the next Master Investigator or Captain."

Tyson shook his head and smiled knowing the captain was teasing him.

"Listen it's nine thirty now. Let's go over some of these higher numbers. I'm sure Tina Justlin will be heading the investigation. Oh, that's right. Damien you and Porter, as well as your unit will be working closely with State Principal Investigator Justlin for this investigation per the governor. It went that far. She'll be receiving all reports and delving into those files seeking completed investigations. It is my prayer that we won't find loose ends that would cause the state any monetary payments to families or those who have been incarcerated because of court cases."

"Wait Captain, I'm not following you." Damien understood but needed to hear it again.

"Listen we need to put a lid on this can of worms. I wish we could handle this internally, but the governor's office has the same report. They don't want this leaking to the community activists. Damien, look, all we need is for them to know that blacks and Latinos have been slighted. Locked up without a thorough investigation or whatever else is missing. If it's happening in this small area of Philadelphia, what are the numbers statewide."

"Tina Justlin, sharp woman. Yes indeed!" The chief smiled as though he was in a dream state.

"Michaels, really? Tyson don't pay him any mind. She's a beauty but we'll let you determine that on your own. Only black woman that turns his head."

"Tyson don't believe him. I just try to keep my professional appearance. You know for the record. Man, she is fine. We get along too. So, don't you or Porter try your Batman and Robin charms on her. I'm still working up my courage to approach her."

The chief paused waiting for the captain to answer. The three men laughed. Damien had only heard conversations about Investigator Justlin. She was always the center of attention when federal cases went to trial or were held up because of investigations. She seemed to be the voice for the media.

"So, when you say we'll be working with her as she investigates just what does that mean?"

"Seems like the major cities have not done any reports such as these. Now the governor wants to see the numbers throughout the state. You and Porter are to answer any questions so that it gets done. I think they're on the drug and weapon cases, but I'm sure our data has to do with other crimes in the community as well. We need numbers and well, Tina will explain exactly what they want at eleven."

The captain closed his folder and waited for the chief's response.

"Yes, well at eleven you and Porter need to be here. Did you get your four people this morning? Stands and Wilson will be with you and cover any new cases your unit gets while you're on assignment. The two rookies are there to help with the data or wherever you can use them."

"Uh, Chief. I appreciate the help and I could really use another two investigators. Miller and Chambers? I don't know if they're ready for an assignment this sensitive. They're still learning. Have they been told they'd be working with this particular report?"

"No, I got a call to send you two. I gave the list to the desk sergeant and told him to get the lieutenant to choose who he wanted to send to you. Is there a problem with either of them?"

"No just, Chambers hasn't done much anywhere. Something about him…"

"Just ain't right. I should have bet you chief. They sent one of theirs. A white boy looking for a spot to play their game." The conversation had obviously been discussed between the two men.

"Listen Worthy, I'm white and I ain't one of theirs. I was young and looking for a spot when I came to the department too."

"So, what are you saying? You know what they do when they find one wet behind his ears."

"Let's let Tyson decide. What do you think about him Damien?"

The two leaned in again as if to hear him clearly. Damien smiled and shook his head slowly.

"The two of you. You've been together too long. Chambers was on a list Sheers handed to me. I didn't pick from that list, yet he reported this morning."

"So, who did you choose?" The temperament of the chief changed quickly.

"Chief, I know what you're thinking. It's not because he's white, it's because Sheers gave me the list. I chose Miller and another kid. Knight or Knowles, something like that."

"Do you still have the list Sheers gave you?"

Damien opened his folder and handed the chief the list. He pointed to a few names on the list showing the captain the names.

"Tyson, you'll get your choice. I'll get Knight and Knowles over to you. Was there another on the list? Do you need another?

"I'll have Porter text the next two choices if that's okay. Just in case these two don't work out."

"Listen, the Captain can get that text. Worthy, get whoever it is over to the unit before lunch. Tyson, I need you and Porter back here no later than twelve. That will give me time to discuss what the governor is probably shoving down our throats.

Bring the data with you for the meeting. Just so you know, you're right, Chambers may be one of what's the name you gave them?"

"The 'untouchables.'"

"He's new and from what I understand the cocky type. He needs to be around you and Porter. Teach him a thing or two. In light of this investigation, they wanted to slip one in. He confirms their fear. Watch Miller closely too. Worthy check out the names Porter sends you. There may be some problems brewing. You're on to something Tyson now let's see how deep their shit is."

CHAPTER 4

Investigator Tina Justlin looked over the notes she prepared while traveling to the meeting she was sure would change policies and procedures for report submissions once all the data was revealed. As the state's Principal Investigator, Justlin was assigned to the administrative duties for all sponsored projects in compliance with applicable laws and regulations. However, her duties in the state weren't limited to just overseeing and monitoring state projects, funding, and administrative contracts. She handled union negotiations and was tasked with being the community liaison for the Department of Criminal Justice. Her experience as an investigator, as well as her affiliation and ability to manage matters as a liaison with the media and personnel, gave her a level up with the governor's office. Many of the policies and procedures regarding community, media, policing, and litigation gave her a prestigious title and new position in the governor's office.

Although her title was Principal Investigator for the state of Philadelphia, her reach went from the highest position to the clerk in each of the police units. She held a position of authority, but her demeanor hadn't changed since she had been an officer on patrol. She never forgot working as an officer in the office or walking a beat in the communities. Tina was able to talk with activist, religious leaders, community groups and organizations as well as the officers that patrolled the neighborhoods. The media tried to extract state "secrets" only to find the information she would often give exclusively was deliberate and benefitted whomever she sought needed her backing. She was a secret weapon, only no one knew which side she would take. She declined many positions offered and after holding a tenure as captain and chief no one dared to question her decisions. Her reports and conclusions were backed by the governor's pen, and no one wanted the publicity from any of her investigations to fall on their department. Budget cuts were the least of anyone's worry, serious allegations meant there would be those who lost their careers and pensions. Her job was to save the state the embarrassment of litigation and court appearances.

Justlin's response when asked about the data that arrived sealed in a confidential marked envelope was a smile. She arranged a meeting with Captain Worthy and Chief Michaels requesting Investigators Tyson and Porter be in attendance to explain their findings. She didn't discuss the report with anyone else including the governor. He'd ask questions upon her return, questions she couldn't answer before the meeting.

The ride to Moore Township from her home was the same as her ride to the state office in Harrisburg, Pa. Often she would stay the week in Harrisburg to avoid the two-hour ride there and home each day. The courtesy of having a driver was extended, but she preferred to drive her own car. Returning to her old stomping grounds gave her a good feeling. She looked forward to the time away from her office. She estimated the reports and data comparisons would take a few weeks and she'd return to Harrisburg with her findings. There would be no need for media attention or any litigation.

She decided she'd be there as a state official the first few days and then she'd blend in to get a feel of what was made evident in the data. Someone was neglecting the communities they pledged to serve. Tina had a few questions of her own. *Were the officers connected to the data reported homegrown? Were they officers who lived outside of the community, had no ties to any of the internal organizations, and had formed their own not so secret group that met once a month?* She needed to confirm what she assumed.

The "untouchables" had a reputation that made a stench in other police departments throughout the state. Tina remembered the name Porter and Tyson gave them after a few were indicted in Allentown for conspiracy. They were right, now five years later, their criminal escapades were surfacing more with each major crime brought to the courts. They had connections and money, that kept them safe. She hoped the data did more than touch the surface. It was a chance to finally get justice throughout the communities. This would be her reward for the fights she didn't win as captain and chief. Her position in the State office would make a major difference in the fight.

The temperature was warm for Philly in early April. There was a morning breeze, without a chill, Tina grabbed her jacket from the back seat. She was glad she decided not to wear her navy-blue pant suit. It was a better fit for winter than mid-season. It reminded her of her dress uniform she wore for years while in the department. The chief and captain would be wearing theirs, the men would be in suits, so she chose russet and crème. The crème blouse was her favorite as she could wear it with many of her outfits. She decided on a russet pant suit. Pants were comfortable and after her years in service it became her norm. She chalked it up to working in a predominately male environment. Her shoulder length auburn brown hair was out, normally she'd pull it to a bun. Her make-up and accessories met her mirrored approval. She locked her car and walked to the main entrance.

She prepared herself for the professional greetings she received whenever she entered the building. The staff was prepared for her arrival, she could tell from those who scurried pass her and those who shot her a quick glance and fake smile. She skipped her usual stop at the coffee shop a few blocks away knowing there would be coffee and plenty of breakfast sweets waiting in the conference room. If she hadn't scheduled the morning meeting, she would have stopped in the offices of those she normally visited each time she came. It was business first and she wanted them to feel the serious ramifications they could be facing.

As she approached the elevator, she checked her watch comparing the time shown with the large clock over the entrance to the Mooretown's precinct. It was the Central District Headquarters. She smiled seeing her close friend waving at the glass door. It was ten forty-five, the meeting was scheduled for eleven.

"Girl, don't you go into that meeting with that look on your face," teased Officer Marcie Williams. She and Tina were friends on and off duty. They were closer now that Tina was not considered Marcie's political ally.

"What look? I must have been thinking. I'm good." Tina whispered, "They don't know what I'm looking for, so they're already scared, I'm sure."

"Hell, what are you looking for?"

"Marcie, girl I'll call you when I have a chance to talk. What are you doing for lunch?"

"I've got a few reports to complete. Nothing I can't put aside to eat. Also, maybe I can run something by you. I was gonna call you later anyway but maybe it will save me the unnecessary steps if I ask as I go."

"Whatever, oh, it will be a late lunch though. Maybe dinner would be better? I don't know how long this meeting will run and it is to be a detailed one."

"Wow, that serious. Yeah, dinner would be better. I don't want to be sitting with a growling stomach waiting for lunch at three." Marcie laughed at the smirk on Tina's face. "No, you will leave a sista hungry and remember hours later."

"Hey, at least I remember. Some of your so-called dates aren't that considerate."

"Ooo you know what? Is your boy gonna be at this meeting or just the captain?"

"No, the chief too. I still think I should have given him a play, white or not, he's got a swagger about him."

"Didn't you say you were avoiding the media? That would make the headlines."

"Why he's nice looking, fine for a white man. He's educated and not a racial or political radical. He's worth dating." Tina paused looking at her friend who remained silent. "Just not my type, I know. I just watch his demeanor and wonder. I hope the vibes about him are right. Although, I don't think it would work even now that I'm in Harrisburg."

"Tyson is another…well, you know. The list is short Tina, who are you watching these days. What about fake Blake… you're still seeing him?"

"Still seeing off and on. Nothing, he's nice but I don't see us being serious."

"Listen, we'll talk my sister. I want you to understand…"

"I know, don't look for another Jerrod. I guess it's a comparison thing like you said."

"Well, at least you're dating, it's getting better and that counts."

The two parted after Tina entered the elevator. She'd only have time to fill a cup of coffee and get a doughnut before the meeting would start. Perfect timing, there would be limited small talk.

CHAPTER 5

Tyson gave Porter a quick briefing promising to fill him in with details as they assigned their new personnel to jobs. He called the meeting after he told Chambers and Miller to report to the lieutenant in Personnel. Explaining the assignments to the seasoned staff was easy. Ms. White and Investigator Montez would continue sorting and gathering data. Stands and Wilson would go through the files that were pulled for the purpose of missing information as indicated on the boxes. There were more boxes than Tyson thought but he wanted the project to be completed, uncertain of what Investigator Justlin would be looking for.

"Listen, there's a set up somewhere in this. I told Porter this morning that either we're being tested to find this information or if we overlooked it, we would be blamed for not finding it. So, let's just get it done. Under no circumstance will Chambers and the others coming on the unit be allowed to handle any of this project. That includes emails, paperwork to be copied, or folders or any other material to be couriered anywhere. Until we know exactly who they are and why they are assigned here, they are to handle new cases that come in. That will keep them busy and out of the way. Stands, you and Wilson will be their go to. They are not to go to Ms. White or Montez with any questions. If they do let me or Porter know what they're asking. The captain thought it was strange that Sheers sent two that I didn't request. Those that I requested should be here this morning before twelve. Same assignment, new cases only."

He looked at everyone to get a sign of agreement. "Porter and I have to be upstairs in this meeting to explain to them how we found the information, and I'm sure they'll want the other information we have. You can check the book for what came in last week and where we are with the investigation. It's your call when you let them work on their own. Split up Chambers and Miller let them partner with the other two. That should shake up a few things. Did you guys see the case files we're talking about?"

"Yeah, Porter showed us what was going on. You guys got a good set up for it to have been less than a year in this spot. And you dug up dirt, I'm impressed you're living up to your names. Batman."

Everyone laughed including Tyson. "Well look, hold us down, you and Superwoman here," Tyson said smiling at Wilson. "Any problems don't hesitate—"

"To text, we know," they both replied.

Porter remained in the office after the others left to get settled in for the morning's work.

"So, will we get Knowles, Knight and two others? Suddenly, they want the unit staffed. Damn man, what did we stumble on?"

"Jeff, man, it seemed like the chief and the captain thought the problem wouldn't get this big. They knew something was brewing."

"Man, I can't believe there were no other reports. I mean what numbers did they turn in?"

"I guess we'll find out. Your girl will be sure of that."

"That's your girl. When she comes in, she checks on you."

"Go ahead with that. All about the titles man. No other interest, I'm sure."

"Batman, there's no reason to deny the attention the two of you give each other. Whispers and conversations, always tell another story." Porter teased knowing the response.

"Porter, Batman never got next to Catwoman because of the same problem. Justlin's life ain't private. Whoever she dates it will draw attention."

"Hey, why is that? I mean, seriously, why is she a media magnet?"

"You know they call her Justice, right? Well, she got that name shortly after making investigator. It was before her husband, Jerrod made Sergeant. There was a case where he arrested a guy during a domestic call. Bad one, the woman was damn near beat to death. He responded to the call along with a few others when back up was called. Anyway, they arrested the guy and found out he was in violation of trespassing, you know, the whole nine. So even without the beating he gave her and the dude that she claimed wasn't the new boyfriend, he was in trouble. Justlin's husband got into an argument with the new boyfriend at the hospital. Jerrod asked a few questions after questioning the woman at bedside. Man, the guy started arguing about the police not protecting her, you know yelling and screaming that if she died it would be the cop's fault.

The officer who was on duty at her room pushed the guy back out of Jerrod's face. About a week later the woman died. You know the case, I'm sure it was on the news for a few days before you transferred in. The dude waited outside the station and when Jerrod came out, shot him. Of course, there was enough armed enforcement to fire back. He was killed too. The media went on a frenzy. Of course, it wasn't about the ass, I think his name was Barnes, it wasn't about him. It was about us, law enforcement and how we reacted to the domestic call."

"So, Justlin stepped in and waged a war with the media."

"Porter, she had all kind of records. Stories they didn't air, protocol, policies and all kind of issues that hadn't been reported. They used her husband's death to get into the department's flaws. Now they may have had a reason, as some say, but they went about it wrong."

"Wow, or at the wrong time. If he hadn't been shot, they wouldn't have pressed the woman's death?"

"Porter, it's the same problem we've uncovered in those boxes. Lazy policing. They call Justlin, Justice, because she fought for the police and the woman. It was chaos for months but the next opening for captain she got it. Justice, as everyone teased man, she lived up to her name. I know you remember a few of those impromptu media coverages where everyone thought she slipped Sayers information that fell back on the department. Man, she uncovered some internal stuff, no one could prove how Sayers got the information. There's been a few incidents some for us, some against us, even some union situations. She's saved jobs and taken them. So, Investigator Justlin, Ms. Justice is handled with care. If one gets the opportunity to handle her at all. My luck with women…"

"Wow, that's deep man. She's an internal exterminator and the governor likes her huh?"

"Yep, that happened when she made chief. Didn't take long. She saved the state money, right or wrong. The state didn't pay and that's all that matters to them. So, get the rest of the files and information from Ms. White and get ready for this ride."

CHAPTER 6

"The governor has no idea what these numbers mean. That's why I'm here. I'm sure he can guess they're not what we want aired in the department, the community and least of all the media. Look if we can contain these numbers here, we'll be able to squash the backlash that the media will create."

"Okay, look Tina, how will they know? Everyone turns in their reports without knowing what any of the other city's report. So how would they know that these numbers are a problem at all. We don't know fully what they represent."

"True but we can trust that someone does. Listen I didn't even talk with the governor about what this could mean. I'm here with the two of you to tell you this is a problem. I see the same thing Tyson sees. Did you look at the districts this report covers and the numbers over the years? It's a problem Walter. You have been here the longest. We don't want you or any of the ranking staff to be questioned."

"Hell, I wasn't chief when this mess was going on."

"Yeah, but you were ranked. Look over the last say, ten years, five as captain, five as chief. Explain to the activist and media how you slept through these numbers. This report, if I remember correctly, goes back about eight years in one district. Missing person cases, rapes, murder, all with missing pieces. You've got at least twenty incarcerated that may have a case against us if there's no linking evidence. Stuff just written to change the look of the investigation. That won't do, people need to know we've done all we can do. It can't just be swept under the rug because we didn't follow through. I need to see the details for all the listed reports before we go statewide."

Worthy shook his head and tossed the folder he held in his hand on the table.

"Justice, the governor wants this mess to be looked into statewide?"

"No, I do."

The men were stunned." Why stir the pot?" questioned Michaels.

"I can't believe either of you are surprised. Worthy you're a captain. You're looking to retire as such or as chief. Michaels, you want your run to be clean, I assume. It's your report that stirred this pot. I can't ignore it and if it may be a statewide issue the media will find it. Better we do before they do. That's why your investigators will oversee getting your departmental information straight and have a strategy that others will follow. The numbers in other townships and cities may be alarming and we need to be ahead of what's coming."

"I can't say I disagree with that. So, what do we do with the findings? Re-opening these cases will take staffing and overtime."

"That's up to you Chief. Listen the time will be approved, and the so-called cold cases were never closed. It's those and the others where we have people incarcerated. Their lawyers will find a way to get retribution if we don't find the problem and have a reason for it. It can be handled without a raise of the eyebrow. Look, if you got information for any of the cases the boxes would be opened and followed through. So will these, reopen them and follow through. The problem is not closing the cases now, it's who didn't close them correctly before." Justlin looked between both men for an answer.

"Yeah, and why?" The captain got up from the table and went to the phone.

"So, what's the plan my dear? Are you driving from Harrisburg daily for this?" Michaels smiled hoping his question would break the ice that always seemed to get in the way of any conversation they had. He wanted to change the subject and breathe a minute.

Justlin smiled. It was obvious he was pleased to make small talk while they waited for Worthy to return to the table.

"No, I don't know how long this project would take so I'm home. Glad I didn't move to Harrisburg as someone suggested."

"I suggested that because, well you know. So much was going on. The media was on top of your every move. It just seemed that you had a new position and a new start there would have done you some good."

"Yeah, both did give me some relief. I usually stay there during the week. I have a place at the Residential Suites. The setup is not exactly home but it's not exactly a hotel and it's big enough for me. I come home on the weekends and whenever I don't want to stay there. It works out."

"Hmmm, and statewide assignments? I guess you're busy all weekend too."

"Not always. I take me-time. You know, social events with friends and relatives."

"I see. That's good to know." Michaels was glad he was getting further than the state agenda.

"So, what about you. Are you still fishing a lot?"

"Whenever I can. It's relaxing, lonely at times but I can take it over the hustle and bustle if I went into the city. I mean don't get me wrong. I do things other than fishing."

"I'm sure you do." Justlin glanced at the clock as Worthy returned to the table. She silently thanked him.

"Okay, the café staff will be up to take the breakfast doughnuts and things back. I had them set up for the staff. Originally, I thought you'd want all the Cold Case Unit staff here. So, I had them do all of this. We can order lunch when they come. I'm sure we'll be working through lunch. Porter and Tyson are on their way."

CHAPTER 7

"Knowles, sir, Mark."
Stands and Wilson turned their attention to Knight who injected his answer louder. "Knight. Gary Knight."
Montez added a deep sigh to the response.

Stands showed them their cubicles and told them he'd be with them in a minute. He and Wilson decided to wait for Miller and Chambers to return before explaining the job to any of them. They went to Ms. White and Montez' area, who had a larger cubicle. There they found the compiled files for them to review.

"So, what you think Stands, I mean they're new boots man. Can they really be tangled in this mess?" Montez watched the two officers as they came in and introduced themselves. He couldn't imagine them being caught in the thick of things already.

"Look man, the way I see it, they come in with an attitude. Did you notice how Knowles answered and then Knight answered entirely different. It's the arrogance. That, I know I'm better than you attitude. He's young though and he's got to be taught. If he is here to learn, well we taught you, didn't we?"

"Man, I didn't come on the force like that. I worked with you and Porter and learned what I needed but I never thought anyone owed me something. Sheesh… to get with Sheers and his boys. Ain't nobody got time to lick boots."

"Well, some do. I'd say Knight and Chambers are the two, but we'll see. So, Miller will partner with Knowles, and Knight will be with Chambers. After a month or so we'll switch it up if we don't burn them out before that. You know Porter and Tyson will be on them."

Wilson picked up a file from the stacked pile on the desk. "So. we're on paperwork patrol?"

"Nah, mama. We had to review the information in each case. See we look for what's missing, and you guys find out who, what, when and why. We give you as much information as we can but... let me see... look on the folder for the red marks. This one the dates don't line up with the reports or the court paperwork. Something is wrong and here, the evidence that's in this report is missing from the box."

Wilson read some of the report in the file and investigated the tagged box with the same file number. "So, Montez, you mean all of these have something wrong?" She questioned pointing to the boxes stacked in the office along the wall.

"Porter said they're some in his office, Tyson's office, and Montez how many are here?" questioned Stands.

"At least twenty-five to thirty. There may be more we haven't finished compiling files. These are the files completed. The boxes for the other files are in a storage room. It was a mess, now it's an organized mess."

Ms. White sighed. "You all have more than enough to be busy the rest of the year as I see it. But Tyson said there's a way to find out all of it, question the cops. I'm just your data clerk but if there's some dirt, questioning them may alert them."

Wilson smiled. "Ms. White, you're right. We need to have all the information in our hands before we talk to any of the names on any of the reports."

"Well, that's up to the boss, come on let's get these four in order. Let's learn what they know or want us to know. I'll go get them, meet us in the conference room. There's enough chairs there, right?"

Montez went with Wilson to be sure there would be room for everyone, and no files or boxes were in the area. Stands walked into the room and found the four getting acquainted. He thought it was a good sign. They felt comfortable enough to mingle, that didn't single any of them out. Miller, being the only female would have a difficult time. It swayed his thoughts, *She'd be perfect as one of the "untouchables."*

"So, hey guys, let's take this to the table. Can't really call it a conference room yet, but it will have to do. Glad to see you've introduced yourselves or did you know each other previously?"

Miller responded, "No, just met. All of us. Well, for me anyway."

The others didn't respond. Stands nodded making note that the men either didn't trust him or weren't comfortable with the assignment at all. There were water bottles placed in front of each seat.

"Look, we're not going to be this hospitable on a regular, so take advantage of this. These guys can attest to the fact that I don't do the sharing or doting thing."

"Yea, she doesn't. This is Investigator Leana Wilson, currently on the list for promotion to Lead Investigator. This is Investigator Javier Montez, Ms. Phyllis White is our Data Analyst. You guys know Lead Investigator Jeffrey Porter and Master or Chief Investigator Damien Tyson, and I'm Investigator Amir Stands. That's the unit. That's who you work for and with. Any questions about us or this unit, simply ask, but ask us. No one in any other unit will be able to tell you about us, the running of this unit, or what we do. You know what I mean? How, why, or what we do with each other, on duty and off is not to be discussed unless it's with one of us. It works so much easier and better when it stays in the unit. It's not like other units deliberately. We deal with… well let me ask. Who has over ten years in?"

Stands looked at each officer knowing none of them had that number of years in the department. Slowly Wilson, Montez, and Stands raised their hands.

"Check this now. Have any of you worked permanently assigned in more than three units?"

Again, there was no response from the younger officers. Wilson, Montez, and Stands raised their hands again.

"So, it's safe to assume that you are all waiting on the five-year promotional list for Investigator?" He paused waiting for them to reply. "Oh, c'mon, you at least took the test. Right?"

Miller and Knowles raised their hands.

"Okay, well what's holding the two of you back?" questioned Stands shifting his attention to the remaining two.

Knight and Chambers grinned. Knight replied bluntly, "Don't need the drama right now. I just want to get what the job has to offer."

"Oh, and not put in? I feel you. Something for nothing is always good."

"Nah, man ain't nobody…" Stands held up his hand stopping him mid-sentence.

"It's all good my man, you don't have to defend your reasons. Listen, there are many who want to float through twenty-five, thirty, to their pension and benefits. Understood, you ain't got no war with me. What about you Chambers?"

"I want to have a little more experience before I deal with that next level. Seems like it's more in depth. I've never been one about checking others, you know reports and such."

"Hmm, so you think just being an officer you can skip checking others, or reports?" Wilson questioned from across the room where she was leaning on the sink.

"No ma'am, it's just, you know. It seems in an Investigation Unit that's all you do."

"So, what about your reports. As a foot soldier you've got to write reports, follow-up situations, investigate, interrogate, whatever the situation is called for." Wilson walked closer to the table; all eyes focused on her.

"Listen, the job is about being sure we all do what's right for us and those we swore to protect. If that means I gotta check you, you checked. If it means I gotta investigate, that's what I'm going to do. Half-ass jobs will get us all caught out there, including those that just want to ride through to their pension. Listen, I hear you.

It's too early to decide which path. It's also a good idea to look down as many as you can, but baby boy, this ain't no pickup game. You can't just jump in and play a while."

"Yeah, and you can't get the playbook and take it to another team. You feel me." Stands replied looking at both Knight and Chambers. "You didn't pick this unit and you won't be asked to join. You were assigned here. Any and all issues, questions, problems, or complaints, come to me or Wilson. If we're not available let Montez know you need to speak to Porter or Tyson. Follow the chain of command and you won't have a problem. Do anything your way and you will be on patrol, for a while. Now, let's talk about cold cases."

Stands and Wilson grabbed a chair and sat at the table as Montez explained the process that had been followed on the unit for just over a year. The on-the-job training, as planned would fill the balance of their day. They would release the officers from their first day of training shortly after lunch.

Montez explained it wouldn't take long for them to understand the process. It was the work each case required before being sealed and labeled that would be time consuming. Stands and Wilson waited patiently for Porter and Tyson to return to the office. They all would have information to share.

CHAPTER 8

Justlin put down the file and slowly closed the cover. "You do realize that what's been reported can't just disappear without reason. We have just cause to open a State Bureau Investigation. It won't be limited to Moorestown Township. Once the media gets hold of it, or the community activists, they'll question comparisons with the other cities. These numbers are reflecting a small part of what may be a larger problem."

"Wait, what larger problem? Here, in Moorestown?" Captain Worthy questioned taking off his glasses. He was still reviewing the files Tyson and Porter brought with them to the meeting.

"No, statewide. Just what I told you and the captain this morning. The governor knows nothing about what these numbers represent. It's easy Chief. If there's ten unsolved rape cases here, there may be more than ten in Allentown. We can be sure that these numbers are low in comparison to the larger cities."

"So, you're speaking with certainty that officers throughout the state are doing this same half-ass investigating and reporting?" The captain asked knowing what Justlin's response would be.

"I hope not but I know this could light a flame that would burn through the state."

"What's next? We can't even tell you at this point how we're going to close these files properly. No one knows what we've stumbled upon. My concern is being certain from this point on things are done correctly. This was before I was assigned to the unit, and I wanted someone to be aware of what we found when we signed on. I'm not concerned with cleaning up a mess that we didn't create." Tyson spoke up before the conversation buried his concerns.

Porter could feel the tension building in Tyson's voice. He tapped his partner's foot with his to signal he wasn't using his professional demeanor. Tyson stopped talking and began tapping his pen on his pad.

"Look, I understand your frustration. Really Damien, I do. But what we have here can fall back on you, the unit and all of us if its tucked and ignored."

Damien waited to respond. Justlin's response confirmed his reasons for concern.

"So, tell me, why was I assigned to the unit? Huh? To clean up the shit y'all knew was going on? Tina, this report is required each quarter. I've been submitting numbers all year. No one questioned any of it until now. One year and now there's questions? Just humor me. Look at the first quarter, those numbers alone jump out at me as a problem. That's why I took the time to investigate each of the files. We went through a few more and found more. I had the team do a five-year analysis with the data we found. What you're looking at is what we found. I'm sure the deeper we dig…"

"The reports speak for themselves. What we don't know Tyson, is who? Who was behind the cover-up?" The captain asked hoping Tyson would have the answer.

"I don't think it was a cover-up." Porter spoke up for the first time in the two hours they had been there. "Look Tyson and I stumbled upon this and thought it best to set up a systematic way to file these botched investigations. There was no record what was missing in each box. The boxes are labeled, and, on each box, it's stated what is compiled in it. We went through a few because there were names, dates and other data that was misfiled or laying on desks, shelves, and whatever that was noticeably out of place. After we found those problems, we made notes and decided to compile the data. We were simply reorganizing a space that we were assigned to. There was no indication that there was a method to what was done or not done. Now we're causing the fire? Let it burn then."

Tyson tapped Porter's foot and smiled. Porter began tapping his pen on his pad. Both men were angered at the thought they would be blamed for the fiasco created over the years.

"Alright guys, I don't think Justlin is saying you or your unit is to blame. We all realize you're following a mess. You were not assigned there to be the fall guys. We didn't know there wasn't a method. Hell, there was what three shifts working there? One maybe two officers each shift. Who knows if they even knew what to do? Looking at this mess maybe they were just logging things into a filing system and assumed the contents were recorded elsewhere."

"Captain, you may have a point. It is done that way in many of the municipalities. The records of what is actually in the boxes or files is logged into computers within the precinct. The boxes are just filed. They're recorded in an on-unit log. You know, date, box number, aisle when they are placed there or taken out. More like a records room in the Cold Case Unit."

The men at the table nodded in agreement They hadn't given that any thought. Tyson gave a puzzled look as Chief Michaels rose from the table.

"I was thinking the same thing, Walter. What's that lieutenant's name?" Captain Worthy paused for the answer.

"Marshall. Hey, this is Chief Michaels," the chief said into the telephone on the wall, "Send Lieutenant Marshall to the conference room. Tell him now. Tina, you know Marshall. Damien you know him too, he started with you. Anyway, he was over the unit, but he had officers assigned to work the unit. I think he was a Sergeant then, but he'll know how the unit was run under him. That was some time ago, but those officers weren't regulars, it wasn't a permanent assignment. Tyson you and Porter were assigned there to get control of so many cases going cold. That's the beast we were trying to get in front of."

"Well gentlemen, that answers the question. Someone, or quite a few caught on to the files not being thoroughly looked through as reported. They could get away with not filing what was needed to call a case cold."

"No, Justlin, it's more than just filing the cases though they were incomplete. There's definitely more than a lack of concern. It's a deliberate action. Someone didn't do their job repeatedly. The data we found indicates that most of the cases are in the same zip codes, the same communities. Someone is deliberately ignoring the needs of those citizens and throwing the files and reports in a box. Labeling them cold, they were filed without officially being closed. The courts won't open the cases once that's done, and the lawyer's fees to re-open cold cases or those where a new trial may be ordered, well let's just say it's what poor folks can't afford."

"Porter's right. Who cares once the investigators close the case for lack of evidence, witness statements, or any other leads or someone is found guilty? File it under a corresponding number and done. Another minority locked up, pained, challenged, wronged and no one knows the police shut it down without a thought."

"Gentlemen, there's got to be records somewhere. Where are the initial files? You're telling me that the logs don't match the files; where's the electronic record? Please don't tell me that we're headed down a deeper hole."

"Look that space was simply storage for Cold Cases, closed records, and filings. We stumbled onto this misfiling mess. There's no data that we've found. In the computer, the cold cases go back about six years. Now granted some of the boxes do cover the years in the computer. Those are the ones we were able to trace. There's quite a few of those alone. I didn't bother to search anywhere else for missing files. Our report is based on the boxes."

The captain held his head. The chief put his glasses on and grabbed another file. The silence held the questions no one dared to ask. Marshall, a tall, lean, Caucasian man who looked more like a librarian than a lieutenant, entered the room and stopped before approaching the table.

"This don't seem like the place to be. What's up Chief?"

"Man take a seat and just listen."

After reacquainting himself with the others seated at the table and a briefing of what was in the folders and the report, Maurice Marshall could only shake his head.

"Say something man, I called you to find out what you know or think about this. We're trying to avoid a mess here. As you know Investigator Justlin is from the governor's office. We need to be able to answer any questions that will be asked about this report."

"Who turned in this report? Man, we never gave them this information," replied Marshall.

"Hold up. Marshall what are you saying?" Captain Worthy looked at Chief Michaels as though he'd answer.

"Hold on Dennis, don't look at me like I knew this shit was going on."

"Well Chief the reports we turned in didn't go into these details. You never required it. I mean you were the captain when I worked the unit. We never gave you this much information. We'd total the crimes, not the ethnicity, the zip codes, or none of this." Marshall pointed to the dates of the investigation, manpower hours, and other personnel included.

"Listen we didn't make up the form. That's what was stated and was required for each quarter and then totaled for the year. We didn't go out of our way to give extra information if that's what you're implying."

"Hold on Tyson, I'm not implying you or your unit did anything. I'm just saying this wasn't how we reported it."

"Well than you skipped some steps. This data report was in the computer and requested each quarter by the Chief's office. I looked for past reports. Even the reports you did file are not on the computer."

Damien waited for a response. Seeing no one had a rebuttal he continued.

"Look, I don't care what happens to the report. Do what you want with it. I just want it noted that my unit did what was requested. In light of what Investigator Justlin has brought to our attention we can water it down re-submit it to show whatever you want, but it doesn't cover the fact that investigations have be whitewashed, put to the side, and they're not closed according to the guidelines set by the department."

Justlin and Marshall spoke at the same time. "How many cases?" Porter shook his head slowly. He looked at Tyson, who just shrugged his shoulders, so he replied.

"We don't know."

CHAPTER 9

Tyson loosened his tie as he and Porter walked out of the room. They agreed to be available early the next morning for Investigator Justlin's visit to their unit. There was no plan of action, nor was there any further discussion regarding who was, or would be held accountable for the obvious infractions. The hall leading to the elevator was empty. Most of the personnel from the upper level had left the building, it was almost four o'clock.

They rode the elevator in silence, connected to their own thoughts and fury. The doors opened to more activity than expected. Porter frowned and looked at Tyson for his response.

"Hey, I don't need any other problems. Whatever it is, I'm sure Stands, or Wilson will fill us in."

Porter followed his partner without asking another question through the gathering to their office. The rotunda was lined with media, reporters and photographers, civilian staff, and police. There were those who were murmuring their questions just above a whisper and others that quickly walked through the crowd to the exit. A corded area was being put in place for them to stand behind and not block those employees exiting the building. A group of police officers made their way from the precinct to help control possible mayhem.

"Tyson, Porter!" The men could hear a woman's voice calling them just as they approached their unit's door.

"Hey, you guys up on this mess?" Samantha Sayers, a reporter from the Village Post, quick stepped across the marble floor. Smiling and waving her pen and pad with her photographer in tow, she asked again, "Did you hear the complaint being made by the Watson family lawyer? It's about that rape case." She paused only to see if their expression gave any indication that they knew what she was referring to. "C'mon, y'all the police, I know you know."

"I don't talk shop in public." Damien smiled and winked.

"So, do you know or not? I'll call you. There's your chief. I guess he'll try to squash this mess."

The reporter and the photographer hurried to where the makeshift staging area for politically correct comments would be made.

"Jeff, you see this shit right. This didn't just happen. Reporters, community, and the chief prepared to speak on the matter. He knew something was coming down the pike while we were meeting with them."

"Damn, that woman is fine! Every time I see her, I lose myself in a dream…" Porter replied.

"Man, shut-up!"

They laughed as they entered their unit.

"Hey, honey, we're home!" shouted Porter.

Ms. White was the first to emerge from the offices. "I'm glad you're home. Listen, I'll see y'all in the morning. It's been a mess all day with these phones. I left the messages as you asked Tyson, on your desk. Y'all let me know in the morning what to do with the data from those files."

"Wait, what files Ms. White?"

The no-nonsense Reports and Data Clerk had thirty years in the department. Starting as a young woman right out of high school there wasn't much gossip or so-called truth that she didn't know the facts about. She was a source of information most departments wanted. There were those who feared her technical knowledge and she did most of the computer training for the precinct. This gave her access to files that others couldn't reach. She became Damien's secret weapon years prior to her agreeing to join him and Porter on the unit. Being older than Tyson and the others, she brought some of the wisdom she gained in life and the experience dealing with many of the department heads. She enjoyed her job and lived in the community; her connections often were confused with her intentions, so she didn't give information to those that weren't a part of her circle.

"The message is on your desk, Watson, Roberts, and Crews, that's what all the stir is about out there," she answered pointing toward the front door. "You know those cases that lawyer has been complaining about. Well, I guess this time his questions will be answered. They can't duck and dodge it much more. That child, the young Watson girl told them it wasn't her boyfriend who beat her and molested her. You remember the Foster case. Anyway, they got the proof or something they needed to get that boy out of jail and lock up the guy that really did it. The case was closed once he went to jail but, Tyson, it's on the list with missing evidence. How did they lock him up?"

"Lawrence Fulton is the lawyer, yeah, I remember him coming into the office a few times. Damn, yeah, Ms. White, I have no idea. Listen, you have a good evening. I'll brief Montez and talk with you in the morning. Have a good night."

"Good night, all. Hey Kai called; she'll be in tomorrow. I thought she was on vacation. Well, good night." Ms. White spoke loud enough for Stands, Montez, and Wilson to hear her and reply. The trio came from her office and took chairs from the cubicles to sit and talk with Tyson and Porter. The two took a moment to put the files on their desk. Tyson hung up his jacket and put his tie in the desk drawer with the others he kept there. He returned to the front office empty handed and more relaxed. The noise in the rotunda grew louder so they all moved to their makeshift conference area.

"So, is this the kitchen, lunchroom, locker area, conference…what is this, man?" questioned Stands.

"You got jokes." Tyson said reaching to shake his hand before anyone took a seat. He walked over and hugged Wilson. "Glad to have you both onboard. Sorry you stepped into…"

"A pile of political B.S.," injected Porter as he entered the room. "What did Ms. White say about that mess out there?"

"It's connected. I'm sure Investigator Justlin will be on it in the morning. There's no way to get ahead of this mess. We've got to be prepared though, seriously. I want you all to know I stated in that meeting that none of these records prior to our existence here is to be put on us. So that mess out there," Damien pointed toward the outer wall, "that mess will be questioned the first thing by her, the captain, or the chief. So, we need those files pulled Montez if you or Ms. White didn't pull them."

"She asked me to pull them. They're in your office." Montez answered and stood.

"Where you going? We ain't dealing with that mess now. Let's talk about what I think is about to happen."

Montez sat down. Tyson gave them the information he and Porter were made aware of. He asked for questions and comments after he told them what Ms. White brought to his attention.

"Okay, so we keep the newbies on new cases. If they connect to any that are on the report it rolls over to you and possibly Investigator Justlin? You know if any of them are working with Sheers it will cause suspicion. We need to try not to alert them to what has been discovered."

Tyson answered Wilson before Porter could give his answer or thought. "Wait, Leana. Listen, we don't know how deep they're involved. I don't want it to look like we're just following their cases. Plus, I don't know how widespread this may be. All cases, regardless to who was on the case, if it shouldn't be marked closed is to be recorded and we need to find where the missing pieces lead us. Any connections to Sheers, I'll keep a separate report. Note it without being obvious."

"Listen man," replied Stands, "we need to keep an eye on Knight. I'm sure he's got a chip on his shoulder or he's giving the appearance of a 'know-it-all'. Either way, he's to be broken and watched."

"Hmmm, I thought it would be the two that came in this morning. Once we have a connection of any new cases to the ones on the list, Leana's right, get the newbies off the case. Don't make a big deal about it just don't give it back to them to delve into. If they ask a lot about it, it's to be watched."

Damien waited, looking over his team as they let the information given sink in. They all agreed the work would be tedious, but they'd get it done. Montez assured them that the reports would be updated again in the morning to include the recent cases. He hadn't cross-referenced any of them.

"It may be worse than we think, I mean a cross-reference could cause another problem."

"Montez, how?" Porter asked with a raised brow. "Man, we got the State Investigator here now. What could possibly be worse?"

"I don't know. I was just thinking aloud. Say we didn't find the rapist, now we have another rape, with new evidence that matches evidence noted or found in a case that we've deemed incomplete and definitely not cold or closed."

"Montez, that's good. That's what we want, connecting evidence, right?"

"Porter, I think what he's saying is we can be digging into a deep hole. But yes, that's what we want Montez any connections. It could very well lead to a so-called closed case. So, we'll need as much as we can get when we cross-reference the new and the old. Just because it's cold, hey, it may be the same suspects or someone they never looked at."

The officers responded to Tyson's explanation nodding their heads. Montez sighed deeply knowing the work he'd have to do.

"Listen, I'm hoping none of the new cases or ongoing cases will link to any of these we've flagged, but if we overlook the possibility, then we're screwed. Listen, it's no different than how we handle cases presented when officers check to cross-reference them. If it leads to closing a cold case, then good."

"But the skipped steps…"

"Porter, man that's on them. We didn't skip the steps. If we find the holes and present them in the right light. Hey, the victims, community, and the department are happy with the results. If any of these lawyers find out what these files represent, we've got problems."

"Wait, so they didn't do the work and we catch the flack?"

"Stands you know how this goes down. If the DEA didn't have enough evidence for a bust but you knew what was going on… man the repercussions are like a boomerang, it comes back on you. Well, whoever decided to stamp these files closed without investigations thought it wouldn't matter who they blamed or didn't blame. How long has that kid been locked up screaming his innocence?"

"About four years, but the other cases dig deeper. A missing person for more than five years and that other man, an older man I might add has been fighting false arrest and identity for more than three years. All of them have that same lawyer, Lawrence Fulton. He's on to something and we're now the bait."

No one could dispute Wilson's point. The unit would be the spectacle for the media. Lawrence Fulton was a young, eager lawyer who had been winning many of the lawsuits against the cities throughout Philadelphia. The attention he drew from the media always began local with the threat of lawsuits looming for the state. He was no stranger to the media, community, or the police departments.

"Tyson, you're the boss. I'll do whatever. The computer does the work. It's just a never-ending cycle. The case Ms. White and those protesters are out there shouting about…man that alone will bury us if we don't stay on top of the new cases."

Shouts of "Justice now!" filled the rotunda. Porter shot a glance to Tyson.

"Put your gear on. The fight begins tomorrow, I'm sure."

CHAPTER 10

"That impromptu media conference was your idea. Who knew those files would become a part of this mess? When do we dig deep into this information? I'm sure Fulton will be requesting the file."

Chief Michaels listened as he had on previous calls regarding the Watson family and their lawyer for Julian Foster. He left the conference room after his cell phone wouldn't stop ringing regarding the crowd and media presence in the rotunda. He knew once the crowd began to gather, he'd be asked to make comments regarding the arrest and incarceration of Julian Foster. He read the materials provided by his office and followed the broadcasts on the case. Lawrence Fulton had found a hole in the department's investigation, and he was determined after Foster's sentencing to prove his discovery would cause his client to be released.

"Chief look, Tyson's crew has nothing that will get this guy off. Look just like most of the cases, there is no evidence there. We locked up who we all agreed was the likely suspect and that was Foster."

"Listen, I sat most of the day with Tyson and Porter and files that proved your stupid ass didn't check what was being filed. The money ain't worth it if we're sitting in a cell."

The voice on the other end shouted out the threat that held the chief hostage for years.

"Listen, you're in this too deep to tell me what this is worth. One word from me and your stupid ass is done. We put you in a position where we're running things, not your scary ass! You do what you're told or that big house, the vacation home, your boat, car, mother and whoever else we deem values you will be gone! You got that? You do what you're told and that's all. Don't question me, or the movement. The Foster family has nothing, even with that fancy nigga lawyer. Let it boil over."

"And on to the next? They've got the files. That's what I'm telling you. I didn't agree to being incarcerated. You said you needed a few things to go your way. This!! This is not just a few things. I didn't agree to this."

"You're our yes. That's all you need to know. How to say, 'it's being handled from within', you keep telling the media, the lawyers, and anyone who asks that simple line. You can't feed me that 'I didn't agree to this' shit. You agreed to whatever a 'yes' man has to do. I'm telling you what you need to understand. Now if my name comes up, I want to know."

"The report didn't have names. I'm sure they know who handled or botched up each case report. They didn't include the names on the reports."

"Tyson is too smart to give away all the information at once. We need to know what files he's working on, not just the numbers."

"What about this media shit. I ain't for putting my face all over the networks knowing I'm lying about this mess you've created."

"Let the captain handle it. Tell him what to say and let him do the media thing. You're the chief, delegate my friend."

The call disconnected. Michaels looked at his phone and sighed. He realized he was put in a position that could cost him so much more than he gained. Each time he thought about stepping away from it all, he found a reason to stay. There were times when he knew the FEDS or CIA would be knocking at his door for his arrest. He lived in shadowed fear, not the lifestyle for a man who could retire. He'd walk away with military and law enforcement benefits, a bank account with a weekly deposit that provided him a lifestyle of luxury, but he chose to stay. The fear was closing in. His fall wouldn't be cushioned with a departmental backing.

Delegate. Captain Worthy was a friend, a true friend. If he chose to delegate, Worthy was the only one in position he could trust. Tyson and Justlin would eventually find the missing pieces and Fulton would bury the department. It would fall on all who were connected at the time of the investigations. Worthy and Tyson would be in the clear leaving him to face Justlin and the wrath of the state. If anyone could help him quell Justlin's curiosity and Tyson's determination to bury the "untouchables," it would be Worthy. The decision to delegate, as suggested, would change his relationship with a true friend, so would telling him the truth.

He poured himself another drink and paused. He looked around the room. His home was never above what he considered to be the norm for a lifelong bachelor. Filled with duplicates of furniture showrooms, he had expensive taste. Both his homes in Philadelphia and where he vacationed often in Florida had no feminine touch. Thinking about it all again, he was the opposite of Worthy. Michael's had never been married, and had no children. His life was his career, dating that dwindled as he aged, vacationing and as Justlin pointed out his fishing were his past times.

Holding the position of chief, he kept his intimate circle small. Political influences helped his career, and he made paybacks when reminded of his climb. The report presented by Tyson, could implement him in an indirect way. Just as Marshall said, "he pushed things through." If anyone cared to ask, Walter Michaels turned a blind eye to many of the negatives. The report revealed his neglect while he was captain.

Tina Justlin always caught his eye. She'd smile at his compliments, laugh at his jokes, and always mentioned his absence at social events. He respected her marriage and never went as far as asking her to lunch or out for a drink. Although he wanted to, Worthy would remind him that "Justice," as they often called her teasingly, would have him locked up. He wondered if he pursued her, would she look the other way when his name came up.

He smiled as he looked out onto his deck. The peaceful scenery often reminded him of the loneliness he lived with over the years. He could offer any woman whatever they longed for, but Tina Justlin had been given that. Her husband, her career, his death, she didn't long for much. Like Michaels, there were no children. He went to the computer to check a few things.

Tina Justlin, her record and Damien Tyson's was impeccable. Tyson had a smudge with the Mona Mandell case but nothing that would cost him his position or respect. The two of them were more of a dynamic duo than Tyson and Porter. Both at the peak of their careers, African American, connected to the community, and no ties to their past. Damien was divorced, but Michaels thought if Tina was to compare him with Tyson, as Worthy said often, the chief would lose. He needed a win.

He'd find out how close they were on and off duty. Pushing the possibility of dating would give him an idea of where he stood with Justlin. Tyson was simple, they had been friends for years.

Tyson respected Michaels and Worthy, not only as supervisors but as men. He could convince the detective that mere oversights on his part as a young captain were the reason for his connection to any of the cases.

He'd have to get close to Justlin and Tyson to keep abreast of their findings. Yes, delegating was the next move. Michaels was sure Worthy wouldn't suspect the role he played in any of the cases. He'd explain as much as he could to Worthy, including the fact that he'd be saving a friend.

CHAPTER 11

Tina was tired. She couldn't muster any energy to dine out as planned with her friend Marcie. They agreed to order in, and Marcie would arrive at Tina's home around seven-thirty. It gave the two of them enough time to unwind a bit. After combining notes summarizing the findings of the day, Tina stepped into the shower seeking a bit of relief. The day, unlike most days in Harrisburg, wore on her mentally. She was accustomed to meetings, viewing files and reports, as well as taking notes, sharing her opinion, and making unwanted decisions. The difference was she was torn. The negligence of the department was once again a slap in the faces of those in the community. Her reason for joining law enforcement was to protect and serve. Over the years her service did little to protect those who truly needed it.

After a bit of pampering, she put on her favorite lounge set and slippers. She decided to read through a few more notes the chief and captain wrote on the files they pulled to discuss. None of them were related to the cases Fulton was handling. She hoped they were a step ahead of him. They'd have to delve into them first before the crafty lawyer requested the cases be reopened. She walked through her spacious home, pleased with the calm and quiet of the surrounding property.

The family-owned property was given to her and Jerrod when they married. It was a year later when the newlyweds moved in and had the land surveyed for additional space, renovated, and it became Tina's dream home. After the death of her husband, she teetered with the idea of selling. Now, living in Harrisburg during the week, her home was a getaway. Memories kept her in Harrisburg for months. Tina couldn't walk through her home without the whispers and laughter she and Jerrod shared over the years. The extra bedrooms they chose for the family they planned, the library or study as Jerrod called it was filled with resources, she still used for many of the cases she investigated; the rooms were special and the emotional pain she felt was just beginning to ease. She took the years they had together to make areas of the home their personal comfort. Jerrod had a workshop for his woodwork, and she had a beautiful garden that surrounded the property. She needed Harrisburg to work through the grieving process without losing her love for the home.

Tina's family followed her lead. Not knowing if she would feel better surrounded by family or supported with calls and cards. Eventually the connections became minimum and not needed. Facetime calls replaced visits and were never questioned by Tina. Marcie was her go to friend, more like a sister. Her family warned that Marcie saw the benefit of having a friend in power. Their relationship wasn't what others thought. They were like high school best friends, and they were close in all aspects of their relationship. Tina's family didn't trust the closeness but knew better than to keep questioning Tina's decisions. Marcie and Tina worked together in various facets of the job and although Tina's career seemed to be a fast track, Marcie was not interested in being her competition.

Tina spread the folders across the farmhouse antique white kitchen table. It offset the hutch and other shelving in the room, giving it a look the couple thought would continue through the home. It didn't, they laughed at the seating for eight, more than she'd ever have in one setting. It would be a perfect area to spread the paperwork that would consume her time for the next few weeks. She put on a pot of tea, hoping Marcie wouldn't say, *"I wanted that fancy coffee you drink."* Tina smiled at the thought. The clock read seven, she'd have thirty minutes before her work would be over for the night. She wondered if Tyson took home any of the folders as he found the problems mounting with each discovery. She picked up her phone and dialed his number.

"Hello, Justice?" Tyson questioned as he read the caller ID.

"Yeah, it's me. Listen, I thought maybe we'd talk about our rules for this. You know, without the upper management's eyes, what did you have in mind to get a grip on this mess?"

Damien had dozed a bit after eating. Sitting up and hoping he wasn't dreaming he asked again, "Justice"?

"Tyson, yes, it's me. Do you want me to call you back? I was hoping we could talk before meeting in the morning."

Damien stretched into an upright position. "No, no, I'm good. Ate and you know what we do after a day like today. I was on my way to it being a couch night."

Tina laughed, "I bet. I'm sitting here listening to my stomach waiting on Marcie and our delivery. We agreed to eat and catch up, but I may wind up on the couch with Marcie across the room on the other."

"So, you got it. Whatever you need my lady. My only stipulation is no blame come down on us, my unit. We inherited this fiasco, and I won't be making excuses or covering up an obvious problem. Tina, they knew what they were doing and had been doing it for some time. It smells. It smells like them, and you know who I'm talking about. I want solid proof this time to get rid of them. I gave the numbers first, but the data Tina, those who were assigned, wrote the reports, gave a pass, it's the 'untouchables.'"

"Do you think or have proof who at the top is tied in? Someone is, you know that, right?"

"Yeah, it's got to be someone turning a blind eye. But it could extend into the courtrooms, the system has been tainted for years."

"Damien, we know that. Everyone does, but we are the voice the people are supposed to have. If we see it and let it go, I don't know about you, but I can't look at myself in the mirror."

"You're right. What do you want me to do?"

"Report to me each morning. Before you report to Worthy and Michaels, let me know findings and any new leads, daily. Don't release any names yet. Let's hold on to them no matter who asks for them, tell them to see me. No one is to know any connections you've made, or exactly who has been or was assigned to those areas."

"Okay, so we're not moving on?"

"Oh no, we're moving on. Continue to collect the numbers the same way you did on the report. Find the missing links, but if I'm right, ranking officials are involved and as you said it could include lawyers, prosecutors, district attorneys and judges. I want to be able to control what goes to the media and the governor's desk. I can't do that if everyone has their hands on what you and yours are presenting."

There was a moment of silence between them.

"Justice, you got it. I understand. I'm asking you to give me the courtesy of your moves as we continue on. What you're looking for, what you may have connected or found, that will help us."

"Okay… hey that's Marcie and my food. See you in the morning."

As Tina opened the door, she could hear Marcie thanking the delivery man. Marcie grabbed the bags he was carrying, and Tina extended her hands to help. He passed her the drinks and condiments. Each gave nodded gestures of thanks, and the two women entered the home juggling their dinner.

"I'm sorry. I didn't hear your car or his pull up. I was on the phone. Did you have anything else to bring in?"

"No wait. Girl, you know me better than I know myself. Where's our bottle of wine?"

"I knew there was something missing! Yes, get our bottle please."

Marcie headed to her car to retrieve the wine. It was a tradition between the two friends. Good conversation, food, and wine kept them in a friendship for more than fifteen years. Tina set the dining room table with the necessities and unpacked the containers and bags from the restaurant. She loved dining out but dining in held unspoken comforts. Marcie came through the front door and kicked off her shoes.

"Girl, I was glad when you said, 'Let's eat in', I had some time to unwind and now take a minute to really breathe. It's been a while girl. I'm glad we're getting together tonight. I know you've got your work cut out for you with that mess today. You may not get another time to gossip with me with all the mess going on. Huh? Is it all connected?"

"It may take longer than I thought. Connected? Girl please, Marcie how do they allow themselves to get caught up like this? Then wonder why everyone questions their actions?"

Marcie passed the napkins and plastic utensils to Tina. Tina passed her the fork and knife she was setting on the table.

"Habit," Tina responded to Marcie's questionable look with a smile, "They are habitual liars, cheaters, what else can I call them, politicians. Child, they think between their money and politics they won't get caught.

Look, I understand the ladder. You know trying to be on top and stay on top. The climb is different for us, you know. Most of the time we have a step stool to climb if that. So okay, they push us off that ladder or we pay to climb it. Some of us get a step up, connections, good job, luck, or prayers, but stepping on the people? I just don't understand what they get out of not serving everyone, you know. Who takes an oath to serve and forgets who they're serving?"

"So, it's true. That Foster boy didn't rape that girl and he's been in jail all this time because somebody covered the truth?"

"No Marcie, they didn't even look for the truth. He was an easy target, blame him, case over."

"What? Not another one of those cold cases lost. I'm with you now. Who reaps the benefit there? I don't understand the payout, who gets paid?"

"I wish I knew. There's nothing to lose when you don't put anything in the file. When you don't look, you can't find anything. They try to satisfy the community and more so the political circus with short cuts. No reports, nothing leads to anything in the files. Marcie, this case is not the only one and that's why I'm here. There's a connection somewhere."

"Shit. You might as well move back home. Tina, they've been doing that mess since you and I started."

"Well, now it's full blown and contagious. They've been locking innocent people up, detaining folks without cause…it's an abuse of power and the report Tyson has tells it all. It's going to cause a rumble in the department, the courts, and the community."

"So, what do they want you to do? Girl, they know what they're doing. That fight has been going on for years. Hell, that's what the Civil Rights era was about. Well, if you need eyes outside of the Cold Case Unit, I'll be watching and listening."

"I've got a feeling there's quite a few who will be doing the same."

"So, your chief and captain were expecting you to come down on them?"

"Marcie, I tried not to sound like that's what I was doing. But one of them, maybe both, can't tell me that they knew nothing. It's hard to believe that all those reports were turned in without all the information we have now."

"Michaels was Captain then. Maybe while he's trying to put his rap on you…"

"Girl please. Just knowing he was or could be tangled in this mess turns me off."

"Tina, you know what to do. It's got to be someone that was in authority then. Fulton will be on it so get ready."

"Now that's a brother that I could deal with."

"Pass me the wine please. He's raising your brow? You know he's got a little thug in him."

"Marcie, shut off your *Spidey senses*. The brother is sharp, intelligent, and about to cause some jaw dropping truths on these ass-holes."

"And what in that definition attracts Tina Justice Justlin?"

"All of it! As my grandmother used to say, 'He brings on the fever and the cure.'"

"Wait, I thought what's the dudes name you're dating was putting out fires."

Tina waved her hand teasingly and drank from her glass which needed a refill.

"Okay, what about Tyson?"

"Marcie, I haven't set eyes on anyone particular. Fulton and Tyson have a certain swagger, I like, hell I ain't dead. Blake is cool but he's too… corporate, political. He's a black Michaels. Maybe that's what attracted me."

"Girl, watch out. Until you clear Michaels that white man may be the fever without the cure."

CHAPTER 12

The morning alarm caught Tyson, stirring him from a three-hour rest. He stayed up going over the files he thought would be needed for the morning meeting with Justlin. He wanted to be certain he could answer questions and give her the conclusions he and Porter discussed over the past few months. He sat on the side of the bed hoping he wouldn't have to pretend to be "okay" with overlooking missing facts. Her call gave him a feeling of comfort but over the years he learned one moment of comfort could cause an investigation to go south.

He stood and stretched; glad he didn't oversleep. Porter said it would be good for the two of them to come in earlier. Tyson agreed which was the second reason he set the alarm. His thoughts drifted to his wardrobe as he sighed unsure what he'd wear. The media would still be lingering in the building, Ms. Sayers and her colleagues would be stalking to get any information that may be whispered or passed on. Emergency meetings were possibilities. Although his team wasn't considered an integral part of the department, the information it held was vital.

Tyson chose a grey suit. He was sure he would be the blunt of Porter's jokes throughout the day. Casual business attire was the norm for the office, especially if they weren't in the field on an investigation. Tyson picked up the phone to give his partner the heads up.

"Hey man, you sound like you've been up awhile."

"Tyson, man my sister, her kids, that man she married… never mind. What's up?"

"Reporters, lawyers, Justlin, you know what I'm saying?"

"Yep, grey suit. Gotcha. I'm ready. I'll let Stands and Wilson know as well. I thought about it when I left the office yesterday. I felt they needed to know the pressure they may be faced with. I'm sure the media will turn the transfers into some kind of cover-up theory. Man, this is a mess."

"We'll get through it and I'm sure it will cause a change, hopefully, a lasting change."

"Yeah, in policies and procedures, you know what I mean? In writing, is the only way they'll put it in the books. Tyson, man, this may be the start of something good if we can get rid of the 'good ole boys.'"

"Yeah, the damn 'untouchables.' I'm sure there are more but starting there would send a message."

"Hey, I'll meet you at work. That's my sister calling again, damn!"

Not knowing what to say he let the phone go silent. The drive in was without a follow-up call from Porter. Once Tyson saw his partner's car in the parking lot he was relieved. Porter's family could stir trouble that neither wanted to be a part of.

The halls were silent, and Tyson sighed and smiled as he walked the hall to the unit. Although the hall was empty, he felt the pressure. There would be questions, those he couldn't answer, those who would make it uncomfortable for him to be in the presence of others. The shadows of the past haunted him; the regrets of time gone by.

His years in law enforcement taught him to keep silent and soon the questions would fade. They did but the looks, the whispers, the meetings behind closed doors; what looked like departmental favors became what others claimed were paid credits for the rising detective. He had no connection to the chosen, or the misfits, which made him a target. They called him a snitch and treated him as such. He rose above the rumors, and with the help of the chief and captain made it through what they told him would shake up the department.

The Cold Case Unit had been under investigation from time to time but nothing that held the attention of the courts. Porter often said it was because no one had the money to fight the department. After all most of the cases went cold because no one could afford lawyers, nor did they have enough information to open the files. Lawrence Fulton, Esq. changed that for many. Over time his name became an itch to the authorities, and the Harvard lawyer would not be silenced.

The media spotlight followed Fulton and it would follow him to what was now Tyson's unit. Being prepared was always an asset for the detective, but expanding the investigation wasn't what he wanted. Justlin would want the governor's office protected. Tyson felt the same about his unit. If they led the investigation that overturned the departments throughout the state, he was sure his career would be short-lived.

Entering the office, he could smell coffee brewing. He smiled knowing Porter could drink coffee all day, but it was Justlin's visit that sparked the purchase of the new office appliance. He heard voices coming from the kitchen and hoped the Principal Investigator was waiting for him. Ms. White, Montez, and Porter greeted him. Ms. White pointed to the pastries she brought for the team.

"Wow, good morning. I didn't expect the two of you to be here this early."

"We were sure you and Porter may need access to a few files before the governor's girl gets here."

Porter laughed, "You know Ms. White saw into the visit before you."

"Don't nothing change. You and Porter know that. I called Montez and told him we can't leave the two of you swinging in the wind. We don't have nothing to hide Damien and if it's their dirt that will be rising, we've got the proof, it didn't happen while you were in charge."

"Thanks, I'm sure Fulton will be filing for the records to be open. So, let's stay a step ahead of him. Get the files on the Watson, Roberts, and Crews cases. If there are discrepancies create the same data profile and that's it. You're right though Ms. White, we have nothing to hide including the truth."

Justlin arrived later than anyone expected. At nine-thirty after greetings and introductions Tyson invited her to his office. The files were on his desk and Porter and Justlin took seats at the table that held stacked data awaiting their review.

"Tina, I don't know where to start. How we got the information? The highlighted points? The cases we all know Fulton will be questioning? It's your choice, we're prepared with all the files there on my desk but fair warning this may take weeks."

"Damien you all know what this data says, and for that matter what it doesn't say. I'm not here to spotlight what you've found. I want to put the light out on those who think they've got away with this type of nonsense. The three cases that Fulton has is the basis for a fire that will take down more than this one precinct. They may not care but I was raised here, hell, so were you. I still have family that lives here. This thing is contagious and if we don't stop it every city, town, or small village with impoverished neighborhoods will fade. Where will those people live, how will they strive? We can't just let them fall victim to this nonsense. We all took an oath."

"Everybody boot up. It may get messy." Porter threw his hands up as he continued. "We're in it, like it or not."

"Guilty by association? Why did they transfer me and Wilson? We didn't have anything to do with these cases." Stands looked to Tyson for the answer.

"We don't know that answer yet either. I thought about that last night. The only connection I came up with was your relationship to us. If Porter and I go down, maybe they're afraid of the backlash from others; one they fear you and Wilson may start. Who knows how they think? Why would they send recruits instead of seasoned officers to help us get this together?"

"Damien's right. They're easier to manipulate. They are eager to find things and won't overlook things for any of you. There's a connection. Watch them. I was going to mention that when I called you last night."

Justlin's comment turned everyone's attention to Tyson. They smirked and smiled but let the pause in the conversation linger without questions. Porter patted Tyson on his back.

"Well, seems like things are heating up. I'm sure we all can stand the fire."

The silence after Porter's comment spoke loudly. "Amir if you and Leana want to work solely with the newbies it's fine. That was my intention when you came on board. This is, as Porter said, a blaze waiting to heat up. We need your help in telling us if they are legit or here on another agenda."

"Damien, you don't really think they're here to find out what you know, do you?"

"Yes, I requested four, got two. Not the two I requested and then two more that seem, I don't know. Maybe I'm just paranoid about the whole thing."

"We're in. You guys get started with this mess. Leana and I will handle the new boots. I like setting fires too." Wilson tapped Stands shoulder as she passed him heading to the front office. The two left Justlin, Porter, and Damien to the files.

"And just like that, let the droppings fall where they may."

"Funny Porter. Listen you guys know I'm with you on this. The problem is this data is exposing years of cover-ups. Someone in a higher position than investigator has let this slip through the cracks."

"Tina, it didn't slip through. The door was open. So, it's not just the 'good-ole-boys' at work here, or not at work. It's who? Michaels or Worthy, maybe a bit of both. I just don't see them being involved with this, not like this."

Damien sighed and stood to take off his jacket. He grabbed the hanger from the closet door and handed Porter one. "Look man, get comfortable. What's the plans for ordering lunch? Tina, what are we eating? We might as well get use to this routine."

CHAPTER 13

Maneuvering through the small crowd that gathered in front of the Watson's home, Samantha Sayers and her photographers made their way to the front porch. The camera crew from the local news station was prepared with the cameras and the microphone for Lawrence Fulton and the family to speak live to their audience.

It had been eight years since Julian Foster was accused of raping his girlfriend Tammilyn Watson. Although there was no evidence linking Julian to the rape, and Tammilyn testified he was not the rapist, Julian was still incarcerated. After an arrest, and trial, he had served six years of the fifteen years sentence. No one quite understood why the Watson family hired Lawrence Fulton for Julian's case. The Foster family, namely Grace Foster, Julian's great aunt, was known in the community, but the family hadn't hired a lawyer to represent him. It was newsworthy, no one knew why Grace Foster wouldn't use her influence to help him. Lawrence Fulton was determined to leave no stone unturned, starting with what he was certain was a cover-up.

Tammilyn Watson was twenty-one when the attack took place. She and Julian had been dating since their sophomore year at Penn State. After paying for Julian's education, it seemed his aunt couldn't afford an attorney. The Watson family, knowing Julian from the community told her they would incur the expense. No one believed he would be convicted. Mr. Fulton met with the family after Tammilyn and Julian wrote letters to him regarding the case. The family fired the attorney they had after Mr. Fulton told them the problem was deeper than Julian's case and he was caught in bureaucratic politics. He explained he had two highlighted cases that fit the same pattern, no evidence, no reports, and yet the defendants were found guilty and serving time. He would take on the case pro bono.

The Watson family, joined by Ms. Foster and their lawyer stood on the porch waiting for the undertones and whispers to end. Lawrence Fulton stepped forward.

The well-groomed lawyer spoke in a smooth baritone cadence. He was well known in the community. Working with many of the community organizations, activists and the media, his reputation spoke volumes. Lawrence Fulton, Esq. was the people's lawyer, if they sought his assistance he never refused.

"Thank you all for coming out to support these two families in their quest for justice. What we know is that Julian Foster has been accused of a horrific crime. I'm going to tell you a few truths about this case and let you conclude as we have that an injustice has been done to Julian Foster, Tammilyn Watson, and their families. However, it goes further. It reaches this community and if we delve deeper, it involves the surrounding communities too. Now I know you're asking how? Why is that? Well, you see Julian Foster is not the only one who has been penalized for a crime he did not commit."

An outburst of shouts and applauds caused him to pause. "Yes, you see as a lawyer it is my job to defend and protect my clients. Over the last few years, I've found myself protecting innocent, yes, innocent people. People like Julian Foster who have been accused, indicted without cause or evidence, and convicted. I'm here to tell you all, it's a battle that we all must be prepared for. Today it's them, tomorrow it can be you or your family member. Support them in this battle. Let's be together in this fight."

Shouts followed his statement with chants of "Let them go!" The reporter from WPAN shouted to the lawyer his question, "What do you expect from the community? What do you want them to do?"

"Listen, it's easy. Make your representatives accountable. You know what the truth is here. Julian didn't commit this crime. That means there's a rapist that is free. Each time the police arrest and convict the wrong person, the criminal remains within the community to offend again. Silence is not the answer. If you know that the police are not asking the right questions take the answers to City Hall. Take the answers to the questions that should be asked to those in authority. I believe you have to push a few of these folks we voted for. Someone knows the truth that will set this young man free."

A reporter blurted out from the crowd and held his oversized microphone above the heads of those in front of him. "What's next in this case now that a suspect that has confessed has been arrested?"

"We'll do what we're required to do by the courts. There's requests to be made through the system to release files, and whoever this suspect is, they must be processed through the same system that processed Mr. Foster. We can't assume that because they made an arrest that they won't let him go."

Another question came from the crowd. "Does Ms. Watson know the man who confessed? Does she recognize him to be the man who attacked her?"

The lawyer looked at Tammilyn and decided he wouldn't allow her to answer. "My client has not been questioned regarding the man they've arrested. She has maintained from the start that Julian Foster was not the man who raped her on that night. They have the DNA evidence and other evidence that can be matched with this new suspect. If they don't drop the ball, and he is telling the truth about his actions, then we should be able to get Mr. Foster out of jail and home to his family."

"Are you certain that the evidence will hold true, Mr. Fulton. After all it's been close to eight years since they collected that evidence. If it is a cover-up, could it be missing?" Samantha Sayers threw in the grenade.

Fulton told her to ask it after at least two questions had been asked. It would be the question that would linger with the crowd and the television audience. He paused as though he wasn't prepared with an answer.

"If there is a cover-up, we've opened a can of snakes. No one needs snakes in their community or their police department." Fulton led the families into the house leaving the reporters, the media, and the crowd to their own conclusions. Samantha returned to her car and waited for the call from the lawyer. She had asked the question he wanted asked. Now she would be allowed an exclusive interview with the families.

The family sat watching from the living room windows. As the door opened, they could hear questions being shouted from the crowd and reporters. Tammilyn followed her mother and brother wiping tears from her eyes. Cecil and Carol Watson took a seat on the couch while Grace Foster sat in the recliner. They waited patiently for the lawyer to finish the call he made on the way in the home.

"Yes, I think it was enough. I'm sure you can help us along the way. Ms. Sayers this is the beginning. It's bigger than this case and we haven't even begun to dig through the pile of cases I'm sure the state is going to try to deny are relatable."

"Fulton, I can maneuver in and out of the police units, the state departments, but I need to be the first every step of the way. I'll help you as much as I can."

"No problem, I understand. I must warn you though, I need everything to be above board. You can't gain information that's coerced. It needs to be clean. I mean if we can't get it through the right measures, I can't use it. It's too much at stake and it's not the usual suspects."

"I got you counselor."

"Okay, I look forward to working with you."

"Thank you, sir, we'll be in touch."

CHAPTER 14

It was two o'clock before Tyson sat back in his executive chair and decided to grab the remote for the television. Everyone stopped their work when they heard Fulton's statement repeated in a playback on the local news channel.

"Investigator Justlin, there's a call for you on line one." Kai's voice came across the phone as a red button began to flash.

"Well strap in folks. This call can only mean that those we didn't want to know, know." Justlin made her way through the boxes on the floor to the phone on the table. "Hello? Yes, I just saw a part of it… I've been literally in boxes all morning… Yes, that's the intention of everyone here… Yes, at the close of the day, sir… Yes, no problem… Good-bye."

The anticipated stares from everyone in the room caused Tina to laugh.

"I know it's not funny, but you guys look like you watched me eat a disgusting meal. Breathe people, it was what is expected each time the media gets hold of a bit of information. The office just wants to be sure we're ahead of Ms. Sayers and the lynching mob of supporters Fulton may have found with his prepared answer."

"Oh, so you caught that too. Porter's statement hit hard deliberately.

"It was too clean of an answer, no thought at all. Yeah, she'll get the exclusive story. Which means we all know she'll be checking here shortly for a rebuttal, Detective Tyson."

"You and Porter both know the drill. Porter, let Stands and Wilson know Sayers is on the hunt. We're good, damn. I wish we were further in these files though."

"You're actually a lot better with this system than most departments. Organized and a way of keeping up in the computer, yeah, you're ahead of many. I think that's why we wanted to start here just in case this thing gets bigger than just your locality."

"Wait! Do you seriously think that these short cuts or putting it bluntly, the lack of procedure is just in our precinct?"

"No Porter, not at all. I'm saying you and Damien have grabbed this bull by the horns."

"Yeah, how many falls before we become experienced bull riders? Tina, you know this is a way to bury us. They deliberately gave me this unit. That man has been locked up damn near ten years, they've been trying to reverse his conviction numerous times. Who slipped the lawyer information about the evidence and protocol not being followed?"

"Wow, Damien! Yea, what about that Ms. Justlin? He's got a valid point. No one suspected anything about this until now. Doesn't seem possible without someone putting a bug in his ear. We definitely didn't know this mess was here, and those who know, well… hey, just who knows?"

"Porter, that may be where we need to start. The Captain, Chief, no one other than me in the Governor's office, and this office. Who else?"

"No, Porter is right. Someone told the lawyer what wasn't in the file. We need the request for discovery, and any other information that was given during and after the trial. Porter ask Stands to track that for us."

Porter exited the room leaving Justlin and Tyson a moment to their personal thoughts. Tyson picked up the folders he set aside and handed them to the investigator. He waited for her to look up from the files.

"You knew? I mean you knew they'd be questioning these cases?"

"No, not at the time we found the discrepancies. How ironic is it that Fulton files charges of misconduct for these three clients at the same time I'm reassigned to this unit? Tina, they knew. Someone in authority is linked to this mess."

"Damien, you're talking about people you and I know personally as well as professionally. Do you really think Michaels or Worthy would put you in the middle of this?"

"I would hope not but it has to be someone in authority to have me moved. I was on to the scum in the department. My last case set me up as a perfect target to be transferred. They knew about Fulton, what he was looking for, what they had me removed to continue their quest."

"What quest? Are you saying that this is some sort of plot?" Justlin put the folders on the desk and walked over to the boxes along the wall. "And all of this in some way is a plot for what?"

"Tina, look at the stats. Hell, look at the names on the reports. Let's just say that I'm wrong, where's the missing paperwork, evidence, reports? Who didn't do their job for years with no reprimand? No one questioned anything? Hell, the chief even said there was no need to ask questions. Worthy wasn't a part of the unit, so who do we ask? It's a deliberate dead end and if I sit back with the code of blue bullshit, I take the hit for a muddled unit. Another strike on my record, I'm on the chopping block, right at the bye-bye pension door."

"And if you're right…"

Porter entered the room and stared at his partner and the principal investigator. There was nothing to be said, they all had the same understanding. Montez entered the room and paused before speaking.

"What's up? You guys okay?"

"Yeah man, just in thought. What you got?" Tyson invited him to the conference table. Justlin and Porter joined him. Montez spread out papers before them.

"Ms. White has the numbers totaled and I asked her to print the list for our review. There's more cases than we thought, we knew of these we're inputting but look over this list. These cases have been waiting for their appeal dates. We didn't look up the reason for their appeals, but we do know that if it comes up that it's because of missing data, well you can see the problem."

Justlin took a deep breath. "Wait, you mean, this list is additional to these boxes?"

"No, no ma'am. They're cases could be in one of these boxes. Ms. White and I just thought it would be easier to start with those who are actively seeking an appeal. Those would hit the media first. There's more than the number of boxes so hopefully it would mean that some on the list have no discrepancies in evidence collected. But if we're going to be ahead of the media and lawyers, we need to check these first. There's a few more on the list that are represented by Fulton. I'm sure he'll stir the pot once he gets Foster out of jail."

"Montez, compile the list to include the arrest date and officers. Also, the lawyers and appeal dates if they're set."

"Got it. Oh, and Porter that new officer Knowles wants to speak with you. I told him before he leaves today, you'll get with him."

"Thanks man. Is it a problem, did he say it was?"

"No, a lot of whispering over files today though. Wilson and Stands are in an out of the front, you know checking over the files and their work. So, I'm sitting in observing. A lot of whispering between Chambers and Knight. The female stays to herself. Just watching, with all this going on, I'm just being observant."

"Damien, I told you he wants to be a real detective," teased Porter. "That computer shit is his shoe in. I'll get with Knowles before the day is out. Thanks, man."

"Porter, we're going to need to know where the four of them stand. If Sheers and whoever is covering for him, sent them, that's a problem. Find out, I don't care how. I don't think any of them is new to the game. I do believe they're hungry. We may have to get them to turn on each other. They may talk about why they're here or try to recruit the others."

Tina slowly put down the folder she held. "Hey, didn't you say they sent you two and a call was made by Worthy or Michaels to get you the others. Find out who has that connection. Who is close to the higher-ups?"

"I don't know Tina, maybe the connection is with Sheers. They may not know who called. I gave him the name Knight and then told him it might be Knowles."

"So, you think it wasn't a set up? Why check them if you don't suspect them?"

"Can't trust it. I don't know if it's just a coincidence. I do know we need to be careful, and I can't trust those I don't know. I'm going to talk with Worthy later."

"I was thinking I'd talk with Michaels. Between the two of us we should uncover something or push them to work with us to uncover this mess. The governor won't like this shit if it turns out to be what I think it is."

Porter got up from the table. "What's that? We all on the same page right or do you know something more Ms. Investigator?"?

"Get your boy, Damien." Laughter lightened the atmosphere. "You better tell him who I am, I think he got me confused with those rookies out there."

"Nah, Investigator Justlin, I am in no way confused. Do I need to leave the room so you can tell Detective Tyson your theory?"

"Detective Tyson, he's still talking." She shook her head laughing. "Listen, you and Damien know. If I know, you know. I came here because of the report. I haven't found anything that leads anywhere. I guess they played it that way, but there has to be a hole in their plan. If there wasn't Fulton wouldn't be on the hunt. He knows something. The problem I have is just what Montez said, there's more than these three. I would bet there are some that have been in prison for more than ten years. They got sloppy and Fulton got the information simply because no one paid attention to these damn boxes of emptiness."

"How did they get through the court system without the evidence?" Porter sat back down waiting for an answer.

"No, the question is, who removed the evidence that could have kept them out of the system? Check the folders for commonalities. It's in the missing evidence."

Justlin and Porter were silent. Deep in their thoughts, knowing Tyson was right. The missing evidence was what gave the cases credence.

"Damien, man that's crazy. Alright, if that's true, we know what's missing but how can we prove it was there at all."

"C'mon Porter, I know it's been a long day but... pass me that folder. Look, this one says blood samples, DNA report; look in the box."

Justlin moved closer to Porter to see what was in the box marked 'Cold Case' with the matching case log number.

"No reports for the samples or the DNA. Now check the log for the dates and see who removed any items for discovery or court reviews."

Tyson waited while Porter checked the box and its contents.

"You're right. It's marked as complete before the trial date, but there's nothing here after the trial date. So, the evidence went to review and whatever was taken in during the arrest or investigation is gone before trial. Enough for the arrest and nothing after the trial for an appeal."

"Tyson, that can't be right. Let's look at the steps. The arrest, the investigation, the prosecutor, the defense attorney or public defender; someone who removed the evidence is a part of the process."

"Tina, you're right but here's the problem. They need the evidence to get the guilty verdict. How did they remove it to be sure there would be a denial of an appeal?"

"How and why? What's the advantage? None of these cases point to anyone connected to money or political gain so why?"

"None that we've found yet. Man, maybe they were covering for one that is connected, and these are missing evidence to deter anyone from second guessing the procedures."

"No, that's not it. Fulton has been disputing the Foster case from day one and he's always claimed the evidence didn't add up. We've got letters in the governor's office that date back at least five years ago. The man has been relentless on all three of those cases."

"Wow, really. Tina, how bad would we look if we met with Fulton not to defend, but to discuss what his theory is. We may be able to find out who he thinks is behind this and flush them out."

"Damien, if we open that can of worms…"

Porter shook his head. "You mean can of snakes." Porter's statement brought on an uncomfortable silence for the three of them.

CHAPTER 15

Knowles knocked on the door before entering. Justlin, Tyson, and Porter were still buried deep in the paperwork and folders that were stacked in designated piles on the large table. Knowles didn't enter until Tyson waved him in.

"Sir, we're shutting down for the day, but I asked Montez if I could have a minute of your time to talk with you." He looked directly at Porter and looked behind him as though he was trying not to let anyone else know what he was saying.

"Is someone there?" Tyson questioned him. "Step in, close the door."

"Uh, sir. Uh…"

"What's going on? Close the damn door!"

Knowles closed the door, but he didn't enter the room. Justlin leaned back in her chair with a questioning stare. Porter read the vibe from Tyson and snatched the door open. Stands and Wilson were talking with the group of young investigators. Knight was seated in a cubicle packing his satchel.

"Man, what's the problem?"

"I can't do this. I can't work in this unit." He voiced in a whisper. "And I can't leave without telling you what I've heard and what I know. But not now. I think they've caught on to who I am."

"Who you are? Maybe you better be making yourself known if nothing else. Have you talked to anyone else about this?"

Knowles took a deep breath. "Are they still here?"

"They're leaving now. Stands and Wilson are still in the office. Is there a problem with them?"

"I'm not sure."

"Should I talk to them as well?"

"I'm not sure."

Porter looked at Knowles who was physically shaken. "Don't leave."

Porter joined the other detectives at the front of the office as Knowles returned to his cubicle.

"What's up with our boy here?"

Stands turned and looked back at the cubicle where Knowles was seated. They could hear him rattling papers and what seemed like him talking. Porter and Stands frowned knowing he was alone.

"Maybe it's too much for him. Is he talking to himself?" Stands questioned and smiled.

Wilson laughed, "Y'all didn't hear his phone ringtone. He's on the phone."

"I was about to say, he's outta here for sure. He says there's a problem, what is it?"

"Yeah, I'm sensing it but can't put my finger on it. We both thought we'd talk to you and Tyson about it if you ever came out of that room."

"Stands, man, y'all just don't know. We're going to have to create a crime scene board to figure this shit out. So, what's up?"

"It's Knight man, he's rough around the edges. I'm trying not to judge any of them too soon, but the only one who seems on level is Miller. At first, I thought Knight and Knowles, then Chambers and Knowles, but right now, Knight is the one to watch for sure. Knowles pulled me to the side saying Chambers and Knight had some issues with me and Wilson, especially her. You know her mouth…"

"My mouth, you never had a problem with my mouth." Wilson laughed and gave him a side-eye.

"Wait, are we talking work here. You two, play nice. We all know about your mouth. What did you do, scare 'em?"

"No Detective Porter. I told them the truth about teamwork and showed them how bad it can get at times. No sugar-coating here, just facts. The young wanna be hood, Detective Knight gave me some feedback on his lifestyle, and I told him he ain't really lived a life. Don't play if you can't take a foul."

"See, her mouth. Anyway a few comments were made I guess among the four of them and Knowles didn't feel comfortable with it. He wanted to talk. I told him later. He said it needed to be as soon as possible. I kept it moving, he went to Montez."

"We should hear him out. Give me a minute. Justlin's still here. Tyson might not want her to hear this right now."

Porter left them and Knowles and returned to the conference table.

"Hey Damien, we need to handle this situation with the new investigators. How long will you be?"

"Oh, not long, I need to get with Michaels and then leave. So, if you guys have a matter at hand that's fine. We can stop where we are Damien and resume in the morning? I'd like to stay ahead of Sayers and Fulton," Tina stated. She began to gather her things preparing to leave.

"That's a must. Call me if the conversation leads to anything that may help this mess."

Tina smiled. "I'll call you regardless. I think this conversation with Michaels will stir a few things."

The three of them exited the room. Justlin said her goodbyes as Tyson beckoned the group to join him in what was quickly becoming the makeshift conference room. Tyson smiled as they entered the area. He knew before long they would need a new floor plan. Everyone took a seat at the table. Porter got bottles of water, giving each one a bottle he sat across from Knowles wondering what he meant when he told Stands," *They've caught on to who I am."*

"Okay, so what's going on young man. You wanted to talk with Porter, but with what Stands has expressed we all want to know what's going on. It's pretty obvious that you knew Knight before. Did you know the other two as well? Did you all come here on some assignment?"

Knowles didn't hide his anger. "It's my problem. I want you to understand I know what I've gotten myself into and I'll get out of it somehow."

"Well, the first thing is for you not to talk in riddles. Start from the beginning or what you want us to know but right now you sound crazy." Porter looked to Tyson for a supportive response.

"I've heard worse when someone is caught in their own shit. What's the problem that you seem to think you can't deal with or don't want to be around?"

"We were asked to find out information. You know what's going on here under your supervision. Knight, Chambers, and I agreed to be a part of an undercover sting, or that's what they called it."

"Hold it. Who is they?" Stands asked and pulled his chair closer to the table.

"Sheers and his boys. Mainly Simmons and Boone, you know the group that hangs with Sheers. You can't be a part of that circle without doing some kind of dirt. Knight got close to Chambers to see if it was a "white only" group. Our plan in the beginning was to report the racial divide. But Chambers came back saying we were to be a part of the group if we took on this assignment and reported what was happening here, on the Cold Case Unit to Sheers."

"What about the young woman? What's her name, Miller? What's her job?" Wilson questioned. "I thought she was acting strange today too."

"She's not in the group but she and Chambers are friends from their academy days. They whisper and laugh together. I think they're secretly dating, but I don't know what she knows. We only talked to Chambers about it a few weeks ago and then this came up."

Wilson took a deep breath and looked to the men who had not said anything. "So why you running? I mean if you mean well, why not stay and help us get this mess out of the unit and maybe out of the precinct?"

"I didn't know what to do. I'm new, you know a rookie to this detective thing. I worked for my elevation and I'm not ready to throw it away for some white boys and their shit. Listen, Knight will roll the dice if looks like it will pay. As I said, I don't know about Miller, and I don't trust Chambers since I know he's connected to Sheers. Sheers has a foul reputation. That's all I needed to know about him. I ain't a good ole' boy and I don't intend to be an example either."

"So, as she said, what are you running from? Listen you're in a room with hard hitters. They've rolled with me on the streets and we each took our hard knocks together. We've never been knocked out. Why? 'Cause we got each other's back. So as Investigator Wilson asked, what are you running from? Why would they pick you if they didn't think you'd bend their way?" Tyson paused waiting for an answer.

"Me and Knight got into a few arguments with Sheers and Boone about the shit they were doing. Excuse my expression but it was foul. As you well know, they ain't keen about blacks moving up or being in the precinct. We were given an assignment, an opportunity to work with the Captain and the Mayor a few times. We were called back to do escorts and you know, be involved in security for political functions. We found out his boys were turned down for a few of the assignments we received later. I guess, he questioned it and was told they didn't want his boys. It started a piss contest with them. You know, the text messaging, problems in the locker room, and we got reassigned. So far this makes the third assignment. So that was why I thought Knight wanted to get with Chambers about his connection with Sheers. He really wants to be down with them, it ain't me."

Tyson shook his head. "You still didn't answer the question. Why you running? What is the threat?"

"Yeah, you said they knew who you were? Who are you?" Porter leaned across the table making sure Knowles looked him in the face.

"Captain Worthy is my uncle."

"Oh!" Porter backed up. "They don't know that I'm sure."

"So, who told you to report here?" Tyson questioned hoping it wasn't Sheers.

"The captain, sir."

"Sheers knows you're here. I'm sure if you're right Chambers told him, you and Knowles are here. You say they don't know your relationship to the captain?"

"No. I don't think so, but the conversation got nasty about how the captain was the chief's lap dog. It seemed that Chambers and Knowles were saying things to see how I would take it."

"And you think if you leave, they won't know who you are? That's giving them the answer." Porter blurted out waving his hands. "This shit is for a television police drama."

"Wait, what do you want to do? We can turn this thing around and put whatever we want in Sheers face." Wilson looked around the table for any agreement.

"What?" Stands frowned. "I thought we didn't want them to know anything."

"Listen, he sent Chambers and Miller. Even if Miller is not down with them, after all she's not white, Chambers is his boy. Knight wants in and if our boy here is right, they'll use them to get information fed to them by our boy here, right Knowles?"

"Uh, I guess but I told them I didn't really like the unit."

"Wow, you don't like us. Now, I'm upset." Porter threw his hands up causing a bit of levity to the matter at hand.

"Me too. I was going to take you all to lunch, then it was just you. Now forget it." Stands pushed back his chair. Knowles let out a sigh of relief.

"No, I didn't want them to question why I left. So, I figured if I told them I didn't like the work they wouldn't question it."

"Knowles, man listen. The work is the same no matter what unit. You're a detective, an investigator, whatever the level. You're going to find negatives in those you work with as well as the work you do. Your uncle should have told you the higher up you go… man, the shit hits the fan. You want to go higher? You can't run away from the b.s. on this level. I love what I do but look where I am, here. My man Tyson asked for help, not by name but your uncle sent him who he thought would fit. Me and Wilson. He sent you, who sent Knight?"

"Never mentioned it. I definitely wasn't telling him I knew before the lieutenant told us to report. I've worked with him for about nine months now, but I've always wondered about his comments and actions. He's one of those type you have to tell to calm down."

"Yeah, I noticed that about him on the first day." Wilson replied. "Now that we know he's seeking to get with Sheers, we're on the inside and they don't know we know."

"Knowles, if you still want to work with us, I think I've got a way to fit you in where it benefits you and the unit. All they need to know is we convinced you to stay. You won't be working with them. Report here tomorrow about seven-thirty. We'll be here and explain what's going on and what the plan is going forward."

CHAPTER 16

Tyson cleared the office and locked the door praying he'd get a good meal and watch television until falling to sleep. He knew the prayer was useless, but he believed in miracles. Porter, Wilson, and Stands didn't ask any further questions after Knowles left. For that alone, he was grateful. There was no plan. He was going on instinct. Sheers was dirty and so was the group he formed over the years. Money, drugs, cover-ups, and possibly the mess that the unit inherited was an outline of their activities within the department. Porter hinted that they may have been in a few unsolved murders as well. After seeing the mess that the unit was left in, Tyson agreed, they could have gotten away with murder.

He'd wait until seven-thirty, after watching the news and preparing for Justlin's call. He decided at some time before the night was over, he'd reach out to the captain. He was sure he wasn't involved in the plot to take him and the unit down. Worthy didn't like Sheers and he didn't work with him in the precinct. Sheers came up under Michaels and a few who had retired or transferred. They didn't take him or any of his boys with them as they climbed the ladder and that was the basis of his arguments. *Blacks and other minorities were given privileges and opportunities that others worked harder for...* He cried often to the union and anyone who listened to his complaints. He had the ear of the media until he tried to coerce Sayers into a night in his bedroom. After too many drinks he found the "black thang" interesting. Her complaint hit the papers the next day and he was on his third round of suspensions.

A troubled officer to say the least, but his ties to city hall kept him employed. Porter would remind Tyson that *"Family mattered."* The two of them didn't have family in high positions but Captain Worthy and others in administration kept an eye on their work ethics and moved them along. That's what Tyson was told about taking over the Cold Case Unit, it would be a step up, another reason to be looked at as "special." Tyson and Porter knew the intent was to cause the "untouchables" to think twice. After talking with Knowles, Tyson knew they were steps ahead of what Worthy and the others intended. He needed to know who was working behind the scenes with Worthy. He wasn't sure if Michaels was playing both sides.

The house was dark, it was close to seven and the winter months hadn't let go to the darkened early hours. He pulled into his garage and noticed Porter's car was parked on the street in front of his four-bedroom home. He shook his head knowing his long-time friend wouldn't end the evening without knowing their next move. He planned on calling him before turning in for the night. He needed a moment to breathe.

"Yeah, yeah, I know. Listen, I was driving and thinking we need a serious plan so maybe I hang out with you tonight. I mean it ain't like you got company coming on a Thursday night."

Porter explained his actions as he met him at the front of the house.

"Jeff, how would you know. Suppose I did?"

"Man, I don't see nobody. Your phone ain't blowing up and besides she would have been calling during the day. I know you man. You looking to pull the trigger, but you've been gun shy since Mona Mandell."

"Alright, and suppose I wasn't gun shy tonight. C'mon man, you could have called me to at least checked to see."

Porter shook his head and walked to the front door ahead of Tyson. "You want me to use my key?"

"Open the damn door. Look I got food on the way home. I've got leftovers in the fridge."

"You always have food. You live like you're always expecting guests." Porter dropped his jacket on the couch and went to the kitchen. He washed his hands in the sink. "It's just a matter of throwing the leftovers together."

"Glad you know. Pass me a beer, I'm eating first, then we can talk, plot, or wait for Justlin's call. I've got to call Worthy too."

"All of the above my brother. All of the above."

CHAPTER 17

"Tina Justlin, to what do I owe the honor. It must be important if you decided to give me a call after hours."

"Cut the nonsense Walter. Maybe I should have asked for an appointment in the morning, but then there would be those who would question what the Principal Investigator from the Governor's office was looking for."

"Oh, so this is not a personal call?"

"You know it's not. I'm trying to clean up a mess you've got in your precinct, and you want to play games? We can work together, or I can assume there's some real bullshit going on."

"Alright, so you're not in the mood. What's up, what do you need? I'm just as interested in what this mess is as you are."

"We need to be on the same page. Understanding you got the report maybe a few days before my office did, what were your intentions to handle this?"

The chief walked over to his bar to pour his second drink of the evening. He turned down the television that wasn't holding his attention and thought about her question. His intent was to get her on his side. He needed her to understand what he was up against. It was too late; he was in too deep to tell those who held the final years of his career in their hands he was done with their agenda.

"I know what it looks like. Crap, it looks like crap. The records are screwed, and I can't explain who or how they got that way. To be honest with you Tina, if it wasn't for Fulton trying to get his clients a deal…"

"A deal. Chief Michaels, if they are not guilty, they shouldn't be incarcerated. The lack of evidence proves their innocence, and I would question where is the evidence that went to trial? We can't possibly fight Fulton when he knows we don't have the evidence to hold them. And why is that Chief, how did these people go to jail without the evidence? You need to come to the unit and see what I went through today. Fulton has three cases, but Tyson has boxes with missing information, witness testimonies, blood samples, oh God, I can't even begin to tell you how bad it is."

"So, you're saying we've got a bigger problem than Fulton's cases?"

"Yes, did you read the damn report!?"

Michaels sighed and drank his drink down and instantly poured another before taking a seat in the chair that often gave him temporary mental comfort when his body became tense.

"I don't know what to say. We were meeting with Tyson before you called for a meeting. The hope was it wouldn't cause a problem before we could get a grasp on it. I had no idea how bad it was. We were in the dark until we got the report."

"How long has Tyson been on the unit?"

"Not long enough to be a part of a cover-up, if that's what you're thinking?"

"Well, someone signed-off on this paperwork and allowed evidence to leave the unit. What's your thoughts about who it may be?"

"I don't know. The name doesn't matter, it's the reason that concerns me. What is Tyson saying?"

"He's willing to help but he's clearly stating he wants every report to reflect that his unit is not responsible for what was signed entries. It happened before he took over. I can't say I blame him."

"Understood, and I agree. How long are you going to be digging up this grave?"

"Until I uncover the grave diggers. Chief there's people in prison that shouldn't be. We've got criminals that walked because someone decided to clean the streets according to the culture of the community. That ain't justice and it's not how I work."

"So, I guess I'll be seeing you more often?"

"I'll be in your building until I no longer believe there's a need. I want to know your intentions; you still haven't said how you'll be moving forward."

"Is that your question or the governor's?"

"Mine."

"Tina, I wanted to ask you about you. We have an on and off connection and I wanted to know if I am being too forward to question you about you?"

"You can ask, but before I answer, I need to know where you stand with this investigation. Are you pushing to solve this problem, clean up the mess no matter who is involved, or are you watching from above hoping it doesn't touch you?"

"Whew! That hit hard Investigator. You really think I may be involved in this. I need to change your thoughts about me and what I do for this city immediately. I'm one of the good ole' boys. Stop by my office tomorrow, bring what you need to discuss, or I can meet you on the unit."

"Okay, that will be fine. I'll be there about nine."

Neither said good-bye, but the call ended mutually.

Justlin looked at the phone. "Good ole' boys, my ass."

The clock read nine. It seemed as though she and Marcie swallowed their food and said their goodbyes simultaneously. Tina promised she'd call her back if anything of interest came up. She grabbed her wine glass and went to the kitchen for the refill. The local news gave her more answers and she wondered if Fulton would make his appearance in the morning or wait until Monday.

Her cell sounded out "I'm every woman…" Marcie's ringtone. Justlin smiled knowing it meant she arrived home safely. It rang again, the default ringer which meant it was business.

"Justlin…. Yes sir… What speak slower, I can't understand you." Justlin sat up straight in the chair, a habit she performed whenever she needed to listen intently. Realizing it was the governor's "message boy," she relaxed. "Phillip? Why are you calling me this time of night with this nonsense?"

Phillip Winters, someone's grandson, worked in the governor's office at the request of someone in the chain of command. Governor Clinton Banks believed in having at least one staff member from any of the community programs. Phillip landed the job and had been an annoyance to Justlin for three years. She thought after the first summer she would no longer oversee him or his juvenile actions. Now as they approached the fourth year, she knew he had connections. The exact problem the "untouchables" whined about happened in every political office.

"I left the information on the secretary's desk. I'm in Moore Township and that you don't need to know other than forwarding my messages to my cell phone. That information is on the secretary's desk as well."

"Ms. Justlin, I'm calling because it wasn't on the desk. She didn't come in today. I sat there all day and didn't find any of what I was looking for or the information you gave her to pass on."

"Is she sick? Catherine is hardly ever out."

"I think it's a family matter ma'am. Can you send the information again? We don't know how long she'll be out, and the governor was questioning a few things from last week."

"Phillip don't worry about it. I'll call him in the morning. I need you to run a background, through our system not local records. The people on a list are here. I'll send you the names. I only want hits. There's no need to alert me unless…"

"There's a mess. I got you Ms. Justlin. Have a good night."

The list would include the names thrown around as "untouchables," the chief and captain, and Fulton. She was sure there would be more once they got into the files. She was hesitating to hit the send button wondering what Tyson would tell her when he called. Michaels's call met the agreement they had. Her suspicion about Michaels could be what they needed to ward off Fulton and Sayers. Justlin hoped he realized they were in a dog fight, and they were the smaller dogs. It was almost ten, she hit send and didn't regret not waiting for the call from Detective Tyson who never called. She sent him a simple text.

Michaels is suspect, what about Worthy?

CHAPTER 18

"Please tell me that's not breakfast I smell. It's too early to think, let alone eat."

Tyson smiled while pouring Porter a cup of coffee. "Have a seat, man. I don't know where we left off last night but before we go in that office we need to understand where we're headed with this. I got a text from Justlin. She said watch Michaels. Actually, she said he's suspect."

"Who ain't? So, what does that say for Worthy? Damn and he sent Knowles? Did you call him last night?"

"No, it was late. My intention was to call this morning on the way in. Now I don't know whether to wait to talk to Justlin or not. Maybe she found out something."

The conversation lasted through breakfast. Nothing more than rehashing what was already known and that which needed to be done. They agreed it was more than a coincidence and they would need the governor's input to come out clean. Justlin said she wanted to keep it from the spotlight that would follow, but it didn't seem possible.

The ride to work was peaceful after a night and wake-up to Porter's agitated temperament. Over the years Damien was accustomed to his partner's bouts. He expected a bit of rage, anger, and sarcasm. Detective Jeffrey Porter's personality was a combination of it all and Damien wouldn't understand him any other way. He relaxed as he chose the longer route to work and agreed to meet him at the office.

It was too early for most of the employees. The few that passed Tyson in the hall were police or police personnel. They exchanged morning pleasantries and continued to their offices. Porter was at the front counter when Tyson entered the unit.

"You didn't start the coffee?"

"Man, y'all ain't…look I ain't the only one that can make coffee. Anyway, the coffee, sugar, cream, whatever is there. Everyone can make their own."

"Oh, that's how you feel? You pick and choose who you're going to make coffee for?"

"What? What is that supposed to mean?"

"Sayers, Justlin, Kai, Wilson…" Tyson paused to laugh at Porter's reaction. "Yeah, even Wilson. You see my friend; you bring coffee for everyone when the women are here or coming around. Now what will they do?"

"Man, ain't none of them calling me at night. I'm saving money. They'll pitch in when I'm no longer the pitcher."

"You're funny man. Listen I'm going to call Worthy before we talk with Knowles. I want to get with him before Justlin gets here."

"Get your cup of coffee before you sit in your seat. You'll be there most of the day."

Entering the office Damien felt overwhelmed as he had the first day on the unit. It seemed the task before him then was too much to take on. Now a year later, he still hadn't met his expectations, he needed guidance and he prayed another call with Worthy would be the answer. He sat at his desk thinking what he would do if the chief and the captain were a part of the problem.

Porter's voice came across the intercom. "Captain Worthy, line one. Saved you the trouble, man."

"Good morning, I was about to call you. How are you?" Damien tried to act as though he was a step ahead of the problem.

"Damien, what's going on? Knowles called me. I really meant to tell you who he was, or did you know I sent him?"

"Listen, Captain when we requested more staff, I had no idea we would find someone's hidden secrets. I didn't need any other problems. Why didn't you mention Knowles was your nephew?"

"I didn't want Michaels to know. When you made the request, it was my intention to have Knowles report to you. His partner…"

"No, his partner is a no, no. Chambers too, I'm not sure about Miller."

"Really? If that's a problem, do you want to replace them?"

"Captain, I don't want to alert anyone that there's an issue. Fulton as well as Sheers will be looking for problems. Knowles will help us with them."

"What can I do? We don't need this thing to blow up in our faces. You're right, Fulton won't let go. He thinks he's got proof of wrongdoing."

"He may have it. Captain, we need to find out what it is and who told him where to find it. I'm sure it links back to Sheers and his boys. Justlin may have to tie up a few people before we uncover it all. Hey, can you find any reports in your office that shows who signed off on some of the paperwork that may be in the court records?"

"The Foster case, yes, I'll send what we have here. If you need anything else, let me know. Listen, Knowles was worried about others knowing…"

"Captain, we don't want anyone to know he's related to you. Thanks for helping us."

"Tyson don't be crazy. Helping you is helping the department and me. I can't stand by and watch this cave in on you without it affecting me and my position."

"Hey, Michaels was the captain back then. Where did he work as lieutenant and sergeant?"

"He came here as a sergeant. Don't know if he was in records then. As a lieutenant he wasn't in records. I don't think he worked records or the cold case unit here at all. You've got me thinking, we met when he was a lieutenant." The captain paused. "You're on to something there Tyson. Someone knew the work wasn't being done."

"Yeah, in hindsight we know that. Finding out who, before Fulton does, is the question we need to answer."

"I'll check out Michaels. These questions were mine too when I talked with Knowles about Knight and Chambers. Knight has caused many to question his motives. Chambers is new to the list we've been watching. Keep me abreast of what you find."

Porter opened the office door and mouthed," Knowles is here."

"Captain, my day has just begun. I'll call you later." Tyson didn't wait for a response. Disconnecting the call, he stood and put on his suit jacket before walking out to the main office.

Stands and Wilson nodded their good morning as Knowles said," Good Morning."

"Lady, gents, good to see you this morning. Listen, Porter check with Montez about next week." Tyson checked his phone. "We've got a little time before the others arrive. Here's the game plan. Knowles you'll be assigned to Montez. It won't look out of the ordinary because we'll need you to input information because of this overload."

Tyson pointed to the boxes. "It's obvious we're swamped. Your cubicle has a computer, and you'll work from that area. You're our in-house CI. You're the ears we need for Chambers and Knowles.

"What if they ask questions?" Knowles looked at Porter and Stands for an answer.

"Who they asking? Not me, I hope. Quick way to get into trouble. Have you ever asked a supervisor or senior officer questions about an assignment? It ain't a good look here."

Porter smiled and Stands waited for Knowles' response.

"Listen, your uncle knows you're being assigned differently as well. He's working toward the same goal. We've got to get on top of this mess for various reasons."

"Tyson, did you see the morning report?" Wilson handed him her copy of the daily bulletin that was printed for officers. The important notices section ended in bold print.

> **A thorough report and record keeping is the only way to secure proper follow-up within the precinct. That includes files and evidence that is secured in the Cold-Case Unit. Please sign-off on all appropriate documents. Updated documents, witness statements, and all evidence included in these secured files are used in court. This is a reminder of what is already a policy in the department.**

Tyson passed the copy to Porter. "Wow, give a copy of the bulletin to everyone Knowles, that's your first daily assignment. Make enough for all of us each day and post one on the..."

"Man, you know we don't have one. I'll put up a day-to-day operation board on the wall for the unit." Porter injected. "This is going to be a real unit after all."

As usual, Porter's sarcasm caused everyone to laugh including Tyson.

"Something is wrong with you. Anyway, Knowles post it daily. Let's keep an eye on the messages. This was a hidden message meant for the 'untouchables.' Now they know Fulton is watching, but they don't know we are too. You can start with the three cases that Fulton will be looking into. All signatures, the evidence log, whatever you can find that was signed off on or should have been, we need to know what officers and personnel were involved."

Knowles nodded his head with a raised brow.

"Oh, and your attire... change it. What did you wear in today?"

"Jeans and a sweatshirt, sir." He responded to Porter's question as he looked around at the four of them dressed for court. "I've got time sir, I'll go home and change."

"Listen you won't be going to court or in front of the cameras but the presence, when they're around is always official. Looking like the street detective, for some reason, is an attention getter. Where the badge in your wallet, not around your neck. Concealed weapon, and Knowles relax, we got you, change out of that uniform."

"Sir, when I return report to Montez?"

"No, to me. I'll take you to the back and they won't question you later. I'm sure of it."

The men nodded knowing Wilson was looking for Knowles to ask the questions if there were any.

"I'll take on the duty of assignments. I've been doing it all week, no need to change it now. I'll tell them about their attire as well, so we're all on the same page with that. Chambers is the only one…"

"Please don't talk about a wardrobe makeover."

"Porter you read my mine. He's been coming in casual attire or his uniform. He still looks out of place." Wilson could only shake her head.

"He is, he just doesn't know it yet." Stands added as he passed her a cup of the fresh brewed coffee.

Knowles smiled, feeling better about the matter at hand. His uncle told him to watch Knight. He was warned he was dirty. Now he could do what his uncle wanted. He'd use the information he discovered about Knight as he got more comfortable talking with Tyson. It was his shoes he wanted to follow. It was as his uncle said," *the perfect path"* to success. He'd help them or warn them. He'd be there for his uncle and his kept secrets. Worthy would soon be gone; Tyson would move up or out. If the unit blew up, he'd be there to catch the pieces.

CHAPTER 19

"Marcie, can I call you back? …No, let's talk after work. Girl, I'm about to lose all my religion between Phillip and Blake. I'm in Tyson's office. He went to meet with someone from records. You should have seen him pass you this morning… I know right. Listen, let me go. I'll call you when I'm leaving."

Tina looked at her phone and decided the third text from Blake was enough to return his call. She tried not to sound annoyed but after not answering his question he caught on.

"I just wanted to see you. I thought the weekend would be good. I mean you're working late during the week. I assumed you'd take it down on the weekend."

"Blake, the problem that has brewed here will probably cause me to work through the weekend. I, more than you, really wish I could 'take it down'. I don't think so."

"Well, you could come here, or I could come there. I mean, I could help you with some of those files, or whatever you need to take it down."

"No. You can't help me, and I wouldn't ask you if you could. You've got your own cases and work. What happened to the project that you couldn't put down last week? You're suddenly free enough to call and make time now?"

Justlin got up from the desk and walked to the window overlooking the street. Blake had been distant for more than a month. She assumed the flame he claimed that burned for her had burned out. Their sporadic sexual exploits had replaced going out on dates. The relationship was no longer leading to any definition of romance and their friendship was fading fast. After almost a year, she was tired of his excuses and inconsistent calling. It was close to twelve, her thoughts wandered to having a drink for lunch.

"Okay, I see where this is going. So, what is your agenda Investigator Justlin."

"Files, folders, notes, soft music, a drink, and maybe an evening with a friend. I'll call you if I get a minute."

She put down her cellphone just as Porter opened the door. "Hey how about lunch? Damien called and asked we meet him at the diner over on fifth."

"Do they serve drinks? Does that sound bad? I mean it's mid-day and I'm done."

Porter laughed. "I can relate. I'll let him know where to meet us. Stands and Wilson are joining us as well. Team meeting away from headquarters."

"Oh, okay, that works for me. Anything to get away from these folders and notes."

"Did you find anything that will tie some of the loose ends?"

"No that's the problem. There's got to be some rhyme or reason to this system they had. It just looks like they dumped files."

"It ain't that easy. Someone went through them. There's a system. We just didn't find it yet. Well close those folders and let's go. You can ride with me unless you prefer to follow."

"Be right there." She watched as the well-groomed man exited the office. Blake had no idea what he let go. The only thing that was better than a black man in a uniform, was a black man in a suit. Another peeve she had with Blake; he just didn't have the swag. She often wondered about his taste but understood that his imitation of the styles he saw daily could have stifled his sense of fashion. She closed the files and left them on the desk.

Porter checked on everyone before exiting the office. Kai gave him a nod and smile, her normal response when he told her not to forward his calls. Montez, Ms. White, and Knowles gave him a nodded gesture as well. Miller, Knight, and Chambers watched as the seniors of the office left them to the cases on their desks.

Montez was glad to have Knowles working with him. He seemed to be eager to learn and it allowed him to focus on other possibilities and connections in the three major cases. Knowles worked on the other boxes and assisted Ms. White and Kai. Everyone seemed pleased with the arrangement. Miller, Chambers, and Knight worked in their cubicles on case files that were seeking approval to be closed and filed as such. Making final reports, calls and cross references took up most of their time and they seemed to be catching on to the routine. Montez checked on them but understood the feeling of having someone constantly looking over their shoulder. Porter called at two and told him to let them go at three if they hadn't returned to the office. It was then that Montez decided to ask if they had any questions. He left his office and went into the main office to find Knight and Miller in their cubicles on the phone. Checking for Chambers he walked into the conference area. He assumed he was in the bathroom until he heard noise coming from Porter's office.

"Hey, whatcha' looking for in here?" Chambers looked up shocked. He stood from the kneeling position he was in. "I'm only gonna ask one more time. Whatcha'—"

"Man, I thought one of these boxes would have the information I need for the case file I'm working on." Montez could tell the young detective was lying. He played along.

"Really? It's a new case, right?"

"Yeah, they brought it in earlier this week. I've been looking for this guy's name and the information in the computer mentioned something from two years ago. I thought maybe it would be tied in or in some way lead to something."

"What name?" Montez watched Chambers' eyes. He couldn't look Montez in his face as he was trying to avoid the look Montez gave him.

"Man, I was doing the job you trained us on last week. If you got a hunch, go with it, you know?"

"What hunch led you to Detective Porter's office? What's the file name on the box you were in?"

"Uh, I was just opening files. I can ask Porter later, I guess."

"What were you looking for? What name?"

"Man, it don't matter." Chambers pushed his way pass Montez. The case name on the box wasn't one Montez was familiar with. It wasn't on the hit list. He sat the box on Porter's desk. He needed to know if sending them home was still an option. He dialed Porter's number.

Porter excused himself from the table when his cell phone vibrated. He didn't want a call from his sister to interrupt the conversation they were having. Business had been discussed before the food was served and for the first time since they started working on folders, they had a chance to put the detective business aside.

"Yeah, hey Montez, what's up man?"

"Look, I caught Chambers in your office going through one of the boxes along the wall. I don't know if it was the only one, but he was in your office. It concerns me."

"Shit, it concerns me too. Damn! What the hell is he up to? Don't say anything to them, let them go home I'll talk with Damien, and we'll be back in the office soon. Did you pull the box?"

"Yeah, I put it on your desk. He wouldn't say what he was looking for. Something about a hunch as it relates to a file he has been working on."

"Oh, really. Okay, ask that ass to give you that file. He can start another one on Monday."

"On Monday?"

"Yeah. Montez, we need him to give us what they're looking for. The asshole has to think that we're too dumb to know he's up to something. Did they mention anything about Knowles being reassigned to you?"

"No, I'll ask Knowles. They all went to lunch together."

"Alright, handle that. We'll be there after they leave."

CHAPTER 20

"Listen, I can't get caught up in your shit!" Knight and Chambers stood in the parking lot watching Miller walk to her car. Chambers stormed out after Montez caught him in Porter's office. No one returned to the main office to question his whereabouts or why he left without shutting down his cubicle. Miller turned in the folders on his desk and shut down his computer.

Knight caught up with him. Stopping him from getting into his vehicle, he held his hand on the door to keep Chambers from opening it.

"Seriously? You not gonna say anything? That ain't what it's about bro. You got caught and do you know how that can backfire on us?" Again, Knight waited for the younger man to respond. It was apparent he was flustered, scared now that Knight caught him off-guard. "You don't know what you're up against do you? What was this some initiation shit? You talked a good game, chumped off Knowles and then you pull this with me? Does Miller know what you're up against?"

"Nah, she ain't a part of this. Listen Sheers, man, Sheers doesn't have to know what happened. Just keep cool, we'll be okay."

"I know I will. But we're here to get whatever they're looking for and you just put eyes on you and I'm sure they'll be watching all of us now. So how does that help me?"

"Look man, you wanted to be in, you're in. You talk, you walk by yourself. You can't expect them to back you if you're scared." Chambers cocked his head and changed his demeanor as though he was suddenly reminded who he was backed by.

"Oh, it's like that now. You fuckin' cry baby. A minute ago, you were trembling in fear of being caught. Now you want play hit man for the gang. Man, I don't get down like this. Maybe I need to talk to Sheers myself."

"Ain't gonna happen and although we work together on this thing, we ain't close enough for me to vouch for you. Someone put you and your boy down. You asked, I took the questions to Sheers, he gave you the 'okay'. But on this, I don't know where you stand since your boy crossed over."

Knight paused before responding, thinking about the excuse Knowles gave at lunch. He was told to return to work on Monday and check in with Montez. He hadn't had the chance to find out any other information or reasons.

"Man, we didn't come into this attached at the hip. He's got his assignment and maybe that's better for him and Sheers. Each of us were told what Sheers wanted done. We all had our own way of getting what he asked for. So, if Knowles is doing something else, I don't know and don't care. What I don't want is to get caught up in shit! Yours, Knowles, Sheers or anyone else, none! So, I'm asking you again, what was you thinking going into his office like that wouldn't be noticed?"

"Forget it Man! Just forget it! I'll take the rap for it and that is that!"

Chambers pushed Knight's hand off the hood of the car and got in closing the door without caring about any reaction. Knight pulled out his cellphone before he got to his car.

"Hey, did you leave the parking lot yet? Meet me over in lot B, what you park that far away for? Never mind, meet me over here."

Knowles dialed Montez. "Hey, Knight called. I'm meeting him in the parking lot. What am I walking into?"

"The less you know the better. You were reassigned to help store these files. That's all he needs to know. Ask him what happened, you changed your mind about leaving but you're not feeling Chambers. Let him feed off that."

"Alright, I'll call if it leads to anything."

Knight was leaning on his car when Knowles pulled into the space next to him. He cut off his truck and got out.

"Nice truck. I was thinking about getting a F-150 but now seeing yours I may have to get this new one here. Nice…man what's wrong with Chambers and what's the real deal with you working with Montez and that data clerk. You're right where Sheers wants you to be."

"Nah, it ain't like that. I'm in the storage files. The ones going to the basement. Cases that went to trial, old cold cases. Nothing interesting or worth anything there, just files. I'm checking them in the computer to make sure the dates are right on the boxes. Your boy Chambers is another story. He's borderline man. I can't deal with that shit. I thought getting into that little group would prove something, but I already know what they are, and I can't work with them knowing it."

"We already knew what they were about. I thought you were down with busting these guys?"

"Not if they're going to tear down a unit run by a brother. Man, there's got to be another way to get involved. I don't care what the pay is. In the end we're black they'll find an excuse to get rid of us, our rank, and… man, I ain't down with that."

"Oh, so you told Tyson what was up?"

"Hell no, I just told you I know what those white boys will do. Why would I be that stupid to open that can of whoop-ass?"

"Chambers is a punk. His pull is little to none. He went in Porter's office and got caught. Shit shook him. It took a minute for his punk ass to get back on level. But you're right he immediately made the distinction about who I was compared to him."

"Really?"

"Yeah, something about since you crossed over. What the hell does that mean?"

"Listen man, I told Porter and Tyson I was out. They said report Monday morning. I did and was assigned to the damn storage room. Crossing over to what? I'm not on active cases, not following up anything information that you guys get on new cases. It's as though I'm being punished for not wanting to be on the unit. Fuck man, I didn't sign up for this shit, and then here you are questioning me like we on a team to disrupt. I'm not about this man. I want to work, make rank, collect a pension, and that's that!"

"So, what did you want when I said let's do this? You knew what we were digging into. Now you've changed your mind, man I can't believe that."

"Believe this, they're killing people every day that don't believe. What they call it, 'friendly fire', taking one for the team, whatever. Knight, they've been doing this shit since, well you don't need a history lesson and I don't want to be a part of their next chapter. I'm no longer interested in being the hero."

"So, you go out like a punk. That ain't you man. Okay, you say you're out, you're out."

"What about you? You ain't in it for the badge of honor. What if they turn Chambers in?"

"I told him if he got caught it was on him. I'd rather talk to Sheers, but I'll play along. The money is good if they pay for the information like he said."

"Be careful. You could lose more than your position or rank."

"What? I'll be working with your ass in the storage room."

"No man, they'll pack your ass in a storage bin. We'd have to find you and label the box, 'cold case'."

Knight stood back seemingly shocked at Knowles' response. He was fixed in position as he watched Knowles get in his truck and pull off.

CHAPTER 21

"Marcie, I can't explain this shit to him. I don't understand why he doesn't understand how I feel."

The waiter came to the table with the menu. It was a late dinner, but Tina needed to get out.

"I felt like I was suffocating with each word he said."

"Do you really think he was going to come to your house?" Marcie asked pointing to the seafood platter. The waiter replied with a nod.

"Anything to drink ladies?"

The women smiled and ordered wine. They watched as he left the table.

"Tina, what is it with black men and black suits, any suit. Tux, two-piece, Sunday going to church suit, bathing suit, speedo suit…"

"Girl a speedo ain't a suit!"

The two laughed. "Blake is a nuisance. He called earlier and then again when I was going home as if the workload was an excuse for us not to be together. He's sniffing and I ain't feeling him this round."

"Tell the truth, you got your eyes elsewhere? Investigator Justlin, Justice, Tina, girl I know you. Tired of that model man and need a man who's not as stiff as those in the Governor's office?"

"Tired of Blake. Stiff ain't the problem, shit I need stiff. I need stiff more often."

Her comment brought them to laughter again. They talked more about relationships and the murmurs in the office. The food calmed the hunger, and their friendship calmed their need for female support.

"Girl, Tyson has everyone on edge. They don't know what he's looking for or digging into. That tells me that someone knows something. Then that fine lawyer, Fulton walked in and had subpoenas for the release of information."

"Really? We thought he'd be around but hadn't seen him. Was the press and a crowd with him?"

"No girl, and still attracting attention. The room froze. Well, I did. He wanted records released showing dates that the evidence was entered, again. I remember him getting this information some years ago. But everything he wanted he got. He was patient, quiet and didn't use his phone or step out to talk on it. He was determined this time."

"This time? What does that mean?"

"He's been there before. Irate, with a herd of spectators, the press, the family. You know, putting on a show. Well, not this time. He came in like those damn big-time lawyers do. I was surprised he didn't have an errand girl with him, you know tagging along."

"Girl, stop. Oh shit, Marcie look!" Justlin whispered. "He's here, don't turn around too quick, you'll make it obvious."

Marcie turned and waved for the waiter. "Hmm… do you want another drink?"

Justlin smiled. She knew the move and he took the bait. Lawrence Fulton was headed in their direction.

"Ladies, how are you? I see you're into late night full dinners as well."

"Mr. Fulton didn't our paths cross earlier. If I didn't know better, I'd say you were following me."

"Officer?"

"Officer Marcie Williams and I'm sure you know Investigator Tina Justlin."

"Yes, she caught my attention earlier today. You're working with the Cold Case Unit now?"

"No, why are you asking? I'm still in Harrisburg. Just doing my monthly checks."

"I see. May I?" He asked before pulling out the seat to sit. The ladies gave their approval, and the waiter immediately brought his drink over to him.

"Will you be ordering sir?"

"No, do you ladies want dessert. Let me treat you to whatever you would like since I interrupted your meal."

"Coffee please. That will be all for now."

"So how is the case going Mr. Fulton. I saw your interview on the television and I understand your stance. We really need to work together on this."

"What do I address you as Ms. Justlin or Investigator Justlin?"

"Call me Justice. That's what I'm looking for," she teased. "No, whatever is comfortable for you."

"Justice. I like that. He turned his attention to Marcie. "And you?"

"Marcie is fine while I'm off duty."

"Understood, I'm Lawrence. Most who work with me, call me Larry. You're right, I'm looking for the truth. As investigators, I'm sure you can look through the nonsense no matter where it falls in a case. This was messy from the start and after I began to dig deeper, I found that this is not the only case that it's spread to or from. I don't know how deep it is, but I know you being in the Governor's office you don't want this to become public knowledge."

"You're right. Not that we want to cover it, but we want to find the culprits and end this practice of blaming any and everyone."

"Justice, not any and everyone. The blacks, Latinos, less paid, under educated, you get my point. I'm sure. I've investigated more cases and the results and see the pattern. It's profiling. Similar to New York and the "Stop and Frisk," the Driving While Black, you know what I mean. I'm defending people that had Public Defenders or referred representation. It's deeper than I thought. I know your office and the unit think I'm the bad guy, but I really want the truth. If my clients are guilty, I'll back off, but I don't think that's the case."

"So, what do you have?"

"Well, I'd rather set up an official meeting. This is where we talk, you know black to black, woman to man…"

"Hmmm… now that explains why you're following us."

"Marcie, c'mon now. Can't a brother notice two beautiful women and want to be in their company? Do I really need much more of a reason?"

"So, to be clear, you want to work with us? I mean you really want to do an investigation without the publicity lurking." Justlin wanted to shout. It was the break they needed.

"Yes, I can't speak for the publicity or the public that is and has been attracted to the case, but I want answers. I can't get them if we're working against each other. So, I'd like to sit down with you and Detective Tyson to discuss how we can attack this and benefit our people."

"Mr. Fulton, I mean Larry. What about Ms. Sayers? She'll be at your heel. If not her there's the others."

"Marcie, you don't want me around or what? I was in your office all day today without the press. I can move with them or without them. Back door procedure works when necessary."

"Okay, he's right. We can get him in and out without…"

"What Tina, what are you thinking?"

"Larry, we're going to have to arrange your entrance and exit for sure. I mean if you're right, there's eyes watching, and they'll eventually find out you've been coming and going. I think it would be best if we discuss the arrangements with the unit."

"Thanks for the honesty. Well ladies, I've interrupted your time and for that I apologize. Justice, I'll look forward to your call."

"Give me your best contact information. I'll call you before the end of the weekend."

The ladies watched as their imaginations followed him as he exited the area.

"It's a damn shame. All that in one man, hell all that in any man. I am so mad at you right now."

"Marcie what's wrong with you?"

"You're right across the hall from me daily now. Well across and a few doors down, well to the back a bit…"

"What?!"

"Well you've got all the, single men, all the single men, all the single men…put your hands up." She kept singing to Beyonce's hit changing the words to fit her meaning. "If you like it, you better put your… well girl you get my hint. Porter, Tyson, that young one Montez ain't bad either, now a lawyer day after day. No wonder you're thinking twice about Blake."

"It's not like they've made a pass or implied any interest over the years. I've been in their company before. I don't think there's any reason for this investigation to be different."

"Another man in the arena, someone will speak up or ask you out. It's in their testosterone."

CHAPTER 22

Worthy pulled into the parking lot. He hoped the bar was not full. The restaurant service would be delayed if they had the Friday night crowd in the bar area. The restaurant was well known and did most of their business on the weekend, especially on Fridays. The cuisine was a blended menu, but everyone spoke highly of the service. When Michael's called with the invitation, Worthy couldn't refuse. He hadn't spoken with the chief since the meeting with Tyson and Justlin early in the prior week. He had questions regarding the investigation, the reporters, and what they expected would be the next move from Mr. Fulton's inquiries.

Walter waved him on as he moved through the small crowd that was waiting to be seated. It was obvious his friend knew to make reservations. His phone rang just as he was pulling out his chair.

"Hey Walt, wait a minute, let me get this. Worthy here." The captain answered the phone while taking his seat. Michaels stood gesturing he'd be back leaving Worthy at the table.

"Hey, Uncle Dennis." Worthy recognized his nephew's voice.

"Hey, Detective Mark Knowles, what's up?" The captain teased. "Is everything okay?"

"Are you alone? Sounds like you're in a crowd."

Worthy looked around and smiled as a group of patrons passed his table.

"Out, getting a bite to eat with the chief. Are you okay? I mean they're not coming down on you too bad, are they?"

"No, but I wanted you to know they're really on to something. I heard them saying they had to talk with you and the chief. Man, Uncle Dennis you aren't a part of this mess, are you?"

"So, are you working in official capacity or is this a off the book question?" His tone and laugh let Knowles know he wasn't taking the question seriously.

"Seriously, what do you know?"

"Not enough, that's why I sent you to the unit. Work with Tyson, I think I've stumble onto something. I'll know after this meal. Listen, I can't talk long. I'll call you when I know something about this."

"Okay, don't get caught up. It's someone in the upper ranks or so it seems to be."

Michaels returned to the table as Worthy was ending the call." Listen, let me go. My friend looks hungry." Worthy disconnected the call without waiting for Knowles to reply.

"I hope you didn't end that call for me." Michaels could tell his friend was a bit on edge.

Walter Michaels and Dennis Worthy worked with each other on cases and in the ranks for more than fifteen years. Each knew the other, their reactions to uneasy situations, the good and the bad.

"Family. I'll call them on the way home. Just checking in, you know, everyone thinks when you're over fifty-five you need to check in if your routine changes."

"How is the family? Cheryl's sister still single?"

"Man, you, and Bernice. She asked about you the other week. She came over to visit. She's well, and yes, she's still single."

"I've always liked her. From the moment she said she was divorced, single, and looking."

Walter laughed as he reminisced the rest of their conversation.

"The two of you are funny. I mean it's obvious you both love the chase. She ain't looking and you keep hiding so you can't be found. Everyone is fine, how about your family?"

"Family. Man, you know how that goes. No one close to here, most moved to Florida. I talk to them maybe once a week. I see them whenever I make the trip. My brother has just about taken over my summer place. You know he left his wife and family in New York."

"No. I didn't see that coming." Dennis waved for the waiter to come to the table. "Man, what you drinking?"

The two ordered their drinks and an appetizer, neither wanted a full meal.

"So, tell me," Dennis continued," what's up with the press, that lawyer and this mess that has everyone on edge?"

"I'm assuming you've included yourself, right? I mean we're in this together, right?"

"Walter, I'm thinking like Damien. I'm in this by title only. I don't know what the hell happened back then or how things were done. I don't want to bear the blame for something that I had no way of preventing. What's your take on it?"

"That's why I called you. It's not going to get easier if we don't deflect this lawyer and the press."

"That's understood. We need time to find out who is connected to this mess and why. I'm sure with Tyson at the helm procedures will be changed immediately."

"Yeah, Dennis it ain't that easy." Michaels lowered his voice. "There's a lot of us that can go down with this mess."

"Us? Say it straight Walt." Worthy thought about his nephew mentioning the upper ranks being involved.

"Marshall was right. I overlooked a lot of their "so called" errors. I was told to do so by those higher than me." Michaels sat back and took a drink, waiting for Worthy's reaction. The men sat in silence as the waiter approached the table with their food.

"Thank you." Worthy waited for the waiter to leave. "Higher in rank or in power?"

"What difference does that make? Huh? I was told to let a few things ride and we need to let it go. I need you to deal with Fulton and the press, especially Ms. Sayers. You've had dealings with the two of them with this case and others, so it doesn't appear to be strange that you'll handle the press releases and any information that goes to them. Keep our boy away from this. Justlin, well I'll talk with her. Dennis man this is the only way to handle this. You can keep them at bay while I…"

"While you what man? Hide? How deep are you in with these people? The 'untouchables' have you by the balls, don't they? What did they give you that you just can't let go of? Yet, you'll sacrifice me, Tyson, whomever? What the hell Walter!"

"Just handle this man. I'll get out of it."

"That's just it my friend. Once you're in, they've got you. Your life, your lifestyle, your rank, damn man, if you had a damn family!"

"Man, you and Tyson are my family!"

"Oh, hell no, brother. Neither me nor Damien would have pulled you in after we reaped all the benefits just to cover for us. You've lived in glory all these years because you turned a blind eye to what they were doing and now, you want us to… man, Walter!"

"So, tell me what to do? What else can I do? It wasn't supposed to play out this way. I'm too old…"

"Too old for what? Jail, to be slandered, to lose your job, to be killed? Man, they will kill you if you don't do what they ask now. Do you realize once this goes to the governor's office what will happen? It's either you or them? The community and Fulton will see to that even if you get Justlin to understand. Humph! Somebody has to burn. Y'all been burning the community for years. What the hell were you thinking?"

"I wasn't. I didn't think that it would get this bad. They'd give me a name, a few facts and tell me what they wanted me to do. Seemed harmless. I didn't read the reports or the files. I didn't know the lines they crossed or how. I was rewarded money, raises, and rank and never thought to look back."

"So now what's in this for you? Yes, I'll keep the wolves at bay as long as I can. Once Justlin and Tyson find the missing link is you, I'll pretend to be shocked. They're going to find out you're in this mess, but I won't defend your actions."

"That's all I need. Time to talk to them and Justlin. That's my only chance. Maybe I'll have to pay them off or something."

"You ain't learned nothing over the years. That's blood money, your rank was giving in lieu of what you've paid, it's blood money. The only trade for that is your life. Listen, business only my friend. Stay away from all of us unless it's business, that's my payment for your favor. If you cross that line, involve me or the Cold Case Unit in anyway, I'll be meeting with the governor and Justlin myself. Seriously Walter, if it comes down to it, I'll be meeting with you."

Worthy downed the rest of his drink and left cash on the table. Michaels watched him as he walked away. Losing the friendship they shared, was stabbing at his heart. He never had the strength or courage Dennis Worthy had. He could only imagine how much more he would lose.

CHAPTER 23

Tyson was glad to finally push the button to the remote. He decided to watch a movie, or let the movie watch him. He couldn't read anymore without his eyes closing and he knew it wouldn't be long before the television would have the same effect. He made himself a quick dinner, opened a bottle of beer and began what he thought would be the path to relaxation. Just as he settled into his favorite recliner his phone rang.

"Damien, I need you to listen." Justlin was talking low, and Damien could barely understand what she was saying with the music playing in the background.

"Justice?"

"Yeah man! Why, whenever I call you, you act like you're surprised? We said we'd be keeping in touch. Are you alone or what?"

"Or what? What? I can barely hear you!" Damien readjusted the recliner to the upright position and turned down the television. "I'm alone, what's up?"

"I'm coming by." The phone disconnected before Damien could respond.

"*What the hell!*" Shaking his head, he wondered where she was coming from. He looked around his living room and the open space to the kitchen and den. The house was a wreck. It was normal during the week. He spent Saturday mornings cleaning and straightening the place.

"*Shit!*" The den wouldn't be a problem, the files were on the desk and couch in an orderly fashion. He had cross referenced the information provided by Montez and Ms. White. He made a makeshift chart that he mounted on the wall, a habit he did whenever he was involved in an investigation. They could talk in the dining room. He never used it. The kitchen was a wreck. Rushing he rinsed the dishes and put them in the dishwasher. He tied up the garbage and placed it on the deck. The quick-clean took thirty minutes and Justlin was ringing his doorbell. Spraying air freshener, he hurried only to slow down at the door. He ducked in the bathroom when he noticed his perspiration. His white t-shirt and basketball shorts held the evidence of a workout sweat. He took a moment to wash his hands and wipe his face. It was then he remembered he had on his tattered slides. He opened the door and Justlin shook her head as she pushed pass him.

"Girl, these phone calls, and drop-ins. You got to give a brother some time, a warning or something."

"Boy bye. One call and one visit and you already complaining? We getting ready to get real close."

Justlin looked around the large open rooms. She could tell he was a man with good taste. The furniture was contemporary but the color scheme, paint, pictures on the walls, and curtain décor spoke well above the "Bachelor" theme.

"Nice place, I'll skip the tour for now. I'm sure you've thrown all of your mess in the closed rooms."

Damien shook his head and dropped himself on the couch. It was obvious she had been out somewhere, he wanted to ask with who, but stopped himself.

"Listen, we're in this together, right? This may get bad quick."

"Justice, this is bad. Yes, we're in this together. Are you really here to confirm that I'm on your side?"

"It's not about sides Damien. We can't get these people if we have one person that gives in to being uncomfortable with this. I've done plenty of investigations where people have folded, and they get away with this kind of shit, over and over again. We've got them Damien. This time I think we've got them."

"I'm listening. Tell me what you've got and let's go from there."

Tina told him about her conversation with Michaels and Fulton. Damien told her about Knowles and his relationship to Worthy. There was a moment of silence between them.

"So, you think Michaels and Worthy are involved?"

"Listen, I know someone is. Just like Porter said, hell you said it too. Someone signed off on those folders and pushed them through. There's a system and it seems Michaels may be a part of it. I'm not sure Worthy even knows. Fulton knows something and if we're going to find out what he knows, we may have to tell him what we know. The problem is, if what we're thinking is right, we can't let on that we are working with Fulton. It's not good for our side if we're working with the defense lawyer on this."

"Okay so working with him how and how much is the question."

The doorbell rang interrupting the thought of both Tyson and Justlin. Tyson stood and motioned outlining his fashionable appearance. Justlin shook her head and pointed to the door when the bell sounded off again.

"Hang on, hang on." Tyson opened the door and Worthy pushed his way past him.

"Man, I'm sorry. Do you have a beer, or something stronger? I couldn't go straight home I figured I could talk...oh, I'm sorry am I... Justice, Damien, I didn't mean to..."

"You didn't. She just did the same thing. I guess Porter will be coming too... hey, I'm joking y'all lighten up."

Justlin and Worthy sighed in unison. "Captain, Justice, what do you want to drink? Beer, wine, something stronger?"

"Wine for me, you Cap?"

The captain was pacing from the deck doors to the end of the kitchen. "I'll take a beer. I had a few before I decided to come here."

"What's up? You could have called."

"Damien, I couldn't talk. I've been going over this...wait seriously if I interrupted anything here, I'm sorry."

"Cap, it's okay. I'm sure your boy will make it up to me later." Damien tried not to look shocked. Justlin smiled. He realized she was going along with the captain's assumption they were handling personal business.

"So, what's up? What's got you wound up?"

"Michaels. I don't know what he knows but he knows something. I had to think about what to say to the two of you. I told him I wouldn't say anything. I decided to talk with you Damien, you know we've been dealing with these 'untouchables' for a minute. I told Michaels I'll be the buffer until he can clear himself. Man, he's in too deep and he knows it. Justlin, he's looking to smooth things over with you. Keep you in the dark. I don't know how."

"He can't Cap. He blew his cover with me when he called the other night. I just didn't know what he had done. I knew he had his hands in it. A signature, a phone call, maybe a few, maybe more than that. Marshall said enough for me to listen closely when he called. I checked the procedures, the guidelines for the reports, dates, going back before and after he was captain of the unit. Marshall was right. They didn't turn in detailed reports. The information that was left from the reports deflected the attention of our office. Simply because so many of the reports were botched missing more pertinent information. Some were questioned, refiled, even requested at hearings, but none of those we're looking into now. I got my answers from my office earlier today, the captain during those years let the lieutenant handle any problems that came back."

"Marshall? He's involved in this mess too?"

"Appears that way. We have to look further though."

Damien led Worthy and Justlin to his den. They stood in awe for a moment not knowing if what they were looking at was an evidence board for a crime scene or a computer white board.

"Man, is this all you do?"

"No, I try not to." He smiled at Justlin.

"We're working on that Cap," Justlin responded teasingly.

Worthy turned slowly in a circle. "Okay, so what the hell is this?"

"Well sir, I've got the three main cases as headers. My thought is that Fulton will be striking for them first. So, trying to stay ahead of his questions what you see is what we have and don't have on each case, cross-referenced with information of the others. As you can see all were checked in by the same officer…"

"Yes, and I see Marshall's name is here as well. Hmmm… Tyson, this could really get ugly."

"Cap it will get worse if we don't have a handle on it before it reaches the media. My office won't stand for a cover-up of this magnitude. Do you know what Michaels did or didn't do?"

"No, I was too damn mad to listen. Hell, then again, I didn't want to know. The less I know the better. I'll find out when you find out. Then, well…"

Worthy shook his head before continuing. Taking a seat in the chair Tyson offered he spoke in a concerned tone.

"My nephew, Knowles. I thought he and Knight would make a good pair. Now the boy is telling me that Knight may be caught up in this mess."

"Did you send him to me knowing something was up?"

"No man. I moved the two of them to your unit to keep them from having to deal with Sheers and the bullshit he was serving. I'm sure they were upset that my nephew got details that Sheers thought his boys should get. So, they had words a few weeks ago. The lieutenant called and said a complaint was made about Knowles and Knight. No real complaint petty nonsense, I knew they were behind it. But you know how they do so I had them moved when you needed the help. No thought to connecting them to Sheers and his boys again."

"Did he tell you his thoughts regarding Knight? We've had to change his assignment after our discussion?"

They talked in detail about the younger detectives and the problem they faced. Justlin juggled with the thought of mentioning Fulton's proposal. She decided to wait until Worthy left. The captain didn't stay much longer, apologizing for interfering in what he thought was to become a date night.

"You know, I told Michaels he didn't stand a chance with Batman here." He chuckled to himself as they walked out of the den.

"A chance for what?" Justlin didn't catch the joke.

"Oh, his thought has always been that he'd, you know, be your choice between him and Damien here. I guess that's why he thought he'd talk with you and wanted me to talk to Damien. If I wasn't so damn mad at him, I'd call him and tell him, well you know."

"No, really I don't." Justlin's face told the men she was clearly not thinking the way they were.

"I'll explain it to her when you leave. Say goodnight, Justice."

"Oh, that's how y'all gonna play this?" She paused in thought and the men laughed as Worthy made his exit. "So, Michaels thought he'd convince me to cover for him if we got together? What the hell? I'm going over this in my mind now. The captain can't really think that you and I…"

"Hey, is that such a bad thought. I mean, here I am in my relaxed attire with you at night, in my home, I mean he can think what he wants. It may be to our advantage."

"Our advantage?"

"Now I don't have to ask you to come over and put on a fancy appearance. You've seen…"

"Tyson!"

"What? I was gonna say you've seen me at my worse. My best is yet to come, I mean if they think we're dating, I can show you better than this. You know that, right?"

"Listen, you and I both know…"

"Know what? Is it that crazy that a pretty woman like you couldn't fall for a man who doesn't wear a speedo?"

Justlin rolled her eyes and laughed. "Listen, do you think I should have said what Fulton suggested we do?"

"No, let's work this without anyone in the ranks. The less they know the better. Over the years, giving Worthy or Michaels information never solved the issue. Now I know why. Michaels had the last say and my concerns were dropped at Worthy's desk. He mentioned being the buffer for the media, the less he knows about the investigation the better."

"So how do we handle Fulton?"

"They'll expect him to come in, make requests for documents, do his norm. We don't want that to stop. It will raise brows if he doesn't dig for answers. We'll have to meet or talk with him after hours. The place can be worked out. Let everyone else assume what the captain is assuming. We'll be getting real close. Didn't you say that when you arrived?"

"Only if you promise to get another pair of slippers."

CHAPTER 24

The morning sun peeked through the curtains startling Tina. She jumped up thinking she'd overslept only to realize it was the weekend. She slept later than she wanted but it was obvious she needed the rest. Folders, files, and missing data kept her mind spinning each night she came home. It had been close to a month of dead ends. Tyson and the others had begun looking outside of their unit for answers and the results took them deeper into an abyss of cover-ups.

Fulton kept his promise, there had been no media frenzy. It was too quiet and that alone raised everyone's suspicions. Tina agreed to meet with Fulton and Tyson to discuss what had been found and what was next. Their weekly meetings proved necessary although it didn't give them any concrete evidence that Sheers, or anyone connected to him was involved.

Spending the early part of the morning sleeping caused Tina to rush a bit. The cases she reviewed the night before caused questions she had Phillip check into. She printed the results to share with Tyson and Fulton. She was sure Fulton would be aware of the depth of each case. If the men were truly guilty, she didn't want to give Fulton a key for their release, but the forensics was questionable.

It wasn't strange for forensic evidence to be inconclusive or reports not to be available at the time of the trial, but the cases and guilty verdicts were based on the same evidence. Justlin and Tyson concluded that the evidence had been removed from the files after sentencing. It was no longer about Worthy overlooking reports or missing entries in the evidence log. Withholding evidence or extracting evidence would hold a higher penalty. The state would be held liable.

Tina's Saturday morning ritual wouldn't include any reading or preparing the weekly report she submitted on Mondays. She would include the notes from their meeting and following the sequence of notes, Moorestown Main Precinct Investigation Week Five would be filed. It became obvious to her that at the close of the investigation there would be terminations, possible transfers, and another set of trials. There would no longer be a denial that the results would shake up departments across the state.

The late afternoon meeting would give her time to return calls from family and read her personal emails. Her phone rang just as she made her second cup of coffee. She grabbed the phone and the coffee and retreated to the couch.

"Hello." The voice on the other end caused her to juggle the phone and the cup.

"Justice, if I didn't know better, I'd say you were deliberately ducking my calls."

"Why would you say that Chief?"

"Seems I can't catch you. Called the unit the other day, they said you were in the field. What are you doing, or may I ask, in the field?"

"Hmmm, investigating? Seems like we're just going in circles."

"Well, it was said that it was a difficult case."

"Really? Who said that? Mr. Fulton or the media?" Justlin hoped he would reveal information they didn't have.

"Porter and Tyson. I mean, they were talking about the report. You are working on that report, right? I didn't know the report was connected to Fulton and his cases."

"Seems those cases are on the report. Since the media was digging into the Foster case, we'd get ahead of them if we can find the missing pieces connecting a specific case or two."

"Or two? Tell me there's not more."

"I'm sure you didn't call for an update or details on this mess. We're still sorting things out."

"Yes, keep me informed. I'd love for this to just go away."

"My office wants it cleared up as well. So, what can I do for you on a Saturday?"

"I was thinking, you're spending all your time here working on this case, maybe you'd need a break. I'd love to take you to dinner, maybe you'd join me on the lake. You don't have to do the fishing of course but the outing may do you some good. You know, taking you away from the folders may relieve a bit of stress. I know how working with those guys day after day may be aggravating."

"Not at all. I'm actually enjoying getting to know them. You can't tell a person by the reports. They're good people, hard workers, and seeking justice. My kind of people."

Tina waited for the delayed answer.

"Tina, that's what we all want, right? I mean, that's why we're in this business, to do the right thing by everybody. I hope you believe we're all on the same team."

"It's obvious Michaels, everyone is not on the same team, or maybe they're playing by different rules."

"If we work together, we can stop this mess once and for all."

"We? I thought you and Worthy were working together on this, I'm with the unit working. What have you found out?" Tina waited for what she knew would be a lie. Rather than let her anger mount she answered for him." Let us know what you've got, that is, when you get something concrete. Fulton isn't playing this round. Fair or not, he's got a reason to come demanding his client's release. Do we know if this guy that turned himself in is legit?"

"I, uh, I haven't checked into that yet. I figured I'd let the process move along."

"Yep, that seems to be what has been done over the years. Just let it smooth over. Chief, let me remind you that everyone from the arresting officers to you, will be questioned thoroughly on this matter. We can't let Fulton empty the jail because of neglect. The governor will see heads roll and I don't think he'd stop with just the officers involved."

"Listen, I didn't call to debate or argue. The fact is…"

"The fact is that this mess is your mess. You were the ranking official that signed or ignored records that went to court, and prosecuted individuals. I'll tell you this much. Whatever's missing was there, which means someone on the inside removed it."

"Tina, listen, I really need to talk to you about this. Can we meet tomorrow? I mean, I've got a copy of what Tyson submitted and we can review it together. I can tell you about my part in all of this and possibly share who was working the unit during that time. I've noted it on the report. Believe me, I understand your frustration, but it's misdirected."

"Misdirected? I haven't directed anything toward anyone. Here we go with the bias shit! Listen Walter! This mess will not fade, it ain't going nowhere. You know why? 'Cause Fulton is carry the marching banner. It's the same message that has been displayed for years. People in the community are tired of being the brunt of systemic racism. This report brings up questions and they will be answered. You can't just say those checking what you neglected to check are misdirected or bias."

"Okay, okay. I'm not trying to anger you. I'm on your side. I really want you to understand things from my point of view."

"Let me explain my point of view. I am the eyes and ears of the government. I speak, in part for the governor. I am not on anyone's side, nor do I care about what their point of view is. You, as well as the others know me. I'm not for sugar coating. This mess can land a few people in jail. Walter if you are looking to persuade me to look through your tinted shades, meet me at the office and tell everyone your point of view. Now, if you're feeling pressure from anyone regarding this, then let's meet, talk, and see how to solve this. Maybe you'll get by with a few bruises."

"I have people to answer to as well…"

"Let me remind you, whoever it is, they don't sit as high as Governor Clinton Banks. I can assure you they don't. So, you answer to them and get back to me on the b.s. Chief Michaels. Let's keep our friendship in tack. Don't try to play with my heart strings, I assure you the strings you pull will be the same ones attached to the rope that will hang you if you're dirty."

"Justice, I understand. Can we talk tomorrow?"

"No, I'll be in your office on Monday. I think we better keep this in house."

Tina disconnected the call, saying aloud. "*Good ole boys, my ass!*"

CHAPTER 25

"Samantha Sayers here. Fulton call me when you get this message. It's the third one. I don't want to stir things, but c'mon man, I haven't heard from you in weeks. An update on what's going on will keep my people at bay."

She disconnected the line wondering if she had given Fulton credit that he hadn't earned. She doubted she would get a return call. His office was closed, but she'd be there early Monday morning waiting for him to waltz through the door. The highly recognized lawyer was news-worthy no matter what case he was representing. The executives at The Village Ledger were worried that their top reporter couldn't land the story. Whispered questions circulated the small offices at the Main Street Plaza location. Samantha decided to work from home the later part of the week. Avoiding the questions and worrying about making the deadline for their upcoming Sunday streaming podcast, she wouldn't return to the office until she had a conversation with Fulton. She would work from the field or at home and no one would be the wiser.

The agreement was to allow Fulton time to investigate without the eyes of reporters or the public interest groups. It had been two weeks since their conversation. She told him there was no guarantee how the story would spin. Once released it would morph into its own media frenzy. Fulton wasn't new to the arena. As a lawyer in Philadelphia for more than fifteen years, he won the support of the community and was featured in many avenues of the media. He wasn't shy to call out politicians or those who didn't play fair in the courtroom. It didn't bother him to be held in contempt or pay a fine for a rebuttal. He marched, protested, and wrote his own submissions to many magazines and papers. Many were surprised he hadn't published his own book or had a time slot allotted on the television.

There were cases before the Foster case that brought attention to the well-dressed, Harvard educated, single, African American lawyer. His personal life wasn't hidden but for a reporter, Samantha hadn't found much to stir emotions for, or against him.

He didn't seem to be "involved" with anyone, and if he was, she was a well-kept secret. He reminded her of Detective Damien Tyson with a flock of cheerleading women waiting in the wings for a moment of attention. Neither man seemed to be seeking the attention of the opposite sex.

They, and a few others she placed in the group, were hard to read. They had their own drama, she was sure. Her southern grandparents would warn her during her college years about pretty men with secrets. A lesson she learned the hard way, thinking it was true love. She flirted, went on dates, and had her pleasures teased and pleased over the years, but she wasn't interested in a long-term romance.

When she finally got a chance to meet with Lawrence Fulton Esq., his low-key demeanor caused her to realize he did perk her interest and it wasn't totally about the case. She tried not to make it obvious. So, she was home on a Saturday morning waiting for his return call. She hoped she hadn't been too pushy. Telling him about her relationship with the Cold Case Unit and those in the higher ranks got her the meeting with him. After the press conference with the family at the Watson's home, she expected to have a story that readers could follow until Julian Foster's release. Fulton was sure his client would be exonerated once all the evidence was presented.

It was close to eleven and Samantha's thoughts were interrupted with an alert for a text message that appeared on her phone.

> We need a story to air Sunday, Ms. Sayers. If you don't have one this week, I'll be moving Collins's slot to fill yours. This placement will remain until you get your over-the-top story you promised.

"Dammit!" She tossed the phone on the couch. The phone rang as it hit the cushioned seat and she prayed silently that it was Fulton.

"Hey, you okay? The message you left sounded as though there's a problem."

"The problem is you. That interview left people hanging. The public, as you say, your community is asking questions and what you disappear?"

"C'mon Samantha. You know better. I can't have cameras and microphones following me on this. I don't want anyone to stop me from uncovering this. I am a man of my word. You'll get your exclusive before we hit them in their knees. They may want you to…"

"What? They who?"

"Hey, how about this, let's go from another angle. Question them, the chief and captain. I'll give you the names of anyone else that a nudge from the media may rattle. If we break them down bit by bit maybe, they'll squeal. Will that hold you over until I get more?"

"Yeah, I'm sure it will raise eyebrows and keep everyone's attention." Samantha grabbed a pen and searched the room for a pad. "So, who's off limits. I'm sure there's a line you don't want me to cross."

"Leave the Cold Case Unit and any of the personnel there alone. I don't need them giving away what they may or may not have."

She put the pen down. "So just those in rank? Didn't they give a statement already? Do you really want them to repeat what they've already lied about?"

"Listen, you'll have the right questions to prod them, believe me. I've got a few meetings coming up this week. If all goes as planned, they'll wonder where you got your information. You don't need cameras and a press conference. You just want to know what they know before you talk to me. You know, giving them a courtesy call."

"Hmmm, and they'll bite. You're playing with sharks in their water. What makes you think they won't be prepared for the questions?"

"Let's see if they, as you say, bite. I'm almost sure they'll be more concerned about who else is swimming with them."

"Okay when will you have the questions you want answered?"

"Give me a few more days, I'm compiling information. I want the questions to hit hard. If they don't answer you verbally, you'll be able to read their expressions. Then you do what you do best."

"What's that?"

"Report it."

CHAPTER 26

Fulton's cabin near Bushkill Creek became the perfect place to meet every Saturday. Tyson teased the lawyer during their first meeting. He couldn't believe Lawrence Fulton would be interested in the wooded area along the Delaware River. His home away from home was close to the Pocono Resorts. He accepted Tyson's teasing and invited the detective to get away sometime and share the relaxation he had acquired. Tyson and Porter had to admit after a week of work overload, they welcomed the Saturday morning drive to what they labeled the "woods."

Tyson and Porter drove together. Fulton welcomed them each week at one o'clock with a catered lunch. Justlin usually arrived between one and two. The meeting was scheduled to start at two thirty. It gave everyone time for the drive, lunch and conversation that didn't include the crimes of the week. They were adding up suspicious behavior, comparing notes and documents that were added after the cases were closed. Each week there were new discoveries and suspects added.

"Larry, do we have anything on who handled the forensic report?" Damien pushed the folder to the middle of the table. "Seems that there is no signature on any of these, just initials. The final report requires a signature for court, doesn't it?"

"Yeah man, it does. Look here, there's no initials signing these into evidence. It's just saying this was found at the scene or taken from the suspect at the time of the arrest. Even the pictures taken at the scene aren't signed into evidence according to the report. Just enough for the arrest."

"Okay, so maybe I'm not understanding. The prosecutor used this evidence, how? Julian Foster was Tammilyn's boyfriend at the time of the rape. So whatever evidence of him being there, even in her bed is not unusual. I mean they were dating for what, years?"

"Porter, man I've argued that point at every turn. His DNA was everywhere and should have been expected. They didn't even consider it the norm."

"Who reported the rape? I mean, we know she didn't." Justlin put the folder back in the middle of the table. "How did this investigation go on without an initial report?"

"A copy should be there. The initial report is with the court documents and in the computer file. I didn't request it yet. At least not this time. Initially, when I took on the case, I got everything I requested. Now that I'm asking again for an appeal, it's been difficult, to say the least."

"So, it's safe to say, we don't have any initial statements in the files we're searching?" Justlin waited for an answer.

"That's not true. Check the data if the report was missing it was indicated. If it's checked, it could be in the computer file."

"Justlin, I checked with your girl, what's her name?"

Tina paused; she had no idea he'd spoke with Marcie. "I'm sorry. Did you say my girl?"

"Yeah, Officer Williams, I asked to see the initial report and she checked and said it was with the Cold Case Unit."

"Wait a minute. Either we have all the documents, or we don't." Tyson looked over the data sheet. "Porter call Montez and ask does this mean physical or computer inputted data."

Porter stepped away from the table to make the call.

"Okay, regardless. Larry, you went to court with this information, was it there then?"

"Yes, it had to be. That's what they arrested him for and later based his sentencing on. The claim was they found his DNA on her clothes and person. She was beat and raped. We tried to keep that out of the news. Actually, it was an attack and rape. They didn't arrest Julian until he came to visit her in the hospital a day or two later. He left the morning after the rape to visit family in Florida. They assumed he ran. They both admitted to having sex earlier that day, saying goodbye and promising to call each other daily. Julian returned as soon as he could get a flight back. He went to visit her; the cops arrested him there."

"Wow. So, was there more than one DNA held in evidence? There had to be, right? I mean she was beat and raped by someone other than Julian and the only DNA is his?"

"Justlin, I took over the case after he had been in jail five years. I've been over it, time and time again. There's a hole somewhere and it leads to a few other cases that I'm representing as well."

"Connected how, what did you find? I think that may be the information we need to find out who is behind this. Tyson, what's your thoughts, are you with us here?"

Damien seemed engrossed in a page on the report. So focused he didn't hear Justlin's question.

"Okay, hey. Montez says that if the data sheet has the information checked it could be hard copy or file. We'd have access to either, but if there's no check mark in that column, we have no information at all."

"That's what I was looking at. Forensics, who the hell was in that department then? On all of Fulton's cases the forensics is missing or dated and withdrawn."

"Withdrawn?!" Fulton, Porter and Justlin questioned in unison.

"Is there dates and signatures, no I'll take an initial for who did those entries?" Fulton held his pen, waiting for an answer.

"Same initials. P.S. I'm assuming that would be Philip Sheers. Officer signature, he gave his initials. Somehow, I knew it would be one of them."

"Hard to prove it was removed with malicious intent. He's a cop, could have removed it for any reason." Fulton put his pen down and sat back in his seat.

"Would the dates and the times link up to before the court date and after? I mean if they do, we could prove they tampered with it expecting Foster to remain in jail."

Justlin shrugged her shoulders hoping the suggestion was a solution.

"Does it work that way Fulton? Does Tyson have an angle with that?"

"Possible and not possible. So, they arrest him because of his DNA. His alibi is spotty during the time of the assault. Hanging with a few friends, home by himself packing, and most of all his aunt having no knowledge of his mini trip to Florida. I think that canned it for him."

"What about the assault? No witnesses? A random act? What was the perp after other than sex? Why beat her?"

"Porter, been there too brother. Now this dude shows up and says he did it. I'm sitting with him and his lawyer tomorrow."

"So, he'll testify, serve time, Foster is released and no repercussions for the file or the case being blotched from the beginning."

"Yeah, man that's the best shot we've got unless you can come up with something else. This happens more times than not. A person can do a life sentence, twenty-five years and be crying they didn't do it. Someone finds that missing key to the case and boom, they're released, nothing said or done. DNA findings, new evidence, missing facts, any excuse is good for the release. The fact is a life is wasted behind bars. Somewhere they wouldn't have been if we, the authorities, did our jobs. Yes, I'm including all of us."

"Well said, brother, but the fact remains we can't find the hole. The other cases do they involve missing DNA evidence or forensics at all? That's the angle I see in Foster's case."

"Damien, Celina Roberts returned after being missing at the age of nineteen. The courts have her for robbery and kidnap of an elderly couple. The Thornes claim Celina was with the ones that robbed and held them for five days. She says she too was a victim. They all were released at a gas station on Highway thirteen in Delaware. They released the Thornes and Celina is doing time. Check this, no evidence showing her touching anything in their home. They even admit not seeing her but the day they were abducted and when they were released. But I can't find any evidence that will help her."

"The other case, Mr. Crews, seemed strange to me when I read the reports." Justlin passed the folder to Tyson. "Says here he's waiting for the trial of another suspect, the one who was arrested?"

"Yeah, they picked him up saying he was involved in a drug pick up. They raided the home and busted the group with drugs, money, and guns. Mr. Crews allegedly made the arrangement for the buy. Picked up his drugs and left with no other surveillance. But here's the kicker, Mr. Crews wasn't here the day of the sale, the raid, or the arrest. He doesn't even live in this state."

"What?" Porter opened the file and began scanning the pages. "Wow, they don't even have his name in the report. Just a black man and on the last page his name is written in. Again, what evidence did they use to implicate him?"

"Not only that. This man left Philadelphia years ago. They sent the court order to his old address, and it was forwarded to the new one. He answered with a call and reported here hoping to clear up the matter. They cleared it for him, he's been in jail waiting for eight months now."

Damien stood to stretch. "Let me guess, no other evidence."

"None at all. I've asked to speak with the investigating officers in the cases. Asked for transcripts, details, you name it. So, I'm using other methods because I know, in these three cases, there's been some tampering. What I call, lazy police work."

Fulton and Justlin left Porter and Tyson at the table, as they walked out on the deck for a well-deserved break. It was close to four o'clock. It seemed later and Damien was ready to pack the folders in the boxes they were brought in. He took a deep breath before he spoke.

"Alright, there's connections to be found. Porter get with Montez cross reference initials and signatures. We've got files that match this mess stacked. I'm sure if we light a fire to one, the others will go up in flames. Justlin and I will dig into these initials; Officer Philip Sheers, Mark Simmons, and Michael Boone, Lieutenant Maurice Marshall, Chief Walter Michaels, and that boy Chambers."

"Chambers? Why Chambers, he wasn't even in the department back then."

"He's connected to someone. Let's find out who. Carlton Chambers check his record and that Miller girl too. We know who the other two are, check those two out."

Justlin smiled as Fulton handed her a glass of wine. "Yep, this will help."

"Tina, business over, I can call you that now. I noticed you guys stick to the last names even on Saturday."

"Habit. That's all, yes, you can call me Tina. I didn't know you had spoken with Officer Williams."

"Yes, right before I saw the two of you at dinner. Nothing really other than looking for the information in the case."

"She hadn't mentioned it. I wonder why."

"Probably too small of a matter. Do you think we can catch these guys?"

"I know those two in there..." she paused pointing back to the dining room entrance," ...they won't stop. There's been complaints about certain individuals for years. We've never been this close to putting names to incidents we knew they were involved in."

"Wow, really. You know you hear so much of the end story; very seldom do we know the reality is in the twist and turns, you know the middle."

"Fulton, there shouldn't even be a middle in these cases. There should have never been a case. It would drive me crazy to know my husband or child was in jail for something that someone just took a pen and added or erased documents. I can't believe someone deliberately made these changes."

"Tyson is right. It's forensics, the evidence, it's missing, someone moved it or didn't submit it."

Justlin watched and listened to Fulton. His concern was genuine, it showed. As he leaned on the banister of the deck that overlooked his property, the pool area and the manicured grass, she could feel herself relaxing in his presence.

"How long have you had this place here?"

The question was an abrupt change of topic, but Fulton smiled. He too was glad to switch his attention.

"About seven years now. Right after I started my own firm. I debated for years about staying in Philadelphia. I love the warmer climate, but I love the winter scenery. Plus, I still have family here. They're getting older and I want to be close to them. My mom has no intention of relocating."

"So, this is home for you too?"

"Yep, born and raised. How about you?"

Tina surprised herself. She and Fulton had a good discussion about personal and professional experiences. Education, adventures in travel, and questions about relationships that could be a conflict with their professional lives and duties. It was close to five when she decided she had told all but her grandmother's secrets. Tyson and Porter were seated in the living room dividing up the paperwork and folders when they re-entered the house.

"Are you still in these boxes?" Justlin teased.

"Yep, here's your box and Fulton here's your paperwork."

"So, we all have new assignments. Any questions you know how to reach us. Now, until next week people…" Porter stood to shake Fulton's hand and give Justlin a hug. "See you Ms. Lady on Monday. Damien, I think we're ready to ride, brother."

"I am with you. Fulton, man, I hope this is the lead to the end."

Justlin gathered her things on cue. "I'm leaving as well. Thanks again Fulton."

"Alright, we'll talk over the week, I'm sure."

Tyson walked ahead of Justlin to his car and smiled as she approached him at the driver's door.

"You look like you want to say something Ms. Justice."

"You were going to leave me here? You didn't even say c'mon."

Porter laughed as he opened the passenger door.

"Man, get in the car." Tyson turned back to Tina to complete his thought. "I thought you were socializing. I mean business was done and you didn't seem to be in a hurry to pack up. Did I miss the signal?"

"Tyson! There was no signal, geesh!"

"Okay, so why are you so, what? Frustrated? The two of you were talking, looked like everything was going well. I didn't want to interfere. Did you want me to interfere?"

"No, no, I guess not."

"Well, what's the problem? But you do know if you're going to fool Worthy you can't flirt with the lawyer."

"What?? Tyson, what? Why are you playing?"

"We have to get real close, remember?"

"Yeah, uh, umm. Call me later, before you hang out with Porter, please?"

Justlin got in her car and pulled out. Tyson smiled and waved to Fulton who was watching from the deck.

CHAPTER 27

The conversation during the ride back to Moorestown included Tyson explaining Worthy's visit and Justlin's teasing statements.

"Man, Worthy can't really believe that you and Tina Justlin would ever be a couple."

"Why not? I mean, it can happen. I wouldn't push it, but hey if it happens, I'd be okay with that."

"I guess you would. But didn't you say she was like Sayers? You know, a media magnet. I think that's what you said or what you meant."

"She attracts the media's attention, that's for sure. But c'mon man, she attracts me, you, and any other brother with a good eye. She's a beautiful woman and she has a sense of humor. I don't know much about her personal likes and dislikes, but she seems to be someone I could get to know and learn to…"

"C'mon man. Batman ain't never fell in love."

"Shit, you ever watch the way he looked at Catwoman. Besides, Bruce Wayne had his choice of women."

"Damien, you've always had a choice. But getting to really know one of them or learning to… man I can't even say it. Stick to dating. You know that love thing is a dangerous playground for you. How are the girls?"

"The girls are good. They want to stay with me this summer. I don't think that's gonna work out, but I've got time to convince them they're better off staying where they are. Maybe Sonya will have plans for them this year. Tina has no children, so maybe you're right. Dating may be a better choice."

"Or simply enjoying the work environment and let a brother like me sweep her off her feet."

"Man, she'll kick you right to the curb. You're not her type."

"Hmmm, if Fulton stands a shot, so do I."

"You think that conversation on the deck was his shot?"

"It may have been. But hey, what would I know since I'm not her type?"

Porter's phone buzzed. He shook his head as he read the message.

"You got daughters, and I got sisters. How's your cousin Kendra doing? Haven't heard you mention the wanna-be detective lately."

"After that friend of hers was sentenced, she took it hard. I think she was upset with me for dating her criminally minded friend. It took a minute for her to get over it."

"She may have felt guilty for introducing the two of you."

"Maybe, but me getting involved wasn't her fault. We talk every now and then, at least two times a month. She's a 911 operator now so I guess she's busy solving those cases."

"Hey, can she pull up records? I mean it's reaching a bit, but what about the 911 calls in these cases. Can't they be pulled?"

"It won't hurt to look into it."

"See, my advice leads you. You just have to follow."

Damien shook his head and couldn't help but laugh.

"I'm serious man. I do for you what Robin does for Batman."

"Stick to the police work. Batman never got dating advice from Robin. You know why?"

"Why?"

"Robin didn't have a girlfriend either."

Porter turned up the music on the radio to drown out Tyson's laughter. Fifteen minutes later Tyson was parking in his driveway. The men parted as Tyson's phone rang with a familiar tone.

"Hey, daddy."

"Hey, baby. How are you? What's up?"

"Would you mind if we came up later this summer?"

Tyson looked to the sky and mouthed "thank-you." "Well, I don't know, what's up?"

"We want to go with a few of our friends on vacation and that will be right after school ends. Then Grandma is taking us to New Orleans for the last two weeks of June. So, we wouldn't get to you until July."

"Oh, I see. Well, if you mother is okay with it…"

"She doesn't know yet, can you talk to her and tell her that you said it's okay. We know that's the first thing she'll ask, *'Did your father agree to this arrangement?'*"

"Sasha, did you even give it a thought. Your mom may have plans for you three to get together. I don't have a problem with any of it if your grandparents are okay with whomever you're going with. What are the vacation plans?"

"Dad, New Orleans, I just said that."

"No sweetie, with the friends. What are the plans, where are you going with them?"

"We're still deciding. But can you talk to mom, please? She never sticks to her plans. If she knows we have plans that you're okay with, we can skip her excuses."

"No not until I know when and where. The trip with your grandparents is fine but you need to be telling me more when it's just you and your friends. What juniors and seniors?"

"Yeah, pretty much. Well, your other child will be a junior but everyone else is either graduating this year with me or becoming a senior next year. Diamond is the youngest, and yes, she'll be well protected."

"I'm going to need more details before I agree with that trip. Did you even think about what if I said no?"

"Yep, maybe we'd just stay with Mom for the whole summer like we did…"

"Gotcha, let me know the arrangements. We can work it out. Where's Diamond now?"

"Tennis practice. I'll tell her to call you later. Love you."

The dial tone was once again his signal to hang up. He grabbed the boxes he dubbed his and continued into the house. He'd have to call Sonya's parents. They had a good relationship. Mr. and Mrs. Stabler loved their son-n-law and no longer argued their daughter's point of view. She convinced them for years that her modeling career was put on hold for her husband's career and desire to have a family. Once the girls were old enough to go to school on their own, she wanted to explore what she missed. After a few rejections, small commercial and print ad jobs, she gave up and left her family without saying goodbye. Damien never asked for their assistance in raising their granddaughters.

Damien became an instant single parent of two girls aged six and eight. Now years later, Sonya called asking for money or a place to stay when she was in town. There was no address or contact information for anyone to reach her. The girls moved with Damien's parents, and no one questioned why he made the choice to send them away from the only home they knew.

Their grandfather, Victor Tyson was a real estate broker and had two offices and staff. His wife Yvonne was a nurse but retired once the girls came to live with them. They understood Damien's job and the hours. He took off early in the summer months to be with them for what they called Daddy's vacay time. As they got older, he was no longer the fun dad. They enjoyed the trips to New York and the beach, but traveling was out of the question. He seemed to always be on duty.

Damien understood the excitement in Sasha's voice during their call. But being a detective, he'd have to check their every move. He smiled at the thought of what Sonya would say, if he could even find her. They hadn't had a conversation since the school year started. He'd call her parents without asking her whereabouts. Ms. Stabler would tell him all she knew. Their conversation would include soft sobs while asking him to forgive her daughter. He'd make the same promise with each call; he'd visit her and her husband in California with the girls. The calls were less frequent as the years went on.

CHAPTER 28

The phone rang again, Michaels ignored it as he had all morning. He didn't want to know the reason for the call. He could only imagine. The calls began the night before and hadn't stopped. He refused to answer knowing the voice on the other end would be another demand. He'd wait for the face-to-face visit that followed whenever he couldn't be reached.

He remembered the first meeting with those now in the circle referred to as "untouchables;" Tyson was right. No one touched them or bothered to challenge them. Their shady business deals within the city limits and too often beyond, were labeled as necessary progress with no names attached. The group was composed of those in political positions as well local business owners. Most of them had family connections in every area from local to state government. There was always someone who could be called to make "arrangements." Over the years, small favors or accepting an application or placement here and there turned dirty. People were fired, looked over, set-up, incarcerated and murdered to ensure progress was not delayed.

Walter Michaels had no connection. He scored high on each promotional exam. He was easy going and looked out for those he thought were headed for danger. Unbeknownst to him, it included a few of the "untouchables." He was introduced to politicians, and those who shuffled money and positions behind closed doors. Just like taking the exams, he passed their tests. Now years later, he was ready to ride out his last few years on the force and retire. He had been warned there was no retirement when it came to the group who had his back.

Sheers was the first officer who rubbed him the wrong way. No one had outwardly showed their disdain for other races the way Sheers did. His narcissistic behavior and racial overtones caused problems before he graduated from the academy. Being protected, he was now a detective. His behavior worsened over the years, and he was now a thorn in Michaels' side.

Sheers and his new partner, Boone, toyed with the idea that they could do whatever they wanted with little to no repercussions. Michaels would write the reports, file disciplinary charges, and have closed office meetings only to be told, he wasn't in any position to reprimand them. He was no longer worth the badge or accommodations he held. He had no authority over matters that weren't checked by the "untouchables."

Michaels was promoted to chief after the Foster case. Everyone knew the case would explode after botched evidence wasn't documented. Julian Foster, the nephew of Grace Foster, would shed light on the unit. Grace Foster had ties in the State Office. She had been in the political arena and currently sat on the board of organizations that would crucify many of the "untouchables" and their positions. They were scared and had Michaels sign off on the mistakes made. There were pay offs for those involved and only a thorough investigation would find the cover-up. It was suggested that if there were more cases with errors of sort, no one would be the wiser. It became a game of choice, and the "untouchables" chose the victims. The residents in Moorestown and the surrounding area needed to understand that the Central Precinct was cracking down on crime. When questioned about the arrests, and crime, the officers were pleased to say it was "work in progress."

The money was paid to those who connected the dots for the unscrupulous group. It was always on time each month, payments included having a blind eye when those the "untouchables" determined weren't worth their time to handle complained. Drug dealers lost money and drugs, others lost property, the family members who couldn't afford legal representation were extorted, and the cases grew in numbers. The group agreed and chose which case would be worth the pay-off. Many, like Grace Foster, had the money to pay, they needed to be convinced.

Michaels sat in his recliner as he reminisced speaking with Grace regarding Julian's case. She explained she believed he was being set up, but she couldn't understand the reason why. When asked about the cost of a lawyer, she simply replied he'd have representation. Michaels knew immediately the case was botched deliberately. Ms. Foster would be ruined financially if she agreed to silence the case. She'd give up and give in it all for her nephew. The table turned when it was announced Lawrence Fulton would be the new attorney for an appeal. The group hadn't banked on any lawyer taking on the case, especially one with the reputation of winning against the state and city officials.

Ms. Foster's husband had been the Director of Public Works and ran for a seat as Councilman years prior. After his death, Ms. Foster continued her work in various community organizations. Her support and finances were well intact and that was what caught the eye of Sheers and Boone. Progress included ridding the city of its black voice at every attempt for change. Grace and others had attracted the attention of the media causing the "untouchables" to fall back.

It stirred those who sat high, and the "untouchables" were feeling queasy. Detective Tyson and his Cold Case Unit would have a time going through files. It was a deliberate puzzle no one would be expected to solve. The pieces were scattered well, or so it was thought. No one banked on Principal Investigator "Justice" or the hot shot lawyer to join forces with them. Trouble was brewing and Michaels knew what the call would lead to. The phone rang again but stopped after the first ring. The doorbell followed and Michaels sat shocked, pinned to his seat.

"Who is it!" Michaels answered annoyed that they would send someone to his home.

"It's Marshall Chief, you okay?"

Michaels frowned as he wondered why the lieutenant would come to his home. They hung out a few times over the years, but never without a previous arrangement.

"Hang on. I'll be right there." He checked the end table drawer where he kept his weapon and continued to the door. Satisfied it was in place, he went to open the door. "Hey, sorry about that. I've been sleeping off and on. Had a hell of a headache. C'mon in."

Michaels stepped aside and let Marshall in. He took a moment to check outside the front door for any unusual cars parked near the entrance. Marshall stood in the middle of the room waiting for Michaels to regain his composure.

"They ain't here man. C'mon away from the door. It's just me. What the hell is going on? Sheers asked me to reach out to you. Said you sounded like you would be making some mistakes with this investigation."

Michaels led the lean lieutenant to the living room. Marshall was dressed casual, jeans and a sweatshirt, and Nike sneakers. The chief made a mental note of his clothing and his demeanor. The question he posed fell in line with what Michaels expected. Sheers or one of the others sent someone to check on him. He took his seat ready to explain his position.

"Have a seat man. That damn Sheers and his dumb-ass side kick will get us all caught up. He called me the other night, the beginning of the week. He wanted me to keep Tyson and the Principal Investigator from the state at bay. Man, no one would have thought this shit would come back to haunt us. Marshall, I'm done with that mess, and I guess you are too since you're no longer in that unit."

"Well, I'm a little higher up the ladder now so, I don't see much of what I had before. Being in that storage area, the Cold Case Unit as it's now called, hell you see everything. All I can say is, if that unit was set up like it is now, back then, those assholes would have been in jail. Some of the…"

"I know Marshall. That's what this is about. It's rolling downhill now, and I guess they don't want to be standing in it." Michaels' frustration was beginning to show.

"So, why didn't you talk to them when they called today? What do they want you to do? I mean, if you look too anxious about this mess, you'll look guilty."

"He told me to delegate, to who? That's what I want to know. Who do I tell this mess to, and then in the next breath tell them to handle it? You want a beer?"

The two met in the middle of the room and walked to the island in the kitchen. Michaels sat two beers on coasters and took a seat on the stool. The two talked for more than an hour before Marshall's phone rang.

"Yeah, he's home. Everything is fine… I'll let him know, sure."

Michaels didn't wait for the explanation. He stood not knowing if he needed to be closer to the end table that held his protection. He was sure that the lieutenant understood his feelings had changed regarding the group they both expressed regret about. Neither would admit the mistakes they made were worth the trouble they would face if they were connected to any of the misconduct the Foster case would expose.

"It wasn't Sheers. I know that's what you're thinking. Listen they want me to tell you there's a meeting tomorrow night. We need to know what Tyson or Porter are doing about Chambers."

"Chambers? What the hell is going on with Chambers? That's the young detective that just got assigned to the unit, right?"

"Yeah, seems like he messed up. Did anyone call you yesterday or today to tell you about him?"

"What the hell did he do? Putting him there was Boone's idea. I simply told them to pick two from the list. What they've been there for three weeks if that. I didn't get a call about him. What's the problem?"

"Good, maybe they're overlooking his stupidity. Boone claims he was caught in Porter's office. Something about him searching for information in the files. Following the directions, he was given by Sheers, and well they're thinking you got a complaint."

"This is the shit I'm talking about. Now my future or next whatever in the department depends on me following their decision about this guy. What was he doing and why? Why would they think a novice wouldn't get caught? Hell, everyone in that department has more time than Chambers, or any of those foot shoulders for…"

"Listen, don't work yourself up. You didn't get any notice, calls, or a report, maybe none was written. I'll let them know."

"So, if that's all the meeting is about, I don't need to be there, right? I really can't deal with them in the emotional state I'm in. I hope you can express my feelings to them. I did what was asked. I was told it wouldn't affect me, or my lifestyle. And now? Now what Marshall, what part are you playing in this, hit man?" Michaels paused, shocked by the expression on Marshall' face. "Don't look shocked. Why did they send you here?"

"I wouldn't be a part of that type thing. The little we did was enough for me."

"Yet, you're in another position, still attached to them."

"We're attached. I'm here to find out what do we do about it."

CHAPTER 29

The message came across the reporter's cell phone. She took the time to immediately write the names on her pad, giving each of them two pages of blank space. Fulton hadn't called her again. As he promised, a list of questions followed. He expressed she shouldn't deviate from the questions he gave for each name. The answers would trigger other questions he was sure, and it would give her the opportunity to create a story that would cause the media frenzy they wanted.

Samantha had to admit, the lawyer gave her the rope that could hang the heads of the precinct and their underlings. Her position at the Village Post would be highlighted and nudge the local news station to consider her proposal for her own segment. After the Resort Murders, and a few other prominent cases she reported on, Ms. Sayers would once again be the lead reporter with the breaking news.

It was still early, and Sunday morning services were still in progress. She had a meeting with Grace Foster at three. A meeting she dared not to tell Fulton about, but it was the only way to get the family's voice in her article. It would be a stab in the heart from the family to the officials that took a decade of Julian's life away. Samantha knew the minute the story broke there would be other networks, papers, and reporters seeking to springboard their career as she unveiled the details to the public.

Fulton didn't forbid her from talking with the family. He warned against it. For this appeal, he felt their emotions would shadow the fact that many of the convicted were held without adequate representation. No one would pay attention to the missing facts in the case when they were watching a family break down for a loved one. Fulton explained it was his reason for selecting The Village Post. Samantha had been the only reporter who questioned what the lawyer thought would be the motive for the courts and its representatives to continuously send people to prison without all the evidence adding up. He promised her, she would get the full exclusive story. It would and had to include more than just the family's perspective.

Grace Foster was no stranger to the paper or Samantha. She called when Julian was arrested, during his trial and conviction. Once Lawrence Fulton agreed to take the case, she called again stating she wanted to speak on behalf of the family. She would wait for the lawyer to hold media releases; it was after all seemed to go quiet that Ms. Foster called for a meeting.

Samantha decided a light lunch for the two of them, with cake and tea would be a nice touch before a question-and-answer period. Her modest townhouse apartment was suggested by Ms. Foster. Samantha spent the morning preparing for her guest. There wasn't much to do since living alone meant only one area at a time would be considered a mess. The two-bedroom apartment was smaller than most in the complex, but she chose it for the view of the river from her second-floor deck. It brought peace for her writing.

The warmth of the day would allow them to sit on the deck while having tea. She thought it would add a bit of comfort to what would be an uncomfortable situation. It would be Samantha's first one on one interview without the cameras. She would have to hold on to the story until Fulton gave her the okay to release all they would uncover.

Her nerves were stirring. She couldn't understand why she felt as she did. Knowing Ms. Foster's position in the city, the level Lawrence Fulton was on and the story that would become breaking news on all channels, she could say she was a bit scared. Mishandling the story could cost Julian Foster and the others. The reputation of a lawyer, a city advocate and the top reporter would be crucified by other media outlets, community activists, and city officials.

As she looked around her apartment for unusual placements, she calmed herself by a nod of approval. The toss salad and triangular cut sandwiches were sent over early from the deli near the courthouse. Samantha moved the tray again from the island in the kitchen to the dinette set that sat near the glass doors of the deck. The weather was warmer than predicted for the afternoon, so sitting where there would be somewhat of a view, she hoped would ease the tension.

The doorbell rang five minutes after three and Samantha put on a welcoming smile before she opened the door. She was shocked when Ms. Foster entered followed by Tammilyn Watson. She tried not to show any expression as she led them into her living room.

"Oh, how nice. I have to say I wasn't expecting you to be accompanied by Tammilyn. There won't be any problem with Mr. Fulton, will there? I mean you being here and talking with me won't hinder the case for Julian will it."

"I'm sure Mr. Fulton would have told us not to come had that been the case." Ms. Foster replied handing Samantha her cape that complimented her two-piece suit.

Samantha wondered if the two attended church service together. Her question would help calm her nerves.

"Of course, he would have said something. Did you enjoy Sunday service together?"

"We attend together every now and then. Do you know Pastor Butler? He has been close to Tammilyn through all of this. Me too for that matter. My family has been with that church since I was a young woman. Introduced her to some nice young ladies, single parents, youth in college like her, and elders. We've all got her in prayer as we continue to fight for this mess. Did Mr. Fulton call you? He told us he would let you know what wouldn't be a part of your story. Cause I don't mind telling it as I see it and Tammilyn, well she can tell you what went on that night and since then."

"I was hoping to talk freely without the thought of us having to…, well no worries, I'm sure what we discuss will be okay to print. Especially, if the two of you agree. We can sit here at the table and have a bite to eat and get acquainted first."

Samantha took Tammilyn's jacket and put it in her room with Ms. Foster's cape. The two ladies went to the deck whispering how beautiful the view of the river was.

"Do you see many boats come through? I'd love to ride on one of those boats that tend to go through every now and then."

"Tammilyn, there were so many daily when I first moved here. Now a lot of fishing boats, only a few that are just tourist rides. I love the view in the summer as well. It's one of the reasons I chose this complex."

The ladies didn't seem to have the worry in mind that Samantha did. She had agreed to wait for Fulton to give her the green light for interviewing the family. She'd have to explain her actions and hope he wouldn't be upset enough to pull the story.

They ate and talked about the changes in Moorestown. Samantha listened as the older woman told her details of the years when she and her husband first moved to the area. She explained how different it was when the community watched out for each other and their families. It was a familiar story that was told by the men and women who were over the age of sixty-five. Many weren't raised in the area they retired, but Mr. and Mrs. Foster moved there when they first married. They watched the town grow and change. The political arena was open to anyone who dared to run against those whose family had roots in the area.

The Fosters moved in and made a name for themselves in the community. Their children attended all the schools, sports activities, and community events. The family greeted and celebrated the minorities that began to migrate to Moorestown and the surrounding area. Organizations for better housing, jobs and politics were on the rise and the Fosters were key members sitting on many of the boards. No one displayed racial discord in the early years, it seemed like a dream. Ms. Foster, now in her seventies, spoke of the years when everyone wanted what was best for all.

"Child, things have changed, and no one cares to fight back. We fought for the right to be here whenever there was a whisper of us being pushed elsewhere. Where were we going? Many of the folks here bought or were given land to build on. We built our home, rented until the final nail was hammered in. Beautiful cabin like home," she laughed," that's what my husband called it, a cabin. I love it. I'm still in it. Once he got sick, Julian came to live with us. He promised to finish his college years here. We promised to pay for it."

She took a moment to eat a bit. She kept her focus on the view from the deck and neither Tammilyn nor Samantha interfered in what seemed to be a necessary silence among them. She sighed and continued.

"Derrick gave Julian the fathering he didn't get in New York. His mother and my sister, live in the Bronx. Julian was raised by the two of them. He wasn't a hard head or nothing like that. He wasn't a push over though. Oh, he'd fight and that's why Derrick took to him. He said the boy needed a man to give him what the streets would block him from having. You know how men talk. I agreed and we had a fifteen-year-old here. Julian finished high school here and was glad to go to college. His grades were never no problem."

She paused again. Samantha was taking mental notes. The woman's expression was deliberate, she knew what she wanted to say without any questions being asked. Her age hadn't interrupted her beauty. She was aging gracefully, and her mind was intact. Her bronze tone would have one think she'd been tanning in her early years to give her a youthful glow. She wore her hair, naturally, in braids. There were no added extensions and no coloring to hide the gray that mixed between each braid in her up-do. She was a short woman in stature, but Samantha was sure many knew she would stand for no nonsense.

"We never knew him to be in any trouble and Ms. Tammilyn here was the first young lady he brought to our home. Derrick spoke to him many nights about flirting, dating, courting, and marriage." Samantha and Tammilyn smiled at her comment.

"Yes indeed, told him the old way, the proper way. We didn't think nothing of it, but he followed what my husband told him. I know you ask, how do we know, well she's here, ask her, but we knew. He'd be home before curfew, kept decent hours. Even after Tammilyn graduated, Derrick reminded him they weren't a married couple."

Tammilyn giggled at Samantha's expression. "Ms. Foster, I'm sure you were shocked to know that they weren't doing everything according to old dating rituals."

"No child, we weren't that old or stupid. He had the sex talk, but the respect was drilled into this boy, and that's what no one wants to understand. He didn't do… Lord have mercy…anyway, Ms. Lady here got her an apartment in her senior year of school. Now I ain't told nobody this but the city helped with that. I put in the application, signed off that it was approved through my organization for young women working with us. Tammilyn worked with us off and on during that year, so everything was fine. There were other applicants, sure, a few were granted housing, but many were not. White, black, Hispanic, the city would send us applications just like I got hers, for approval. I denied a few 'cause I knew, the apartments would be a front for other activity. You get what I'm saying?"

Samantha listened to what Ms. Foster knew had been drug fronts, gambling fronts and hangouts for young college girls to meet some of the city officials after hours.

"I told Tammilyn to watch herself. I wasn't the only one approving the housing. I sat on the Council trying to clean up a few of the units and areas. You did an article on a few, so I know you remember. I broke that news to the reporters then. I was tired of the girls being used and returning to their parents abused, drug addicts, or pregnant. It was bad and to this day a few of those units are still housing old man thrills. It's the system and we can't break it when the families won't fight with us."

"What happened to the complaints? I do remember the stories, news, and the protests regarding the units." Samantha offered them more to eat.

"No thank you baby, you trying to make me go to sleep this early in the day. I still got Sunday dinner to put down. We're eating with her family at six."

Samantha cleared the table as Ms. Foster continued.

"The complaints, I guess went to that storage bin marked G for garbage. I talked to Worthy about it. You know, him being the Sergeant and then the Lieutenant at the time, I thought he'd have an ear that would hear what the people were bringing to the council meetings. The complexion of the meetings began to change. More white residents than minorities. Now everyone knew that didn't measure up. Only the white girls at the school lived there, none of the families even visited. You could tell that by the limited repairs and upkeep. Nevertheless, they were there talking about the cost, the complaints, tearing the complex down and rebuilding. It was something different every week that would curtail anyone from inspecting or expecting change. Well, I took it further. Sat with the mayor a few times, called the governor's office and yes violations began to be served. The police had to include the area on their route more often and it stopped a lot of illegal traffic."

"Ms. Foster did any of this, at the time seem as though it would be held against you or anyone in your office."

"No child, we were doing our job. The police wouldn't go through the area, drugs and anything else was running rampant. The inspectors didn't turn in reports. You know why Ms. Sayers, them boys, what they call them. The 'untouchables' my husband believed owned a lot of those properties. We found out when they had a few problems with the water main over there. Derrick came home with the names of a few, who at the time, were in powerful city positions. They hadn't paid taxes in months, some years, and the water department had to contact them about the main break. They were invested in the property and just let it run itself. No one cared."

"But Tammilyn didn't live there when she was raped, did you?" Samantha questioned the younger woman.

"No, I moved during the main break. The cops would come and raid apartments in the middle of the night. They didn't need a reason to break locks on doors or bust in and tear up personal property. I complained to my family and moved back home for a few months until Ms. Foster found another place for me to live."

CHAPTER 30

The conversation continued and the reporter began to understand that the attack could have been retaliation. She kept the thought to herself hoping Ms. Foster or Tammilyn would bring up the connection. Tammilyn explained harassment at the job or anywhere she was seen began shortly after she moved. She thought it was because she no longer lived on the other side of the complex. Once again Ms. Foster spoke up for her and the other tenants who clearly didn't live as the others had. The solution that most requested was to benefit all who resided there. More security, better lighting in darkened walkways, nothing more than what were highlighted points for residents to consider the complex for family living. Samantha concluded that Tammilyn had been targeted because of her connection with Ms. Foster. The question was why?

"There were a few drug deals on my side of the complex, but it faced Hillsdale Avenue, so no one really wanted to be noticed hanging out in front of the buildings. The courtyard was the spot. Everyone including the cops knew it. Right where the tennis and racquetball courts were, girls were being attacked. It started at the end of the semester. I had been out of school a year. It was the first year of me working full-time. There were nights when Julian would come over early and meet me to walk me past the courts to get home safe."

"Those were the nights when I would worry about him making it home. We live too far for him to leave from that part of the city that time of night. So, he'd call, and I'd tell him just stay. I knew they wouldn't argue with me, and Derrick had passed on. I didn't need no family upsets. You know?" Ms. Foster shook her head.

"Yes, ma'am and we understood. The next morning we'd leave together and go to work. The weekends, I'd spend with my family, or we'd be together with Ms. Foster. We didn't even stay around there, but it was close to my job. So, I was happy to be living on what I thought was the other side of trouble."

Samantha watched as Tammilyn took a deep breath. She prepared herself as the young woman had knowing the story was about to get ugly. Tammilyn was petite and had piercing dark eyes with long eyelashes and thick brows. She wore no makeup on her dark chocolate skin. Her hair was thick and healthy, shoulder length and she wore it in a ponytail. She wasn't plain in her dress, casual skirt and blouse, church attire. Samantha could tell she didn't appear to be the one to carry on about designer's latest fashions. However, she could imagine the college graduate ignoring the catcalls from the drug runners and others who were on the courts in the late afternoon. She could see the beauty they wouldn't mind attaching themselves to. What the reporter couldn't imagine was the attack, the brutal act that was authorized by a higher authority. She listened intensively, knowing the connection was to the police who had another purpose.

"Julian told me about his friend. His roommate from college who was living in Florida. He wanted us to visit him, but my job wouldn't give me the time off. It was his friend's birthday and he invited us to come for his celebration. He told him he didn't think we'd make it but at the last minute, his boss gave him the okay. He could leave Friday and be back on Tuesday. He asked me to go again. If he had been leaving Friday and returning in time for me to be at work on Monday, I would have been with him. We couldn't find a flight for my return. He stayed with me Thursday night and Friday morning he caught an Uber to the airport. We talked, off and on that day while he was traveling. I got home at five. I begged my boss to let me leave early. I prayed I'd miss the Friday night crowd on the courts, and it seemed I did. Julian said they must have seen him leave with his bags that morning. I was attacked as I reached my door. I don't remember anything else."

"Wait you were attacked before you got in your apartment? I was under the impression; they came into your home." Samantha waited while Tammilyn got her thoughts together.

"Ms. Sayers, I woke up in the hospital. I was told by my family and Ms. Foster what the police and others told them. They found me in my apartment on my bed, they said, naked. I had been beat in the face and head. I had a concussion, my jaw was broken, and I was medicated for weeks. No one questioned me until after Julian was locked up."

"Wait! Who put you in your bed? How did they...Julian was locked up without you saying anything?"

"They never said how she got in her apartment. It was already decided that he had done it and ran. They watched him leave with her that morning and didn't see him that evening. Like she said most weekends she didn't even go home. That's what I told that dummy of a lawyer we had before Mr. Fulton. I wasn't paying for no lawyer provided by the housing division."

"Ms. Foster, the housing division offered a defense attorney for Julian?"

"Yes honey. Seemed odd to me too. I see how you looking, … we didn't ask nobody for nothing. Lawyer came to the hospital shortly after I was asked to meet with the director in a closed-door session, you know, he had a friend that had a friend who was a lawyer that was willing to take the case. I asked him was it a prosecutor."

Samantha couldn't contain her snicker and Tammilyn joined her. It brought the tension of the conversation down a bit. She poured more tea in each of the glasses as Ms. Foster continued.

"Yes, he said that and laughed at my response. I told him I'll see about Julian's representation. He had the nerve to say he knew how hard it was on me handling Julian without Derrick. I almost cussed at him. Julian wasn't the problem, but you see at the time I didn't know where the boy had been. How was I to know he left and went to Florida to visit his friend Terrance?"

"Wait, how did they arrest him without you knowing he was back?"

"Never mind that. Listen, they questioned me when this child was laying in the emergency room. They asked about Julian, and I told them he was at work that day and must have went to the Watson's place like he did most Fridays. When the Watsons told me they hadn't seen him, I just knew they attacked him too. I called the police from the hospital. I got in touch with Worthy. You know me and him go way back. He said he didn't know it was my Julian, but they had him there. Now, when I heard he had been to Florida, I shut up. What could I say that wouldn't look like I was making excuses for him? They had him in custody as soon as he stepped into the hospital doors. No questions asked. He had his ticket to and from Florida and his bag. Came as soon as the Watsons called him. Took the next flight he could get. Family emergency flight home. Never really got to spend no time with his friend. He was there in the morning, gone in the evening."

"Aww, Ms. Foster. Wait let me get you a tissue."

The older woman couldn't hold the tears any longer. Tammilyn went to the bathroom and brought back a few tissues. Samantha wet a cloth so she could pat her face and neck.

"Would you rather have water than the tea? I can get you cold water with ice cubes, no bother."

"No, I get worked up at the thought of what they done. You just don't know what we've been quiet about. Listen, when the Director of Housing asked me about an attorney, I simply knew something was wrong. So, when I called Worthy, I thought I would get to the bottom of why he was arrested. Worthy didn't know. With all the reports and investigating, the news y'all was doing, he still couldn't tell me why my boy was locked up. I told him there was a lie somewhere. I explained about his trip, why I didn't know, and the only thing Lieutenant Worthy could tell me was, do you need help with getting him a lawyer."

"He offered to get Julian a lawyer too?"

"I couldn't trust it, so we were stuck with the dummy. What was that man's name Tammilyn?"

"Spencer, or Spence. It's like she said Ms. Sayers. He was a dummy. Never answered any of our questions and during the trial, well you were there, he didn't dispute any of the holes that were obvious. What evidence did they have? I told them Julian was going to Florida. It showed texts and calls we made throughout the day. He couldn't be here in Pennsylvania and in Florida ten minutes before I was assaulted. His fingerprints, DNA, his clothes even being in my apartment, they used against him. They never looked for anything else. Lieutenant Worthy promised to send out more detectives to question me, dust the apartment again, it never happened."

Samantha and her guest talked until five. They promised to stay in touch with her and she gave her word that nothing would be published without their review and permission.

"Chile, they know what we've said. The story ain't changed. It's Fulton who has made the difference. For some reason, they've been calling asking how I am. I no longer work for the council or talk to any of those folks. They have the nerve to check with the Watsons as if they can give them relief. It's just their way of trying to find out what Fulton's next move is. He was right, as long as they don't know what he's doing they're sitting on edge. He's going get them, every last one of those jokers that raped and attacked this child. My boy will get out of this. I just hope he'll be the same young man that went in. Ms. Sayers that's my prayer, he's got to be mentally okay when this is over."

Samantha didn't want to hold them any longer knowing they had promised to be at dinner by six. She went to her room and got their outer garments. She paused in thought not knowing Ms. Foster was watching from the living room.

"What's on your mind? Say it, Ms. Sayers. We came here willingly, so if you want to know something please don't ask someone else. They'll make up things from what they assume. Ask us while we're here. If it's over and above, too much for us to tell you, we won't."

Samantha smiled and handed them their garments. "Just one question that I know everyone has been asking considering this young man who has turned himself in. Have you seen him before? I know you told Fulton you didn't know him, and he didn't rape you, but could he have been one at the courts?"

"No, I don't think so. I didn't know many of the young boys that hung out on the courts. He's older. He's older than most of them that hang there. He's definitely not one of the ones who sells regularly there. I know most of them. I don't think he would even know any of the guys who live in the area. I don't know that guy at all. Mr. Fulton said it would all come out. I'd sure like to know why he'd admit to something that would put him away for years."

"Or what the alternative would be if he didn't. I'll watch it unfold with Mr. Fulton. He'll find out, I'm sure."

Samantha thanked them for coming and sharing their story. Strangely she hadn't asked many questions, but she got more information than she needed to press the questions Fulton sent for the others. She wondered if Fulton knew the young man wasn't from the area. That was an angle he needed to pursue. Those with money being made in the complex requested something be done about the Watson girl and her boyfriend. The cops added insult to injury by arresting Julian Foster. They wanted to stop Ms. Foster and the residents who were complaining. It was where they were making their money. It was obvious, the money deals and corruption didn't start in the street, it started in the offices of the city officials.

CHAPTER 31

The unit was buzzing when the younger members entered. Everyone was in the center of the office waiting for their arrival. The four stopped their laughter and communication as soon as they entered what seemed to be organized chaos.

"Hey, good morning young people. Glad you all had a safe ride in. We're going to take the first part of this morning to speak with you, reminding you of a few things we thought were understood when you were assigned to the unit. Then we're going to separate you to talk about your future here and in the department. Just for clarity, we need to understand your means and you need to understand our efforts. We'll start in about ten minutes or so, so if you'll get prepared to listen, we're going to give you a moment to think if you still want to be here at all."

Porter made the announcement and turned back to the counter where everyone else stood waiting for any type of response. He gave no indication that there was a need for questions or a need for a prior conversation. Knowles separated from the group first, he headed to his cubicle. The message seemed clear to him; they each would be on their own. The others followed his lead and unpacked their belongings at their desks. Chambers paused in thought, shrugged his shoulders, and walked over to the detectives to speak.

"Uh, Montez, can I talk with you before this meeting?" He asked in a low tone. The unexpected response caused everyone to notice he had approached the group.

"No! Why would I want to talk with you? I asked you questions Friday, and you pushed your way past me. You on your own youngin'. Wait and ask your question when Porter calls everyone together." Montez paused before turning back to the counter. Hearing Chambers' begin a response, he turned to faced him squarely.

"It's just… oh you got back up now so the soft-spoken Montez ain't about helping out no more."

"You want me to show you what my soft-spoken…" As he walked closer to Chambers, Porter stood between the two detectives.

"Yo man, go back to the cubicle. We didn't call you over here and if you have a question, or something to say, they should hear it too. We all should. Don't talk your way into a problem you can't get out of. You're in deep enough."

Chambers followed Porter's advice and retreated pulling out his cell phone.

"Yeah, text them and tell them your ass is in the fryer now. Let them know the soft-spoken one will decide if you can still spy on us here."

Chambers froze in the middle of the floor and slid his phone back in his pocket. He returned to his cubicle without looking back at the detectives who watched him take his seat. Montez waited for a response, hearing none, he once again turned to the counter.

"Punk-ass," whispered Montez.

"We got him. He'll leave on his own before we're done with him," replied Porter.

Justlin walked in with coffee and doughnuts. After handing them to Miller to be set up in the conference room for all, she returned to the counter, joining the others.

"Okay, coffee run, phone calls and DNA reports. Done Chief Detective Tyson." She smiled hoping her comment would change the air a bit.

"Thanks. So, they're going to send the same reports we already know are false?" Stands and Wilson had their own thoughts about how the original reports would read.

"Stands, I guess that's what we would expect here at the Cold Case Unit, but Ms. Justice here asked differently."

"Oh, I forgot we have an insider. Well do tell my lady, what twist did you put on the request?"

"The governor's name, my name, and the head of their department. Apparently, they always had a different report. That was Fulton's complaint. The findings in their report was retracted."

"Wow, who pulled that off Justice? I thought there had to be a few meetings and signatures before evidence wasn't given to the prosecutor and the defense attorney."

"Stands, listen. It's the same when you guys find drugs. Everything don't make it to the court room."

"So, what happens now?" Porter didn't want the back-and-forth Stands was prepared to give about drug raids and evidence.

"They will be producing a full report. I gave them the heads up about a few of the others on this unit's report. That gave them credence to track more than just one case. If we can show a pattern of evidence overlooked, thrown out, maybe it will connect us to another officer, or someone they used in all of this. They have no idea it's for any particular case, just the report."

"Yeah, that keeps Fulton out of it as well. They'll think the report is the only reason you're here."

"Tyson and all of you, listen, there's a thin line in all of this. We've crossed it looking in these folders, it's here and they thought we'd miss it. That's what I think. Tyson, unfortunately that means you and Porter must take a trip to the Forensic Lab and State Evidence Office. I requested the complete findings, as they filed it. I stated it was a necessity to complete this unit's report for me and the Governor's office. So, it won't be coming through the email channels or the internet. It can only be hard-copy documents."

"I'm sure they weren't happy about that."

"Listen, they weren't upset about pulling the records. My office said they thought having it ready by tomorrow was a bit much though. Oh well, get busy."

The group laughed and stopped one by one at each cubicle to peek in on the sadden officers who hadn't moved from their cubicles. As they left the main area, they announced the meeting would be in the conference room. The young investigators followed and sat scattered deliberately separating their seats. Porter smiled remembering how he would avoid sitting next to Tyson or Stands during meetings. He thought he could avoid being called out with them, even if he was a part of their antics. The trio was known for their "choice" of methods to find evidence or interrogate a suspect.

Montez stood in the front of the room with Tyson. The others chose to stand to the side and watch expressions as they changed with each word spoken. Tina, although not included in interoffice situations could feel the tension in the room. The younger detectives knew Chambers was on a mission, and that was the reason for the meeting.

"This unit is responsible for the filing of cases that have been closed or gone cold. I know you all understand what that means. We, detectives, investigators, police, whomever was assigned to these cases can profess that they have thoroughly done their sworn duty by the victims and those involved. We also keep the records of cases that have led to incarceration. They too are based on reports, and information submitted to the District Attorney, other lawyers, the state, etc. So, we have two separate filing systems that are crucial to the foundation of policing here in Moore Township."

Tyson paused and walked closer to Chambers. Bringing an added uneasiness to the young detective, he leaned over him and spoke in a softer tone.

"There are many who have disrupted the system. Many who have broken the rules and no matter how long it takes, they will be caught."

He walked away from Chambers and stepped to Miller whose expression told the seasoned detectives she had no idea what was going on.

"Criminals, shouldn't wear a uniform, have a badge, or have taken an oath. But that's on the television, in reality they do; they sometimes don't realize that others know they are criminals. Everyone is not blind to their actions, their attempts to rid others of their rights, or their bias toward those we are expected to serve. You see, they assume everyone will go along with their antics, or turn a blind eye. I've worked too hard to turn a blind eye on crime. I would hope that you all feel as I do."

Tyson continued his slow walk to Knight, who sat with his eyes focused on the wall straight ahead as though he was a recruit in class.

"Your assignment here is simple. Montez gave you the information, the steps we follow when cases are presented. He explained why and how we process each case and the reports we file before putting the file to rest. We re-investigate, and without fail if we find the need we can and will re-open the case before it is deemed closed. We review the notes from attorneys, files from the court, and yes in our report we question missing information and the reason it has not been returned to the file. That's what we do here."

Knowles moved a bit before Tyson approached him and was stopped by Tyson's hand on his shoulder.

"That's the only job you have here. You weren't asked to do anyone else's job. Not mine, not Porter's or Montez's. You can't do our job, we know that, and so does the person who asked more of you. Don't let them give you a check your ass can't cash. I'm telling you, whoever asked you for whatever from this unit, they're setting you up. We know the work can be boring. It's not the heat of the street. But think about it Chambers, had you been caught by a cop on the street looking through his things, his locker, his car, his desk, how long would you last?"

Chambers smirked without giving an answer.

"Yeah, I know. You'd talk your way out of it, or so you think that's what you would have done. For every cop you offend, you offend a larger group. So here, you've offended Principal Investigator Tina Justlin, you met her. She's from the governor's office. You've got our attention with what you did and she's wondering why, just like us. What the hell were you thinking?"

Chambers took a deep breath and sat up straight in his chair.

"So, we're in the middle of an investigation. Since you were wondering about the files you see lined up in the offices where doors are closed. We're investigating what could be dirty cops, falsifying documents, removal of evidence, misappropriation of funds, I could go on; but to tell you the truth, we don't know what other crimes have been committed by one or a few of the good guys. Maybe you can tell us who since they told you to search files."

Chambers began to fidget in his seat. "I wasn't told by anyone to search any files…Sir," he mumbled. He glanced at Knight and then looked around the room.

"Oh, I see. You just took it upon yourself to go in Detective Porter's office and eenie, meenie, minee, moe… a file? I find that hard to believe because that's not what you told Montez. Now, before you call him a liar. Think about it. What did you say as an excuse for being in that office? What file were you looking for and why?"

"It's been a long weekend; I'd have to check my notes, but I was following up information on the file I was working on."

"I see. Miller, what file were you working on Friday."

"Dalton Smith, sir. Closed murder case, double homicide. Still looking for signatures."

"Thank you, Ms. Miller. Knight, what file are you working on sir."

Knight paused, shaking his head. He cleared his throat and looked at Chambers as he stood.

"Fatimah Williams, sir. Currently seeking appeal. Just began checking all documents requested by her attorney. Sir, I checked that information this morning, if you had asked when we walked in, I don't believe I would have remembered it."

"Good try my man. I don't think Chambers would have tried to help you in the same way. Listen, I'm sure Ms. Miller didn't remember her case either but you both checked while sitting and waiting on this meeting. While your boy here didn't worry about last week's case 'cause he was ready with that lame excuse. Knowles, what file, sir?"

"Working on the evidence log signatures sir. Any missing or illegible writings are referred to Detective Montez."

The room went silent. Tyson returned to the center of the room.

"Chambers, you don't have to tell us. We know. We know who and why. We understand your reasoning too. My last question for you is, do you still want this job? I mean the whole thing, detective or higher. You see you've violated this office and your answer will tell me what I should do. I mean, I don't know if you can be trusted."

Porter laughed. "He can't be trusted. He couldn't even tell Montez the truth about what he was doing. Why should we trust him?"

Wilson chimed in." Why should we work with him? He ain't got our backs. Maybe Knight, Miller, and Knowles can trust him, I can't."

Stands looked and Chambers and smiled. "Hey, I'll help you man. How much they promise you for the information. They pay you; you pay me and to hell with these assholes. It's all about the money right. I know you thinking if I was serious why would I say it in front of them. 'Cause the snitch gets caught sooner or later, so why not say who you are… we already know."

Chambers took another deep breath. He felt like he was being interrogated. A tactic he learned how to overcome being with Sheers and Boone. They drilled him about being questioned and revealing any information they gave him regarding the group. He simply smirked and nodded his head slowly.

Justlin, who hadn't made any indication that she was a part of the meeting walked over to Tyson and then spoke.

"Detective Tyson, there seems to be more than a breech. I'll need to speak to each of them when I return from the Chief's office. I doubt if he needs to know any more about them than you've already told him. The governor may want to know more considering the on-going investigation. Thank you all for your work and commitment to getting this unit in order. Officer Chambers, I hope you can put a period at the end of each statement you make and not a question mark."

CHAPTER 32

The door was closed behind Montez, Justlin, and Tyson as they left the others waiting to be dismissed by Porter, Stands and Wilson. The silence broke when Miller sneezed.

"Bless you, why don't you come with me." Miller paused, in what seemed to be a confused state. Wilson paused waiting for Miller to respond.

"Why don't you come with me? I'm sure the fellas can figure this mess out. I mean you're not involved in Chambers secret agent shit, are you?"

Miller stood and shook her head as she sneezed again. "Excuse me. I'm going to go to the ladies' room first. Where do you need to meet me?"

"I'll be in the back." Wilson smiled knowing it would irritate Chambers to know that Miller was not on his side or so she indicated.

Miller stood and exited without giving anyone a second glance. She proceeded to the restroom sneezing along the way. Porter and Stands waited for the door to close before they began their method of interrogation. Porter moved to the center of the room closer to the seats between the three men who appeared to be irritated.

"Fellas let's talk. You know this is a problem, right?"

The mumbled replies affirmed they understood there was a problem.

"Good, at least we're starting with a confirmed understanding. Before this gets nasty, I think it should be said that I understand the reasoning, just not the method."

"Wait Porter, man, are you saying the reasoning behind all this 'I spy shit' is okay. Now I'm confused because team members…well hell go on, man." Stands shook his head and walked to the back of the room.

"Let me explain. Everyone here agrees what has happened is the problem unless there's another. Is there Chambers? I mean did you go in my office without notifying Montez about what you needed because there's another problem?"

There was a moment of intentional thought given before Chambers answered.

"Well, we know there's a problem. I mean isn't that why we're searching through these files. I didn't want, well I wanted to go on a hunch. Maybe I would impress you, or the others by finding out the information I was missing without Montez. I thought I remembered the name on one of the boxes. I checked the breakroom and those in our area, so I started with your office. No harm, no foul."

"Oh, no harm, no foul, but you couldn't explain that to Montez when he asked. I mean it may have shed a different light on the matter had you told him what you just said. Your memory was a little fogged when we began this meeting, what about now. The name you were looking for, what was it?"

Chambers was doing Sheers' dirty work and the names "Foster" or "Watson" were to be searched with a connection to "Sheers" and "Boone" the two who were assigned to the case. The evidence log, and any other paperwork if found was to be shredded. There were a few boxes in Porter's office marked "Logs." The assumption was to be fulfilled. Chambers was seeking an individual file.

"Porter, I'm being honest. I don't remember the name. It's on my desk, written on a pad to go at it again this morning. Check it yourself. The name is there."

Stands left the room headed to Chambers desk.

"What is it they want Chambers, let's stop playing the game? Knight, what do you want, are you in this scheme of things? You know they don't particularly care for those of another shade, right? Knowles what's your angle? Really, the three of you are here for what?"

No one answered. Porter recognized the fear on their faces. Catching it from both sides was a known problem within the department. Everyone understood it and the rules. People lost their careers and their lives for less.

"So, look Porter," Knowles paused waiting for Porter to stop him. Looking around he continued," I'm here to get the work done, whatever it is. I'm not here to be a part of any groups, clicks, or anti-whatever groups. I'm here to get the work done, that's it."

"Well since we giving reasons," Knight grinned," Chambers is on his own Porter. We all are, it was set up that way after we did the partners thing two weeks ago. Stands and Wilson gave us folders and let us know we were on our own. Knowles is with Montez, Miller is usually working with Stands, me, and Chambers… Well, we had our own folders and were told to turn in the folders as we completed them. I guess that's why we knew what assignments we were working with and well Chambers… like I said, is on his own."

Knight stood. "Sir, I don't want to be a part of what doesn't involve me. If I need to, I'll contact my union rep."

Porter chuckled," I had a feeling that would be next. You and Knowles can leave. Thanks."

Stands returned with a paper in hand as the young detectives left the room. Chambers seemed unnerved as he watched Porter read the paper that was handed to him.

"So, this name was in some way attached to what was in my office?"

"I guess. I didn't get a chance to find the folder, Montez walked in, and I stopped looking. Listen—" Chambers started to explain his position.

"No! You listen. I don't know if you recognize it or not. The three you came in with, well they won't be helping you. Yeah, they punked and you can tell Sheers and his boys they're done. Watching over you guys is our new assignment passed on to us from Principal Investigator Justlin. We can't cover what you did or why with any reasonable excuse to save your dumb ass. So, since the state was investigating this report, they're on top of us. I'm sure Sheers knows that. It wasn't smart to put you on at this time. Too many eyes, and you're new at it."

Stands waited for Porter to add to what he said, but Chambers spoke first.

"It ain't your place to change what is already done. Let the chips fall where they may. Those cases aren't your cases. They belong to the state and cleaning them up now won't matter. That's what this unit is assigned to do, clean it up and make it look neat."

Porter clapped his hands slowly. "Thank you. I'm okay with cleaning it up and making things neat. Maybe you should pack your shit man. You might as well say you're done. You can't stay on this unit 'cause we can't clean you. Think about it and let us know. I'll let Tyson know."

"Man, I was assigned here by those over your heads. I'd rather not be here anyway."

"Yeah, tell them to talk to Tyson about it."

CHAPTER 33

Miller watched as Chambers packed his satchel clearing his desk. He hadn't spoken with her since being caught in Porter's office. She didn't know what to ask or what to say. Her text messages had gone unanswered. It left her no choice but to believe his troubles were deeper than the problems he had on the unit.

"Chambers, can I talk to you a minute?" Miller met him at the door as he was leaving. "Can we talk out in the hall, please?"

Chambers was worn. His complexion was pale. It was as though he was drained. Miller remembered when they met in the academy. His physique was small, but he reminded her of a model for skinny jeans and sportswear. His smile was contagious, and he always spoke to her as though they had a childhood connection. They could tease each other, chastise each other, and critique each other with no ill feelings. Now Miller felt distant. They never crossed the line, although she thought eventually it would happen.

"What's going on?," she questioned as they walked to a bench that was in the hall. "They're reassigning you?"

"I don't know and at this point, I don't care. I can't…"

"Did you go in his office for Sheers or Boone? What were you thinking?"

"Who told you I was working with Sheers?" Chambers' demeanor seemed to change. "Who told you that?"

"I heard them mention you were working with the 'untouchables.' That's Sheers, right? Why would you do anything for them?"

"Why not? I'm not waiting for someone to assign me to a case that will win. This unit can't give me what I want!"

"What do you want Chambers?"

"Them to move out of the way. They can't keep getting positions that belong to us."

Miller backed away from him with a questioning stare.

"Who the hell is 'them and us', huh Carlton Chambers? Who are you talking about?"

It was then that he realized he said too much. He saw his friend for the first time recognizing who he was. Miller moved closer to him.

"I thought we were them, and it was about us. The unison color was to be blue… but I guess you and your boys see black and white. Good to know."

"Miller, I…" Chambers started to explain.

Miller left him standing in the hall and returned to the office. She tried to fight the emotional sting. Remembering Chambers in the academy, his spirit had changed. There weren't many that made Miller feel like she belonged, and Chambers was one of the few that made sure she wasn't left out. They went their separate ways as rookies, but they kept in touch over the years. Meeting for a casual drink or dinner, nothing romantic, but she felt he was a friend. When they received their assignment to the Cold Case Unit, she thought they'd pick up with the bond they created. It didn't take long for her to realize, Carlton Chambers the detective wasn't the same man she met years prior. He certainly wasn't the same recruit that cared what others said about her being a minority. She now wondered what his intentions were.

Wilson was sitting in what had been Chambers' cubicle for the past few weeks. Unable to express her mixed feelings, Miller needed questions answered.

"So, he's out. Just like that? I mean, what is really going on with him and you guys. I feel like I'm the only one that hasn't been told what Chambers was about."

"Do you know anything about the group called the 'untouchables'?"

"Wilson, I don't feed into the gossip. I never have. So, I've heard things about them, but no I don't know who they really are or what they do."

"Pull up a seat."

Wilson watched as the younger version of her walked to get another chair. She liked Miller. Everything about her including her willingness to work with Chambers reminded her of the young officer she was when she just wanted to 'fit in'. She understood the struggle many of the females found themselves combating trying to be one of the respected members in blue.

Laniece Miller was a lot younger than Leana Wilson was when she decided to become an investigator. She admired the drive in any officer who sought to move along the path provided by the department. Becoming a detective was a major step and being an investigator was the ultimate before administration. Wilson didn't want to be a part of the administration, but she could see Miller becoming a candidate for a top leadership position. The question was would she truly lead. Porter and Stands questioned the young men about their intentions, she was sure Miller's would be totally different.

Miller seemed to take a back seat to the others. Wilson watched as she worked alone and had very few questions as she completed the folders assigned. Her mannerism fit her profile. One would immediately understand her roots weren't of American decent, as she didn't always understand the humor as it related to family and community traditions. Her questions often began with, "*Why would one…*" and conclude with "*oh, so different.*" Wilson smiled thinking it wasn't so different when your mind was on a different path than those you worked with.

"I don't want to be a part of the rumors or talk, you know? But I don't want to be the only one who doesn't understand the mess Chambers has created. Or maybe, I'm just not thinking right at all, but he's leaving so…"

"Miller, it is a mess." Wilson explained what had been done. She told her about the 'untouchables' and the creed they portrayed. The conversation was welcomed, and Miller appreciated Wilson taking time to explain.

"What was he thinking?"

"He wasn't. The question is, how will you deal with him from this day forward. It may affect your future within the department as well."

"I'm certainly not attached to him or that group. He told me nothing about his intentions and I'm glad he didn't. I've been following cold cases since becoming an officer. I've prepped for the Investigator test," and I've never expressed my future with anyone. It's too important to me and my family."

"Oh, I see are you married. I didn't think you had… well, you know what I mean."

"No, I'm not married. My family and I moved here from Trinidad. I still live with my family. My sisters, my mother and father all work and we all look forward to moving on with our lives. I can't be the one who has failed because of my ties with someone who has no regard for the job or my race. I'm a little naïve but I'm not totally oblivious to what that could do to my career and life here in America. I don't need that in my life."

Wilson changed the subject. She understood that Chambers would not have been able to convince Miller to be a part of his quest.

"Your accent is beautiful. I've only been to Trinidad once, for a friend's wedding. I'd love to go back again and just vacation."

"It is beautiful, but it has its problems just like everywhere else. Thank you for taking the time to explain this mess."

"Well, you're here now and you can make the best of this career for your personal growth."

"Yes, so what's next?"

Wilson put the folders Chambers was working on in front of them on the desk.

"We start where he left off. We still have to find out how these cases got through with missing pieces."

CHAPTER 34

"Why do you think I'm here Chief? For answers, my friend. I thought I was clear when I said you need to delegate. I told you what to do, that ain't my job. My job is to see that it's done. You didn't do what was to be done."

"What are you talking about? There's nothing in the papers, nothing on the news, it's quiet. That's what you wanted right? No one is asking questions."

"No one accept that damn lawyer and your boy, Tyson."

"Not what you asked me to do. Let me talk to the others. I can tell them what's going on. Settle their rattled nerves, or are you scared they'll blame you like you're blaming me. There's nothing for us to do but wait for the next move."

"What about your girl, Justice? What is she still hanging around for if everything is smooth?"

"She's here investigating the report. You know about that already. It has nothing to do with the Foster case. If you don't raise everyone's brow, she'll be back in the state building within a few weeks."

"You're raising brows. You know more than you're saying, and we know it. Maybe we should have a talk with her or the captain. I'm sure if we pressure one of them enough, they'll talk."

"If you think that will work, go ahead, but know that will open doors you won't be able to close. She's the governor's mouthpiece. We feed her what we want her to know, that's it. You push and she'll know to investigate it all, matters we haven't presented. The captain is just collecting facts given and passing them to me. I've already told him he's the spokesperson. Believe me, he's not one for the lights and action."

"Oh, get Chambers back in."

"Back in where?"

"The unit. He walked out and needs to be there to tell us what's going on."

Michaels shook his head and stood looking out of his office window. "Sheers, what the hell? How the hell am I supposed to do that? You're putting me in a bad position. They won't trust me at all if I defend that prick. What the hell was he thinking?"

"Hey, that's what you can tell them. Make it happen, that's all. We need eyes on the unit."

"Send a damn replacement. What about that boy Knight, he's there?"

"He's not solid enough."

"None of you are. Send a seasoned guy, someone they will recognize as a worker and not a damn flunky."

"Watch your mouth old man. One word and your ass will be the seasoned guy. Like I said, Chambers is the man. Call him and Tyson to your office, break bread together and put him back on that damn unit."

"So, I'm firing Tyson?"

"What?!" Sheers' anger began to rise. "What the hell? What aren't you understanding?"

"Oh, I understand what you want, but Tyson may get tired of what he knows is B.S."

"That's your problem. The nigger wanted to be top dog, let the chips fall where they may. When this is over, he'll where the guilt of a unit that puts his people in jail."

Michaels shook his head and smirked. "You don't understand at all, none of you. When the chips fall, he'll be throwing them up in the air. That's the reason the report was filed the way it was. It shows he wasn't involved in the mess your so-called "untouchables" created. Take a break. You've locked up enough to prove a point."

"And just what do you think the point is?"

Michaels turned to face the officer. "You're just as tired of this shit as I am. Your uniform doesn't even fit you anymore. You drink every night and those you skip you're with the tramp that will have you for a play or two. You've lost your family and those you call friends are as rancid as you are. It's the money. I fed off it for years and now as much as I know I just keep wishing I could lose it all. I want to puke every time I think of what we've done. I have nightmares about what we've done to their families. Like I said I want out."

Sheers walked around to the window where the chief stood. "You're right I'm tired of your shit. Your uniform got bigger and bigger. You got fat from the good eating you did over the years putting the asses we determined were the scum of the community. You, Marshall, Boone, and me have ran this part of the operation for years. You can get out. Is your insurance paid up? Beneficiaries in place? That's the exit plan for us, all of us. Those higher than us will kill us and they'll kill Chambers too. So, you see you don't have a choice. Put him back on the unit and stop your whining."

A knock on the door interrupted the exchange between the two men. They both seemed shocked when the door opened as Tina Justlin turned the knob. Sheers didn't give her a chance to say anything. He walked pass her without acknowledging her presence or telling the chief goodbye as he slammed the door. Justlin turned her attention from the door to the chief with raised brow.

"So, I guess he was upset?"

"Humph! Damn well should be. I'm sorry. It's been one of those mornings. Hell, it's time for lunch. Can I interest you in being my company?"

"No, no you can't. I have work to do and I'm not ready to take lunch just yet."

"Oh. Well, you look fantastic. I really like that ensemble. Polished lady, that's what has always been your signature."

"Alright Walt! Let's stop the damn games. Was that who I thought it was?"

"I don't know. If you thought it was Sheers, yes. He was here about Chambers. What is going on this morning? I didn't get the full details and Tyson, nor Porter has complained or written paperwork on him."

"You'll have to take that up with them. So, he already knew about them having a problem with Chambers. I mean that's my reason for coming to you. We just found out about him late Friday. How would Sheers know anything about him this quick?"

"No idea. He called, told me he had to talk about an officer. I told him report to my office with it, and he did."

"Oh, so what's the verdict? Tyson and Porter want him out, and before you say it, that's with or without a replacement. They really can't trust he's there to help with the files."

Justlin hoped the chief would come clean and explain his connection with Sheers. She could see his anxiety mounting.

"Hey, sit down Chief, let's talk a minute."

CHAPTER 35

Waiting was not one of Tyson's better qualities. He and Justlin separated at the elevator headed to the chief and captain's office respectively. He looked at his watch and sighed. Thirty minutes passed without the secretary giving him a nod of approval to enter Captain Worthy's office. He decided to wait another ten minutes before making his agitation noticeable. The phone beeped twice and the officer at the desk looked his way and smiled.

"Detective Tyson, the captain will see you now. I'm sorry it took so long, sir."

"No fault of yours. He'll hear my ranting, maybe you'll hear some of it too," Tyson replied giving the female sergeant a reason to smile at his remark. She had become accustomed to his sarcasm over the years. He pushed open the heavy doors that led to his mentor's oversized office.

"I would say good morning but it's now afternoon. I've been sitting there longer than expected. Have I been moved down the list? I mean, there was a time when my entry didn't have to be announced or paused."

"Man, this mess. I'm trimming the fat they're trying to throw in the mix. What is this shit with Chambers? You had him removed from the unit?"

"No, how did you get wind of that already? Never mind, he called Sheers. Of course, he did. I haven't talked to Porter or Stands to get the details. The text sent to me just read, he walked out."

"Walked out? Just left, what happened? Nothing has come from you about him, so exactly what was the problem?"

"Him snooping through the files in Porter's office, closed door policy in effect. He violated it. He did it Friday claiming he was seeking information for a file he was working on. He didn't find what he wanted, and Montez walked in on him. We set up a meeting with the four of them this morning. Seems like they all knew what he was up to, and they didn't defend his actions. You know a cornered animal will fight or give in."

"He gave in and walked out."

"Seems that way. Like I said I hadn't got the results to turn in any report or complaint about his actions. He left and called his boy. Why, let me guess, they want him to be put back on the unit?"

"Michaels said we had to talk about it. He emphasized it as though it would be an order not a request."

"He won't last captain. We won't let him. He won't work alone, and I'll make Stands or Montez be his watch dog. He'll quit before the week is out. Don't let it worry you. We know he wants to be the eyes for Sheers and his boys. We'll give him enough to take back to them."

"What about getting rid of them and the mess they're causing?" Worthy leaned back in his chair waiting for what he knew would be a better solution than what Michaels proposed. "Listen, Michaels thinks you can bring him back and someone in your unit will tip Justlin off. The blame would fall on you and you'd be removed."

"Humph! That won't work. Justlin was with us when we found out he was busted in Porter's office. She was there this morning when we had the meeting. She was there and will question why he's allowed to come back to the unit without some type of disciplinary action."

"Always on point. I didn't even think about that. I told Michaels he's got to find a way out of this mess once and for all. Sheers has him shook. He's in deep and Tyson, I don't know if he realizes it."

Tyson stood to leave. "The two of you taught me. He knows, the question is, does he care?"

"To be honest with you, I think he gave up a while ago. These last few months he's been quiet, maybe too quiet. Not responding to reports, ending calls without nagging me to call back with answers, he's been different. Even with your report, he made that call to Marshall and that was it."

"So, Marshall may be in on it too. I hadn't thought of it before, but he calls Marshall, Marshall calls Sheers or Boone and the top boys are on the alert. Think about it. Chambers is caught Friday afternoon in Porter's office. He's questioned and refuses to answer. Michaels is asked either over the weekend or this morning about it and he questions you. Of course, neither of you know anything about it because that's my job. They assumed I was going to request him removed. Since I didn't they're trying to find out why. Why didn't the black flunky fall for the trap? They'd have me in here explaining how I requested his removal without an investigation. No need, Cap. He walked out the door after he packed his shit. He removed himself. Now they want to act like it didn't happen and put him back in place? He won't be able to live through it, that I guarantee."

"Listen, I don't know how or what they want this boy to do for them, but it seems like you've put a stop to their plan."

"Captain, we didn't put a stop to anything. That boy was shook. He didn't answer any questions. He was mumbling, tapping his foot, you know, nervous as hell. Porter said he thought he was about to cry."

"Tyson man, he probably did once he called them, and they threatened him about leaving. Maybe, he told them you were going to reassign him."

"He can come back, but you nor Michaels can save him. Like I said he'll be assigned to Montez and Stands. We've got enough trouble with these files. I don't need him free to roam through folders to save them. If you can, don't tell them we spoke. Tell Michaels to tell his boys to send him back apologizing and maybe we'll ignore his antics. I'll agree on those terms only. This cat and mouse shit has to stop. They need to know we're not affected by them having someone in our house. He'll be caught in the trap they set.

CHAPTER 36

The phones were busy for a Monday afternoon. Every department seemed to have questions about the investigator who was sent back to the day sergeant's desk for reassignment. The response for each call was Chief Detective Tyson was not available to take any calls. The team was prepared for the fight that seemed to be brewing. Tyson returned to his crew working. He smiled as he walked through the front office enroute to his desk. He needed a minute to unwind. What he assumed would be minutes in the captain's office led up to hours that he needed to get to the State Forensics office. He pushed the intercom as he took off his suit jacket to hang it behind the door.

"Montez, who else is here?"

"Sir, Wilson and I, as well as the young guns. Ms. White and Kai stepped out a minute. Porter, Stands, and Justlin went to Forensics when you didn't return by one."

"Great, okay when the ladies return, come to my office, both of you."

The line dropped. There was a knock on his door. Knowles entered with two folders.

"Sir, Montez said I should bring this to your attention. I think these two folders may relate to the Foster case."

"How so?" Tyson offered the seat across from his desk. The office was beginning to look like he was in the line of the other heads of departments. He looked at the walls and decided while Knowles was opening the folders, he'd need to dress them with a few plaques and personal awards.

"Well sir, Ms. Watson stated that there was a lot of drug trafficking in the area. The same day that Foster was arrested these two were picked up for trafficking large amounts of cocaine. Same area, where she lived about an hour after she was found. What I thought was interesting is the officers that filed the paperwork for her report and Foster's file are the same as these arresting officers. Sir, if they were at Ms. Watson's crime scene, how did they leave that scene and arrest these guys?"

"Let me see the reports. So, you're saying they signed both reports?"

Knowles smiled," I thought it was strange too. The names are the same but the signatures, well, I'd question them."

"What made you look at these files?"

"Missing information from the log sir. The quantity of the drugs differs on the report than the evidence log. Then I noticed the date and location, I looked up the Foster case and cross referenced the reports. The times are too close. Those officers couldn't have been at both scenes. These guys are doing time for the drug bust. I don't think the officers know they're names were being used."

"So, the arrest was done by these guys which means the names on the Watson report are false. Who testified then? Thanks, listen, leave the folders here. Check out the officers on the computer with Montez. The Roberts and Crews folder are also cases that Fulton will be checking. See if those same officers signed off on those reports."

"Sir, we did, and they are. They're a part of that group. I'm sure they're 'untouchables.'"

"Shit. Thanks man, good work. You okay? I mean after this morning and your boy's antics, are you feeling a bit better?"

"To be honest, I'm glad he left."

"He'll be back. So, don't let any of what will be going on phase you. He's an 'untouchable' and we're going to put our hands all over his ass."

They shared a laugh and Knowles left meeting Montez at the door. Wilson entered the office and took a seat.

"He's gonna be okay. I worked with him and Miller most of the day. Knight was left solo. I'm still not sure about him and I don't think Miller or Knowles trust him either." Wilson looked to Tyson for a reassuring response.

"He's got their smell on him. Nothing we can do about that. He'll have to prove himself and we know how that works for officer's that try to cross over to see that greener grass."

"Well, the young guns are on alert. That's what they used to call the rookie officers."

"That's what Montez calls them too. Hey man, c'mon on in and take a seat. You've been working hard these last couple of days. I wish I could tell you it's going to ease up."

"Where?" Montez' question caused Wilson and Tyson to laugh.

"Listen, I wanted to talk to everyone at once but since the rest of the team is on a field trip with Investigator Justlin, I'll talk with you two. They're throwing Chambers back over the fence. I don't know if it will be this afternoon, or in the morning. I want him to work solely with Stands and/or Montez. He's in your boot camp and treat him no better than an arrogant boot. Send him home each day wondering why he chose to come back. He's on new cases and files only and everything he does must be checked. Montez check his entries each night before he leaves. We're babysitting him. I explained to the captain there's only one advantage to this, we know what he's here for. New cases will keep him away from what we need. No open conversations in the front office. All conversations are to be done in an office, as private as possible when talking to the others. Montez, check what Knowles found, it may be the lead we need."

The intercom sounded before Montez could speak.

"Detective Tyson, line one, it's Chief Michaels." Tyson nodded as Wilson and Montez motioned, they would be leaving him to his call.

"Chief, good afternoon. How can I help you today?"

"Tyson, are you okay? You sound like you've got problems, I mean, other than the pretty investigator. Worthy and I were thinking you brought a lot to us that pointed right back to you."

"Not at all, and because she is pretty, I don't mind her being around. Hell, maybe she can get an office here since this investigation may take more time, you know."

"Tyson, you and I know you don't want someone looking over your shoulder."

"Chief, you and I know there's always someone looking over my shoulder, even if it's you."

"Hmm, well that's the point of my call. Worthy told me about this Chambers thing and…"

"And send him back. I'm sure we can teach him a thing or two. I won't call him back. He walked out on his own. He'll have to return the same way. There's been no paperwork filed on his insubordination which should have been my immediate response. I won't call him, if that's what they want."

"They, who are you talking about. This is me and you talking…"

"Chief, play the game fairly. Worthy already asked about this guy. News of this incident shouldn't have reached you or the captain. Again, there's no paperwork. Now who did he call that called you or Worthy about this. I didn't send him home; I didn't ask him to pack up and leave. He made that choice. So, out of respect; my title alone deserves respect. He needs to come to work tomorrow, ready to be a part of this team."

"It won't work that way Tyson."

"Well, you send him and that will be that. I'm not calling anyone to ask for his return."

"That's not… listen can we meet later? I can explain better then."

"Okay, your place?"

"No! Uh, no. I'll call you."

CHAPTER 37

Samantha pulled into the parking lot and smiled seeing Fulton standing at his car. He seemed to be in an intense conversation as he didn't notice her approaching.

"Oh, wow. She's here so I'll call you back after we're done here." He put his phone in his pocket. "I hope you don't mind us eating this far out. I just didn't want the locals to notice us."

"Hey, I understand but, you know we both have been on the networks before, right?"

"Listen Samantha, I need you to be Samantha Sayers the confidant, not the journalist right now. You said you think you have information that may help the case. I need a few connectors to this puzzle right about now."

"Well, this is a little quaint place. How did you find it?"

The two walked to the entrance of the diner. It wasn't one to brag about, small, and distant and that's what Fulton wanted. There were a few patrons at the tables and two couples at the bar. Soft music was playing in the background, enough to cover the individual conversations. The waitress seated them and gave them the menus after they ordered their beverages.

"I come here on my way to and from my home. My exit is the next one up. I have property in what you city folks would call the woods."

"It's a nice ride from the city. You drive in every day?"

"Most of the time. I don't mind, it's peaceful and those I defend, and their families won't be looking for me on the streets."

"Gotcha. Well, you know I met with Ms. Foster and Tammilyn over the weekend."

"Ms. Foster called and told me. Their story is solid, I just need to find the holes in the prosecutor's story."

"Let me just put it out there. After hearing Ms. Foster, it sounds like retaliation. She stopped the drug traffic flow, complained about the housing, and who knows what other problems she tried to solve. Her reward, the applicant she put into the building was harassed and her nephew blamed for a crime he didn't do. She had other applicants she approved to live there, were they harassed? It may be a lead into reasons for the attack."

"It's an angle I hadn't thought of but linked to Ms. Foster doesn't link to what Julian was tried for. His arrest had nothing to do with the complaints about housing or her job. We can't even prove that drug money was going through the building or if any police are linked to the trafficking that we know is going on."

"It seems so obvious." Samantha shook her head and looked at the menu. "What's your favorite here, since you come here often."

"The salmon is good, the salads, even the burgers if you want that…"

"Burger man, I eat enough of them when I'm working."

"I hear you. The food is pretty good. Choose what you like."

The two ordered their dinner and glasses of wine. The discussion changed to what each of them faced daily and how their lives changed as they grew in their professions. Dessert was apple pie, which Fulton said Samantha couldn't compare to any other. They both agreed it had to be homemade.

"So, what's next? I'm going to meet with Michaels tomorrow and Worthy on Wednesday. I couldn't get a same day appointment for some reason. I thought after I talk with Michaels, I'll stop in and speak with Tyson. I'm leaving the others for the end of the week. So, by Friday, the questions you gave me should paint some sort of picture."

She smiled taking in the last bite of her pie. Fulton was nodding his head without speaking. His thoughts had left the diner and he remembered looking at Tina Justlin on his deck. Lately, his thoughts of her crossed his mind more than he cared to admit. Samantha was always attractive to him but there was something about her that he didn't fully trust. Maybe it was her ambition, but he wished he could just focus on her as he had the principal investigator.

"I need you to question Tina Justlin too. I'm not sure of the angle yet. I think having her voice be a part of the story may push the community, the judge, and the governor. Once you get the answers from Michaels and Worthy let's revisit what those questions would be. Again, they're coming from you, not me or the case, just coming from the angle of what's right for any citizen."

"Okay, I can see it being another angle. Do you think she'll say anything different from any of those representing the police? They're all covering their jobs at this point."

"Ms. Sayers, she works for the governor not the police. If the governor and his top investigator become questionable in all of this, she'll defend her job and his."

The lawyer never mentioned he'd be meeting with Tyson and Justlin or that they had their own investigation going on. Justlin would know Sayers was on the prowl. Her reaction would let him know if Samantha was team Fulton or playing solo. He hoped they both would win, but he couldn't let her get all the accolades. He'd check her angle without her knowing she may have found another piece to the puzzle.

CHAPTER 38

It was close to nine. Tyson hung around the city limits waiting for the call from Michaels. He informed Porter and Justlin he'd call them after talking with the chief. He left the bar where Michaels frequently had a beer or two thinking that may have been where he wanted to meet. As he approached his car his phone rang, he paused hoping Michaels was calling to say "stand-by," he was on his way.

"Hey man. Did you meet with the chief?" Porter was agitated. "What time were you meeting him?"

"He didn't give me a time, he said he'd call. I'm still near Pine, I thought he'd want to meet me at the Oasis."

"Man get to his house. I think, well just get there. I'll meet you there."

"What's going on?"

"Worthy called. The neighbor called him concerned about shots being fired. Worthy is on his way there and called me. I told him you were meeting with Michaels. He told me that wouldn't be a good look if you were there."

"What the hell? Shots or a shot?" Tyson was yelling the questions as he started his car.

"Man, I don't know."

"How long ago did Worthy call?"

"We're all leaving at the same time. Be careful and hurry!" The call disconnected.

Tyson spoke into his dashboard. "Call Worthy!" The command was repeated, and the dial tone could be heard. The detective sighed deeply. He didn't know what to think and was scared to pray for a soul he wasn't sure had departed. As his thoughts drifted, he heard Worthy's voice.

"Hey, man, so you're not at his house." Worthy's sarcasm was expected.

"No, sir. I was supposed to wait for his call to meet him. I never got the call. Do we know some of what's going on?"

"The neighbor heard the shots about well, a half hour ago now. He's a retired veteran, medic. He's got an extra key, but I told him not to go in, I'd send a unit. You and Porter are the unit. I can't trust it going over the air. The neighbor, what is his name… anyway he said he didn't see anything moving after the shots. He's keeping an eye on Michaels' home from his location for anyone. D'white Stanley, known him for years, good guy. They're property touches so even with the land Michaels has, this guy can see who comes or goes. Tyson, I'm hoping, man I just don't know. I've got a feeling he shot himself. I mean no call to you and no movement after the shots the neighbor heard coming from his house; seems strange, so take the drive time to prepare yourself. This could be ugly."

Tyson understood. If Michaels wasn't shot, he was trying to plot his way out of a shooting. They wouldn't know what or who they were dealing with until they entered his home. It was a forty-five-minute drive from his location and if Porter and Worthy were home, they'd all arrive about the same time. Worthy wouldn't go in without Porter and Tyson being with him. Over the years responding to calls involving shootings at the homes of cops never had positive results. Tyson learned to keep his emotions intact. He and Porter drank in their homes in silence. If there was a need to vent, they trusted and supported one another, with questions and answers they only trusted between the two of them.

Worthy would be there to see their reactions. They wouldn't be able to say anything but the truth. Batman and Robin, those who thought they were the caped crusaders, wanted to kill the "untouchables" and if Michaels was one, their emotions wouldn't be rattled. His prayer over the past few months was that the "untouchables" hadn't given Worthy a pass. He prayed he and Porter weren't walking into a trap.

The path leading to Michaels' home was lit, as it had been whenever darkness fell surrounding the house. Worthy and Porter were there standing on the porch. Tyson assumed they checked the exterior of the chief's home. As he got out of his car, he could hear the neighbor's dog barking. He wondered if either of them spoke with the neighbor before his arrival.

"Tyson, man the neighbor met me with the key. We've checked the perimeter. Still don't know what we may find, so let's be careful."

"Ring the bell and knock." Porter gave the two of them a head nod before turning the key. "Yo, Michaels. It's Porter, Worthy, and Tyson. Say something man, Michaels!"

"Blood splatter there!" Worthy pointed to the floor as they approached the grand room." Michaels man, say something!" Tyson stepped around Porter and peered into the dining room. Worthy yelled again," Walter man, are you here?"

The men followed each other guns drawn, each in the defensive mode their training taught them over the years.

"Sssh!" Worthy pointed to the deck door which was partially open. Porter moved across the floor quickly and stopped suddenly. He pointed to the couch before going out on the deck where the motion light immediately lit the area. There was a body, face down on the floor in front of the couch. Worthy went to the couch where Michaels was slumped in a seated position with his gun in hand. The men holstered their weapons. Worthy pulled out his phone and called dispatch. Tyson continued to check the rest of the house.

"The guy near the deck door is dead. Took two to the head, maybe more once we turn him over. It can wait 'til the wagon gets here. I don't recognize him." Porter holstered his weapon and watched as Worthy assessed the chief's condition. Michaels took two bullets in the chest. His breathing was faint, he wouldn't last long enough for EMS to arrive.

"Man, give me a name." Worthy talked softly in his friend's ear on bended knee. Who is that guy? Is he one of them?"

"You are my only…friend." Michaels whispered as he drew in his last breath and closed his eyes. Tyson entered the room and looked from Worthy to Porter. The knock on the door interrupted his thought. Tyson went to the door and gently pushed the neighbor back onto the front porch.

Worthy got up from the kneeling position and walked to the deck. "Who is this guy? Is there a vehicle parked on this property somewhere? How did he get here? What the hell?"

"Hey, Captain. Do we need Dwight for anything else right now?" Tyson yelled from the front door.

"The normal questions man, what did he see if anything." Worthy responded without giving the question a labored thought.

"Thanks man, if we need any other information we'll come over, I mean we don't want to involve you in this if you don't have to be. Hearing the shots is enough unless you saw or heard something else."

"So, he's dead? I mean, Walt is dead? What about the other guy?"

Tyson took a deep breath. "Both are dead. Hey, did you see or hear a vehicle? Is there another road that leads behind the house or near the back of the house?"

"No, there's one behind my house. But you can't drive from that road to Walt's. My dog barked before the shots I heard. Could have been someone going from the road to Walt's house.

"But you can walk. Hang on. Porter!"

Porter came out the front door. "The bus should be here within the next half hour or so. What's up?"

Tyson looked toward the neighbor. "Take us to the road."

CHAPTER 39

The phone began ringing at eleven-thirty and hadn't stopped. Tina would answer and just listen to the details of the shooting again and again without a response. Marcie offered her company, but Tina simply stated it was late and they both would have a busy day to face. There would be questions and assumptions. Marcie would be dealing with calls from the community and in-house departments, while Tina would be dealing with the calls the governor would send her way. Neither knew the details so their conversation was filled with speculations.

To her surprise there was very little media coverage. The report of a shooting was announced but according to the reporters the home and victims could not be disclosed. Captain Dennis Worthy would be giving a statement shortly. Tina kept the television on hoping the names wouldn't include Porter or Tyson. She was tempted to call the captain or either of the detectives but thought it better that they report to her. Her phone rang again, and she rolled her eyes at the number that appeared on the LCD screen.

"Hello," she answered as though she didn't know the caller.

"Tina, is everything okay. I mean are you okay?"

"Blake, why wouldn't I be okay? I'm not an officer."

"I know, but you're working in the office with some crooked... well that's what you're there for, you know, to ruffle some feathers."

Tina couldn't believe what he was implying. She got up and went to her island to pour herself another glass of wine. She and Marcie had said goodnight to what she thought would be her last glass. After pausing long enough for him to say," hello?" she replied.

"Blake, I don't know what you think I do, but believe me it's not ruffling feathers. Where did you get that lame ass statement anyway? If you want to know, I don't just provoke people into killing one another."

Silently she added another reason she needed to break up their relationship. He wasn't black enough... "*ruffle feathers.*" She wanted to tell him to turn in his black card.

"You know what I mean. You working with, it doesn't matter as long as you're okay. Do you need me to come there for a few days?"

"Blake, no I don't, thanks for offering but there's enough knights in shinny armor if I need protection. I'm on the team with the good guys, so I'm covered. Not to mention, I was a cop, so I can protect myself if I need to."

"Yeah, that's where we had our problems. You didn't really want a man that would take care of you. You've got everything covered including support when your emotions need to be settled. Damn, I just thought I would be a shoulder for you. You do know that was Chief Michaels home. Yeah, he's dead along with the perp. So, you be careful who you lean on."

"Who said I was leaning on anyone? I already knew that information. Listen, when I wanted to lean on your shoulder, your ego had you so self-absorbed you could only support you. It taught me quickly how to support myself in our lopsided relationship. So, thanks for the call, I've got company coming."

"Tina! Wait! Tina..."

She disconnected the call and turned up the volume on the television. The phone rang again, and she answered ready to give her built up aggravation to her ex.

"Hey lady, are you watching this unfold?"

It was Fulton. Her demeanor changed instantly.

"Yes, and what does that say about upper management."

"So, was it the chief, do you know who the other guy was?"

"Haven't got the back story yet. I'm assuming, yes it was the chief, and they had a shoot-out."

"Really? I hadn't thought of it as being a shoot-out, maybe someone was looking for information they thought he had. Was Michaels involved in, you know, the mess we're uncovering?"

"Lawrence, I really don't know."

He could tell by her response she was tired of the questions.

"Hmm, Lawrence. That's right we're off the clock. So, what's your position for the rest of the week. I'm sure the station will be busy buzzing with this. What does that do for your investigation and if you're free, how about lunch without an agenda?"

"Lunch without an agenda? Sounds like you have an agenda in mind."

They shared a laugh and continued to discuss possibilities until a second call and an announcement brought the investigator's attention back to the news on the television. It was confirmed that one of the bodies in the home was Chief Walter Michaels.

"I've got to go Lawrence. Call me tomorrow, we can meet for something, I'm sure. I've got to take this other call. Goodnight."

Tina checked to see who the next caller was, praying it wasn't Blake or anyone from the governor's office. She really needed to process Michaels' death. Again, she tried to calm herself. She paused before saying hello as the background noise made it difficult to hear Tyson.

"Hey, you okay. You need anything. I'm leaving Michaels' house now. Checking on you on my way in."

"Wow." She couldn't explain her short response. Three men, just checking. How lucky was she. She'd tell Marcie how lucky they were. She could see herself enjoying the pleasure of having three men seeking to comfort her distress.

"Wow?"

"Just a thought of the mess you must be dealing with." She hoped he wouldn't question her further.

"Listen, you and I had a close relationship with him. Even if he's connected to this nonsense, he was a friend, a mentor of sorts, so this is uncomfortable to say the least. It stings. I thought I'd be upset if he truly was with Sheers and his boys, but Tina this is worse than that."

"Damien, he was with them. I think this confirms it. They killed him because he wanted out. He told Worthy, remember? I thought it would be suicide he wasn't himself at all. He was scared and scared folks, well they get desperate. I'm not glad it went down like this but I'm glad he didn't feel so desperate he would kill himself."

"So, what you doing? Watching this unfold on the television?"

"That's about the size of it. Drinking a glass of wine so I can unwind. Each report seems to be worse than the last, but I can't cut it off."

"Go to bed, get ready for tomorrow."

"You've got to drive home. Have you eaten yet?"

"No ma'am, you offering a meal? A conversation, a glass of wine?"

"Hmm we can share whatever you bring. Don't bring Porter and Worthy with you though."

"Oh no, is this not an open invitation. We have to make this relationship Worthy thinks we have real."

"Tyson?"

"Yes."

"Where are Worthy and Porter?"

"On the porch, I'm looking right at them. Why?"

"Wave goodnight to them and get in your car. Oh, and go home."

Justlin hung up the phone and laughed. She poured her last glass of wine as she heard the reporter on the news state, they were removing the bodies from Chief Michaels home.

CHAPTER 40

"I understand, that's not why he went there. I'm sure of it… No there were no orders given from me or Boone… Yes, yes, Chambers? Sir, if we do anything different it will look as though… yes, yes, I understand. He'll be reassigned sir, yes… No, the lawyer hasn't been around lately… I don't know. Yes, I'll have someone check that today. Yes, I will. Goodbye."

Sheers slammed the phone on the receiver and looked at Boone.

"This ain't good man. This shit ain't good." He sat back in his chair.

The two were in his home waiting for the call that turned into a scolding. The plan that was set to be a nudging visit to Michaels' home was now a double murder with questions. Nothing came over the airwaves to inform them that what was ordered to be a simple threat could cause unexpected problems.

"So, what now?" Boone questioned sitting in a chair across the room. He stood and approached Sheers offering him a cigar. Sheers waved the gesture away shaking his head no.

"Man, what was he thinking? Michaels ain't the type to just pull a gun on someone. I'm wondering what this ass said that caused him to get shot. He wasn't supposed to threaten him, so why was his gun out? Who the hell shot first?"

"He was supposed to knock and visit. That was it right?"

Knock and visit was a term the "untouchables" used to talk with someone they thought wanted out. A reminding visit and talk, one on one. Marshall had attempted the same gesture days before, but Sheers sent Officer Kevin Longo as a follow up. Longo had time on the force and was a recruited member of the lawless group. He was married with four children and the phone call was to inform Sheers Officer Longo should never have been assigned to the task.

"Boone, he was to go there to see about Chambers, and talk about Michaels' intentions, that was it. It wasn't a knock and visit call, Marshall did that days ago. I don't know how this happened. He was to ask about Chambers. Now, Chambers is to be reassigned."

"What? Where? I thought he was to be plugged back into the Cold Case Unit."

"He's to be protected. They seem to think he's weak, the reason Longo was going to talk with Michaels. You know, to tell him to go easy on the kid. Let him know that Tyson and Porter were harsh. Who the fuck would think it would lead to murder?"

"So, Chambers was the topic and they wound up shooting each other? Man, that sounds way off base."

"Boone, I swear. I told Longo, tell the chief that Chambers is scared to go back on that unit and make it clear he's to be treated with kid gloves. Nothing about a problem with Michaels or any of the other mess, you know what I mean? I don't know if Longo was aware of Michaels wanting out, so why would he mention it. Michaels was antsy, that's all it was. He didn't trust nobody with questions and look what happened."

"So, what's next?"

"Call Chambers. We'll meet with him today and calm his damn nerves. Have Braize call Tyson and let him know Chambers is being reassigned. He don't need to know where. I'll go in and meet with Worthy. Damn, we need someone we can deal with and he ain't it. They'll fix that, I'm sure."

"Yeah, they can appoint Captain Mancy. He's got seniority over Worthy. He ain't political, but he's one of us."

"Boone man, they running short. You ready man? We can be promoted really fast if people keep dropping."

"I'm good. Too many spotlights at the top. Mancy will work in our favor, Worthy ain't one to fuck with."

"What? Man, everyone has a weakness and a nigger in charge, hell they're the weakest. Let's get started. Things will work in our favor."

The two laughed as they exited Sheers' home. They departed to their vehicles heading to the precinct. They never noticed the black Escalade parked across the street.

Sheers arrived at the precinct and found the mayhem that was stirring at the entrance. Officers and reporters were waiting for Captain Worthy to arrive at the podium for an official press conference. He was certain not to stop in the mix of officers whose questions were about Longo and his reason for being in the chief's home.

Sheers passed Marcie at the front desk mumbling. "Officer Marcie Wilson, is the sergeant in?"

"He's out there with them, somewhere. Is there something anyone else can help you with?" She refused to acknowledge his sarcastic attitude.

"Did Chambers come in?"

"I don't think so. He may be out there in the mix too." Marcie rolled her eyes. Sheers didn't talk with her, in fact, he avoided most of the minority officers and civilian staff. "Most of the officers that reported this morning have been assigned. Did you check the board for him?"

Sheers gave her a thoughtful stare and went into the line-up room. There, the board detailed shifts and assignments. Chambers name wasn't on the board which meant he hadn't been assigned or hadn't reported in.

"Did Tyson call this morning?" He asked as he returned to Marcie at the front desk.

"No, why would he call?"

"Just a thought. I don't know where this officer is and with everything that has happened, hell, just a thought."

Sheers left before Marcie could ask about his thoughts. He feared she'd see through his reasons and question his cause. Chambers walking away from an assignment was a mistake, the same one Michaels made. The applause from the atrium let Williams, Sheers, and others know the captain was in place to speak. They stepped out of the office to hear his announcement.

"Good morning, I don't have much time, as you all can imagine, there's an investigation, calls, and paperwork to follow. I also don't have too many answers to the questions I'm sure you all want answered. So do we, so do the families of both, Chief Michaels and Officer Longo. We will get the answers it's just too early in the investigation. So, now on to what we do know."

Captain Worthy gave the details as the media, community leaders and police staff stood by in silence waiting for their turn to ask the questions he explained couldn't and wouldn't be answered. He stepped away quickly from the podium introducing the Deputy Chief, Commander, and Assistant Commissioner who would be answering questions regarding the investigation going forward.

Sheers scanned the audience and found Chambers standing with a small group of officers across the floor. Not far from them was Tyson and the staff from his unit, Tina Justlin, Lawrence Fulton, and Samantha Sayers, the reporter. Sheers thought it strange they would be standing in the same area. He tried to follow their responses as Worthy explained the call from the neighbor and his call for officers to respond. Sheers was sure Worthy's choice of officers was planned. He deliberately chose not to use officers from the precinct, although he had his favorites. Knight and Knowles would have been chosen if he didn't need seasoned officers. Sheers understood what most wouldn't; the captain needed Porter and Tyson to respond.

Eyes would be on the officers Chambers was with, the newly recruited "untouchables." Boone was spotted approaching the group and walking them toward the elevators. Their eyes met; Sheers nodded as he headed toward the Desk Sergeant to speak on Chambers being reassigned. Sheers whispered to the sergeant the need for him to be pulled away from the information being conveyed. His response was one of frustration as he had to move through the crowd as they walked toward Tyson.

"Hey, Tyson, can we talk a minute." Braize and Sheers approached Tyson as did Fulton. Tyson turned, hearing his name, and stepped away from the group and the crowd.

"Sorry Tyson, we'll talk later. I'm going to need the report for review if you don't mind," Fulton said. "Officer Sheers, Sergeant, you boys have a good day, or at least a better day."

The lawyer proceeded to the center of the crowd, closer to the cameras. It was his movement that caused whispers, only to be quelled by the next speaker. Turning his attention to Sheers and Braize as they approached, Tyson waited for one of them to speak.

"Tyson, Chambers is being reassigned. We thought you should know he won't be back to your unit." When Tyson gave no response, the sergeant continued. "I don't know if you were expecting him to be with your unit today. I'm sorry the request came in this morning."

"No problem. I hope his reassignment fits him better." Tyson turned to walk away.

"Anything is better than working where you're not wanted, you know that."

Sheers spoke and Tyson didn't respond to the comment that was to be a deliberate trigger.

"Sergeant, you'd have a better day if you kept better company. But then again sir when you're 'untouchable,' your days are numbered."

"What the hell Tyson, you know I don't play games." The sergeant an elder to both Sheers and Tyson, who was well past his retirement years mumbled as he walked away. "Sheers! No need for you to ask where that damn rookie is going, tell him to report to me now! Tyson, you know I don't condone their bullshit! Keep my name out of their mess!"

"You and your boys Sheers are getting sloppy. Home visits and murder…hmm wondering if they left evidence? I would be wondering what may be found at the scene since none of the boys are on that team. You didn't get a chance to get there or place someone there, which means you're in the dark. I thought Chambers was coming back, someone's scared. If it's not you, someone is on to you, it ain't just me. It just got real. Boone is over there smoothing out the edges with your pups. If they're like Chambers, this murder has them scared. The list is getting shorter, close to your name, my man. Hey, I can't be seen talking to you too long, may jeopardize your operation."

Tyson walked away before Sheers could respond. He looked toward Boone, who was listening to the speakers as were the rookies with him. Chambers had left the group.

CHAPTER 41

Samantha put the menu down and waited for Fulton to lower his. He hadn't said much since they left the precinct. No one had disclosed more than what was reported by the news the night before. Samantha was on the phone off and on all morning with no answers to the questions her paper wanted. She refused to report what she couldn't back with facts. Agreeing to have a bite to eat with Fulton she hoped, would put her on track to another lead for a bigger story.

"What are you having? I think I'll have a tuna melt. Doesn't look like there's a need to miss a meal huh?" Fulton smiled as he put the menu down.

The diner was filled with many who were at the press conference. The whispers and buzz of the conversations were the same throughout the dining area. The small bar area for the after-work crowd, held a few of the towns store owners. All were too busy to notice the famous lawyer and the Village Post reporter.

"I'll have the chicken salad lunch special, whatever that includes. Are we going with the schedule we talked about?" Samantha didn't know if she'd get anyone to answer to the questions she prepared.

"Sure. I don't see why it would matter. Michaels is the only one we can't get a response from and maybe talking with Worthy now we'll get answers that he may have avoided before."

"What does that mean? Do you think Worthy would be a part of the cover-up?"

"Don't know. If it's causing problems, we may get a few whose story would be different now. Start with Worthy, we may get new names on the list. I told Tyson I'd glance at the forensic report he just got. I'm thinking it's not what's in the file now. Different totally from what was filed for court, I'm sure. It's breaking down slowly, especially considering this shooting. The questions I gave you, I'm hoping will point us in the right direction."

"Maybe tie into this murder. I agree, I think there's a connection." Her phone rang interrupting the conversation. "Sorry, I have to take this."

Samantha excused herself from the table. "Hey, what's up?" She got up from the table looking over the diner for a spot where she could hear the caller clearly.

"I was told to let you know your meeting with, well I don't need to tell you, but I didn't think anyone else would to make this call." It was the sergeant assigned to Chief Michaels' office. Samantha usually got the first call from his office for any reports. She didn't expect to hear from his office at all. It was obvious she'd be depending on answers from Worthy.

"Thanks for the call, I know your office must be buzzing. I'll keep my team at bay, as long as I can. Do they know who'll be appointed to his position?"

"Ms. Sayers, you know I can't say officially. If I had my choice, it would be Captain Worthy, but I'm just the sergeant who has worked in this office for ten years. They won't ask me for my opinion. I'm sure they won't rush to putting anyone in his place for the next week or so. They'll work Worthy in both spots until they tell him they've got someone else. You know how that goes, they've got to find the right fit, if you know what I mean."

"Understood, wishful thinking."

"Ain't nothing changed but the date. Same shit-show, with the same actors playing their assigned roles. Anyway, I wanted you to know the appointment is officially cancelled per them. They were in here early looking over things before the press conference, without Worthy of course. Listen, when you get a chance when things die down, we'll really talk. I'm sure I'll be outta here too."

"You've got those three strikes you always talk about."

"Yes ma'am. Black, a female, and don't give a shit. Have a good day ma'am."

Samantha could only laugh as she disconnected the call. Returning to the table, she found her salad waiting. Fulton's raised eyebrows made it obvious he knew what her call was about.

"They want you to stay away?"

"No, not really. I'll check Worthy with the excuse that I know he'll be too busy on Wednesday. I may have another for the list though. The sergeant that worked with Michaels, she's on top of everything that goes on in that office. Maybe she knows who signs off on those reports or paperwork. Anyway, she said we should talk. It can't hurt."

"You're right, a story is a story. Your schedule has shifted, is that a problem."

"Not at all. Like you said, a story is a story."

The two finished their lunch listening to the surrounding conversations filled with theories of the happenings the night before. There were questions regarding the officer who lost his life in Michaels' home. No one remembered him; there were questions about his assignment to the Moorestown Precinct. Fulton and Sayers left the diner promising to be in touch if any new information was reported.

Samantha crossed the street avoiding the traffic and the crowd mulling around. The sea of blue included officers who were from other precincts assigned to accompany senior staff. Others were to keep the media, community activists, and others behind the barricades that were now bordering the doors of the precinct and the parking lot. Sayers smiled as she thanked the officers who gave her free passage to the front of the crowd.

"Hey c'mon man. The Village Post gets privileges here!" Shouts from the reporters with their cameramen and microphones could be heard as she walked by. "Samantha, you on payroll or what? Take my camera with you."

Knowing the staff and what not to do was the advantage Samantha had over many of the reporters in the crowd. Her camera crew would be invited to the precinct when others were writing what she had in her notes while watching the chaos they often caused. Her technique got her interviews others wouldn't be afforded. As she walked through to the elevators a part of her conversation with the sergeant in Michaels' office crossed her mind, "*officially cancelled.*" She questioned the meaning. Samantha nor Michaels ever had an official meeting scheduled. She thought about the past few days, speaking with Fulton, Ms. Foster, and Tammilyn over the weekend. She was right, she never told Michaels she was coming to his office. She got off the elevator and dialed Michaels' office.

"Good morning, Chief's complex." The sergeant's greeting was changed as to be expected.

"Hey, it's Samantha. Did you know I had an appointment with Michaels?"

"No, I'm assuming he had it on his calendar. Maybe written on his desk calendar. Listen, it could have been a reminder to call you. They didn't know when it was first mentioned. The exact words were, '*cancel everything including call-backs*'. But when your name came up one of those damn rookies brought the list to me with your name at the top of it."

"They have his calendar?"

"They're still in his office. I'm sure they'll clear everything out. Hell, wish I came in earlier than them this morning."

"Thanks, Sarge. We'll talk a little later."

"Looking forward to it."

She stood still a moment before entering Worthy's office. For the first time in years Samantha feared she could be a target.

CHAPTER 42

The orders from Worthy were clear, the Cold Case Unit would be working on a skeleton crew until further notice. He had his reasons which he explained to Tyson and Porter in a closed- door meeting prior to the press conference. Tina Justlin was asked to report to his office and together they would make a call to the governor's office. Tyson called his team together on the unit to explain what would be going on within their unit.

Everyone listened intently to what Tyson had to say. The 'young guns' were still on edge wondering if they would be reassigned since Chambers was not a part of the morning briefing.

"The unit won't be running normal operations for the duration of this murder investigation. Porter, Wilson, Stands, and I, are temporarily assigned to report to the captain's office. Knowles and Knight you are to report with us although you will work between this office and his. We'll be given further instructions from the captain. Montez you will work with ongoing cases and these files with Miller. It will slow the process for Investigator Justlin's report, but this murder is the priority now. Don't hesitate to contact us with your findings. It's uncertain where these folders may lead us so we have to be up to date on what may answer our questions. Kai, calls for us can be handled by Montez and whatever you can't handle Montez, pass on to us. No information is to be given to any reporters or discussed outside of these walls."

Tyson paused checking the expression of his staff. "I hope this will be short-lived assignments and things will be better in a few weeks."

"You think it will take that long before they sort things out?" Montez shook his head at the thought of working solo with the boxes of folders.

"I'm hoping that there's a connection somewhere. Listen, this is for the three of you...," he said pointing to Miller, Knowles, and Knight. "I know you've got your own thoughts about what goes on in this department or in this line of work. Understand,

Michaels' murder, just opened a can of 'aww shit'! Someone messed up and I'm sure the department won't stop until they pin someone for it. Now whether the murder was a set up or mistake, the investigation will point a finger. We hope it won't be within the department, but my gut feeling tells me it's one of us. I don't have to labor you with the dirty cop thing or who the group is, but if they're involved in any way, things are going to get rough. Watch your backs, we're not the favored unit or people. Knight and Knowles you can head to the captain's office. You'll report here each morning and be called for your assignment."

Everyone dispersed leaving Tyson, Porter, Stands and Wilson to retreat to Tyson's office. Each reported to the office aware the day wouldn't proceed as normal.

"Worthy is not playing with this one. We're assigned as the investigators on the case with Knight and Knowles being our runners if needed. No other officers will be assigned without his permission. He's got a team of officers from the special ops unit in his front office monitoring who comes in and out as well as personal protection. He chose the officers from the forensic unit as well to collect the evidence. No calls were made over the airwaves, he handpicked everyone that's working on this case. I think he believes the 'untouchables' had something to do with this shooting."

Porter shook his head. "Man, what was Longo doing there? How does he fit into this puzzle? That dude don't never leave the precinct."

"Where was he assigned?" Wilson asked as she offered the others coffee.

"I'll take a cup," responded Stands," Didn't he work intake a few years ago?"

Silence fell between them. Tyson hit the intercom button on his phone. "Montez, I need you a minute man." Tyson questioned Stands, "He worked on evidence intake?"

"Wilson, remember me telling you about the dude who would just take my word for the drugs I turned in? That was him. I complained a few times, but nothing changed about how he handled the book. He didn't check the quantity. He'd tell me to leave it blank, he'd fill it in when he got around to checking it. I wrote my numbers in with my initials each time. He'd sign for others. I don't know if he worked in this unit."

Montez opened the door but didn't enter the room.

"Montez, check for Longo's initials or signature on Fulton's clients. Check the names on the logs signing before the court dates and after. We checked for Boone's and Sheers' right? I don't think they'll be that stupid but check for his and those other two."

"The other two that made that drug bust the same night are definitely there, I'll check for Longo."

"Well, the fog is lifting." Porter waited for the others to agree. "What? Tell me you don't see there may be a connection here."

"Sit down man. Everything is still speculation. We don't know if—"

The phone interrupted Wilson's thought. Tyson held up his index finger to silence the room.

"Hey, Cap. Yes, I've informed them. What? We're on our way. No, Chambers didn't show up. I spoke with Sheers during the press conference, Chambers is being reassigned. Understood, we're on our way now."

Tyson hung up the phone and took a deep breath.

"Porter man, you were right. The shots to the head entered from the back and front. He also had a shot to the chest."

"Who?" Wilson and Stands questioned in unison.

"Porter pointed out that there may have been another shot when we saw Longo's body on the floor. It was obvious there were two holes in his head. They've examined or are examining the bodies this morning. He was shot in the head and chest from the front, but the other shot in the head came from behind. Michaels was shot on the couch, he couldn't have fired that shot, someone else did."

"So, two came into his home? We only found one vehicle on that back road." Porter looked at Tyson for the answer.

"Wait, you're saying three people were at Michaels' home. Two, obviously, are dead. The third left? They had to leave in another vehicle." Stands looked at Tyson and then Porter for a response.

"Worthy wants us upstairs. I'm sure we'll be visiting that neighbor and where the vehicle was parked this morning."

CHAPTER 43

The officers nodded their greetings as the Principal Investigator passed them heading to Captain Worthy's office. She remembered being an officer hoping to be on the special details. She recognized Knowles and Knight when they passed her being led to the captain's office before her. Now as they hurried pass her making their exit Knowles stopped her in the hall.

"I think you'll see who's who now," the young officer said with a smile.

"I always knew. It comes with years on the force. You're ahead of the game. Recognizing your partner there going astray is a part of learning who's who. Be careful, he may still be confused about what side he stands with."

"You're right and I will. Let's hope we catch them this time." Knowles started to walk away, Justlin touched his arm softly and whispered, "There will always be more, stay alert out there."

"Yes, ma'am."

She walked into Worthy's office and as she suspected he was on the phone. He hung up, offering her a seat at the conference table.

"Tyson and his team are on their way up here. Tina this is a mess."

"Has the governor's office called?"

"The governor? Hell, I'm expecting the President to call. Everyone has called that has a title, including secretaries and clerks. There's some that I believe are scared they'll be caught with others they know are dirty. Everyone is on edge."

"How about you? Are you okay? You haven't had a chance to take a moment. Have you taken a breath captain? A chance to really rest in the thoughts and memories of your friend, not the chief, Walter Michaels. I know Tyson and I have talked about our moments, have you had yours?"

"I prepared myself Tina when he told me he was being pressured. He wanted me to do the media stuff, keeping me away from what really was going on. I dismissed him and it. It's bothering me that I didn't push to know more. Maybe, his death could have been avoided."

"Captain, maybe your life would be in danger, that may be why he didn't tell you everything."

Tyson and his team walked in and joined them at the table. Worthy grabbed paperwork from his desk and gave the order in the phone for all calls to be held.

"Alright, you all know what we reported last night. I've got a preliminary report from the evidence collected. Looks like Porter was right, there was a third shot. The problem is that the two bullet wounds to the head entered in opposite directions. It looks as though Longo was facing Michaels and they had an exchange of fire. My assumption is they hit each other twice simultaneously. Michaels was shot twice. Once in his chest puncturing his lung, the other in his throat. His shots fired from his position hit Officer Longo in the chest and forehead. The pictures here show two exit wounds in his head, the back, and the front. The wounds indicate there was, there had to be a third shooter. Someone shot Longo from behind. Whoever it was didn't leave on foot and they left Longo's vehicle on the road behind the neighbor's home. There had to be a second vehicle."

He passed the photos and printed emails he received showing the evidence for everyone to review. As they shared the information, most that had been reported on the news at twelve, the captain handed each of them another set of paperwork.

"These assignments will be adhered to until this investigation is completed, or at least until they remove me from my position. I'm sure they're working as fast as they can to get me away from the evidence that may put a noose around a few necks. Now as I see it, some of this may spill over to our favorite group. Do as we have done, keep all findings and information among us. Knowles and Knight will be a part of the team I've assembled to collect evidence. They'll be signing off on all paperwork and collecting data to bring back to one of us. I've set up each unit who will only report to me or Tyson in my absence. Justlin, I'll need you to work as our liaison with the governor. They want to know what's going on. Tell them, as we get the facts, tell them. If we need more officers, we'll need the governor's approval. I won't ask anyone whose title is lower than his. As I said, they'll be looking to replace me especially when they find out none of their people are included in any of this investigation. Any questions?"

Justlin looked around the table, seeing no one was speaking up she asked, "Had Michaels told you he was being pressured to the point of desperation?"

"If you mean. did he mention suicide, no. He did mention he was tired and wanted out. I think he told you that as well. I told him to get out of whatever it was. I don't know how deep he was tied up in the b.s. but, he did say that boy Chambers would be killed if we didn't get him back on the unit."

Everyone's attention shifted from the papers before them to the captain, who continued to speak.

"I thought they would push for him to work on your unit Tyson. Sometime during the press conference, they changed their minds. I believe it was a possible connection between Michaels being a threat to their group, the shooting, and Chambers being a weak link. They're scared, and if we're to get rid of them, now's our chance."

The group understood their assignments. Tina left them to go back to the Cold Case Unit to make her calls. The others would meet at Michaels' home which was under surveillance. Worthy returned to his desk to start his report of the initial incident and findings.

CHAPTER 44

Samantha waited patiently as the foot traffic in the captain's office continued. She was told to wait as the captain did want to speak with her. She sent a text to Fulton letting him know she would be allowed a minute or two of the captain's time. The phones were busy, and the sergeant was clearly irritated repeating the same message. It wasn't until Officer Sheers entered expressing his urgent need to talk with the captain, that Sergeant Smith's anger reached its peak.

"Not happening right now. I can have him call you when he's ready but interrupting the flow of what's going on… Sheers it ain't happening."

"Is that the response that you were given from him? I think if he knew it was me, or you allowed me to at least tell him what it is…"

"You've got his direct line. Call him, if he says he'll see you, no problem. Let me warn you though, if the call bounces to this phone, you beat," Sergeant Smith responded emphatically. "Take your chances, call him, but move away from my desk."

Samantha watched as Sheers stepped near her to sit in the vacant seat. He paused before sitting as though he wasn't sure he wanted to make the call or leave. He pulled out his cell phone sending a text and waited for the response. It was obvious he didn't like the response as he dialed a number and put it to his ear. The phone at the front desk rang and the Sergeant sent a piercing stare allowing the ringing to continue.

"What! Do I need an appointment? Who is she waiting for, no what she's going to get an exclusive and I can't see him? Suppose I had information he needed?" Sheers yelled walking from his seat to the sergeant's desk, the length of the waiting area pointing toward Samantha.

"I'll leave him the message. If he wants to talk with you or hear what you have to say, he'll call you. In the meantime, you have supervisors to report to and a union rep, tell them your story. He'll answer their calls before yours. I guess you forgot you're an officer, Sheers, an officer. You're not a priority, nor are you a part of this investigation. If you do have information, follow protocol."

"Protocol? Protocol, there's going to be changes around here…"

Before he could finish his statement, Sergeant Smith nodded to the officer standing at the door. He opened the door.

"Officer Sheers, that's enough." The Special Operations Officer spoke firmly. "Do you need an escort?"

"No, what the hell? Who are you? Special Ops has authority in our house now? Smith you got the game twisted!" His anger was clearly demonstrated, and Samantha wondered what the connection was to the happenings over the last twenty-four hours.

"Ms. Sayers, the captain will see you momentarily. I'm sorry you had to be in the mix of that."

"No problem. I'm sure everyone is on edge." Samantha continued to text notes into her phone. She was convinced that Officer Sheers' intention was to get information about the investigation more so than give information. The pieces were falling all around them, they just weren't falling in place. Captain Worthy opened his office door and waved Samantha in.

"Ms. Sayers, I'm so sorry, it's been quite a day."

"I can only imagine. I know you don't have everything in place regarding the murder, but I was going to talk with Michaels today and maybe visit you later this week."

"Oh, I see. So, you're not here about the shootings?"

"No, not yet. I can wait until you're ready with credible information. I really wanted to talk about Tammilyn Watson, the Foster Case."

Captain Worthy sat back in his high-back leather executive seat. He took a deep breath and closed his eyes. He wasn't sure what the reporter would ask, but he was sure his answers would make headlines.

"Ms. Foster was and is, a friend. We've been mixed in community affairs for years. She told me about the problems in those projects, the drugs, the late-night activities, and the violations. I did what I could from my desk as a Sergeant. It didn't amount to much, it was stopped at every desk with a stamp of "not now," hell that was better than "request denied." She'd come back months later with added complaints, or her version of what the police should do. We had officers posted there, touring the area, and supposedly stopping the drugs. We're working on a few things internally that should have been dealt with over the years. It's recently been brought to our attention, and I can't speak about that until we're sure about what happened."

"Captain there's several appeals, cases where lawyers and family members believe they've be entrapped by the police. There's news of falsified documents, missing signatures or evidence, and lack of witness statements. If this comes to light do you think there's a possibility of inmates like Julian Foster, and others being released?"

"Ms. Sayers, if this comes to light and it's found to be true, yes, they will have the right for an appeal and/or release. I don't know the circumstances of the others you refer to. Each case would be separate and investigated thoroughly."

"How long has the department been investigating the complaint made by Julian Foster's family. Their lawyer has obtained proof that the department was a part of the cover-up."

"Does he now? Well Ms. Sayers, I haven't been contacted or included in any of the investigative reports. In light of Chief Michaels' murder, I can't promise when I'd have information that would bring clarity to where we are with this. However, I can say that I will find answers."

"Have you had other cases where the information just disappeared?"

"Ms. Sayers, I can't answer that. I would hope the answer would be never. You and I both know how a man like me, even with rank, is observed. I'm just a page turner, shouting orders, signing paperwork, and making sure others like me do the work. In this community, they need us, you included. They're woven into this community but we're the border and edges so they can continue to do what they do. There's a lot I can't say, and plenty I won't say. Give me some time to investigate the reports I didn't have eyes on. I'll get Ms. Foster, Mr. Fulton, and you some answers."

Samantha stood to exit. Closing her phone and thanking the captain for his time, she had a final question.

"Captain, the officer who wanted to see you, is that Officer Sheers who has been labeled an 'untouchable'? Are they a part of the murder or the cases with the missing pieces? He seemed desperate enough to be a part of that group. We've been sporadically writing about them over the years. They've been involved in some serious problems within the department."

"Yes, that was Sheers and I have told you, with this murder and everything else I didn't have time for his questions. As I said, I'll contact you."

Captain Worthy opened the door but stopped her from leaving. "Oh, it may not be wise to meet here so I'll have Tyson or Porter call you to meet."

CHAPTER 45

Stands stood at the base of the steps as Tyson rang Michaels' neighbor's bell. Wilson and Porter were checking the road where officers were monitoring the scene and hooking Officer Longo's car to the authorized tow truck to be towed. The evidence collected on the scene the night before would be rechecked and the car would be wiped down for fingerprints. D'white Stanley came to the door holding the collar of his dog, who continued barking.

"Hush! I'm sorry, he hasn't stopped barking all morning. This movement next door and the officers coming to mark off where that car was, has him riled up. What can I do for you?"

"We've got a couple of questions. If you can secure the dog and walk with us out toward where the vehicle is, we'd like to ask about the area, if you don't mind."

Tyson waited while Mr. Stanley pushed the dog inside and secured the door.

"Hush! I'll be back in a minute. He's sure gonna keep up noise now. Hearing all these people out here like this. It's normally so quiet. But he can hear the animals come through, that's why I keep him. I always said I was well protected. Police chief on one side and my dog right in the house. It didn't help, I've been really feeling bad that the car was found right on my property, you know?"

"I can imagine, this is Investigator Stands and I've got two more investigators with me, you met Porter, but we've got Investigator Wilson with us as well. You may see them here over the next few days looking in the area or at Chief Michaels' home. If you remember anything after we speak today, don't hesitate to speak with them."

The three of them walked the path leading to the area where the car was parked. Tyson asked basic questions about the area, how long Mr. Stanley lived there, and if he'd ever seen cars parked in the area or on his property before.

"Do you have cameras outside of your home or any covering your property line? You've got a few acres here, right?"

"Family owned, sir. I just ain't into city living. Been here for more than fifteen years. Hoping my children will appreciate that I've kept it up for them and their families. I got three children, adults with families. It's enough room for them to build on. Now, no one asked about how far my property goes. Just about this road here. I guess cause it's closer to Walt's house. Ain't no way they'd walk from the other side, too far. The other neighbor has three dogs, Pitt-Bulls, mean ones. They were barking last night too. But you know, like I said, if a deer or anything comes through between their dogs and mine, you can't hear nothing but them barking."

The conversation continued with Stands and Tyson asking questions about the time, and anything else the neighbor could remember about the night before. The walk to the road took almost five minutes. Mr. Stanley stopped and looked around.

"These trees here have been cut. Branches cut down." The three men walked over to the brush to take a closer look.

"Look here." Mr. Stanley pointed to the area just before the path where Longo's car was parked. "The grass and smaller bushes is smashed. Looks like something may have been on top if it."

Stands walked further along headed to the path. "Hey, Tyson, it looks like the second vehicle may have parked there, entered and exited here." He pointed to the branches that laid across the dirt road. "Seems like they swept the area with the branches to cover the tracks."

Tyson looked over the area and agreed. They found where the other vehicle was parked.

"Stands call Knowles, let him know we need a team to collect what they can from this area. They need to secure this spot too. Mr. Stanley seems like we may be here a little longer. You don't let the dog roam, do you?"

"No, if he's out, I'm out with him. Too much land for him to roam on his own, plus the neighbor's dogs would go crazy. They're out from the early morning until just about dusk. They're fenced in but you can see them, and they can see you. That's why I said, most folks know we've got these dogs. They don't try them."

The group walked back to Mr. Stanley's house. Longo's car was removed. Stands and Wilson would wait for Knowles and the team to secure the additional area found. Porter and Tyson said their goodbye to Mr. Stanley reminding him if he had any questions to give them a call. They walked toward Chief Michaels' home and Porter stopped before they approached his deck.

"The shooter had to come from a different angle. Longo came through the doors there on the deck. We've got proof of that. Whoever was following him knew he was coming here. I'd say he knew he was coming to stop Longo from shooting Michaels. Walking from where the second car was parked and the result of the shooting…"

"They followed Longo…" Tyson began with his own thoughts.

"Or they came together," added Porter.

The detectives paused in thought. Each had a theory, and each agreed, either could have been possible.

"Whoa, I hadn't thought about them coming together. Then why park in separate spots?"

"Maybe that was the plan all along." Porter turned to look in either direction. "Longo may have gotten here early, and the other person was sent to be sure the task was carried out. Suppose they were here to stop whatever, not knowing shooting Michaels was in the plan."

"I see your point. It's all possibilities at this point. Call Stands and tell them lock down this area for more evidence as well. The neighbor was right, they wouldn't have come from another direction that's why they parked where they did. Maybe, they didn't cover all the tracks."

The two stood on the deck looking in both directions. The investigation would take longer than planned.

"Man, so where does that put us with all the work we're doing with Fulton and those damn folders?"

"Porter, man, if I didn't know better, I'd say this was the diversion. You know, like they knew we were getting close, Michaels was breaking, and Chambers wasn't doing his part. Cause confusion and chaos will leave loose ends."

"Murder? Man, it's hard to imagine that uncovering the mishandling of those files would bring them to murdering an official."

"Porter, how many murders? How many people have lost themselves, their lives behind those walls? That's why we agreed to work with Fulton. It's our people that are losing, our community, somebody has to stop this madness."

"Yeah, I'm with you. I'm just surprised how far they will go."

CHAPTER 46

Captain Worthy glanced at his watch, pausing as he watched text messages loading on his phone. He answered as many emails as he could, coupled with the text messages from the field, he needed a break. Although, Justlin, diverted many of the repetitive questions, he was sure the governor's call was on the horizon. It was close to four, and unlike the endless hours he worked the night before he hoped to close his office by six. There wasn't much to do until the evidence was collected and filed. Reports would follow and only then would they be able to direct the investigative team. Today would be the best day to rest and be refreshed for the upcoming chaos.

Sergeant Smith knocked and entered the office. She pushed the door gently, careful not to close it. As she approached the captain's desk she began to talk in a hushed tone.

"Lieutenant Marshall is here to see you. He said he can't wait and wanted to leave you with some information. Captain, we just got an email about his inquiry regarding the Special Operations Unit. You wanted to be notified if there were any inquiries about that team."

"Really, flag that email for me. What the… never mind, yes, let him in."

Worthy scanned through the emails he hadn't read. He hoped the email would indicate the time Marshall put in his paperwork. He knew he would have to ask the lieutenant why.

Marshall entered the office in civilian dress.

"Not working today, lieutenant? I'd think with Michaels' murder being a priority you'd be leading the charge to find the killer. We've found there may be another shooter, another person on the scene at the time of the murder. What the hell Marshall, never mind. What is your question about the Special Ops unit?"

The captain nodded to the seat across from his desk. Marshall sat and paused before answering. He passed an envelope to the captain but held his hand on it. An indication he didn't want him to open it while they talked.

"I asked for an assignment a while back. I haven't heard an answer yet. I want to use the time until I hear something for vacation. I won't get much time before a reassignment. After talking with Michaels… well I guess now you'll be the one to get me reassigned."

"What? Did Michaels know about this request?"

"We talked about it, but it's come to that or…"

"Or what Marshall? I can't do this today with all that's going on."

"I was there Worthy. Michaels and I talked about getting out. I don't know how much he told you or if he even got the chance to speak with you. We were a part of this so-called inside sting mess. That's how it started, cleaning up the mess and covering the mistakes along the way. We got things done and well, we were rewarded above and beyond our salaries. We both knew the end of our service was near. Michaels talked about getting out one way or another. I told him I was tired of the way things were turning out. It didn't start like it is now."

"You're talking about the 'untouchables'?"

"Yeah, they've resorted to killing. I believe they wanted Michaels to be the fall guy or cover up until he retired. We both wanted to just walk away from it. We've done some serious things over the years and covered them. Now Chief Walter Michaels is dead. What will his epitaph read on his headstone, what accolades will they allow him to claim? After years of doing their work, his reward was a "hit" by another officer who thinks they'll climb the ladder without repercussions. We planned on getting out."

"So, Longo was an 'untouchable'? And you?"

"We all were a bunch of fucking dummies for the cause. We talked a few days ago about approaching Sheers. Michaels was afraid they were planning problems with that Chambers kid being placed in the Cold Case Unit. We planned on finding out what the plans were then stepping out."

"Do you think Michaels mentioning getting out, caused them to send Longo?"

"Cap, I don't know how they chose Longo. He was a three-year recruit to them, wet behind the ears, and he has experience as an officer. But he was a kid. Looking to make his way through the ranks without working like most of them. I saw the changes, so did Michaels. Believe me with the drug deals, cops covering for their gain, and then the housing scams, the crimes mounted. We covered, but murder? I put in papers to transfer a few months ago. You can check it. I'm on the list. After talking with Michaels, I decided to take some time until I got a response. If I didn't make the cut, I'd resign."

"How did you know when Longo was going to Michaels' home?"

"A call. They were betting on how and if Longo could convince Michaels that he needed to keep quiet. I had already been there a few nights before. Michaels was nervous then. Had his gun in the drawer, right near him. I had to convince him I wasn't there to kill him. He knew what Longo was there for. I hope that the last thing he saw was me shooting that young punk for killing my friend. We planned on talking with you this week."

Marshall's face fell into his hands. He didn't speak, hoping he could control his hurt and anger.

"Damn! So, who knows you're here?"

"They knew I was going on vacation. Like I said, they knew about the paperwork for the transfer. I guess they thought they'd have an insider in the Ops Unit."

"You've got me caught in a catch 22 here. You know the law, you're suspect. I mean, good shoot, you did what was expected but man…"

"I know, I had to put things in place. It wasn't planned. I shot Longo and I'm ready to turn them in."

"You need protection."

Worthy couldn't believe the murder was solved and the "untouchables" were soon to be exposed. *It can't be this simple.* There'd have to be decisions made, and things in place to take them down. He'd need a higher authority.

"Marshall, I understand the dynamics and I'm sure you've thought this through. Tell me their reach is not in the governor's office."

"Worthy, I can't say who or what rank. I can tell you on this level, a few in different units, and there's a few political connections. Never heard one mentioned by name in that arena though. Calls are made by the real ass kissers. Sheers and his cronies call those of us that just followed orders for a payment or favor."

"So, with Michaels gone we'll get one of theirs replacing him."

"For sure. I'm certain they're wondering who shot Longo. It will keep them quiet for a few days."

"Damn, Michaels said he had to talk to me. I had no idea, damn!"

Worthy stood," Wait here. Let me clear this office."

Leaving Marshall obviously nervous in his seat, the captain stepped out of his office closing the door behind him. There were no other visits scheduled for the day. Two Special Operations Officers were standing at the office entry doorway, the other two assigned were sitting strategically in the waiting area. The four were chosen by Worthy just as he chose the investigative team. The sergeant hung up the phone when she noticed the captain coming out of his office.

"Sir is everything okay?"

"No, but I'll fill you in tomorrow. Right now, I need you to call it a day. If I need anything immediately, well you know."

"Keep my cell on. I got you Captain. You need more of these guys," she said pointing to the officers in the doorway.

"Yes, call the team. They need to be here now. Also, contact Justlin. Catch her before she leaves the Unit. I'll contact Porter and Tyson."

CHAPTER 47

The office filled quickly. Each officer was given their orders individually by the captain. New phones, radios, and equipment were disbursed. Understanding their assignments, they left knowing to stay within the walls of the precinct. Porter and Tyson arrived shortly after Justlin. The three understood the urgency but they didn't expect to see Lieutenant Marshall sitting across the conference table. Not having a chance to make assumptions, the trio couldn't hide their expression as they took a seat. Each nodded hello, hesitant about the meeting that would start when the captain entered the room.

"Okay, so everyone knows each other here. The lieutenant here has information we've been seeking over time, and I want you to listen without judgement until he's done."

Marshall spoke slowly repeating his earlier confession and parts of the conversation he had with the captain. Tyson took a few notes, as did Justlin.

"So, any questions before I say what I think we need to do?" The captain paused waiting for Porter who seemed to be putting it all together.

"Okay, I'll say what no one else will. So, what is it you want us to do with this? Give you clearance to leave and pluck out these fucks one at a time? Captain, we can't get them all at once. There will always be a group out there. We'll be the targets, you Cap, you will be the first if they don't do Marshall. We can't do a sting on our own and they know it!"

"Porter, I know, I know. That's why I called the three of you in. That's why I have those officers standing by. I became a target as soon as Michaels took his last breath, hell maybe sooner than that if they knew he talked to me. Even without them knowing Marshall as the shooter, Marshall was a target too. If he wasn't, what was their reason for sending Longo to talk to the chief. Longo wasn't close to Michaels; he was sent there to do just what he did. They'll send someone for me and anyone else in their way."

"So, what's the plan, Cap? The investigation, the cover-up here, the report and fixed files, and then there's the lawyer?" Justlin tapped her pen on her pad hoping she could explain why she hadn't reported the report and files earlier. It was more than enough to have her position questioned by her office.

"What lawyer?," questioned Marshall.

"First things, first. Fulton can wait. If this unfolds the right way, his cases will be absolved."

"Alright so where is Marshall going. He's on vacation as far as everyone else knows. Where were you going?"

"I've packed what I need. Wherever you send me. If it's a jail cell, that's where I'll be until you need me."

Porter smirked. "Man, you know that would be a flashing light, but it may be better than you going to a so-called non-disclosed spot and them killing you."

The silence in the room spoke loudly. Worthy picked up the phone and hung up without anyone answering the call. His office door opened, and two officers entered.

"They've got their instructions. Is your car in the lot here? Where did you park?"

"I told you. They think I'm leaving for vacation. I parked on the backside of the lot. I've got my luggage by the desk out there. I've got my airline ticket. If that's what you want me to do, I'll let you know where I land. No one usually bothers us when we're on vacation."

"Usually, this ain't usual." The captain shook his head and continued. "Alright they know to take you to the airport. Calls have been made for your flight. I'll be in touch in a few days."

Porter frowned and glanced at Justlin and Tyson. Neither seemed to be unnerved by Marshall walking out with the officers. Their reaction let him know whatever was planned had been done before. The office door closed, and Worthy picked up the phone again making the same mysterious connection.

"Let's get out of here. I promised myself, before Marshall came in, I'd be out of here by six. Play it out Tyson, we're still investigating a murder. Marshall came in to check on his transfer before his vacation and gave us tidbits about the last time he spoke with Michaels. Porter that will go in your notes and report. He didn't give any indication as to who may have been involved in this murder. Justlin I need you here in the morning. We need a team from the governor's office, those he trusts. Jail ain't a bad place for Marshall to be, but we can't say he was arrested here or have a reason that's connected to this case."

"So, do we know the names? I mean other than the obvious ones we've been toying with?"

"Well, he mentioned those we suspected, he said the ranks are high, and Wyatt Mancy is their chose for the interim appointment of Chief. So, I'd say he's one of them. There may not be as many as we think. Marshall mentioned a few politicians who have lined pockets too."

Tyson began tapping his pen on the table. Porter smiled and Justlin stood to leave. The trio bid the captain goodnight and promised to call when they got in the office in the morning. Passing the officers who remained in the office and at the door, they smiled at each of them. It didn't surprise them that they didn't recognize and couldn't name any of the captain's chosen crew. They walked to their cars in silence agreeing to meet in the office early.

CHAPTER 48

Captain Worthy picked up his briefcase filled with additional files and notes he preferred to keep with him. Unsure who would enter his office he decided it would be safer to carry the briefcase to and from his home. Four of his chosen crew walked with him to his car, they understood their assignment and separated only to follow him without being suspicious to anyone watching the captain's movements.

The forty-five-minute ride was his unwind, a promise he made to his wife early in their marriage. Emergency situations were an exception to the rule, an understanding they had. Talking business without the details kept the family from heightened worry. Dennis Worthy promised Cheryl Worthy as he moved up in rank, he'd always keep her ahead of the six o'clock news. They spoke about the "untouchables" over the years. He hadn't told her about the conversation he had with Michaels and now he remembered her warning him about Michaels over the years. How she could detect Michaels had a problem was a mystery to him. They hadn't talked about the murder, and it wasn't a conversation he wanted to have before Marshall was secured.

He started his car, and he could hear two other vehicles start their engines. The ten-man team he chose were from the military group he was a part of. The mixed group was comprised of retirees, a few who were still on active duty, and any call from the members was priority. The "unit," as they often called themselves, did private security, investigations, and assignments as given. They met monthly whether it was business or pleasure, the men were close. Forty in total, the Philadelphia chapter could call on other chapters across the country. The mandatory requirement was they were or had been a part of the military's special operations unit. Laws didn't have to be explained and they all were all trained the same, Worthy trusted them more than he did any unit that would be assembled in his precinct.

He traveled home safely surrounded by four black sedans. Two parked on his property and the other two roamed the surrounding area. The cars would alternate assignments throughout the night. Worthy parked and entered his home knowing he could rest and prepare for what he knew would be next. The home he always called his haven was threatened. He'd have to explain to his wife, what she feared had validity. He opened the door to the smell of dinner. He wondered if everyone ate late. His children, he was sure, would be engrossed in the computer. Cheryl came out of the kitchen wiping her hands on the dish towel she held.

"Hey there. I thought you would at least call with all this mess going on. Any clues who killed Walt?"

"Baby…" Worthy paused. For the first time he broke down. He took a seat on the couch trying not to show the pain in losing a friend and the fear for himself and his family. Cheryl sat next to him as she had through many difficult moments and decisions. She'd wait slowly rubbing his back. Worthy cried a moment and began shaking his head slowly. "Baby…"

"Take your time." Cheryl and Dennis were a team through the good and the bad. The department wanted the strength of the captain, his ability to be fair even when he was looked over or handed dirt to clean up. The couple agreed his home, his family would always be open for him to release the emotions he couldn't express with many of his ranked co-workers.

He took his time and explained what the local news channels hadn't reported including Marshall showing up at the office. Cheryl sat in silence as her husband explained the possibility of danger coming to their front door. She knew most of the men in the "unit" and their wives. Many of them attended events, traveled together, and raised their children to understand the special bond they had.

She never expressed the fears she had each time he mentioned the "untouchables." Cheryl knew the racial overtones of the group were the baseline of what they claimed to be protection for the good of the community. Now, as her husband continued to explain possibilities, they would be on high alert.

"Dennis, how long?"

"How long what? I can't say how long or if we'll shut them down at all. Even if Marshall gives us names, baby, you know. We'll never get those on top or those rooted in this operation. There will always be more. The officer that shot Walt only had years in. Hell, Walt had more than twenty-five. They've got politicians, and top ranked officials tied into their group. We've got those that know and turn from the problem. A scared force can't make changes."

"So where does that leave you, me, hell our family? Are we supposed to wait for the same type of visit or be forced to run?"

"Cheryl, I have to take this one step at a time. That's why the guys are protecting the house, my office, me, you, the kids…"

"Oh God! Okay Dennis, listen I told my mother we'd visit. I'll contact the school and let them know they'll be out of class until further notice."

"Okay, but I'll make the call."

Cheryl gave him a questionable look. "Alright, call them before you get tied up doing whatever. I mean it Dennis I'm not staying here with a covert operation at my doorstep."

"Baby, I understand. I just want to make sure that no one has an opportunity to follow you. If you don't mind my dear, one car at your mother's wouldn't hurt, would it?"

"Wow, okay one car."

The bell rang and the captain looked at his phone. He had missed two text messages. Cheryl left him alone knowing it would be Fabian, or Arthur, members of the unit.

"Hey, Cap. Man, you didn't answer the text. We need to give you info and I'm sure you've got info for us."

"C'mon in guys. I had to alert Cheryl first, you know."

The two men looked like they were related. Both stood well over 6'4" and were well toned physically for their age. Most of the men in the unit ranged in the age forty-five and above, however the ops components were those who were recent retirees. There weren't any females in their chapter. Worthy teased they were getting younger and younger, there were a few who weren't forty-five. The group was headed by the elders, no rank given. Their unity was based on what Porter, Tyson, and Worthy were fighting. Combating internal racism and community domination. They didn't attend rallies or the marches. They worked behind the scenes and closed doors. Over the years they put a few behind bars, and others went missing. The group took no credit for the work they did.

"So, you got everyone together. I thank you brother. I was sure we wouldn't be able to get everyone on at such a short notice."

"Cap, you called, and we saw the news about Michaels. You know, you spoke about him, what, a week ago? Flags went up then. A few of the brothers assigned called us. We got you and Cheryl, you know that. Let's get a few of these crooked ass cops. It will send a message to those politicians and other officials."

Fabian was a retired marine. His no nonsense demeanor caused many to think he was arrogant. He called it his fuel. He was dispensing the men as they were needed.

"We've got Arthur and his three outside. So, you know you're good here. We're waiting for the call from the airport, and then you know they'll follow through wherever that takes them."

"Okay, well first, as you know we may need to pull out more men. Cheryl wants to go to her mother's with the kids. I'll need a call to the superintendent of the school for the classes to be on-line or whatever. I don't want them missing class. Cheryl can work from there. She works virtually anyway."

"That won't be a problem. I can get more men. They're all on standby." Fabian and Arthur nodded in agreement.

"Arthur man, when was the last time I saw you."

"At my wedding. Wow, that has been about three years ago. We moved, Cap. She wanted to live in Jersey. Couldn't convince her to stay, so well, you know, you do what they say and smile."

The men laughed. Worthy offered them a drink, they accepted, and they waited for the call from the airport.

CHAPTER 49

Justlin stayed up well past two finishing notes about the yearly report and the missing information. Fulton called and said he put in the appeal, and he wouldn't be waiting until the department solved or dismissed the chief's murder. Tina understood, the lawyer had been put off and he looked at the reasonable delay, the murder investigation, as another excuse. She called Phillip and emailed the necessary findings to him. Although Montez and the others were still looking into the folders, she was sure the District Attorney's office would want to know what they found and what the reports revealed. She closed her computer and sat surrounded by what she considered was a signature for her resignation. There would be phone calls and emails she couldn't answer without sounding as though she was confused. Not a trait of Tina Justlin's and it was wearing on her nerves, she couldn't sleep.

The phone rang shocking her out of her thoughts. She glanced at the clocked mounted on her bedroom wall… *"Who the hell…?"*

"Hey girl, are you up, free to talk?"

"The question is, what are you doing up?"

Marcie ignored the question and continued, "Listen, I couldn't catch you earlier and I knew you'd be busy with all this mess going on. Fulton wants to meet with us away from the office. He found some information on Sheers, and I guess a few others. He thinks it may tie into Michaels' murder."

"Why didn't he call me? I spoke with him earlier and he didn't mention it."

"He came into the precinct right before the end of my shift. I can't say why or what, he only said we needed to meet him away from the precinct."

"Why you? Are you getting familiar with the sexy lawyer? I mean…"

"No, not yet anyway." Marcie snickered. "I think it had to do with entries made in the files he asked for. Same problem as the cold case unit entries, the documents don't match what was received and recorded in court. Someone has changed them. I think that prompted him to put in the appeal sooner. If he waits, they may have time to remove it once they know he's on to them; or your report surfaces."

"Okay, where are we meeting and when?"

"Well, you don't know your schedule tomorrow, I'm sure with this mess going on."

"Marcie, if he has information that may save this fiasco from being a part of my downfall within the department, I'm there."

"Let's set it up for the afternoon, late afternoon. I don't want anyone to suspect me in this either."

"Well, if they see you smiling and eyeing Fulton…"

"My professional demeanor has not been frayed by that … man. Anyway, I'm a single woman. They can't expect me not to look."

"Your looks? Girl, I'm sure he feels the heat," Tina teased.

"Alright, he asked for me each time he came in the office. He's not the only attorney that does that though."

"Don't explain it to me or are you trying to convince yourself. Just be careful. I say that because of the cases he's pursuing. These assholes that killed Michaels will do anything to cover their guilt. He seems to be a good guy. Call me and let me know where or what we're doing."

"Hey how are you making out with Blake, or is that done?"

"Done. I'm not playing his games."

"So…" Marcie held on to her word waiting for Tina. The response was laughter.

"Oh, cause you're on the hunt, so am I? No ma'am, I'm good for now."

"Okay, if you say so."

"I know so. This mess is deep, and I need to focus. It's bad enough that the men in that Cold Case Unit are fine, fit, smell good, and are real men. Blake pretending to be a clone of the clowns at the state office was driving me crazy. So, I'm going to focus on this work. Besides, it's important and if we can catch these assholes that's a plus."

"Alright, when your fire gets heated, let a sista know. We can compare notes!"

"Not! You know that ain't happening. Talk with you tomorrow girl, it's past your bedtime."

Tina hung up the phone and immediately opened her notes. She wanted to know what Fulton was on to and whether it would explain the missing information from the cold case files. It was too late to call Tyson. She'd get three hours of sleep and then call him.

CHAPTER 50

"And he filed the appeal based on what he found? Tina, you got me. I don't know what it could be, maybe signatures that weren't in the original files. I mean we found that in a lot of the files. Marshall stated that officers would sign simply because they were turning in the evidence. They had no knowledge of what it was or what case it pertained to. However, they become responsible and if they're subpoenaed, they have to testify to what they signed off on. Being new officers, or dummies they don't realize the predicament they put themselves in."

Tina tossed and turned for the three hours waiting for the time she could call Tyson. Now the awkward feeling of knowing the information she had could have waited for when they were in the office silenced her.

"I'm lost in all this Damien, really, I am. I don't want my reports to reflect my lack of understanding what's going on."

"That's what they want, confusion. Listen, Fulton wants to meet with you, go for it. We may be able to tie up some loose ends. Don't give him any information about Marshall or what we know regarding the murder. That has nothing to do with the files."

"Not yet, I'm thinking Sheers, Marshall, Michaels, that other officer, Boone, they're all involved in the murder and Fulton's cases."

"You may be right but, until we know where they tie together, we can't let on to what the District Attorney may need to save us in Fulton's cases."

"Hmm save you or the department. Damien if there's guilt it belongs to those involved. No matter how we catch them, they need to be caught."

"Tina, you're right but I need them to know just that. This mess ain't my mess. It doesn't belong to the team I have and if Fulton takes us all down… well, I don't know the brother to say if he will or he won't. He's got to understand who to go after. That's all I'm saying."

"I'll be sure he does. I'm tangled in this too."

"How?"

"I didn't report to the governor and if all of this is connected to the murder in some way, I'm sure I'll hear about it."

"Don't worry. We got you. The captain can straighten that out with a reason why you couldn't give details. I mean, the report was one thing but the explanation and plans to correct the reporting, hey, you didn't have enough to tell him. Besides, with this murder, maybe what Fulton will disclose, will take precedence."

"I hope you're right. I'll be in the office as soon as I can. I kinda need to wind down."

"Okay grab a cup of coffee and I'll see you in a few. Unless you need consoling. You know the captain still thinks we're an item. I could pick you up."

"That may be an option. Let me call Marcie and I'll call you back, okay."

"Wow, I was joking. This thing really has you shook, huh?"

"They're killing people. I may need the protection. I have a gun, but…"

"Say no more my lady. I'll be there in about, let's say an hour or more?"

"I'll be ready. Thanks Damien."

"No problem."

The call ended and Damien could only think of the predicament Justlin was in. She was sent to protect the situation and it kept escalating. She was right, there would be threats, erroneous accusations, and the harmful predictions brought on her fears. Besides, he'd learn a bit more about the single lady who no one seemed to win over. The phone rang, changing his thoughts instantly. He was expecting Porter or Worthy to call with an update.

"Hey man, good morning. Listen, we got prints back late last night. Knight processed everything and did the paperwork. Nothing really from the area where the second car was parked, so that's a dead end. Marshall didn't take the time to clean anything from the scene. I guess if he hadn't turned himself in, he would have stated he had been in Michaels' home many times. Are we still looking for more or pull the officers?"

"No not yet, let's talk to Worthy about it. If we're staging the investigation, we may need that delay in the evidence. We'll find out this morning. Where are you?"

"On my way in, and you?"

"I've got to pick up Justlin, she's shook. She's meeting with Fulton later. He says he has information on Sheers. He filed the appeal."

"Damn, I don't think we have all the information on those files for him."

"We must have enough. Hey, we can only do so much. We've got the initials of those officers that signed off on the evidence presented at trial. Get Montez to round them up today. We can talk to them before they're subpoenaed."

"Okay, I'll call him now. So, the Tina thing may turn out to be true, huh?"

"Porter, she's upset, I'm helping relieve some of the stress she has. Now, being the gentleman that I am…"

"Okay, shoot that bull toward another target. Make sure our Principal Investigator is taken care of. I'll see you in the office."

Damien smiled and grabbed the folders needed for the day. He stood looking at the wall he rearranged after Michaels' death. The evidence they had didn't matter, with his confession what they suspected would have led to another cold case. The unit would submit their findings and whatever the captain planned would be their next move. The problems seemed to be solved. Marshall would confess and turn over names of the "untouchables." The department would press charges and it all would be history to be told during academy training. He grabbed his keys and headed to the door. His cell phone rang again, he stepped outside and paused before locking the door.

"Hello?"

"Tyson."

"Good morning, Captain. Do I need to sit down?"

"After these past few days, when can we sit down? Listen, Marshall is with the Governor's team. He'll be there until we sort a few things out. Once you get in the office and somewhat settled, call me in my office. We'll get briefs and reports together then. Did Tina go to her office or is she still with us?"

"I'm on my way to pick her up. She's a little edgy, you know with the threats and Marshall needing protection. So, she'll be with me until we get a grasp on things."

"I'm sure you're glad of that. Anyway, I need her to find out what the plans are with Marshall. No one has called to say anything other than he's with that group from the governor's office. I want to be sure they don't have connections with those who ordered Michaels' death."

"Hmmm, I didn't think we'd have to check the governor's team. You're right though, better safe than sorry."

Turning the volume up on the radio, allowing the jazz to play as he did each morning, cleared his mind. Tina and the captain had the same fears. The "untouchables" were on a new course, killing officers. Over the years the so-called balance they wanted to set within the department and the community turned to crimes. The "blue-code of silence" kept them employed and until Tyson and a few others constantly ruffled their feathers no one paid attention. Tyson was transferred, with the hopes he had learned a lesson and others were promoted and given perks they often didn't deserve.

Captain Worthy stayed clear of it all over the years. Tyson often wondered how or who he had connections with. The notorious group would touch those that surrounded him, but he was off limits. There had to be a reason. Tyson's team of choice was under the captain, but he wondered what they knew since Michaels was close to Worthy. Justlin was right to take concern with who they may be after next. Tyson would mention it in the morning meeting and to the captain. His unit could be on the hit list.

He parked his car in Justlin's driveway. Taking a moment to look around, he could have Knight and Knowles keep an eye on her whenever he couldn't be with her. He was sure she would say "no," but he'd give her a choice them or him. He heard her call him to the door.

"Damien, can you do a quick check around here for me, please?" Tina's smile caught him off guard. "I'm serious. Please?"

"I've checked out here. Do you need the inside checked as well?"

"Uh, no. I don't think so, do you? I don't know. I mean if they walked in on Michaels, I'm an easy target."

"Tina, don't worry about it. We got you. They know you're with us, believe me, I'll see to it that you're protected."

"Uh, what does that mean?" Tina stopped in her steps toward the front door. "I don't want to be a pain, but if this is too much, I'll ask the governor for protection."

"No, that's not what I meant. It will be from our unit. No one else. Someone will be with you if I can't. Is that okay?"

"Stands, Wilson, or Porter, if not you." She continued her walk to the front door. Opening it she allowed him to enter but she remained where she stood.

"What areas concern you the most. I mean at night, are there darkened areas that cause you to be concerned? The perimeter is easy for a car to watch. No one can just walk up to your property the way your driveway sits from the road. We can have a car here at night, and I'll be with you in the day. Does that give you any relief?"

"I guess, who will be in the car?"

"Two ops guys that the captain will select, or we can have Knight and Knowles. I can be here too if you want. I want you to be okay, that's all."

The two walked through the house and out the front door. "I'll make up my mind after meeting Fulton. I'll know more than, but for now if you don't mind, I prefer you."

Tyson led her to the car and opened her door with a smile. He too, preferred to be the one to protect her.

CHAPTER 51

As promised, Fabian had the car waiting for Worthy's family the next morning. Worthy said his goodbyes, promising them he would join them on the weekend. It didn't present a worry to the children, but Cheryl was still upset.

"Dennis, did you ever consider giving it up? You've got the pension; you've got what we dreamed of why not just let it go?"

"I understand, and I will. Believe me, I'm working toward walking out that door as soon as…"

"As soon as. Do you realize how many of these operations put us in danger? As soon as they finally mark you as the target? Our family, everything we've worked for, Dennis we lose. Please give this some real thought this time. I did and I can't sacrifice all we have for the badge."

"I understand. You don't wear it and there's more to it than just being on my chest. Our obligation is on the highest level for me, but with this, I have obligations too. I'll clear them up from this point on and yes, I'll seek retirement."

"Dennis, you, and I both know you don't have to seek it. Find it if you want your family to be with you."

Cheryl walked to the opened car door and the officer nodded to Worthy as he closed the door. Worthy stood watching his family leave him again because of dangers his position caused. It didn't happen often, but he understood his wife. It happened enough. He got in his car and the remaining two sedans followed him to the precinct.

Arriving at the precinct Worthy dialed his office from his car. "Hey, what am I walking into?"

"Good morning, Captain. So far, it's quiet. I shouldn't have said that though, it's still early. Mr. Fulton was here. He went to get coffee, but he's been waiting for you to come in. The Ops guys are here, plain clothes as you ordered. The phones are quiet as well."

"No call from the governor's office?"

"No, sir."

"Have Fulton wait. I'll be in after I talk with Tyson."

As he got out his car, he noticed Sheers approaching. The officers stood at their cars waiting for an order from the captain.

"Hey, why do I feel you're ducking me?"

"Sheers, good morning. Do we have business this morning, or over the past few days that needs my attention? I don't recall anything. Why would I be ducking you?"

"I tried to come to your office yesterday and was turned away. I called; you didn't answer. What's up?"

"No, the question is, what do you want? I'm in the middle of a murder investigation as you well know. A new chief will be coming in, so I have to tighten up things for him or her to have a smooth transition. You understand, I'm working. What can I do for you and your boys?"

"Humph, my boys? Don't we all belong to one unit? Doesn't seem like it, Captain. You've assigned a team no one knows, changed those who usually handle these things. What's up? We don't play according to your rules?"

"I don't know what you're referring to. Sheers, if you have questions, see your lieutenant. Who, what, or when I decide to make changes or assign officers is not something I have to answer to an officer, such as yourself. Your lieutenant hasn't made any calls regarding any concerns about this investigation. Seems strange to me since your boys went to Michaels about everything. No one seems interested in who killed him. Why is that?"

"Like you said, I'm just an officer. I've noticed a few things and thought I'd ask you what was up, that's all. Just questions sir, no disrespect to you or your position. Michaels understood and looked at us as one. I just hope the relationship we had with him would carry over to you."

"Sheers, I'm not new to this position and never have you asked me to assist, recommend, or look over any of the things you took to Michaels. I haven't changed and I'm sure whomever gets the Chiefs spot will either know or learn how to make this precinct work."

"Well then, let's hope you stay in your place. You know, I mean your position."

"I don't think so. I know my place, it's others that don't care about my position. Change is inevitable when things like this happen. So, we'll see. You and your boys can stand down until the dirt settles."

"Dirt? And what then Captain?"

"Sheers, don't you have a shift to report to? This idle conversation is really taking up too much time. So, if you don't have anything concrete to tell me or refer to, I'll be on my way."

The captain left Sheers standing at his car. The four officers waited until Sheers moved on before following the captain into the building. Morning greetings met him as he entered the Cold Case unit. Tyson and the team were awaiting his arrival.

"Morning all. Who was assigned to ward off Sheers and his boys. I hope I don't have to assign a team…never mind. Tyson, where are we with this mess or anything for that matter. I've learned that Fulton is in my office."

Tyson and Justlin gave each other a questioning look. Tyson spoke, hoping to avoid the questions he knew eventually would have to be answered.

"Maybe he wants to know whose approval he will need. He filed his appeal and I'm sure he'll be requesting files from this unit and others. We're waiting on your word with the investigation. Do we know what's going on with Marshall?"

"You may be right about Fulton. I didn't receive a call from the governor or the team that's sitting on Marshall. Justlin, I'm sorry to put more on you, but can you make that call? I didn't think Marshall would call but someone should be letting us know where he's being held. He's the key to this thing. Sheers wanted to know something and I'm sure it's about the murder."

Wilson walked into the room and signaled to Justlin she had a call.

"Excuse me, Captain that may be the call we're waiting for. Excuse me gentlemen."

Tyson and Worthy were silent, deep in their thoughts about the call. Justlin returned and shook her head slowly. "Marshall is in the intensive care unit at Thomas Jefferson. The unit was ambushed during transport. Two officers and Marshall were shot. Two unidentified suspects were apprehended, they were shot as well."

"What the hell? So, there was someone who knew. Tyson…"

"I know, we're on it," he replied to the captain. There was no immediate response that Worthy would accept.

"Call me with an update. Justlin find out as much as you can from the governor's team, I guess they'll be looking into this too. It's possible that someone knew, but when?"

"Captain, go deal with Fulton. We'll handle this. Oh, you may want to talk with your boys too. They need to know… Justlin were any of the guys we sent injured?"

"No seems like all this went on after they turned Marshall over to the governor's team."

"Damn, okay call me as soon as you find out anything. Oh, how bad is Marshall and the other officers."

"The officers were wounded. Apparently, nothing serious. One had a shoulder wound, the other was shot in his leg. Marshall is in surgery."

Captain Worthy left the unit and to his surprise an undercover officer was waiting to escort him to his office.

CHAPTER 52

The captain entered his office with the look of urgency on his face. Fulton was on his cell phone and nodded as the captain passed him. The sergeant stood and signaled to Fulton indicating it would be at least a few minutes for the captain to get himself ready for an unscheduled meeting. The phone rang on one line and then another. The sergeant sat down attending to the calls.

"Captain, line one sir, and there's another call on line two." The sergeant was impressed with Fulton's patience. "Mr. Fulton would you prefer the captain to call you when he can sit with you. There's so much going on with the chief's death, you may be sitting a while."

"Sergeant… Smith, is it? I'm willing to wait. I want the captain to be on top of this appeal I've filed and although I understand the reason for any, and all delays, I'll wait."

The lawyer's formality was a melting point with most of the women he encountered. He hoped his sincere, yet soft tone won an understanding with the sergeant. She smiled without speaking, a sign that she understood, or he scored another appeal award. She turned her attention to the next call.

Captain Worthy listened as Fabian explained the information that was given to him.

"They didn't say much when we turned Marshall over. They didn't have the location when they picked him up. The Special Operations Lieutenant said they'd get the orders and address once they were on the road and had Marshall in their custody. It wasn't one car; they were ambushed on the back road they were instructed to take. The destination is still unknown. The officers were hit and wounded just enough so the attempt on Marshall's life could be carried out. We gave Marshall body armor as a safety precaution, that may have saved him. Sir, someone knew about the transfer and transport."

"Fabian, I don't want to say this but…"

"I know and we will. Most of our guys are old heads. No one is new to the unit. I've had contact with the governor's team, and they seem to be clear, but that transfer to another team, who ordered that?"

"I had no knowledge of another exchange. I would think the governor's team would have checked that before turning custody over to another unit. Let me make a few calls regarding that. How is Marshall doing?"

"Still in surgery. On bullet hit his neck and the other pierced his side. It's the bullet in the neck that has them worried. So far, he's good. I've got two of our guys at the hospital. There's a team from the governor's office there as well. Do you want me to pull our guys?"

"No. I'll call you back. Don't change anything regarding coverage until you hear from me."

The captain hung up the phone and logged into his computer. He searched the names of the officers the governor's office deployed. There was no indication that they would be connected to the "untouchables." Sheers knew something and Worthy was sure his questions would have led them to talk about Marshall. He dialed Tyson's number as he continued his search on the computer.

"Hey Damien, just a reminder, no information is to leave your office. It was an inside hit; Marshall and those officers were ambushed. Someone knew about the transfer."

"So, the governor's unit was ambushed?"

"No, they turned Marshall over to another unit. We need to find out who that unit was."

"Damn, they knew. Someone had to tell them he was moved and when. It's one of us."

"I didn't want to think it was but… they had to have an inside contact. Did Justlin talk with the governor?"

"Not yet. She's waiting for a call back."

Worthy tapped his desk with his pen, sinking deeper in thought. "Alright, let me deal with this lawyer. I hope his shit ain't this deep."

Tyson laughed as he responded. "Get ready Cap. Get ready."

Captain Worthy opened his office door and invited the patient lawyer in. Fulton took a seat across from the captain's chair at his desk.

"Thank you for your patience, there's a lot going on with this murder investigation."

"Understood, I won't take up too much of your time."

"So, what can I do for you? Listen, if it's about pushing the appeals, I can't get involved in that."

"No and yes. My reason for the appeal is because it's backed by evidence that someone or some group in your department has tampered with the evidence. What's on file for my client's case is not the evidence presented when he was sentenced."

"So, you're saying that you have evidence that will change your client's case?"

"Yes, the reason I filed the appeal. It's obvious and whoever it is they have access to files."

"The evidence files. They're checked and rechecked, when filed or whenever a request is made, it's checked. Signatures…"

"Sir, I have them."

"If I'm thinking right, those you have are flunkies for those who are guilty. I'm sure you're aware of that. You got what you wanted an appeal but when those initials, or signatures are pulled in, they won't agree with what was signed in."

The lawyer confident about his findings reached in his satchel and passed the files to the captain. Watching the captain finger through the pages and shaking his head brought on questions.

"So, do I have what's needed to bust up this group? I have other cases and some that I'm just beginning to investigate. It's all one zip code, one area, our people captain, our community."

"You've got a reason for questions. Answers, that's another matter. We've got to dig deeper to bury the scum. You can be a part of what we find, have access to the evidence, but you must agree to work with us as you get evidence from witnesses that won't talk to us. We can talk to those who have signed for this evidence that will help settle your cases. We're not looking to incarcerate innocent people, but yes, we're seeking to destroy the 'untouchables.'"

The men stood and shook hands. Captain Worthy instructed Fulton to give a copy of the names in the evidence book to Tyson. Fulton agreed to follow up with Tyson and his officers. All updates would go through Tyson.

Worthy peeked out his door knowing no one else had entered. "Smith, get Ms. Justlin on the line, please."

CHAPTER 53

Fulton was satisfied. The captain's response was friendly, and the argument Fulton prepared to deliver wasn't necessary. His next stop was forensics. As he walked the halls toward the office, he recognized a few familiar faces, but the clerk that approached him with her attitude had no idea who he was.

"Good morning, I…" Fulton was cut off before he could complete his request.

"There's no one here but me. I guess I didn't get the memo I would be the only one on time or working the desk, the phones, the pending work, and of course walk ins. So, what do you need?"

Fulton looked her over from her pink and black shoulder length wig or sew-in to her wrinkled clothing. Her jewelry, necklace, six or seven bracelets, big hoop earrings, and long pointed manicured nails spoke loudly. He shook his head before answering her rudeness.

"I'm seeking information in the following cases." He handed her paperwork from each of the three files connected to his clients. "I have filed an appeal on that one," he said pointing to Julian Foster's file. "The others are pending."

"You got the original paperwork on these, right? So, what makes you think there's gonna be a difference." Her comment was followed by a slight rocking of her head.

"What is your name… Miss? I just want to know who I'm talking to. Although I'm sure Captain Worthy would be able to give that to me. I wouldn't be here if I didn't think there would be or could be a difference. Since you are the only one here, I guess you'll have to pull the files and allow me to look through them as I requested. As a lawyer, a well-known lawyer, a damn good lawyer, I don't have time for your antics and games this morning. I don't find them attractive or appealing."

Fulton passed his business card to emphasize his seriousness in the matter. The clerk slowly reached for his card. Upon reading it she smirked and left him standing at the counter. It took her a few minutes to return.

"Okay, I don't see the Foster folder. I would think it may be circulating in the Prosecutor's office or maybe the DA's office. I can't imagine anyone taking it out and not signing for it, but it was done so, my thought is either office may have it. Here's the two you requested. Mr. Fulton, if you'd like I can call the offices and see if they have those folders."

"No, I'd hate to take you from the work you have to do since the clock keeps ticking but your coworkers aren't here yet. Thank you, I'll work with these for now. May I?"

Fulton pointed to the conference area. The clerk stepped around the counter to unlock the door for his entry. It was then he spotted the six-inch heels that caused her to walk awkward. Fulton would describe her in one word, a mess. She smiled as he passed her in the doorway.

"If you need anything, my name is Nina, Nina Majors. Ain't that a coincidence, my name being Majors working in a minor position. Looking for better, I'll be moving on from this job soon. Maybe I'll be interviewing for a position in your office. What you think?"

"We're not hiring. Secure with staff for a long time to come. Thank you though."

She tried not to slam the door, but he knew what her reaction meant. He smiled and shook his head as he began to delve into the folders. There was more information that had changed. Whoever removed it didn't expect anyone to discover the changes. Items added as well as deleted and none that had been presented before any judge as changes. He'd have to share what he knew, not knowing if he should deal with his client's cases before ripping the Moorestown PD a new one. There were more that knew what was going on than those affiliated with the "untouchables." If he took it to the judges he knew, they may alert those who shouldn't know he was on to them.

He put the papers back into their folders and prepared to confront Ms. Majors again. Seeing he was preparing to leave, Ms. Majors met him opening the door.

"I hope these were of some help. I mean for you to come in earlier than nine, before anyone but me was here, did you see what you wanted?"

"Hmmm... I guess in some ways yes; in others not at all. Have a blessed day. I see your workers have arrived. I hope that changes your attitude."

"It's that early morning thing, you know, before I've had my coffee."

"You should have a cup before you left home. Good day."

Fulton could feel her stare as she watched him walk to the outer doors of the office.

"Damn!!" Nina Majors spoke loud enough for. the secretary to come out of her office.

The secretary, years older than Nina, stood with her watching the lawyer pass their office window.

"Full of himself, no room for a woman? That's your normal complaint," stated Ms. Jenkins.

"I think it's more like he knows, you know confident. A man's man, you know that saying right."

"Nina, if you know that statement, you'd be more careful about the men you complain about on Monday mornings. Child, ain't nobody got time to fall out over every date to curse them when you realize they don't fit the false impression they've given. What you need to do is take care of you. Get yourself together, head to toe, and that attitude…" Ms. Jenkins left Nina staring with a smirk on her face.

CHAPTER 54

"No, I can't wait Phillip, and neither can the captain. Find out what's going on. Hell, as the Office Assistant I'm surprised you don't know. Nothing is hush in that damn office."

"Justlin, I can't barge into the governor's office, I'm not you. I have to wait."

"Who is in his office?"

Phillip lowered his voice so the governor's secretary couldn't hear him. "It's the tactical team. Seems like the whole unit. Something went wrong. So, telling Governor Banks anything at this point is touchy. What do you want me to do, leave a message and come back? I've been here since they came in."

Justlin paused in thought. Who would the governor call? She thought of her best friend, Sharice Pulley. Sharice was a State Investigator and part of the tactical team, one of the best, one that the governor may have called for her to help with the investigation by going to the hospital.

"Has Sharice been called in?" Justlin took a chance with the question. Phillip wasn't always aware of the governor's requests.

"She was. She hasn't returned the call. I was asked to contact her, so she may be on the way here."

"Okay, I'll call you back."

Tina sighed, she opened the folder and sat back in the chair. It was the first time in a long time that although she needed the information for the captain, she didn't want to know. Her mind began to drift about the possibility of Lt. Marshall dying and the investigation dying with him. It wasn't the first case she worked on that put officials in jail, caused community chaos, or wore on her after work hours.

She realized, before taking the job there would be difficult challenges. She didn't expect her name to be a part of a hit list. Now that she felt the need for home protection, she realized this case brought about challenges she hadn't faced. She smiled,

Tyson was a sweet resolve and wasn't bad to look at. The conversation on the way to the office was a blur. Usually, the ride to work was musical, soothing, thoughtless. She had thoughts she had to shake if they were to ride together during this investigation.

If there was a bulletin board for interesting, attractive, single, men within the special units. His unit would crush others. Although they had four men that would be of interest it outnumbered those who were worth spending time or thoughts on. Tyson was a target of many, but Tina had been close to him for years. They teased and flirted, laughed, and enjoyed the time spent. It was all work, not play, and definitely not leading to where she imagined it could go. The ride to work tickled her curiosity. She'd have to try to contain her thoughts and libido if he was to be her temporary personal security.

Tyson stepped into the room smiling. "Hey, did you find out anything? Can I help you in anyway?"

Justlin wanted to answer," Yes, you definitely could help me." knowing that answer wasn't in the file. She pushed the file toward the end of the desk. "There's nothing here that gives any clue to what is going on. Who would infiltrate the security team assigned? I've got a call to make and then I'll try the governor again. The tactical team is with him now. That was expected, I don't know who's with Marshall."

"The captain sent his men there. We'll get details from those who they relieve, I hope."

"That's just it. We've got three operations going on and no communication between them. That's not good or protocol."

Tyson took a seat across from Justlin. He didn't speak he looked at her deeply. "Don't stress. I'm with you. I'm communicating, any questions, any information, whatever you need to talk about, I'm here."

"It's just hard to comprehend. You, know on this level…"

Her words began to fade. Tyson was caught in her eyes. He questioned if she would open up, relax, and become comfortable with him. He nodded, hoping she didn't think it was a response to what she was saying. His nod was an approval for him to take it slow but capture her attention beyond the mess they faced.

"I understand. You know it could be more than a conspiracy."

"What do you mean Damien?"

"It could be someone determined to force us to be together, starting with your security."

"You're funny, but that's serious. No one that I know forces you to do anything, and you know that shit doesn't work with me."

"Okay Ms. Justlin, we'll just have to be sure they don't succeed."

CHAPTER 55

The conversation with Sharice answered questions that the governor didn't call back to answer.

The captain's security team arrived, relieving the governor's tactical unit. Lt. Marshall was resting, heavily medicated, but no further surgery was needed. He hadn't recovered to speak, and Sharice was still at the hospital waiting for him to open his eyes. There had been no exchange of details between the security teams, so there wasn't much to report to Tina or the governor.

"Girl, this is a mess." Tina explained how they concluded that they needed Sharice to be included as part of the investigative team.

"The governor's concern was what information was passed when the original transport officers were ambushed. In the failed attempt no one was able to ask questions. The officers were attended to and had their own rooms in the hospital. I asked them what went on, what did they remember. Girl, everybody is so doped up, they can't answer."

"Were there more than the two suspects who got shot?"

"Tina, no one has said anything about more being involved. The responding units didn't question anyone and are guarding the two suspects who as the others are doped up."

"So, what did Governor Banks say? He hates the lack of information."

"Nothing anyone can do. Once these guys wake up, the medical personnel will contact me, whether I'm here or not. I'll stay long enough to satisfy the governor, but girl, this is the pits."

"Understand my sister. Do you think if I called the governor he'll tell me more, or does he even know more?"

"Can't give you an answer about that. You know you're closer to him then I am. Try and see, but if you get anything or if I get any more information, let's call each other. We need to solve this mess. Who the hell is shooting police?"

"Girl, this investigation connects to another investigation. I'm sure of it. It's an internal uprising with a couple of officers and some in upper management. Those against change, you know the kind. I was sent before all of this, to investigate an issue of missing information on reports. Well, they say when you dig deep, you don't always find gold."

"Tina, who the hell said that... girl if you guys have been digging. This ambush proves you found something, I'm certain of that. Trying to take out a lieutenant, what does he know that they don't want disclosed?"

"Well, that's what I'm assigned to now, find out."

"Oh, there's the nurse. Let me ask her a few questions."

Tina sat in thought. Phillip hadn't returned her call and she was certain the meeting with the governor had concluded. Tyson and the others left her to find out the information that Worthy was checking in for every hour.

As she dialed the number, she heard Phillip and Sharice once again stating, "*You're closer to him than I am.*" If only that were true. Banks liked her because she was thorough. Tina Justlin left no stone unturned. That's how she got the nickname "Justice." She fought for it. Good or bad for her career, her name carried weight. Weight, she didn't want to lose.

"Hey, Ms. Winters. Yes, it's Justlin. Is he free? I'll hold."

The line instantly went to the programmed jazz station. Justlin was enjoying the third song played when the governor interrupted her small piece of tranquility.

"Tina, let me first apologize. Hell, yes, it's been hell. Are you okay? I wasn't too worried about your safety. After all you're with some killers there." He laughed nervously.

"What's going on, Clinton? Who did this?"

"We've got some digging to do on this end, but I spoke with the tactical team this morning."

"Who on our team is the weak link? Hell, how many are weak links? There's a few in Worthy's regime too."

There was a pause. "Tina, we don't know. The team that I met with this morning wasn't our regular team. I got with the military special operations and met with them. I don't know who to trust. I've changed a few on my security team who just started as well."

"I asked Tyson to assign officers to secure my home as well. I understand totally, this is crazy." Tina didn't mention Tyson being her personal security.

"Did you finish investigating those reports?"

"I think this is all connected. I spoke with Sharice and wanted your approval to share my findings with her. It's that same group, or so it seems to be. If so, they initiated the attack. I'll let Sharice fill you in with an update, if anything, but I have a strong suspicion that group tried to kill Lieutenant Marshall."

"What does Marshall know?"

"The truth."

CHAPTER 56

Tina called Worthy with the bits and pieces of information she had. Leaving the office for what it seemed like survival air, Tyson asked her to join him for lunch.

"After all, I am your security, right?"

"You are so…"

"What? That's what you said right? I mean, security. You move, I'm there."

"Okay, okay. Where are we eating?"

"The cafeteria."

"The what?" Tina stopped at the door. She rolled her eyes and laughed knowing he was teasing her again.

"Hey, after we eat, I want to meet Stands and Wilson at the sight where Marshall was hit. Are you okay with that?"

"Sure, what do you think you'll find?"

"Tina, Ms. Justlin, never miss an opportunity for more information. They called to say they think they've got something. They went to the district police and asked for their report. They were able to talk to the officers who responded to the call."

"Maybe a break?"

"Don't know we'll see."

The two were leaving the office when Montez and Miller stopped them. "We've completed the interviews of those signatures as you requested. Miller has the report, but she discovered a questionable response in one of the interviews."

Tyson looked at Miller, who had been quiet since her hire. "What do you have young lady?" Tyson thought she didn't speak much because she was from the islands. She did her job, often without any instructions. She learned quickly. Tyson was considering her for a permanent placement on the unit, unlike Knight or Knowles. He decided to leave them on outside details for the investigation and beyond.

"We did as requested, Montez and I. We interviewed each entry that wasn't the reporting officer. The initials MS and MB were often crossed out and others replaced them. Not officers who had been on duty or assigned to the response teams that were connected to the incidents. It seemed, sir, a cover for Officers Simmons and Boone."

"Hmm, so what do we do with that information Miller?"

"Call in Boone and Simmons sir? Those are the officers with those initials on the response team to each incident. Their reports were signed but they didn't sign off on the entries."

"No." Justlin looked at Miller. "Not anyone from this unit. Let me call them in. If it is what you've concluded they probably have a story that would suffice this office, but not mine. It's a part of the investigation to your report Tyson."

"Okay, that will put pressure on them for sure. Miller have you spoken with your friend Chambers since he's been reassigned?"

"Sir, he's on administrative leave."

"What?"

"Yes sir, since leaving here he's been on administrative leave."

Tyson couldn't believe Worthy would approve the leave. "Worthy didn't approve that, I'm sure of it."

"Well, that's a way to keep him honest." Millers statement caused questionable looks from everyone.

"Let's just say I believe he's lied since being assigned here. He tried to get us to join his group although, can I say, they are not of color. Ah, yes, I thought he was mixed up in something, I just didn't know what… sir."

"Miller, stop with the sir." Tyson laughed easing the tension that he felt mounting. "Call him. As a friend, ask how he's been doing. See if he asks any strange questions regarding the investigation, work outside of this office, or the murder. Good work young lady."

Montez and Miller understood what would be done next. Justlin told them she'd get back to them after the interviews were concluded. She left the office with the thought there were no surprises they couldn't handle.

As they exited the building, Tyson dialed Worthy's number.

"Hey, Cap. Just found out Chambers is on Administrative leave?"

"What, wait hold on." Worthy sat back from the paperwork he was reviewing. "Say what now?"

"The young boy who was looking into the boxes in Porter's office is on Admin Leave."

"Who signed off on that! Hold on! Smitty come in the office, please."

Sergeant Smith entered the office with a questionable look "Sir?"

"Leaves, have any crossed your desk? Wait… Tyson when was that… two, three weeks ago?"

"About that long sir, the same week as the press conference you spoke at."

"Okay Sergeant, about three weeks ago. Chambers is the officer, supposedly he's on Administrative Leave? Who signed off on it?"

"Excuse me, Cap. Can I use your keyboard?"

Captain Worthy rolled his seat back from his desk to give her space.

"Here it is Sir. You can look it up by name or if you know their work assignment or shift. It was approved by Chief Michaels."

"I guess that was easier than putting him back on your unit. I told Michaels I wasn't for him going back to the unit he walked off. That ass should have been given an internal reprimand. Thanks Sergeant Smith."

"So, the connection to Chambers is broken?"

"Well, I guess once they place their boy, Mancy, as the Interim Chief they'll bring him back."

"Have you talked with Mancy? Any idea when he'll be in the big seat?"

"No. We don't have a relationship like that at all. He's always been questionable. Dirty cop, and up the ranks. He can't be trusted."

"He's Spanish?"

"Not that he will tell. His mother is Spanish, father is white. He doesn't lean to the Spanish culture."

"Okay, so we know what we're dealing with."

"Tyson it won't change unless we can catch them. They'll wait for the opportunity or take the opportunity. Now we know killing is not beyond them."

"I'm heading back to the crime scene. We may have something."

"Listen, you and Justlin be careful. I'm sure they're watching."

The captain hung up the phone. Tyson and Justlin decided to skip lunch.

CHAPTER 57

The weather changed and meeting Stands and Wilson in the rain and wind wasn't what Tyson was ready to endure. The forty-five-minute ride was quiet. Justlin was in her own thoughts and Tyson didn't want to know what the Principal Investigator had conveyed to the governor. He thought about the conversation he had with Stands.

"Boss, man, this is going to blow the lid off this investigation."

"What? What did you find?"

"Your boy was here too. Chambers, I don't know if what we have can be linked to the murder. It seems he was here with Longo or maybe at another time."

"Did you…?"

"Knight called forensics, he's still at the house. Seems like this thing will sway a few ways."

Tyson couldn't imagine what "this thing will sway a few ways" meant. That was the purpose of Justlin coming along. His attention turned to the surroundings as they approached Michaels' home.

"Hey, do you think we could be on a wild chase. I mean, Tyson, think about it. Suppose it's more involved than just the dirt they've done with the files, the dirt on the street, and now murder. We don't know if there are other murders, other cover ups, and there's always the dirt on the street. How can we stop this type of corruption?"

"It's our job, what we signed up for. We'll get close, lock a few up, and they'll find a better way to do what they do. It's always the same results with different methods. We find the methods and the wheel to justice spends again. It's our job."

He turned into Michaels' driveway and paused after he turned the car off.

"Tina, you know better than me the cover-ups, bribes, and the system that's frayed to say the least. We do all we can do and close the case."

"I never dealt with a case involving us being the suspect. Like you said, it's our job. Someone has changed the job description."

The two exited the car and Tyson set the alarm.

"You really think someone is going to steal your car from here?"

"Yes, it's an Audi, you drive a BMW don't you set the alarm?"

"Look where we are… damn it's the woods. Which causes me to wonder why Michaels would live out here."

"Hunting, I'm sure that's why. Closer to nature, not my style, but hey to each their own. Now my car is locked, secured, and if hunted they can't get in."

Justlin smiled. "You're too much. Again, I ask, who?"

"Asks the lady who wants security inside and outside of her cottage home on the outskirts of the city. You're nowhere near what you call the woods. So, don't judge the choice of Michaels location. You have a point though. Suppose, just suppose, he lived out here because of them. He was a member, recently quit. Maybe this spot covered for a lot of their exploits."

"He was involved that deep? I thought he and Marshall were only interested in the promotions. I can't wait to hear what he tells Sharice. I'm sure he'll talk knowing they're trying to kill him too."

The rain tapered off and the two avoided as many puddles as they could. Tina laughed once they arrived at the back door.

"Do you think if we walked the paved walkway, it would have made a difference?"

Tyson hadn't thought about her walking through the unpaved ground. He shook his head and smiled hoping his new female partner wouldn't be upset with the wet mud on her boots.

"So sorry Ms. Justlin, I didn't think about your designer boots. You should have said something."

"You're going to learn me eventually, I'm sure."

"I'm looking forward to it ma'am."

Stands and Knight stood at the back door. The two were engaged in a sports debate when Tyson and Justlin reached them. Tyson looked at them and shook his head.

"I send the best from the unit and a new boot, and this is what I get. Both of you standing at the back door. Where's the forensic crew and Wilson?"

"Sir…" Knight began to speak when Stands interrupted.

"Sir…" Tyson shook his head and walked past the two. Stands knew better than to leave Wilson alone with the forensic team. Justlin remained silent as they entered the home. Stands and Knight followed.

There was no one in the front of the house. Voices could be heard coming from where Justlin assumed the new evidence was found.

"How long will it take to process?" Wilson questioned the officer bagging the items.

"So, what's going on Officer?" Tyson interrupted sounding so formal everyone laughed. "What was wrong with that approach?"

Justlin was lost and just shook her head. Wilson moved closer to her and whispered. "He always says the wrong name or can't pronounce it. So now it's the slight raise in his voice that tells us he can't remember who works with our unit."

"Hell, they have more than one team that comes out. What's your name, huh?" Tyson waited for the officer to face him.

"Freed sir, glad to meet you. Your resume proceeds you. Hope to work with you and learn a few things."

"Boot lickin' don't impress him Freed. Believe me next week he won't know if your name was Freed, Plead, or Released." Stands couldn't help himself. Tyson stopped him before he continued with his next joke.

"Well sir we've got phone information to pull from these phones, calendars, photos, and logbooks. Seems to be a good bit of information on a few officers. Wilson said to collect it all."

"So, what links Chambers?" Tyson wasn't prepared for the answer.

Knight handed him a picture of Longo and Chambers with Michaels at his home.

"Hmmm, friends huh? So, they betrayed him for the cause? Is that what I'm reading here?"

"There's more pictures and phone calls. Seems that Michaels hired them for the cause," Stands responded, handing Tyson a photo album. Flipping through the pages he handed the book to Justlin.

"Does it show any officers that are seasoned? Like the two we know are involved. I'm wondering, were they ever visitors here."

Justlin looked around the room and decided she'd look around the house. Wilson left the men in the den and joined her.

"What do you think? Will we actually catch them in this? They always slip away and appear when it's convenient for them. Their last appearance caused Damien to lose what should have been a promotion."

"I hear you, Wilson. We see it all the time. We'd have enough to at least fire them and the next thing you know they're getting a new badge. Why it happens, how to catch them and hold to it, we've got to clean the top layers. That's how I see it. The community marches, complains and yet they know who's in their neighborhoods in uniform doing whatever. They won't report it because they're afraid what the reaction will be. But this, this! Murder within the department, insanity! We've got to at least send a message."

"Yeah, you're right. A clear message that it won't be as easy as this. We've got to stop them somehow."

"I'm sure Sheers and Boone and whoever's on the top of that wicked pyramid, know we're here. Hell, they've done investigations. I'm sure anything attaching them has been removed. Chambers is on a limb, but I think his failure to get that file in Porter's office did him in."

Tyson, Stands, and Knight left the forensic team to collect whatever they deemed might be evidence.

"We're ahead of the game. I'm wondering what is hidden, not in plain sight. Michaels didn't know he'd be the victim. Knight you and Knowles stay here with the team and then report to Montez. I'll contact him with your next assignment. We don't need to monitor this house." Tyson left them and joined Justlin.

"Did anyone contact his next of kin?" Justlin's question shook Tyson. He hadn't thought about relatives and didn't know any of Michaels relatives. He never asked if he had a wife, children, or anyone who needed to be contacted. Tyson whispered his answer. "We'll call Worthy about that. I thought you were close enough to know."

Justlin rolled her eyes and moved on to the next room, Wilson followed.

CHAPTER 58

Sayers answered her phone and hesitated to say hello. "Yes?"

"Hey, it's Sergeant Sanders My number made you wonder, I'm sure. Lock it in after this call."

"You're right," she laughed. "What's up?"

"I told you I'd meet with you. I mean if you have questions, I'm sure you do. I'll answer what I can. It may not fit your needs, but they need to be stopped."

"They? Hey, you're right. When is a good time for you?"

"Can we meet today for lunch or better after hours, say about seven tonight."

"Tomorrow may be better. Let me know if that's good and I'll meet you."

"Ms. Sayers, I know I'm giving you information that could cause a disturbance within the precinct, but beware it could cause problems for you and I. So, I'm only agreeing to let you know, who and what they're doing to our precinct and the community. Newsworthy, yes, but I don't know if it won't jeopardize us personally. We need to be careful about who could pass this information on. So, your reporting can't be direct or indicate that it came from within."

Sayers listened and thought about what was being implied. She was certain the sergeant was right. There would be questions. She would have to talk with Fulton. The story that was mounting would need to include what was known prior to the murder, prior to the cases Fulton was bringing forward. Sergeant Sanders seemed to have the answers.

"I understand and have been in situations where I had to make choices about what to disclose in my reports. Let's talk and I'll be sure to be discreet. Sergeant, I have to warn you, information given is often disclosed in various circles. Circles you and I wouldn't be a part of, nor would we bump elbows with many of them. I'm aware of the dangers we'll be able to avoid. Have you told anyone else what you know? The captain, Tyson or Justlin, anyone?"

"No. I thought just a conversation with you may lead me in the right direction. I mean what I know the captain knows and I would guess he's informed the others. We haven't really had the chance to talk or even share a moment of grief. Not just for the chief but for what's coming next."

"I can't say I understand, but I can imagine. Yes, let's meet at seven tomorrow evening. Call me with the place of your choice, preferably away from the local spots."

"Sure, I was thinking about… well let me make the reservations."

The arrangement would be made, and Sayers thoughts were rapidly asking "what if?" She decided she had no answers and wouldn't be able to prepare the appropriate questions. It was close to two o'clock. She wondered what questions Tyson would want answered. She fingered through her contact list and dialed his number.

"Damien, it's Samantha."

"Okay, so I take it this is not official business, Ms. Sayers?"

"No, it's not official business. You are so… never mind. Listen I need to ask you a question. I received a call from Sergeant Sanders, the chief's sergeant. You know her, right?"

"Yes, I know her from Michaels' office. She's been working in Worthy's office for the past week. I don't know much about beyond that. What's up with her?"

"She's offered to give me off the book information. Things that go on, you know, phone calls, visits, what's been seen and unseen, heard and unheard within the walls of that office, she wants to disclose."

"Wow, does the captain know?"

"I doubt it. I'm just wondering what information she has. Has the captain done some things that would shed light on the murder. Have they glossed over some things that she can bring to the forefront?"

"Well, like I said I don't know her outside of that office. I've chatted with her a few times about topics I can't even remember. So, you called me to ask what?"

"If you think this will put us on their radar?"

"Samantha, wait, whose radar?"

"The 'untouchables.' I'm sure what she'll tell me will lead to the same thing that Fulton has been saying. They run the department behind those in appointed positions. They steer the agenda, the actions taken, and the results. It's now come to murder. I'm sure they're in on it. You guys may not report it as such and I understand that too, but Damien, I don't want to be on their dart board."

"Understood, we all are on the edge about their involvement. How much control they have… we don't know, and this case has uncovered their hidden agenda. It's your choice. If you want to talk with her, it should be looked at just what it is. The chief has been killed; the captain is assumed to move up even if it's until they place someone in the open position. You talking to his sergeant shouldn't make waves. You're talking to her about what we know will be changes. Now if you report the details, the things she's concluded may relate to "them," or details of what is not public information, you shine a light on both of you."

"Yes, so this would just be information received until needed."

"Like a tool you may need to repair or destroy, you have to determine when to use it. You may want to share it with those who are actively investigating "them," you know?"

"Funny, I thought about that. Should I… well can I call you after she and I talk?"

"Sure, call whenever you need to. You know that."

"Thanks, hey do you think Fulton should be included?"

"Depends on what she tells you. How close are you with him? I mean he won't jeopardize our investigation or put you in a bad light, will he? I've got to know that before sharing what you receive.

You won't know that until you have the information. Don't get ahead of yourself. The information may save your job and life later. Samantha, they're killing for their cause, don't get caught up."

"You're right. It's a lot and I don't want to get ahead of myself."

"Well, my lady, your choice. See what she's says and let me know if you need me."

"Thank you, my friend."

It had become a dilemma. Samantha Sayers was known to bring the unknown to the forefront. It was her reporting at its best. The inside story, the stories no one else could or would report had her name on them. Her reputation to disclose the difficult interviews had given her literary rewards. It all was at stake; would she be able to hold on to what took her years to achieve.

Damien was right. She had to be careful who handled the information. It could jeopardize more than her reputation. It could affect others. It was the unknown that told her, go home, and relax until the next day at seven.

CHAPTER 59

Marcie called Justlin to ask if she was still going to meet with her and Fulton. They had been at the restaurant for thirty minutes without a call from her. Marcie decided to call before the lawyer got tired of the monotonous conversation.

"Hey, I'm on my way. Sorry for the delay, but you guys are aware of what's going on. I couldn't reach out. We went to the house, and I had to go home and change clothes."

"What house and with who?" Marcie held her finger up before Fulton could ask any questions.

"Michaels' and with Tyson and the team. Forensics was there too. This thing gets bigger and bigger by the minute. Anyway, I'm in the car now, on my way."

"Nah, Sistah, how did you get assigned to going to the scene? Why were you there? You get the reports, you're not usually on the discovery team."

"Tyson..."

"Oh Tyson. Girl let's talk about this later. Seems it will be interesting, and I don't want Mr. Fulton to think about us in another light."

"You are so... I'm not, we're not. Never mind, I'm on my way."

"Yes, you can't cover it. I see through it. How far out are you?"

"Ten, fifteen minutes. Yeah, after Fulton leaves, we'll have some wine and talk. Put the orders in. I'll have whatever you order. I'm starving."

Marcie looked at Fulton who turned his attention to his cell phone. She noticed he wasn't pushy; his patience raised her curiosity. He wasn't married, but had he been? Did he have children? Was he a workaholic? She wanted to know.

"So, Tina is on her way. She said we should place our order. I've got hers."

"Okay." Fulton put his phone in his pocket and picked up the menu. "What's good here? You chose this place; I'm assuming you frequent here?"

"Yes, a favorite of ours. You'll love anything here. We've tried most of the dishes over the years."

"So, I'm assuming it's been a challenging day for all of you in the precinct."

"It has and the whispers and the shoe shuffling has begun again. It's always something. You can imagine. An employee promoted, another suspended or fired, behind closed doors, the meetings, new assignments, it can be challenging to those who refuse to face the issues. For me, I do my job and protect those who work with me."

"Understood, and I'd like to tell you, you do it well."

"Thank you, you as well. Defense attorney can't be an easy job. What made you choose defense attorney as opposed to what, district attorney, or a prosecutor?"

"I don't know. Things change on this path called life and this is where my journey led me. I'm comfortable and I look for those who are innocent but caught in this system of confusion."

"Confusion? Most of them know they're wrong yet being a defense attorney it's your job to get them less time or none."

"You're right but when the system declares they're guilty before a trial, at the arrest, creating the chaos and claiming they're right because of their titles… I fight for them."

"A lot of time put in. I'm happy to go home at five. Your job puts a lot on you and your family. You have to take a lot home with you to be as good as you are."

"Yes, I do work at home when I have to. Otherwise, I cut off work at eight." He looked at his watch and smiled. "Your friend is cutting it close."

Marcie smiled but needed to ask her next question. "So, no family concerns."

"My mom gets a call every other day and my siblings well, we play catch me when you can. They have the family life. I haven't slowed down enough, I guess. Thought about it but what women would put up with my work? Can I question them and get an honest answer? I doubt it. Most don't understand the passion."

"Hmm… sometimes you have to ask. That's if you want to know."

Fulton looked across the table and realized the chit chat wasn't without cause. Justlin walked over to the table interrupting his questions he wanted to ask the beautiful lady seated across from him.

"Ah, Tina Justlin, again we meet. Two beautiful ladies, I'm in awe." He pulled out her chair and waited for her to take her seat before he sat back down.

The ladies smiled and nodded to each other. Tina wondered why he wanted them to meet with him but didn't want to rush her questions. She was still in quick, get it done mode. She reached into her purse and silenced her cell phone.

"I'm sorry I'm late Mr. Fulton." Fulton shot her a look and she immediately responded. "Lawrence. Things have been a mess all day. What did you order for me?"

"Steak with gravy and onions, mashed potatoes and a salad. They only had green beans; I know you don't really care for them."

"You know me well. So, not that I'm being pushy, but why am I here?"

"I was going to wait until we had our meal, but I'll give you the information you'll need to chew on before giving any answers."

The ladies gave questionable looks to him and each other.

"Look I don't want to put either of you in an uncomfortable situation. One that could cost you."

"Cost what?" Marcie looked at her friend and then the lawyer. "How could it cost me or her?"

"You may have colleagues who seek to file lawsuits or blackmail you. There's a risk in knowing what others try to hide. I got you, remember, I'm a lawyer, a damn good one. But I can't tell you this information and have it become office gossip. It can and will damage reputations and if I have my way take jobs, I will. So, I prefer you use the information in your investigation Tina. Many will assume Marcie was involved since that's who I go to for names, assignments, and reports. I got you. Just remember, be careful with what I give you."

The waiter brought the meals excusing himself as he placed the dinner on the table. The table filled quickly with the plates, salad, and bread. Asking did they need anything else; he was excused and promised to return. The ambiance of the restaurant was peaceful as they began their meal.

"How's your lasagna Lawrence? I usually order that or the spaghetti and meatballs. It's all worth trying." Marcie watched as he nodded and smiled. He seemed to be engrossed in his plate and the bread sticks. "I love them too, the butter. Tina found this place and we come here often." She took a moment to sip her wine.

"You're a foodie, aren't you?" Tina could help herself. She laughed and covered her mouth.

Marcie and Lawrence joined her in laughter. It lightened the tension, and the attorney nodded his response.

"I knew it. It didn't take you long to decide your meal, the salad, your choice of wine. See Tina, investigations? I got it."

Marcie's comments came across as innocent although it was totally out of her character. Tina wondered how much her friend drank before she arrived and how much she'd remember later.

"So, tell us, what is this information you've come across?" Tina wanted Marcie to be able to respond to the attorney, if necessary.

"I visited forensics a few days ago. The thought crossed my mind to check what was turned in on the date of the crime."

"And there was no match to what the books in the Cold Case Unit had."

"So, you're aware of the discrepancies I've been complaining about."

"Just recently. I was called in to investigate the books and entries. We've found several. The investigation has been interrupted because of the murder, but yes, we know."

"No one from any of the offices contacted me." Lawrence paused, placing his fork on his plate and dabbing his mouth with his napkin.

"No reason they should. It's not a requirement to notify the lawyer, is it?"

"No, you're right. No one is required to notify us even if we've filed an appeal."

"Lawrence you've been doing what most give up on. So, if you've found the discrepancy, your clients are fortunate. Most lawyers search the surface and don't push for what's not there. How did you deal with that clerk?"

He rolled his eyes before answering Marcie's question. "Let's just say, she's more than enough for her position."

"She's good though. Once you get to work with her. She won't stop searching for answers and she knows how they collect the evidence and what is done with it." Marcie tilted her breadstick in his direction and smiled.

"Really, maybe I'll send a clerk to dig a bit. You do know the "untouchables" have their hands in the missing information in my cases. That includes Officer Sheers and his sidekick."

"It may or may not be true. We need to know how and what impact it may have on more than your cases. That's what we don't know and need to protect. I agree with you, we need to be cautious of anyone we're suspicious of and that's what these findings you've uncovered gives us. I'll let the captain and Tyson know what's going on. We need to be careful because we don't know all of whom is involved."

Fulton didn't add his thoughts to what Justlin stated. Neither Tina nor Marcie said what they knew and didn't question what they didn't know. He understood why they weren't as open as they could be with him. He could end quite a few careers. He was pleased he talked with Worthy, maybe it would give him an opportunity to join forces with those working to rid the system of the "untouchables." The conversation got quiet as the next serving of wine and dessert came, and the conversation was cordial. Fulton prepared himself to leave after complimenting the meal, dessert, and conversation.

"Well ladies, I must say I enjoyed dinner and your company. I will get more information, I'm sure. Can't say I'm looking forward to it, but my gut feeling is the "untouchables" are involved. Listen, I think if we share what we know, we can and will stop them. Our community, and our people need to be treated fairly. I mean, there are rules they've set up and they still avoid them."

The ladies nodded in agreement. Marcie smiled and stood up moving closer to the attorney. After the wine, he looked like a tall glass of a top shelf Cabernet. Tina saw her reaction and interfered immediately. Standing she shook his hand, he smiled and he in turn, shook Marcie's hand. She held it longer than expected, causing him to give her a questionable look. Tina tapped her on her shoulder pushing her softly, encouraging her to sit down.

As the attorney walked away, Tina stared at Marcie who laughed.

"Girl, ain't he a sexy chunk of well-seasoned meat."

"You've had your fill, that's for sure."

"Who said… never mind. The night is moving on and yes, I need it filled."

"Girl, grab your purse. We've paid and Fulton is gone, so let's get out of here."

"Alright, I parked across the street. The usual?"

The women Tina trusted had an agreement. If they seemed to have had too much, they would be driven home. If they were just a bit tipsy but could drive, they'd be followed. Tina pointed to her car and nodded in agreement. She'd be following her friend. As she walked to her car, she made a mental note, *Marcie has to control her libido levels. I can't help her. Hell, I have to control mine.*

CHAPTER 60

Justlin arrived at her home and was greeted by Officers Stands and Knight. The two walked with her to her front door. She looked around as though there was something missing.

"Ma'am is something wrong?," asked Knight.

"No, no I thought I left something in the car. Stands where is Tyson?"

"On his way ma'am we got here earlier than the assigned time for this detail. We called him when we arrived checked your perimeter and called him as he required. He's on his way."

"I see Stands, come on in please. Knight stand by."

Knight nodded and Stands followed her in the home. Justlin kicked off her shoes and put down her satchel and purse. Stands stood in the living room awaiting instructions.

"Man, sit down. Why are you so formal? We just left each other at Michaels' house. Y'all are hilarious and why is Knight here I thought Wilson was your partner."

"She will be here in about an hour or two. Had some personal business to check on. Tyson is aware of it."

"Okay, I'll tell you before I jump…let me change that before I tell Tyson this. I don't trust Knight and I ain't too fond of Knowles. If you and Wilson are not with this detail, I need to talk with the captain or governor for replacements. Knight was offered to be a part of the 'untouchables.' Do we know if he's still in touch with any of them? Knowles being Worthy's nephew, which he keeps quiet is a bit difference but…"

"I understand. He's being replaced as soon as Wilson gets here and I'm sure Tyson won't assign him again. Is Montez a problem or anyone else in our office?"

"No, I'm good with Montez, even Miller. She seems to be coming along, but Knight, there's something about him I just don't trust. Take a seat, if you will, for a moment. He can sit in the car on his own, right?"

Stands shook his head and let out a soft laugh. He watched while Justlin checked rooms. She went in and out saying it would only take her a few minutes.

"Justlin, are you doing our job? I mean, do you want a shift in the vehicle too?"

"Bye, I've checked the rooms, yes. Go I'll talk with Tyson about shifts and duties. You guys are funny, all of you. I guess that's why you work well with each other. Listen, this mess we're dealing with ain't my cup of tea. So, if I seem slightly shook, please don't think I am less than or a weak, complaining, woman."

"No, never that. Believe me, we know your personality and love it just the way you are. We also know you'd be right on the front line with the best of us. This is your home, your safe space, and any fears that touch the border of that is to be protected. We're here for that. But Justlin, we'll check the rooms, the outside, anywhere you tell us, that's what we're here for."

She sighed. He was right and Tyson would tell her the same thing. She watched as he went out the door. Marcie was right. They both needed a break and a refill or just the attempt would relieve some of the frustration they held. She'd suggest a short weekend away from it all… but with who? Blake, hell no, Marcie and the girls, maybe. Tyson crossed her mind. It was a thought.

Trying to get comfortable before her security arrived caused her unforeseen anxiety. If he was to stay, she couldn't walk around in her torn tee shirt and shorts, or any of her lingerie. Damien would tease her about either.

She heard laughter and voices nearing her front door. Too late, she threw up her hands and answered the door in her work attire.

"Hey Ms. Lady. You still in work mode. I didn't come right away assuming you would want a chance to unwind. You know bubble bath, shower, relax a bit? Tina, what's wrong?"

He could see she was upset. He waved Stands away from the door closing it and giving his full attention to her flowing tears.

"Hey, what's wrong? Was it me not being here?"

Tina shook her head "no" as she went into the kitchen with Damien close behind her.

"Well, what?" I want to understand your tears, you're hurt? Who or what is bothering you?"

"I don't know why I'm crying like this. It's just… it's just too much going on. I need that slow and steady pace back. One I could control." She wiped her tears and continued. "I'm taking up personal time that I vowed I wouldn't give to my job again. I left my position here as an officer for that peace of mind. Damien it's been, what, three years of trying to find peace. Just peace… and as soon as they give me a position that slowed it down, this happens."

Damien didn't answer, he couldn't. There were many including him, that sought the peace she was referring to. He reached across the counter for her hand. She reached and touched his. He walked around the counter and held his arms out. She walked into his arms to receive an embrace of support. Her thoughts of work became a fog. She backed up and waved her hand.

"Damien, this isn't what we need. We're approaching it all wrong. Everything can't be tied together for it to work out."

Damien wanted to ask what "everything" was, but he waited for her to continue.

"Fulton's case, the murder, your reports, Worthy's position and those damn…"

"'Untouchables,' yeah, I had that same thought. But listen, don't you let it disturb your peace. If you need to release that stress, that tension, it's not a part of security, but baby I'm here for whatever you need."

"Be careful. You may be asked to fill a position that you're not ready to give in to."

"Try me girl," he answered with a smile and turned to walk away.

"Humph. So, one more thing about work then I'll relax. I don't trust Knight. I don't want him here and I'm wondering if you should be trusting him. Someone connected, talked about the transport. How do we know he isn't still trying to, what did he say, get in and find out?"

"Wow, you think he'd do that still?"

"Why not?" He was asked. "Suppose he talked with Chambers and mentioned he was working the investigation and transport, and other details? A possibility, right? I don't want him around my personal space. I'll interview the staff if you agree. Just keeping your unit tight and me safe. I've still got to talk with Boone and Simmons, it won't seem strange."

He didn't have an answer as he realized she was right. He nodded his head "yes," and she continued with directions.

"The guest room, well you've been through the house. It has its own bathroom as well so we shouldn't have a problem with that. You can leave your clothes; I mean you know to make it easier for you to change."

"Oh, I thought you were offering space in the closet."

Tina gave him a stern stare.

"Really? I'm that bad? I'll carry them out with me ma'am. As a matter of fact, let me check with Wilson, you two seemed to hit it off. Maybe we can schedule her for the overnight shift."

"No, Damien, I mean it. You don't understand. I have top security paperwork and items I don't want others snooping around trying to analyze me. You know me, they don't. So enough unless I need to seek…"

"Yeah, we're it right now, but I understand. I'll be here. Prayerfully it will be over soon."

"Well, I need to shower. I ate, did you?"

"I'm good."

It was then when Damien realized he hadn't eaten since lunch. He went to the guest room and looked around. There was a desk next to the queen-sized bed. The décor wasn't an indication it was a female's home and he appreciated not having the floral welcome he imagined. He checked the bath, and it too was to his liking. He could rest easy there was no way Stands or Porter would tease him. As he came out of the bathroom, Tina was standing in the door.

"I hope everything is to your satisfaction."

Damien hoped she didn't realize he was dazed. She was beautiful and the attraction brought on a smile he couldn't hide.

"Yes, I was glad you weren't into the floral feminine décor. I might have had to stay in the car."

"So, you don't like flowers, or the aroma?"

"I think it's just when you cover the walls, with the pictures, have the bedding and spread the walls and windows with the same…. It's a bit much. But your taste seems to be more, I don't know, but I like it."

"Well, thank you. Glad I didn't run you out."

Damien paused. Looking at her as a woman and not a woman co-worker was different. "You wouldn't run me out. After all who would you choose for your next security detail."

"Hmm… do you want another glass of wine. I'm pouring one for me. It will help you sleep on that last comment." Tina's smile was inviting. Damien knew he was stepping into what he wanted but did she want their next.

CHAPTER 61

The morning began with an odd conversation. The two had taken the step that neither expected but eagerly accepted. Damien came from the master bathroom wrapped in a bath towel after showering. Tina was standing in front of the full-length mirror in her robe. Damien approached her slowly hoping the night wasn't just a reward from the bottle of wine they opened and finished.

"How are you?" He whispered on her neck as he kissed her softly. She turned to face him with a smile.

"I'm good, how are you?" She was pleased, although she didn't know how they would be able to keep their new secret.

"I'm good. Maybe once you're ready for breakfast or we stop for breakfast, I think we need to talk?

His voice went up an octave. He held her hands and his breath, hoping she wouldn't be upset with the question.

"Yes, and we can have breakfast wherever you're comfortable."

"Okay, if you… or do you want me to cook?"

"I'm sure you can, but we can eat out. I don't normally cook breakfast during the week. I tend to get up too late, but you seem to be an early bird." She pushed him teasingly and headed toward the bathroom.

"So, my lady, what do you prefer?" Tina smiled and closed the bathroom door.

Damien's mind was racing. His title could no longer be security, but he wasn't sure what she would say. He questioned whether it was a one-night thing. Maybe he had filled in for her boyfriend that worked with her. Could he have been a fill in since the wine eased her mood? He decided to cook breakfast and wait for the answers.

Tina reminisced in the shower. The night made up for the lost nights. She missed Blake's touch. She gave it a second thought and realized it wasn't Blake's touch, but the touch of a man. The embrace was enough to melt her. The conversation regarding their work brought her to tears. She chalked it up to the weakness that wine always gave her. She couldn't control her emotions, or truths after a few glasses of wine. Another reason she didn't drink heavy with her friends.

Damien pulled her into her arms and the night of pleasures began. He had always been a comfort to her. His demeanor and talks always led her to wonder how his wife walked away. The romance started on the couch but when it was obvious what they both wanted, they went to the bedroom.

Tina stepped out the shower and began to dry herself. Every part of her body held memories. Damien took his time to totally explore her from head to toe. She smiled at the thought; she was sure he'd ask about his so-called title. He definitely couldn't be her Private Security, although he secured her, and they would have to keep it private. She wanted a sound relationship; one she could depend on. She needed him to be a man's man and not bend when her job demanded more than he would ever want to handle. Damien could be that man. He couldn't be her bedroom fantasy if… well she didn't want to spoil the thought. She dressed, still on a cloud of night memories and desires for their next encounter.

"Tina, one egg or two?" Damien called from the kitchen. "Scrambled or…"

Tina walked in the kitchen which put a smile on his face.

"Girl, girl…" He said admiring her plum two-piece suit. "One or two?"

"Are we still talking eggs?"

"Eggs, ma'am, eggs. We've got to get to work this morning." He laughed and shook his head.

"Yes, two please. Do you need help with anything?"

"I got it. If you're like me, I eat at the island. You may want to set the table or something."

"No, here is fine. What's on your mind?"

Damien looked back from the stove. He shook his head and focused on the eggs and cheese he had cooked. He was sure she had more questions than him. He didn't know where to start, but he knew she had more.

"This assignment is yours. Do you think after last night it may need to be changed?" He didn't turn to ask the questions hoping she wouldn't say it was only one night.

"No, not at all. What they don't know, well Stands and Wilson are your friends. I'm sure they'll read you this morning and know you're acting differently."

"Oh, you won't act differently? I can't cover how I feel but you can? You've got to learn more about me, I mean on a more personal level."

"Okay, that's fair. I don't know you on that level, but Damien if we take this further you have to learn about my feelings as well."

"I'd love that." Damien served the plates and took his seat across from her.

The two sat and talked, they knew it wouldn't be a one-night encounter. They talked and laughed about Worthy and Porter being right about their attraction. Damien admitted he was upset when he found out she was married. She questioned, wasn't he married at that time as well.

"It was going bad. I knew it. She didn't want to be married, be a mother, or live here and work out the issues."

"What were her issues?"

"Me. My job. The attention I gave to the cases, the victims, and as I took on promotions, my team. She said she wanted to be a part of the fashion world, the glamour, and lights she'd get on the runway. She designed clothes for a few models and others. She was good at it. Left me, the kids, and never came back. I didn't run after her and that's when the marriage ended. She filed for divorce claiming I never wanted to be married or I would have come for her. I tried Tina. Really, I did. But she wanted me to move, leave what I had established for myself and our children. My mother, and other family members helped me keep it together. My first step into what I thought would be a relationship was years later. It got me transferred, better than fired but, I'm not looking to have issues that would surround my personal relationship."

"Wow, I didn't know you had that kind of problem going on. You hid that well… until that nut case."

"Yeah, that's why I'm careful who I talk to or deal with. Relationships can ruin you if you don't know the person you're dealing with." He reached for her hand. "I believe I know you well enough to try this, that's if you agree."

Tina squeezed his hand. "Yes, I agree."

"Well let's get going. Do you want coffee? I know how to make that as well, didn't know if you were a coffee or tea drinker in the morning."

"We can stop for my Starbucks. It's a habit I don't want to drop now."

Damien shook his head smiling. He hoped he would become a habit she wouldn't want to drop. The two walked out the front door, greeting Knowles and Porter.

"Morning, Tyson can I speak with you before you leave?" Porter's question didn't cause concern until he spoke.

"Two things boss. Reliefs for this security. We relieved Stands and Wilson this morning. What time are they expected to be in the office? We can't cover the office without them. I understand Justlin's fears, they're real, but we need to have outside coverage. I mean, well you know what I'm saying."

"Yeah, I don't think we'll need coverage all night. I'm on the inside that should be enough. If I call for back-up… well let's hope that doesn't happen. I'll be here until she feels better about it. I'll reset the times, maybe until nine and rotate. I'm thinking of adding Miller to the team permanently, and Montez as a fill-in."

"Damien, is it that serious? I mean they'd come for us in our homes before hitting her?"

"Would they? My home is empty other than me. Yours is as well and to be honest our positions in our unit don't send a message. Killing a Lieutenant, close to the Chief speaks and if a Principal Investigator is pulling folders, talking to the lawyer that may blow their cover… they may target her."

"Okay, I got your message about Knight is Knowles, okay?"

"Yeah, yeah, he's fine. So, you've been here since…?"

"Since about five. Oh, and I got a call from Montez. Sayers and Fulton want to meet with you this morning."

"Okay, did Montez say a time?"

"No. If I were a betting man, I'd say as soon as you walked in."

"Like you ain't a betting man. You bet, but how often do you win, my man?" Tyson laughed teasing his friend.

"Hmm… how much money you want to put on you and Justlin. It ain't no little joke no more, I bet you. Congrats man, you did what many men couldn't do."

The two looked over at the car. Justlin was on her phone and didn't look their way.

"Let's keep that between us."

"Damn, I was joking. So, you… and… wow. Well, she's a solid. Damn, I thought I had a chance."

"I'll see you at the office. Adjust the time sheets to reflect the overtime. And no, you don't have a chance."

Tyson walked to the car smiling and then the thought of his morning visitors crossed his mind. The day would be filled with questions he'd have to relay to Worthy. It seemed they were getting deeper into a hole they wouldn't be able to climb out of.

CHAPTER 62

The ride to the office was pleasurable. The music played was on the smooth jazz station. After Justlin agreed to ride with him to the office, he decided not to listen to the local station. They talked about the reporter and the lawyer awaiting Tyson with hopes it would prepare him for the possibilities.

"What else could they want? After having dinner with Fulton, I'm sure he wants to know how far he can go with you. He knows the law, but your office can break or help his case. He's got names and dates, that's all by what I can tell. He did mention forensics and collected evidence, but it doesn't add up to much."

"Tina, he's fishing. What we have or don't have may not lead to an appeal. I haven't read much into the cases but his representation in court, led them to jail. So, my thought is he's seeking what he may have missed. Now, whoever removed material may have tainted the results for his clients. He can't possibly win an appeal when the evidence he reports doesn't appear on the file, I'll give him that. You and I both know the courts would come up with an excuse. Files are moved all the time for various reasons."

"What about the signatures and initials?"

"Baby, that's internal problems. It's just like the report you're working on. Nothing attached to his cases, and even if they were, they would question us."

"And?"

"And what? See that's what I was complaining about from the beginning. We took over after this mess. I can't explain reasons or actions of the others. Lt. Marshall could put them all under and may be an asset for Fulton's cases. I really don't know. Hell, they said the connection goes higher than we think. It reached your boy's office with this ambush, so why not a judge?"

"Wow, so we are in a cross trap. No matter how we present our findings, they have a cover for it."

"It may be that way. I don't know. What I do know is they won't involve my unit. This is a mess for the entire precinct. Worthy may be in that seat until the mess is cleared. They don't want Mancy to be tainted, let Worthy go out kicking and crying."

"I didn't think of it as such. So, do we continue the way we were going with this?"

"Following Worthy babe. It's his show now. All we can do is be in his corner."

"This can ruin a career or two."

"Yep, there's always that possibility. I've learned let the chips fall. Me and my team have ducked a chip or two. We may have had to eat a few."

They laughed and changed the subject. The conversation was one Justlin seemed worried about. She sighed before asking her next question.

"Hey, what do you think others may say about us?"

"Why do you care? Does it upset you if they say anything? I'm not unsure about this or you and you shouldn't be. We're adults, we're private people, and other than a few nosey folks, I don't think many will care. You may have to explain it to that suited boyfriend you had. I don't have anyone to explain why I'm dating you or anyone else."

"Hmm… maybe it is me. I just don't want the questionable looks. Women tend to be petty when it comes to dating the eligible man everyone has been…"

"Watch it girl, making me feel good this early in the morning."

"Boy, please! What I'm saying is you've been on the wish list for single women for years. Don't tell me you don't know they won't talk."

"I'm a grown man, dating, loving, and whatever they can imagine with you, a grown woman. They can say what they want. I won't be treating them any different because I never pursued any of them. Oh well, if there was a bet they lost."

"You are so… hey is that Sheers?"

"Not this morning." Damien sighed deeply as he parked the car.

Tyson found a parking spot and waited. He noticed Sheers had not moved from his spot after seeing him enter the parking deck. The two exited the car anticipating the sarcastic remarks or questions. As they approached the officer they nodded and continued to walk by.

"Uh, Tyson, can I speak with you?"

Tyson stopped and Justlin continued on surprising Sheers.

"So, you're not attached at the hip. Seems like since she's been here investigating whatever, you guys have been attached. What's up with that?"

"Now that you've concluded we're not attached, what is it you want to speak about?"

"Hmmm… don't let her burst your bubble. Your last love landed you in another department. This one may have you unemployed."

"You wanted to speak or preach. I don't need you to preach to me. Again, what do you want to speak about?"

"The lawyer. He's been in and out. Your office, the captain's office, and this morning he's been seen with the reporter. You know anything that's to be reported has to go through proper channels."

"And you know that's not my department and I'm sure they both know what they're doing."

"Tyson, man, if you can't tell, I'm on your side. Blue, you know we stand together."

Damien thought about the hearing held before his transfer. Sheers sat in audience with a smirk on his face. He and his friends whispered with smiles after the panel announced Tyson would be reassigned. He avoided them as much as possible yet Sheers and Boone taunted him for months. Earlier in his career he would have met them in the same parking deck and settled their differences.

"So, what is it you wanted?"

"Since we are in this together, I wanted to ask if you could share the information as you get it. You know what they're looking for or what Sayers wants to put in that paper of hers."

Tyson shook his head, pausing to choose his words carefully.

"Sheers, we don't stand together, and you know it. You want the information they have or have received speak with them. I'm not in your circle, not many of us are, blue or not. Therefore, these little sideline meetings won't be happening anymore. You're an officer, I'm a bit higher, not sure you understand that. As such, make an appointment to see me, if not, it's all good. Have a good day."

Once again Sheers was left standing in the parking lot. He dialed a number and waited for the voice on the other end.

"No go. He didn't budge or seem on edge."

"And you said Sayers and that lawyer are in the building this morning." The voice on the other end didn't seem bothered with Tyson's response.

"They were outside of the squad room when I saw them. I don't know where they are headed but I'm sure it's to meet one of the folks upstairs."

"Alright, so find out and call me back. Tyson is not stupid. He won't jeopardize the unit or his position. We made one mistake. This unit ain't for him. We'll fix that once Worthy is removed and I'm in place."

"Okay, so what now?"

"You and Boone go to the hospital. Visit the lieutenant and who is on him. It's been a few days now, we need a way in. So, since it's not one of our own on duty there, I need to know who is there. I'm understanding the governor assigned the coverage. Find out. Let him know we're with him, on his side, praying for his healing. You know, lay it on thick. I've got to know so I can pass the information to those who make the difficult choices. I'll be in my office later this afternoon."

"Gotcha. I'll call back soon."

CHAPTER 63

The building was buzzing as though there was a scheduled press conference or presentation. Tyson dared not ask any questions as many greeted him and Justlin as they made their way to the office. Marcie waved and Justlin changed her direction to talk with her friend. Tyson waved and smiled thinking the conversations would be silenced if he had kissed the Principal Investigator on the cheek as they separated.

"Girl, did you get a call this morning? I know you know what all of this is about. What's the scoop? I like your suit."

Marcie was more than excited and looking picture ready. Tina scanned the hall and foyer, it was busy. Conversations and whispers; Tina noticed there were a few who were gazing at her. She checked her cellphone and Marcie was right she had missed calls from the governor's office and Sharice.

"Damn, I missed the calls. What's going on? I'll call them back when I get in the office."

"Seems like you had a lot going on girlfriend. Spill it. What were you up to after our dinner?"

"Who said I was up to anything. We'll talk about the after, later."

"Oh, so something went on that you couldn't call me this morning. Phone calls unanswered. You and Tyson walked in together. Are you riding with the security team now?"

"Not the team… but we can get into that later. What is this?"

"Your boy is making his way here this morning. We weren't given a time, so this is the result. Everyone wanting to be on the greeting team like they have an agenda pending with him. I know and you know why he's here. Clinton Banks is trying to smooth over the staff with his beautiful smile and charming personality. Tina after two murders? I don't know if it will work for us, it must be a photo-op. I saw Sayers and Fulton, so obviously the press knows. This will not turn out to be what they've expected. It's a band-aid, that's how I see it."

"Damn, I've got to catch up. Thanks, I'll call you once I'm settled. First there's the calls and then the lawyer and his reporting puppet. I'm sure she's delighted to be included. What the hell is Banks thinking? As the governor he can wave his hand, and all will be resolved. This place has an issue that's bigger than him or his title."

"Yeah, it goes back to slavery and the marches. Injustice never changes, and neither does the attitude of these assholes we work with. Call me if you need anything. Hey lunch or dinner? We have to talk about your last night."

"You're right and yes, we definitely do…. Oh hell, I guess the governor will be here soon. A part of his team is here. Let me get in this office."

Tina weaved between the small crowd that wasn't moving, seeking the best place to stand before others took their places. She opened the door to the organized chaos in the office. Montez was organizing folders with Miller at his side. Porter was going from his office to Tyson's. She didn't see Sayers or Fulton. Stands walked by and she stopped his movement hoping he would answer her with a loud response.

"What's going on Stands and am I to be included in it."

"I don't think so. Sayers and Fulton wanted to talk with Tyson. They're in his office now. No one expected that out there so we're rushing before your boy 'stops by.' You should have got a call, right? Hell, we should have been ahead of this mess. Wilson got you a… oh you got your coffee. Alright superwoman, do your thing and find out what we need to prepare for, if you're still on your boy's good side."

Everyone smiled a good morning as she went into the conference room to make her return calls. She hoped the governor would speak to her while in route. The phone rang longer than she expected so she prepared herself to leave a voice message.

"Hey Justice, where are you? I told Phillip to call you early, but he said you hadn't returned his calls. Are you okay? I tried to tell him that wasn't my top investigator's normal reaction. So, I ask are you okay?"

"Just a bit tired. I overslept and…"

"No problem. I can only imagine the pressure that your small assignment has been thrown into. Understand we need you. I need you and Sharice to get together on this. Let's tie this mess up so we all can move on."

"I'm here for a problem with reports, or has that changed? Sharice is investigating a shooting. Worthy and whomever he's assigned is investigating a murder. How do we…the cases seem to be entwined."

"That's why I'm on my way. I'll give the press a bit to calm the rumors and speculations. While I'm there I was thinking maybe talking to the reporter, Sayers who is working with that lawyer Fulton."

"Clinton, that may be reaching. I'll talk to you once I find out why they're here."

"Okay well we've got a few stops before coming there. We'll be there about noon or a little after. So even if you think it's not a good idea let me know, please. I miss you in the office. Being able to run things by you and your way of challenging my thoughts. Justlin, I want you to know I appreciate you. Call me back, please."

Tina hung up the phone. It was then she realized he was scared. Questions about his position, who gave him the title and was it hanging on the problems he was confronted with. Before making her next call, she got a cup of the coffee, it was then she realized she needed something stronger. She wondered how Damien was doing as she dialed Sharice's number.

Sharice explained the problem better than Marcie or the governor. Lt. Marshall was awake and talking to anyone and everyone. Putting all in an awkward situation. No one was permitted to visit or question him without Sharice being present. She had been sitting with him for more than twenty-four hours. She interrogated him as soon as he came out of his stupor. The others who had been shot were in regular rooms, no longer ICU patients. They were being watched by officers from the special operation unit appointed also by the governor. Sharice explained everyone was on edge and no one knew what their next move would be. She was told to report to the precinct and was on her way.

"I can't wait to have a moment of down time. A drink to unwind and not be in a rush to an assignment."

"Well, if we get a moment. You, me, and Marcie can do a few rounds and have a moment to catch up."

"Love the thought. Let's see how this mess goes for today. You missed the morning call, are you okay?"

"Sharice, better than okay. I'm good, believe me, I've finally changed my thoughts about moving on."

"Oooo… a night of pleasure, I assume?"

"Okay gotta go. We'll be on this phone, and I won't have anything prepared for a briefing."

"Okay, I can wait. I'll call Marcie, she knows something, I'm sure."

Tina stood ready to mix information with the team. She smoothed her skirt and touched her hair. She'd stop into the bathroom before peeking in on Tyson.

"No problem. See you when you get here. I'll be in the Cold Case Unit. It's across from Marcie's unit."

The ladies hung up the phone and Tina was met at the bathroom door by Wilson.

"Tyson said come in the office if you're free. Sayers and Fulton are still there."

"Thanks."

Tina stopped backed in the conference room to pick up the folders she thought would suffice the two awaiting her entry. She smiled and noticed what seemed to be a cold stare from the reporter, Samantha Sayers.

"Good morning," Tina smiled ignoring the look she received. "What's new Detective Tyson, Fulton?"

"I was telling the detective what I didn't extend to you and Officer Williams last night."

"Oh," Tina was surprised there was more. She pulled in her seat at the table next to Tyson across from the two visitors.

"Fulton has witnesses that can identity Boone and Sheers on the scene where Tammilyn Watson was raped." Damien answered her puzzled look.

"Were there others in the room with her? Where have they been, I mean, after all this time they're coming forward?"

"They thought the police were there because someone called. Ms. Sayers went to the building, a little reporter investigation and there's a few who identified the 'boys' from their pictures."

"I have an interview with two of them this morning. Boone and Simmons… let me talk with them and see if they admit to being there."

"Ms. Justlin, the reports written don't indicate they were there. So, I doubt they'll say they were in the area or at the apartment during that time. I don't even have their signatures on any evidence."

"Exactly why I'm interested in what they have to say."

"Well, I think we've said what we came to share with you, Detective. As you both know the governor is on his way. It will be interesting to hear his excuses for allowing a Lieutenant to be ambushed on and the connections."

"Whoa, I don't think anyone said there were any connections yet. Let's not get ahead of the released information. Fulton if you do, they'll escape us again. As we discussed earlier, there's and unequal mix in this precinct. We know who they are, at least some of the flunkies. They'll withdraw if they know we're on to them. You'll lose your appeal and we'll be back to where we started."

"I don't think it would be smart to print a story regarding the appeal or what you've found as it pertains to the case." Tina spoke hoping it would touch the reason the reporter was there.

"Just as smart as prolonging the investigation of signatures and reports that have been missing for years," The reporter injected.

"We're handling that. Samantha, you know how long we've been on the unit. The files you're referring to were in a report I submitted. That's why we have the governor's Principal Investigator here. It has little to do with Mr. Fulton's cases. That's how it is to be reported if you decide to include my unit or the reason for delay. I didn't sit with the two of you because I needed to."

"Detective, I don't know. No one mentioned that the officers were there prior to me talking with people in the community. A job your police should have done years ago."

"Again, nothing to do with my department as I don't have police that I send into the streets unless the case warrants it. We follow up leads that are created at meetings such as this. As I said and will say to anyone. I follow the law, what I took an oath do. You want to bring all of us down, go ahead. However, this meeting is off the books. From now on, make an appointment with the captain, who by the way won't be there long. Fulton, I told you we could work together, my rules. Ms. Sayers, I don't know what's got you twisted this morning, but same goes for you, appointments only."

Damien stood waiting for the two to stand. He shook Fulton's hand and nodded to Sayers.

"Listen man, I wasn't trying…"

"It doesn't matter Fulton. It's best for me and those I work for and with. I'm not trying to burn down the house to get the rats out."

"Ms. Justlin, welcome to the team, I guess. I'm still trying to understand your part in this," Sayers said as she grabbed her satchel.

"I don't know if you really need to know. As I said I play no role in what you and Mr. Fulton are seeking to expose. As Tyson said, you're welcome to make an appointment."

The reporter and the lawyer left disappointed, although they had very different needs. Fulton wanted to nail the officers and get more information from them. Sayers, wanted to be closer to Tyson. She wondered what the Principal Investigator was looking for.

CHAPTER 64

Sheers arrived at the hospital hoping his conversation with the officers would be the least of his worries. He knew talking to the governor's team wouldn't be easy. He was sure there would be someone monitoring the visitors. Marshall was still in ICU and the others were moved to the sixth floor. Sheers took the time to change into civilian attire. He knew his uniform would draw attention. He exited the elevator and spotted the officer's post outside of the room. A second officer was posted across the hall. The two were in a heated conversation about the upcoming basketball game.

"Hey, good afternoon," Sheers interrupted their banter. The officers in plain clothes turned their attention to him and Sheers immediately noticed their demeanor changed.

"Hey, what's up?" One questioned as the other checked the hall beyond where Sheers stood.

"I'm here to see the fellas here. I was sent by the attorney whose representing these fellas. Just have a few questions and I'll be gone."

"Did your office call and get clearance?"

"You know, I don't know if they did. We usually show I.D. and talk with them, in front of the officers, and that's it. Is there a reason why our firm wouldn't be able to ask them a few things? Since their families reached out to us, I guess they thought it would be okay as well."

Sheers was unsure what to do and it seemed his reasoning didn't faze them. One officer pulled out his phone and began to dial. Sheers didn't need any other signs he wouldn't be able to get in.

"Yes, Ms. Pulley. I've got a guy here asking to visit, says he's with a law firm… He said a few questions, the family might be seeking to sue. I'm not sure, ma'am. Hold on."

He turned to talk to Sheers. He had begun pacing from the officer standing in the door to the window in the hall. The officer on the phone began to whisper. "Hey, send two, this guy seems awfully nervous."

He hung up the phone and approached Sheers at the window.

"She's going to call our main office. I'm sorry about this man, what did you say your name was?"

"Oh, I'm sorry. Michael Murphy. Funny huh? Me working for lawyers with the name Murphy. You know Murphy's Law… hell it happens, pretty much, each day."

The officer didn't flinch or smile. He nodded his head and watched the hall as the two undercover officers he called for arrived.

"Let's see your ID, that's what they came up here for."

Sheers was prepared with a driver's license with the name Michael Murphy. He handed it to the officers and stood in his arrogance. One of the officers dialed four digits on his hand-held device and turned his back to talk. The other handed the fake identification back to Sheers. The call was short, and the officer asked the question that Sheers feared.

"Your office doesn't have a visit. You can see each of them for fifteen minutes, but it's with one of us present. Not just in the room but at bedside with you. It's either that or you wait for them to be discharged."

"I'll have to check with the man in charge, you know. I've only been on board for a few months." Sheers continued with his lie. "This is a first for me, so I want to be sure I do what I was told. Mr. Manns will visit tomorrow after calling for that appointment."

He turned to leave the area and paused with another question. "Are they being discharged within the next few days?"

"Don't know sir, you'll have to check once you get clearance." The two officers pull their chairs to the wall and went in to talk to the officers in the room. They confirmed the suspicions, neither knew about a lawyer's visit, and neither knew Michael Murphy.

Sheers knew not to go back to the precinct without trying to see Marshall, especially after failing to see the officers that were a part of the transport detail. There seemed to be a crowd at the room in ICU. There were four officers talking to a female who appeared to be in charge. Sheers approached the ICU room and peeked in.

"Sir, can we help you?" Sheers attempted to go in the room. Marshall appeared to be sleeping.

"Sir, stop. You can't go in the room." The officer met Sheers before he advanced further. Looking at the other officers and the woman, he was glad he didn't recognize them.

"I wanted to see if he was my friend. They said he was in ICU. I'm sorry I've checked out the rooms and this is almost the last of my search. Could you tell me where I'd find Mr. Maurice Marshall, he's a lieutenant? I'm a family friend."

Sharice had his picture which was sent by the officers who checked the identification he provided earlier. The response had just come across her screen. She smiled, not wanting to give her secret away, she played along with Sheers' game.

"I'm so sorry. They just gave him a dose of that good juice. You know what I mean. If you allow me to check your identity, you won't have to do it when you come back. He'll be out at least a couple of hours. Isn't that what the nurse told you guys?" She turned to the officers who nodded in agreement.

Sheers was stumped. He couldn't give her the same driver's license he provided earlier. He knew she had denied his entry to the rooms upstairs.

"I'll call or come back. I've got to get back to my office and I can't wait here for hours."

"Well, we can check your ID and log you in for a visit later, maybe tonight." Sharice was trying to be accommodating but Sheers didn't take the bait.

"You've been helpful. I'll be back with a family member. Thank you for your service."

"Thank you."

Sheers walked to the elevator. He felt their eyes as he left the floor. He wasn't sure who the female was, but he was certain she recognized him.

As the elevator doors closed Sharice headed to Marshall's room. She told the officers there were to be no visitors without her being on the floor. Marshall turned his head toward her, shaking it slowly.

"They don't give up. A bunch of ignorant assholes. That was Sheers, and I guess he wanted to visit the others too. They've got to be stopped. Hell, they killed Michaels. What did they send him to the hospital to do?"

Sharice pulled up the chair to the bed and took a seat. Her silence was deliberate, and Marshall waited for her to speak.

"You and I both know their reasons. You know the inner workings of what? What is the group really called?"

"No name really. It's not a well thought plan just one that works against, well you know what and who. It started years ago and passed on. You know, putting pressure on the community stores, clubs, prostitutes, drug dealers, and internally hitting the weaker officers. Somewhere along the way we didn't get the message. Those of us who sought the pay-days, raises, and promotions. We didn't hear or wouldn't listen to the complaints internally or on the street. Once we got older it became our problem. They'd offer more, we took more, we couldn't walk away clean. Others before us died out. They were old and gray still doing the bid of what you and others call the 'untouchables.' It was and is for those still connected to them, an addiction. We did it to feed the greed... money, power, positions, we had it all.

"Michaels wanted out; he saw the change coming. I understood and told him if he left, I was with him. I had his back. I knew they wouldn't let him retire. They wanted him to rot in the chief's chair. Nothing more, nothing less, just sit there and do their dirt. In a position to make power moves for the assholes they're grooming. Michaels saw it, their plans to ruin good cops, politicians, and the community. We were done. Well, you know the rest, I've told Worthy the details of the night of Michaels' murder. Now Sheers shows up here? He was sent. Either he was told to get information or he was here to finish me off and question the cops."

"Well, we're going to work on getting you and them transferred. I'm talking with the governor's people now. I'm on my way to the precinct."

"Be careful, they'll watch you now, knowing you're in charge and blocked their efforts. Sheers will get new orders and follow them. The other two they may send is Boone and Simmons. You might want to alert your men to them. Have Worthy send their ID photos for you to have."

"Good thoughts, thanks. I've informed them no visitors if I'm not here. I'm trying to understand how they knew you were enroute to the safe house. Someone breached security transport. That's more than the 'untouchables'' reach."

"Investigator Pulley, they aren't just in the precincts, their reach is what is 'untouchable.'"

CHAPTER 65

Sharice called Tina on her way to the precinct. She couldn't wait with the news she had. Sheers had crossed the wrong line. The questions were why, and who sent him? It had to be a supervisor, why would he take it upon himself to interrogate the transport officers who were shot and Marshall. Sharice smiled; he wasn't as smart as they gave him credit for. He was a yes man for another in a higher position. The phone rang three times before Tina answered.

"Girl, guess what fell in my lap, rather who?"

"Huh? No, he wouldn't be that dumb."

"'Untouchable'? When they touch you with the thought that you are the dummy? Girl he's been tagged. Marshall heard him asking to visit. He pretended to be sleep. As soon as he left, I took the picture of his fake ID he showed the officers with me to question Marshall. Before I could ask, Marshall said, that's Sheers."

"No, he tried to visit Marshall?"

"And the transport officers on the sixth floor. He went there first. The officers called me and sent the photo. I didn't know who he was. He told them he was a friend of the family and knew the lawyer they hired. Of course, it didn't budge the officers. They hinted his temper was rising, we refused the visit telling him it had to be scheduled. I thought he exited the hospital. Girl, that fool came down to ICU. I don't think he thought about an investigator being here and in charge. Marshall heard his voice and identified him. The picture confirmed it. Sheers got some shit with him. He tried to retain his anger. I wish he would…"

"Girl, that is too much. Let me inform Tyson and Worthy. You'll inform the governor, or not."

"I don't plan on it. Let him get the news from you."

"What's wrong now? C'mon I thought you guys looked past the issues you had?"

"I don't know what's wrong with him now. If it's not business, there's no need to talk about it. He's got to learn all black women are not alike."

"Well, I'll see you when you get here. Let me go and inform Tyson and Worthy. It may change some of the plans they have."

"Alright, I should be there in an hour." Sharice hung up her phone hoping she'd get there before the governor.

Tina opened the folders for Simmons and Boone as she waited for her first appointment to show. She prepared simple questions. She hoped they would lead to what she now knew would point to someone in a higher position. A knock on the door caused her to prepare the Investigator demeanor.

"Hey, do you need anything? Water, coffee?" Damien smiled and then gave her a questionable look. "What's up no, what's wrong?"

"Come in and close the door."

Damien checked the hall. The floor was cleared per the captain. Only his security and other authorized personnel were allowed to use the conference rooms.

"Sheers went to the hospital. It was his intent to visit the officers and Marshall. He showed a fake identification to the officers on the sixth floor. They sent the picture to Sharice. She didn't know who he was and turned away the visit. After being turned away he still attempted to visit with Marshall. Sharice turned him away again. She went to show the picture to Marshall since he claimed he was a family friend. Marshall told her it was Sheers."

"What the hell? Who authorized a visit to… I'll talk to Worthy. You have enough to deal with this morning." He kissed her on the cheek and left her to her appointments. Boone was seated in the hall. "Hey, Boone is here. Do you want him to come in now?"

"Yes, send him in please. Officer Boone, take a seat here please." She pointed to the seat across the table from her.

"Can you tell me why I'm here?" Boone questioned showing an obvious attitude.

"You can refuse this informal interview, but there will be another requested by the governor's office."

"What is this about?" He leaned forward and gave her a stern look.

Tina thought about giving him an answer and a few choice words. She let the thoughts play out in her mind, *This young white punk thinks he can intimidate me with his childish behavior. Play him girl, send a message to any of the others you may have to interview.*

"Officer Boone, this is not a place to power play. My title speaks loudly, louder than yours. I've been an officer, sergeant, and refused to take the position of captain, although I passed the damn test. I am a Principal Investigator for the state, appointed by the governor. This is not an easy job, nor is yours, but be sure I can have you removed from your position. You can't have me removed from mine. Now this can go easy; you answer the questions, and I am out of your hair. You give me a hard time, I become dandruff. You won't know how to get rid of me."

Boone sat back in the chair. He didn't think Sheers had met this investigator. She was not what he described as could be intimidated. She pulled out a recorder, a pad, and her laptop, none of which were on the table when he entered the room. He wondered why. He looked at her dress, the plum two-piece suit fit her well. Her hair and make-up was outstanding. He nodded his head understanding her more than he would admit to. She was on point, well organized, and very pretty, a professional.

"I'm here to present to you a few facts backed with evidence. So, let's be truthful Officer Boone. I will tell you what I know as it surrounds the questions and I expect you to be truthful as well. I have the logs for evidence and the reports that should match the entries. They don't, that's why we're here. Let's get started."

"Am I looking at time off for these errors. I mean if there's a discrepancy, that can't be my fault. I mean, suppose I don't answer your questions."

"That's up to you sir. I'm not holding you here. I'm just looking for answers. It may be on the officer who took in evidence and asked for you to sign. It happens, but until you know the questions, what's the hesitation?"

Boone stood up. "I may need my rep, you know. Can I contact him and get back to you?"

"Unfortunately, I can't promise you it won't go further without your answers or reasons why. If you want, write a report stating you want your Union Representative to be with you at the time of questioning. You can explain or not. I'll turn it in with my findings and if the governor finds your reason is acceptable, you'll be able to answer the questions, with your representative."

Boone couldn't believe her answer. He couldn't remember what the logbooks said, who signed for him, or what evidence they eventually pulled without signing the log. He left the office looking for Simmons. He dialed his number, he wanted to warn him. There was no answer.

Tina didn't schedule them one after another Simmons was scheduled to report after lunch. She was sure Boone would try to notify Simmons and get him to unite with him. However, she had a different approach ready for Officer Simmons.

CHAPTER 66

Stands and the rest of the team were in the conference area with Tyson. He was relaying the information about Sheers as they sat waiting for the captain's next assignment. Knowles and Knight were in plain clothes, assigned to the unit's security as were those assigned to Worthy. Miller had been offered a permanent position with the team and accepted. Knowles would talk with the captain later about what seemed to be an abrupt change in assignments, but he was sure there was an underlying reason.

Tina was surprised to see the two standing by the door. She assumed they were assigned to the outer perimeter because of the crowd. She smiled, greeting them a morning hello.

"Ms. Justlin, may we speak a moment?" questioned Knowles.

"Sure, now or later?" she replied, observing Knight's reaction to his partner's request.

"Now, I mean if you don't mind. It will only take a moment." Knowles moved away from the door giving them space to talk without Knight hearing them. Tina moved as he had, wondering what he had to say.

"Ms. Justlin, I wanted you to know that my agenda is not the same as Knight's. I'm wondering is he playing both sides like Tyson warned. I'm not, nor do I want to be affiliated with him, regardless. His conversations say more then he realizes. Something is up with him, or he's seeking to be on the next upcoming officer quick gain list, you know what I mean. I'm just saying you and the team can depend on me. You want a detail at your home in the evening, I want to be a part of the rotation. Not with him though, it's enough being with him during the day."

"Okay, I do understand your interest and your point of view. I'll talk with Tyson about your assignments, including during the day. You know I don't have anything to do with who is assigned, even to the evening detail.

I noticed his demeanor as well. I'm watching him and you should too. Let Tyson know how you feel."

"Yes ma'am, I wanted to talk to my uncle at first, but letting Tyson know first is best."

"Sure is. I don't know that today is the best day for it, with all this going on. I'll mention it and we'll take it from there."

The two separated, Tina entered the office and Knowles stood again at his assigned post.

"So, what's up with that private encounter?" Knight asked with a scoffed look on his face.

"You do know your facial expressions say more than your words. What does my conversation with her have to do with you?"

"Hey, I may want to step into the land of milk and honey. Although I'm more of a honey man, you know?"

"Not an interest, business comes first."

Knight smiled and shook his head. "More like personal interest as I see it. You better watch yourself you'll be next. Following our boy Chambers."

"Your boy, not mine. I'm not interested, if you think you're offering me an invitation to join. I see where it gets people, especially a black boy like me and you. So, you still dealing with Sheers and the others since Chambers left?" Knowles decided to question Knight's interests.

"You have your secrets, I'll have mine. Nothing serious, but it comes with what I see has great rewards. They want to know our answer. Sheers called, wondering if we're we still interested."

"Where's Chambers? He made the offer. Why is Sheers contacting us instead of Chambers? Have you spoke with him?" Knowles was confused.

"No can't say I have. You call him, I'm sure he'll answer your call." Knight stated sarcastically.

Knowles laughed. "Man, you really have things twisted. Listen, keep that shit between you and the white boy. I don't call him or want to call him. They're a bunch of losers. They bully others to get what they want, threaten, and persuade new officers to do their will. Chambers got caught up and it seems you have too. I don't want any part of it. I'll climb the ladder according to the rules."

"Man, listen, I understand. We're the minority on the ladder and in their circle. They control it either way. Why not have a bit of an advantage? You don't have to worry about the promotional tests, the bullshit ass-kissing that's just a promise and never full-filled. They handle it for you."

Knowles let out a sigh. It was a losing battle trying to convince Knight he was on a destructive path. Justlin was right and he'd let Tyson and Worthy know. He wondered if Knight had already joined the vile group.

"Everyone has their limit. I can't deal with them. It's a violation of my black code, never mind the limits of my job. Good luck with it, but no need for your ploy for recruitment. Do me a favor, be careful. Working with you can be hazardous because of your choices. I don't want to be shot due to association."

"Punk ass. Association, really? Well, you may not have protection otherwise either."

"Hey, you good? I need to hit the rest room." Knowles didn't wait for his response.

Entering the office, Knowles could see how the exterior's chaos had entered the unit. Montez approached him as he walked toward the conference room.

"Morning, what's up? How can I help you?"

"Going to the bathroom. How are you this morning?"

"Good man, how's it going out there?"

"Depends on what you're referring to. Knight or the crowd that's gathering." Montez noticed the attitude in his response.

"That bad huh?"

"You know what, I need to talk with Tyson or the captain as soon as possible. But I don't need him to know I've asked for the conversation." Knowles turned and looked at the door. Knight was talking with a lady outside the door.

"Hey, we can pull you. I'll stand with him while you talk."

"Thanks, man, but I don't want it to look like I came in here for that conversation, if you know what I mean. Can you arrange it though? It's got to be done today."

"No problem. I'll talk to Tyson now. Don't be surprised if he pulls you immediately though. He doesn't like things lingering."

Knowles thanked him and continued to the restroom. He wasn't sure if Knight was in or just talking to see what Knowles thought about the invitation. He didn't want to accuse his partner, but he was sure there was something to his questions and arrogance. He had been promised something and maybe he needed a recruitment before he'd get the promised reward. He washed his hands and looked in the mirror. Worthy would move him immediately, but he liked the Cold Case Unit. He'd have to let his uncle know Knight needed to be moved.

CHAPTER 67

Sharice entered the precinct as her phone buzzed. It was close to one and she was sure the governor and his team had made the anticipated appearance. She checked her phone and changed her direction. She was being summoned to the captain's office. Heading toward the elevator, she noticed Justlin, Tyson, Porter, and an officer she didn't recognize coming toward her.

"Hey, lady, long time no see." Tyson greeted her with a kiss on her cheek. "Looking good, too. What do you ladies do in that office on the hill?" He teased as she said hello to Porter and Justlin.

"This is Officer Knowles," Porter whispered," He's the captain's nephew so we let him hang."

"Nice to meet you. How do you like your assignments so far. I'm sure your uncle has set you up."

Everyone looked at him with raised eyebrows as they entered the elevator. Knight noticed Montez as he took his position with Knight. He knew Montez had the same thought as many in the department. Most, who knew his relationship with Worthy felt he would be given easy jobs. It was something he couldn't avoid but he didn't want the special attention. He would be considered an exception; he would express his problem after the impromptu meeting.

"I'm dealing with it. If you know my uncle, it's hard to convince him his decisions aren't always the best, especially for me. Working with these guys has been a plus compared to other assignments."

"Well, you better stay on his good side," teased Porter.

They got off the elevator and Justlin noticed Simmons was there for his interview.

"Tyson, I don't want him to get with Boone. I'm hoping he hasn't. I'd rather interview him now."

"I'll let Worthy know. What an hour, thirty minutes?"

Tina looked at the officer seated on the bench, holding his head.

"Hmm, he looks worried. I'd say thirty minutes but if he cares to share, I won't stop him."

Sharice smiled," If we both did the interview it would be short and sweet."

"Girl, we ain't trying to scare him into a confession."

The group laughed bringing attention to their entrance into the office. Simmons looked up and only recognized one person… Knowles. He sent a text to Sheers. "Hey, that boy you're trying to recruit, not Knight the other one. Well, he's on his way with the Cold Case Unit into the captain's office."

The reply was in his phone before Tina approached him. "He's Worthy's nephew. We just found out he was connected. We'll deal with Knight asking another one of their kind. He's a no go, for now."

Simmons put his phone in his pocket closing the message and followed Justlin's hand gestures to enter the conference room. She waited for him to sit before she introduced herself. He seemed to have a better attitude than Boone. Tina could tell he was younger. If she had to guess she would say mid-twenties, early thirties at the most. He sat across from her with his hands folded on the table.

"Officer Simmons, my name is Tina Justlin. I'm the Principal Investigator for the governor's office. I am here to investigate a report that was turned in with some missing information, problematic signatures, and other issues. Your name is one of the names that came up during the investigation. So, with your help, I'd like to clear up a few things."

"Okay, whatever I can do to help."

Tina was surprised at his response. It did tell her one thing. He hadn't spoken with Boone.

Worthy wasn't pleased that Justlin wouldn't be in the meeting. Tyson told him about the interview with Boone and considering Sheers trying to visit Marshall, she needed to see if she could get anything from Simmons it would help. Each of them had information to add to what was building to an explosive situation. After everyone spoke, Knowles asked to speak with Tyson and Worthy.

"Listen, you're going to have to stop with the secret meetings. What is it you want to ask, say, express, c'mon man you're trying to be a part of this unit right?"

Knowles looked around the room. His uncle had his reasons. He wanted Knowles to be secured with people who would lead him in the right direction. Worthy knew those in the Cold Case Unit would steer him the right way. If his foot was in deep with them before he left, no one would bother him.

Tyson pointed to the conference table for Knowles to take his seat again as did everyone else.

"I don't know what we have to do, but I think Knight is with the 'untouchables.'" He asked me again if I'd consider talking with them about joining. Chambers approached us before he was booted, but it seems Knight has been in touch with him and Sheers. I know I can't make assumptions and we'd have to know for sure, but I really don't feel comfortable with his conversations and actions."

"Okay, Justlin questioned his actions as well. He may have been the one who told them about the transport detail." Tyson stated and paused in his thoughts to hear what the captain had to say.

"So… what do we do about this Ms. Pulley? You're investigating the transport and what happened, right? Would you want to speak with our so-called officer?"

"Sir, I'd be glad to speak with him? Who'll pick up the pieces?"

"Pieces? What do you mean pieces?"

Everyone appeared to be confused. They waited for her answer. Porter answered for her.

"She's going tear him a new one. There will be pieces of him scattered, which is just what the captain doesn't need right now." Porter winked at Sharice. "What black officer, heck, black man would want to join the ranks of those prejudice…"

"Understood, but we've got to be careful about how we handle him. Knowles, is he considering being a part of this group or is he in." Tyson was thinking well beyond Porter's questions. Knowles was right, regardless. Knight had to be removed, possibly from the force entirely.

"I think the intention is if he can recruit more blacks, the more, he will, I guess, be rewarded. They want to even the playing field, so it doesn't look like a race thing."

"Okay, well Captain, I've got it. I won't talk with him today. I'm interested now in what Sheers will do after Knowles has rejected the offer. Knight will have to report to him, I'm sure. Can he be reassigned? I don't want him to gain knowledge of anything else just in case we're on to something. Sheers is already attempting things; he may use Knight."

"How is Sheers doing any of this? He's an officer, he has no rank, no authority," Porter questioned. "This joker just does what he wants and could care less who knows."

"I think it's Mancy or whomever they've got to take Michaels' place. They know I won't take it, even if it's temporary. I can't and won't deal with them without losing my pension. Okay, so I'll have him assigned to, hell he can't be on the inside where he can browse through information."

"I'll take him with me Captain. He won't know the difference. Still security but in the hospital where I am and where we can chat." Sharice's confidence spoke loudly.

Worthy nodded his head and looked for Porter and Tyson to agree.

"Doesn't look suspicious." Tyson nodded, agreeing with Sharice.

The phone buzzed. Captain Worthy picked up the receiver shaking his head.

"Yes, what? No! That was not approved, have him wait. No, tell him to come back in an hour."

Worthy slammed down the phone. "That damn Sheers! They want to be with the governor. He's here and has asked for a detail to accompany him to the hospital. How did Sheers get near him? Well, Pulley, I guess you'll have to go. Knowles and Porter accompany Ms. Pully to the hospital. Governor Banks will be returning to my office, so you'll escort him back here."

Tina entered the room with a smile on her face. Everyone waited for her to speak.

"Well, we got another one. Simmons won't take the fall for anyone who signed his name or initials. He's a new dad. Had to congratulate him and as such he sees the need for his future without problems. Now wait Porter, before you ask, he didn't name anyone, but if pushed I'm sure he will."

"What did he say?"

"He said he's worked in the Cold Case Unit, but Marshall never assigned him to any of the logs. He doesn't have as much time as Boone or the others. I don't think he has ten years. Anyway, he's willing to clear his name. We can do a writing comparison if necessary. He signed paperwork for me."

"So, Knight, Sheers, Boone, and Simmons… what's the plan for keeping people from the hospital?"

Sharice's answer to Porter's question was cut off by Tina's question.

"What's going on with Knight?"

"I'll explain it to you. Captain you better get ready your governor is on his way." Tyson teased trying to ease the moment.

"Hell, he belongs to Tina and Sharice… Pull Justice…you know Pulley, Justlin… A real team."

Everyone smiled leaving the office. The tension on the elevator would be dissolved in the office. Montez and Miller were on the door and Tyson looked at them as he waited for the explanation.

"Desk Sergeant called for him. I thought they'd contact you or the captain."

Tyson left the pair staring at him as he crossed the rotunda to the records department. Marcie saw him coming her way.

"Where's your Sergeant?"

"In the office with Sheers and your guy Knight."

Tyson didn't wait to be announced. He opened the door to shocked faces.

"The next time you want to pull an officer from a post I've assigned them to see me first. It's a courtesy, something you wouldn't understand, especially since I'm a black detective. Believe me this shit is gonna end. Respect me and leave my unit alone.

Unless you want a problem. I don't pull your assholes from here don't bother mine. Are you re-assigning this rookie or are you giving him an initiation. Either way, I don't want him back, so find a place for him."

The sergeant picked up the phone as Tyson was leaving.

"Tell Mancy I said hello. Can't wait until he gets his promised position."

CHAPTER 68

"Who does that nig—" The sergeant stumbled over the word he wanted to describe Tyson. Knight sat between the two white men and felt the discomfort without saying a word. The sergeant nodded at Sheers and Knight as he received his next order.

"I don't know what he knows, man, I just don't know. He's on top of this though. I can send them to the hospital, but as Sheers said, how would they get to Marshall?"

There was silence as the voice on the other end of the call continued to bark orders.

"Yes, yes, we'll be sure to get them together tonight. No, the governor has not arrived yet. That's the other problem. There's too many eyes around today. Maybe…"

The sergeant hung up the phone and folded his hands under his chin. He stared at officers Sheers and Knight as they sat in silence.

"We've got to figure this out. It's not hard Sheers. What do you think?" He asked addressing Knight.

"Uh, sir. I'm not sure. I mean if we go to the hospital we'll be checked, and I'm sure they've tightened up things since Sheers was there. Today won't be the day for anything, not with the governor and his staff lurking around."

Knight found himself caught in a well woven web. Getting out of the situation wouldn't be easy, but there was no doubt, they set him up to fail. Sheers and Knight left the sergeant with his head in his hands. They walked together with eyes watching. Knight understood what Knowles tried to warn him about. He'd be their guinea pig. There was no reward in being a scapegoat for the department. As they passed Marcie, she nodded to him and shook her head. It was at that moment he knew no one would understand why.

"Hey, we've got to talk and well, you don't have an assignment so let's get some lunch."

"I'm not really hungry. We can go to the cafeteria and get a coffee or something, okay?"

Sheers looked at Knight with what Knight knew was a scowl. Sheers didn't want to be seen with him in the cafeteria. He turned into an empty office. Knight paused at the door, unsure of what would happen, he entered and closed the door.

"Look, they're on to you. We can't cover that, and we can't have that. So, there's something we need from you to protect you."

"It's not my fault. I did as you said. I spoke with Knowles and the others after I got the call from Chambers. I did as you said."

"Listen, shit is fucked now. We have to change things; they'll be watching you and your assignments. You have to agree to what I'm saying."

"I don't want to be a part of anything that will lead to jail time man. I ain't signing on to give way to my freedom."

"Do what we say, make no waves, and help us build, you'll be fine."

Knight looked at the officer sitting across from him. He didn't know Sheers or Chambers; he didn't know the depth of the undercover group called, the "untouchables." He wondered if he took Sheers to be honest, would he survive with the onlookers. The other officers who would know what he signed on to.

"And if I don't?"

"Let's not talk about the 'what ifs', I mean what else can you do? They, your kind, the officers on that Cold Case Unit, they won't accept you back. You'll find it hard to find a place to work and grow old. We want to build. We need a few of your kind, the Ricans, you know add other cultures. Show the community that we aren't the racists they claim we are. You know what I mean?"

"Yeah, I hear you. Man, I..."

"Look if you don't, we can't and won't protect you."

"Protect? What kind of protection?"

"Listen, any kind. Why worry about that when you have us to make sure you're good. On the job and off, we got you."

Knight knew he was in too deep. The room became warm, and he began shaking his head "no."

"Hey, are you okay? Man, calm down. I'll give you some time to think about it. We just want you to recruit a few, who like you, see the benefits of this. You come to work, receive an assignment, and report back. Not hard at all."

Knight didn't answer. His breathing became louder. Sheers tapped the table trying to get the distressed officer's attention. He grabbed his chest and passed out, falling to the floor.

Sheers called for officers and medical staff. As he dialed the phone for the sergeant, he checked Knight for a pulse. He reported what he considered to be an urgent situation to his superior who simply said," Handle it."

The EMT told him Knight would be evaluated and taken to the hospital. Unsure if the sergeant assigned anyone to go with the officer, Sheers got in the ambulance with him. He hoped it would help Knight with making his choice.

Montez and Miller watched the EMT's entry and exit. Montez dialed Marcie's line to get the information to relay to Tyson.

"Yeah, both of those assholes went with the EMT's. Knight on the stretcher and Sheers chasing the gurney."

"Thanks, my lady. Let me relay the information."

Tyson wasn't pleased with the information given, but he understood Sheers' attempt to pull in other ethnicities. There were those who would give their life to be a part of the group. It had nothing to do with loyalty to one's culture, it was about the money and power to be. It didn't matter that they would lose their dignity. He dialed Sharice's number to give her a heads up. Sheers being in the hospital warranted an alert.

"Knight passed out according to the relay received. Sheers is with him, but he may roam, so just calling to make you aware. The fox is in the hen house."

"You calling me a hen, Tyson? I run the farm, like most hens."

They both laughed and said their goodbyes.

CHAPTER 69

It was close to four. The rotunda was buzzing waiting for the governor and captain to make their way to the podium. Reporters with their cameramen made their way to the front of the crowd. It had been a day of questions and answers. Governor Banks explained his intentions as they made their way from Worthy's office.

"Dennis, we can't let the media, or the public get ahead of us with this murder. We've got to give them what we want them to know. They'll be questions about how far we've come with the case; do we have suspects; and what was Marshall's involvement. I've been dealing with this all day, that's part of the reason I'm so late. They want to know about this and community problems with your precinct. I'm assuming their concerns are a part of that damn report that Justlin is dealing with. Please tell me the reporter, her name slips me, and that lawyer can't make a connection to this report."

"I wish I could sir. We think it could be tied to Fulton's cases, Michaels' murder, the attempt on Marshall, and a group of officers we're investigating."

"The 'untouchables.' The name has been floating around for a few months now. In other precincts, they've squashed some of their activities. We've got a task before us. I don't know if this mess will be settled without it blowing up in our face."

The elevator doors opened to the waiting public. The two made their way to the podium as a few clapped causing others to join in. Sayers and Fulton stood in the middle of the crowd; the members of the Cold Case Unit watched from the office door. Marcie and other officers from her office came out to hear what the governor had to say as well. The rotunda was full, everyone had questions and hoped the Governor could give answers.

"Good afternoon, I know it's late, I've been talking throughout the community, and we've got some things that need to be addressed and cleared up. First let me tell you that I visited the hospital and the transport officers who were on the detail escorting Lt. Maurice Marshall are being discharged. Lt. Marshall is coming along well and still in the ICU unit. He's got a little more healing to do, but he's in good spirits and we're watching his progress closely. It's been a day. I've been informed by Captain Worthy that the investigation in both the transport of Lt. Marshall and the murders of Chief Walter Michaels and Officer Kevin Longo is ongoing. We can't answer all the questions that may arise as we're still collecting information and evidence.

My office receives many of your community complaints. We have personnel who are looking into those calls and forms, and we're handling them as quickly as possible. I understand that in this precinct's jurisdiction there have been several complaints relating to ongoing cases in our courts. We can't discuss or answer any questions regarding them. However, I will answer any general questions regarding your safety concerns."

The governor moved from the podium giving way to Captain Worthy. A few officers gave shouts of," Chief," as he took his position.

"No, no. Thank you, but no." Worthy shook his hand and silenced the shouts and cheers. "Well, you know if I'm standing here next to our governor, there's trouble or an award. We won't be getting or giving any awards."

The crowd laughed. Everyone loved Worthy; he was fair. It was his way of leadership that they admired and respected. There were those who understood him and worked his way without an argument or concern. He blocked as many as he could once it was revealed they were trouble. Trouble didn't follow him, nor did it cross his office doors. He didn't associate with many in rank. Tyson and Porter became his protégés and it was the reason trouble whispered in the background.

"Let's talk about these things the governor has put under a light. As we know, Lt. Marshall has survived an attempt on his life. We will take the necessary precautions to protect him as he heals. We are also pursuing leads to who made the attempt and why. We won't stop until we find them. The murders are, as was stated, under investigation. We won't divulge any information we've obtained. Now, your complaints about this precinct and the response to crime in the community. Please come to us before going to reporters, lawyers, and our political representatives. We can't look into anything that we don't know about. There are a few issues that we've been looking into for months. Issues I'm sure many of you may be able to help us with, however you've chosen to be silent, or go to others as I've stated. Good luck. I won't be chasing you for the information. If we can't solve the problem, it will be filed until we get more information. That's what the Cold Case Unit is for. Cases that we can't solve. That unit works to investigate those cases. They work in conjunction with the courts, forensics, lawyers and yes, the community. If you have information on any case that can help solve it, take the time to contact them. It keeps them working."

Worthy smiled and turned the podium over to the Press Secretary who would take questions. Hands went up quickly. A few wanted to know about the lack of patrol, recent arrests, and why information wasn't readily available about the murders. To Tyson's and Justlin's surprise, no one asked about Fulton's cases. Sayers raised her hand and Tyson nudged Justlin.

"There are cases that are awaiting appeal. Evidence based information has been questioned without answers. How are these cases being handled without the necessary information for appeals?"

The Press Secretary, unaware of why she'd ask such a question gave her an immediate answer.

"In court. If there is information that is missing, not reported, and all attempts to acquire that information have been made, then the recourse is to have the lawyer pursue it in court. Listen, everyone has to understand, our attempt to investigate, solve cases, and be sure we apprehend and prosecute criminals is not an overnight task."

"Years, sir years; without naming the cases, there may be more that haven't been thoroughly investigated. Just pushed through the system and the criminal, as you say, is guilty without a question regarding the missing pieces." The reporter's voice got louder as though she sought support from the crowd.

"Ms. Sayers, you, and I both know the system. So do the lawyers that file or don't file proper paperwork. If the ball is dropped, we don't want it to be us, or you. So, we report what we find, what we know, and how we've handled it. If there is a problem in the process, to correct it again I say, let the lawyers do their job. We don't dodge the responsibility to handle problems, but if we are not aware of them, well…"

"Sir, the community has no idea when their loved one is being railroaded by the system."

There was a slight buzz and shouts of," Let them go!" The secretary paused waiting for the crowd to settle down before giving his response.

"But Ms. Sayers, their lawyer, the ones they hire for court proceedings, bail, etc., they know. Getting their face on the front page promotes them, not the case. Putting it in the community as if they have no hand in it, that's criminal as well. As I stated lawyers, if you want to get results contact the appropriate offices here and file with the courts."

He turned his attention to another person in the crowd. Fulton shook his head and walked away leaving Sayers standing in disbelief. She wasn't unaware of the procedures, but she failed to ask Fulton had he followed the protocol. After hearing the Press Secretary, she wondered if she had been used for Fulton's benefit. She turned to see if the lawyer was in view. She wasn't sure she wanted to hear Tyson say," I told you so…" but she needed clarity. What exactly had Fulton filed or investigated before filing? As she walked toward the office, Tyson shook his head.

"Not without an appointment. Sorry, you and your… what is it? You both had ill intentions. You wanted that front page story, he wanted it too. So, what's the problem now? The story is a wash for you? Whatever your question, the conversation, you need an appointment, see Kai. She or Ms. White will tell you when. It's okay Samantha, we all fall for what we think is the next step. Fulton, just like everyone, has agenda. Hell, he's a lawyer."

"So, you're not going to hear me out." Sayers shifted her position, showing a non-professional attitude, but it was an effective move.

"What? If I can't answer it in one sentence, you'll have to make an appointment."

She took his hand and pulled him away from his glass office door. Justlin noticed them talking and then watched as he and Sayers moved from the door. Porter noticed Justlin's reaction and walked over to her.

"Now, now, do we have an issue with the reporter?"

"No, not at all. She'll learn that I don't chase, and I don't stand in between. If they have something going on it will raise a flag. I'm not the one. If she's looking for a confirmation or a reason, he'll give it to her."

The conversation outside the office stopped short of what Sayers wanted to find out.

"So, things have changed in your office."

"They had to since we're a part of Worthy's investigation. Nothing unusual. We move personnel all the time. It's not the first time and you know that. What exactly are you implying?"

"Let's not play games. She's a part of your team now? Suddenly, appointments only? What's up Damien? I thought we had a good relationship, I mean if she's your type, okay. You bringing it this close to your position is new for you. I guess you didn't learn your lesson with Ms. Wells."

"Wow, really. Ms. Sayers, I find this beneath you. If you wanted to date, have that closer relationship, I've been single for a minute. Appointments need to be set because I'm not always in the office, especially with this mess going on. I set the perimeter for this office and me. I don't want to be the one to say, see Porter or one of the others."

"Hmmm, you can say what you want. It's her and I know it's her. We'll see when she goes back to her primed position with the governor. I'll make that appointment and you be sure you're free. Just you."

"Aww c'mon you know you want someone to whisper with. I'll be sure Porter is aware of your availability."

"Stop it. I'm serious. It's like overnight. Well good luck my friend. She seems like another Melinda Wells."

Tyson watched as she walked away. Fulton was across the rotunda watching her actions. Damien wondered would the call for an appointment include the lawyer or would he make his own appointment. He was sure there was more to the lawyer who held on firmly to his courthouse polished decorum and his hidden touch of arrogance.

CHAPTER 70

"Banks is calling for a meeting before his departure. It will include you and Porter, Knowles, Justlin, and Pulley. Full reports, so if you've begun noting progress in any of the investigations, please have them with you. I'm sure Justlin will get a separate call."

"He'll probably call Pulley too. Captain, are we telling him about Marshall's confession and what he knows?"

"Damien, considering the attempt on his life and Sheers trying to visit him, I don't see how we can hide it. We have to have a damn good reason to move him. Pully wants him to be transported tonight. Another hospital or at a staffed safe house is best. We'll get Marshall to sign a document stating his actions."

"Okay, that should be enough. What time are we meeting?"

"Give them enough time to clear the Rotunda and settle. I'll have Sgt. Smith place an order for food, nothing big, to hold us over. None of us have had a chance to sit and eat today, at least I haven't. The governor is speaking with a few office heads. I'm assuming a discussion about my position and who will fill Michaels' position. The sergeant in Michaels' office has been reassigned temporarily, so I'm assuming he'll mention how we will be handling things through my office until after the appointment."

"Mancy is the man they want, is Banks aware of their intentions."

"Damien, to be honest, I can't tell what his thoughts are. He mentioned the group earlier stating they had problems with them in other precincts. Didn't state the problems or how they were handled. No names, no beware, nothing. What does that tell you? It tells me he may be involved, or he just doesn't know how to handle it."

"Okay, so let the fun begin. Now that the press secretary opened our doors widely to the public, I'll be requesting two officers."

"Damien, that list was filled with officers with less than ten years, I'm sure. Most of the old heads don't want to work on that unit."

"Or with me. Captain, let the desk sergeant choose. He's a part of their group, I'm sure of it. He'll send me those he thinks will fail."

"What's his name? I'm compiling a list hoping we can investigate them and get rid of them in the same breath."

"Braize, Breeze, I think, or Braizer. I'll find out and let you know." Damien paused in thought.

The call ended as Kai knocked on Tyson's office door. "Hey, if you don't need anything, Ms. White and I are done. Montez and the others are still here."

"Okay, how have you been since, well the staff has been scattered?"

"Good, we're good. Montez and Miller have a system and we've all followed it. It's working. Oh, your wife called. She said she'd be waiting for your call back. You know how she goes off, well, she did a bit of that too."

"Thanks, and I apologize. You would think it's been long enough for her to stop the antics.

Kai left the office with Ms. White in tow. The ladies had worked until six for the last few nights. It wasn't often, but when asked they would agree knowing the unit needed them. Damien sat back in his chair and closed his eyes. He could only imagine how tired everyone was. Stands walked in and waited for Damien to open his eyes.

"Yes sir. What can I do for you? I closed my eyes for two minutes and Kai, now you… never mind. What's up?" Stands shook his head knowing Tyson was teasing away the tension.

"Security at the house or what?" You said Knowles and Porter will be with you."

"You and Wilson, go check things out and give me a call, if everything looks good, you can leave."

"Okay, be careful. You know the governor wants this all to be pushed under the rug. Quick and easy ain't gonna handle what we're facing Damien."

"You're right. This is deep and it keeps getting deeper. I'll take your advice, go tell Porter to keep his mouth shut. I'm more worried about what he'll say than my reaction."

"Good, as long as you know. I'll call you from the house."

Damien waited for the others before proceeding to the captain's office. He stood in the hall until everyone accept Sharice were ready with their reports.

"Well, how long will this be? I think I'll put more hours on the overtime report."

"Porter, you say that in the presence of the woman who reviews reports?"

Porter turned to address Justlin directly. Damien shook his head and pressed the button for the elevator.

"I'll be adding to the report. Hell, this is more than enough work to keep the overtime coming."

Tina rolled her eyes and sighed. It was five o'clock. She'd be on her way home by now if she was working at the Statehouse. She enjoyed the work but, the hours were wearing on her. She nudged Knowles and smiled.

"You okay. Getting use to these two yet?"

"They remind me of my uncles. Not the captain, the younger ones."

"Oh, wait until we tell him that." Porter teased. "I understand though, he is an old man."

They laughed as they exited the elevator. The sight silenced them immediately. There were special operations personnel standing around. Those who were a part of Worthy's team were mingling and talking about their time in the military. It seemed to be a reunion of sorts. All nodded and smiled, an officer opened the office door for Tyson and his team. Sgt. Smith greeted them and asked if they would take a seat. The captain and the governor were in the office talking.

After what seemed like too long of a wait, they were invited to join the two in the office. They sat at the conference table without knowing what they would be asked or why. They followed protocol. Investigation reports as well as interviews and notes that had not been compiled were in front of Tyson and Justlin. Porter and Knowles sat with their hands folded. Tyson decided to start conveying where they were in it all once the captain revealed the necessity for the meeting.

"Governor Banks, we can't get ahead of the press, the community, or these internal thugs without you being aware of what we're facing. However, I say this with respect, if we find that you or anyone else in your office is involved, we will cut off all communications and bring in the FBI." Worthy pushed the paperwork to the middle of the table.

"So serious, Worthy. I can assure you that I have no connection or involvement with the 'untouchables' or anyone who would attempt an operation to kill a lieutenant, or the mess Justlin has uncovered. This is a lot deeper than I thought. Are you the only ones who have this information?"

The office door opened, and Sharice smiled and tiptoed to the empty seat between Porter and Knowles.

"Yes, I think we should start from the small findings that led to where we are today. Governor, I really believe that the report I was sent to investigate ignited the reasons for the murders and the attempt on Lieutenant Marshall's life."

Tina opened her folder and handed everyone the report. There were colored markings indicating problems she initially thought were minor. Once the report revealed what she referred to as a 'cover up', she stated she realized the problems were related to Fulton's cases. She gave the details explaining how the problems began to escalate.

"Fulton showed up asking questions. He stated that the missing information that I was seeking was a part of what he needed to file his appeals. Signatures, reports from the courts, evidence and who knows what else he was seeking were missing, or changed since the cases were heard in court. Someone took the information from the files. Signatures were falsified, crossed out and there are some that have been erased. This was all done prior to Detective Tyson being assigned to the unit. His filings and final report was what his team found and reported as required."

"It was brought to Michaels' attention, and he passed it off to me. As you know, Tina has been digging for reasons anyone would take a simple report and make it major. Fulton's questions raised our curiosity and Tina requested to interview the officers and others involved. The last thing we needed is that damn Fulton and Sayers looking to tag the precinct in what had been buried." After making his point, the captain closed the folder he held.

"Okay so where is the connection and why?" The governor was tired and annoyed. His questions hadn't been answered and it was getting late. "Can we agree that we've been going in circles?"

"It's more than that governor. We believe there's a connection between the 'untouchables' and the missing information." The captain gave his conclusion, trying not to show his annoyance.

A knock on the door brought a welcomed relief to the group. Worthy ordered salad, chicken, tea and coffee, with dessert. They took a break from the conversation and made filling plates. Updates and conversations about their personal lives brought laughter and a relaxed atmosphere. Thirty minutes passed before they returned to the conference table.

"So Worthy, Michaels tells you he was involved with these… never mind. He says what his plans were and?"

"Basically, that was it. He was done with whatever they wanted and maybe they wanted him to be involved in what they were doing in the city. I'm saying that because he wanted me to deal with the media, and he would deal with assignments and the officers. I agreed not really understanding what he wanted. I do know he didn't want me to be a part of it."

"Okay, so if I'm understanding that much, he wanted out and it could have been he knew their plans. They killed him because he knew. Who is this kid, Longo, the shooter?"

"One of the shooters." Porter stated. "He was shot as well." He paused and looked at Worthy, who shook his head no.

"Oh yes, I read that in the report. So, he was an 'untouchable' and following his assignment got him killed," the governor said while fingering through the notes and reports.

"Longo was fairly new; I mean he didn't have the time in you'd expect for that kind of dedication."

"Porter, what do you mean? I've found that there's a few that have less time than him."

"Sharice are you serious? They don't even know their regular jobs and they've locked in promotions and benefits with these assholes?" Porter continued with his rant. "They should all be shot. Anyway, he entered the home and there was no evidence of him breaking in. So, I'm assuming, and the evidence points in that direction, the chief let him in, or the deck door was open. Once he entered, they began a conversation. We didn't find any evidence of a struggle as the chief was seated on his couch. Longo was lying on the floor, face down. After finding a shot to the back of his head, we sought other evidence."

The meeting continued with the governor asking questions and shaking his head slowly as he realized the investigation into the "untouchables" involvement would be a tedious process. Porter began giving the details of Lieutenant Marshall's visit after the murder. The governor sighed and tried to give himself a moment of clarity.

"Damn, does this thing have an end? I sent you into a shit storm, huh, Justice?"

"Yes, I'll say it. That's exactly what it is. Somehow, our investigation is intimidating them and their operation." Justlin stated and looked at Sharice.

"Nah, they can't be intimidated, or so they think. You and Sharice did this, yep first you, then Sharice," teased Porter.

Sharice gave him a friendly punch and a slow shake of her head. The governor could only laugh, and everyone let their laughter calm their nerves. No one knew what the next move would be.

"Okay, so I think I can tie the other loose ends into this tangled mess. After what Sharice has told me, we'll definitely need to move the lieutenant. So, set up the arrangement. Don't use the normal spot or hospital. Call central location and get them to give you a spot. Not in Philadelphia no matter what they say."

"The transport officers have been discharged. I don't know if they need coverage." Sharice wanted it understood that they could be in danger.

"What do you think Worthy?" The governor passed on answering the question. "Young man you've been quiet. Is this the nephew?" He questioned looking at Knowles.

"I think we should cover them for a few days, Sharice. Yes, that's him, sir."

"So, they tell me you've stumbled upon some more information to link to those scumbags."

"Sir, yes sir. I'm only going on speculation and being observant, sir."

"Speculation, hmmm. So, with what you've been observing, what conclusions have you reached?"

"They're here, but they're everywhere. It's going to take a task force and then how long becomes the question. They're looking to bring in other cultures and continue to grow. It affects the community and the system."

The governor took notes as the meeting continued with everyone's input. It was close to seven when the meeting concluded. The governor expressed his gratitude for each of them. He promised to relay information as he received it. He reassured them that their precinct was not the only one dealing with the problematic group. He assured Worthy that any officers sent from his office would be from the special operations team. He agreed with the captain; they couldn't trust their own without being able to thoroughly check their connections.

CHAPTER 71

Tyson and the others retreated to their cars after saying goodnight. Each had their own thoughts and understanding of what would happen next. There was no doubt that changing their approach to each situation would send a message to everyone who was involved or concerned. Justlin rode in silence wondering why seeing Tyson with Sayers was still bothering her.

"I noticed Fulton and Sayers separated after Sayers questioned the Press Secretary. Why would she go against him like that knowing you said you'd work with her and Fulton?"

"I don't know. Anxious to get the story or…" Tyson didn't complete his thought and Justlin knew what he was about to say.

"Or they planned it. Once they knew the governor would be there, they wanted him to know they had information that would bring unwanted attention to the precinct. Fulton would be granted whatever he wanted pertaining to each case. The "untouchables" wouldn't want to be in the light, and the governor would want that same light dimmed. So, revealing what they had is an advantage to him and a story for her."

"That's the way I took it. Tina, Sayers is no dummy. She wanted to meet with me to discuss the reason. I told her to make an appointment. Let's see if she, or the both of them, will do that."

"Oh, I'm sure she'll make the appointment. The reason may be different for her. She obviously thinks you have an obligation to assisting her in what she does. Why is that? Have you expressed you'd be committed to her?"

"What? No, why would I be committed to her?"

"Just the way she looked at me and then you. She knows Damien that there's something between us and it's changed since I've been here. Just like your team, they know you, so does she. Your reaction at the meeting was different. You didn't give her the same reaction as in the past. Maybe her intentions were to have a deeper relationship with you."

"Wow. No, I think I would have known that. No, I don't think she has those type of feelings for me. I certainly don't have feelings for her. Listen, let's just see what their plan may be. I want you to know that I have no intentions of pursuing Samantha Sayers."

The ride to Justlin's home gave way to the music played. The thoughts and conversations were personalized, yet they agreed not to press the issue. They arrived at Justlin's home where Stands and Wilson were walking to the car.

"Hey, I thought the two of you would be gone," Tyson shouted from the driveway as they approached.

"There were a couple of slow drive-bys. I thought Boone was one of the drivers and the other Knight. I could be wrong, but we decided to stand by."

"No one seen, other than the vehicles?" Tina asked. She walked to the opposite side of the walkway.

"No, no one on or near your property. We were doing another check of the perimeter. Do you want us to remain on duty?"

"No, that damn Porter is already talking about the overtime report." Tyson replied shaking his head slowly. Stands and Wilson found Porter's thought to be amusing.

"Tina, they're leaving. Do you want them for anything else, questions, or anything?"

"Uh, no thanks. I thought Boone and his boys may have tried to show up. Damn fools, what would his reason be for being here when he didn't want to talk at all."

"Listen, they're getting desperate. If you want us to stay, I mean, the last time he drove by was about an hour or more. He may come back since there was no car in the driveway." Stands stood waiting as Tina paused in thought.

"You've got a point but, Tyson is here. We'll deal with it, thanks."

"Alright, see you in the morning boss, you too ma'am."

Tyson and Justlin shook their heads at Stands' humor. "Goodnight, man. Thanks, Wilson."

The couple waited until the car pulled off before they entered the home.

"Damien." Tina stopped in the living room.

"I got you. If he shows up, we'll invite his ass in."

"What? No, you won't." Tina walked into her bedroom. She completed her thought in a louder voice as Damien followed her. "Why would I want him in my home? I keep work and relationships separate!"

"Tina, I was teasing. I got you." Damien took a deep breath as he walked out of the Master Bedroom to the Guest Bedroom.

"What are you doing?" Tina yelled from her bedroom.

"I'm going to take a shower and ready myself."

"Damien, what the hell does that mean?" She walked quickly to the bedroom door.

"You'll be worried all night that someone may return. I got you. After my shower, I'll be ready for whatever we have to deal with."

"So, you're not going to bed?"

"Eventually. Let me take a shower, please?"

Tina decided to make tea, leaving him sitting on the bed. She changed her mind and poured a glass of wine. Taking a seat on her couch she remembered Sharice and Marcie wanting her to call. She picked up her phone and dialed the numbers to connect them.

"It's been a day. I wish that was all I had to say but before I get into the better topic, let me just say, I ain't down for this."

"What's going on?" questioned Sharice and Marcie

"Boone, that damn fool showed up here. Stands and Wilson saw him take the slow drive past the house. So, they're getting information that shouldn't be disclosed?"

"Tina, you need to check the office. They shouldn't have access to your personal information. Someone in-house had to give it to him. How else would he know where you lived?" Sharice waited for a response.

"No, that's not how he did it. He checked the cars. Stands and Wilson had a car from the precinct, it's easy to trace where they are. He checked they're assignment. I bet that's how he got the address. I don't know if he even knew it was your house." Marcie firmly stated.

"Damn, I wonder if Damien thought about that. Stands and Wilson didn't mention it when we got here."

"Oh yeah, how is the personal security going? I want my own security. Can it be a lawyer? I'll settle for either."

"Marcie you better stick with the officers. That damn lawyer may have his own agenda. His reasons aren't in line with benefitting anyone but himself or that damn reporter."

"Wow, so you came home to the mess you left in the meeting. Wait what's up with Ms. Sayers. I thought she was a bit much at the press conference. She's always seeking information. Didn't she come to the Unit later?"

"She did and it's all a part of this damn tangled web."

"Okay, so you came home to him, your mystery man?"

"Wait, Marcie I think we already know the mystery man. It's Tyson right. So just fill us in on the first night."

"Sharice, it can't be Tyson, or can it? What did I miss? Spill it, Tina."

Tina lowered her voice to a whisper. "He's out of the shower. We're going to have to have that lunch or dinner date. I don't want him to hear me."

"No, don't pump up his ego." Marcie answered in agreement.

"Well, if you're happy, that's all that matters. What is he going to do about Boone?"

"Sharice, I'm not going to worry about it. He said," I got you."

"And I do." Damien stated as he entered the room. "Go and relax with your friends. I'm good now."

"Oh, I guess…"

"Girl, we're hanging up. Get relaxed with a glass of wine and him. Marcie say goodnight."

Sharice and Marcie said their goodnight. Tina smiled at Damien wondering what the night would hold.

CHAPTER 72

Samantha sat waiting for Sergeant Sanders. The two agreed on a quaint restaurant on the highway leading into town. Crossing the bridge to its entrance, Samatha thought of the tranquility of the water. It was a beautiful night. Her thoughts drifted; she'd love to take time off. She dared not; she continued to hope the story would break before Fulton's appeal came through. If not, she'd be competing with the other journalist for interviews within the police precinct. Parking her car, she paused to take a moment to breathe. The ladies agreed to meet at six. She had fifteen minutes to calm herself after leaving the press conference.

There were a few who applauded her questions, but there were others who thought she pushed too hard. Her fans or those who chose to follow her were often conflicted. It was obvious that she wanted the Press Secretary to admit guilt or at least an oversight regarding the missing information. Fulton warned her, he told her the technique she chose should be her own, but he knew the audience, as well as the offices that backed the behavior of the officers. Although someone, or some group was penetrating the community, their aim was to change the culture of the precinct. They needed as much help within the department as they did from the community. Reports of misconduct was the key.

Fulton promised the three cases were strong cases with evidence of police misconduct. He needed the Foster case to lead the way. The lawyer was known to win against the system. He was called in after the first trials were heard with another lawyer as lead. Fulton's encounters with the precinct in past cases led him to believe there was a problem within the precinct. He promised he would disclose all the information that he found and why he sought to fight those in 'blue' once his appeals were filed and trial dates were set.

There was a tap on her window. Startled she opened her eyes to the sergeant's smile. She got out of the car, a bit embarrassed, but refreshed she had fifteen minutes of free time. They greeted each other and walked to the front door of the restaurant in silence. Once seated, they looked over the menus.

"So many good meals to choose from. How did you find this place? The scenery is breathtaking."

"The chief and eventually the captain would come here. The captain asks for reservations here for his family often. I've known and worked for Michaels and Worthy for more than ten years. My first assignment was with Worthy. He'd come here and not be disturbed by other patrons. It was perfect, they could enjoy dinner without police business interfering. Michaels didn't have many reasons to eat out. He seemed to enjoy 'the boys' as he called them. Hanging out, going to sports events, having them at his home for barbeque outings, that was his thing. So, this restaurant was a choice when you said out of the way."

"It certainly is impressive," replied Samantha. "The ambiance is perfect for a relaxed dinner. I know you can appreciate not looking over your shoulder when you go out."

"Don't have that problem. I guess I'm not in the public eye. You, being a reporter, the lawyer Mr. Fulton, the chief, and sometimes the captain, you guys worry about that because you're in front of the community all the time."

The waiter came and took their order for drinks and dinner. "I can't wait to taste their fish platter. Tell me, what is your first name? I don't want to address you by sergeant."

"Oh, I'm sorry. You, being a reporter and all, I assumed… no mind. It's Tanya, Tanya Sanders."

"So, tell me what you wanted known. I mean to me and Mr. Fulton. He'll let me know if I should report it or not. I don't want to ruin his cases."

"Well, I don't know if you've been told but Chief Michaels had close ties to many who are a part of that group, the 'untouchables.' Those would be the people he hung out with and why Worthy didn't deal with him much off duty. That group is seeking to destroy the reputation of the precinct. A lot of our special units failed because they convinced officers they could give them more. Payments, positions, the blind eye to bad behavior, and bad arrests were promised and fulfilled. Many were busting store owners, drivers, landlords, and of course drug runners. They'd collect money from them in exchange for police coverage or dismissal from minor offenses.

It's begun to be too much, you know. It started with small complaints from those who weren't a part of the group. Their departments were feeling the heat from the community. So, Michaels would switch personnel around, you know, assignments were changed, and more complaints came to the office. Michaels became tired of playing both sides. I could tell because he began refusing calls. He'd leave the office knowing meetings with a few of them would be rescheduled per their constant request. The outings at the restaurants and his home stopped. He declined to participate anywhere he thought they would be."

"Why, how, wait. I don't really know where to start with this. Chief Michaels was a part of the group or just knew of the group. There's a big difference, if you know what I mean."

"I do." She adjusted herself in her seat. "Samantha, he was in deeper than he wanted to be. It's not just officers. It's department heads, those in rank and out, as well as civilians. I just want to be able to work and get my check. Some days I was scared they would storm our office with their demands. Promote this one, change an assignment, pay a bail, meet after hours. It all seemed too much, too much to be killed over unless they knew he wanted to be separated from them. Chief Michaels wanted out."

"So, do you know who, any of them?"

"No and if I did, I wouldn't say. This information I'm giving you is enough for an investigation from the outside. I don't trust many, so if I don't say anything to anyone in blue, hey I'm just saying."

"Understood, I guess, but I can't do anything other than write the story. I'm not sure that would change much."

"It would help get eyes on Fulton's cases. I mean, he's complaining that things aren't right from start to finish. You can tell him and that should help the matter."

"Yeah, you're right. The Chief? Damn, up the ranks and protect the assholes. Do you think it goes further?"

The sergeant gave her a look that answered her question.

"How far? I mean Marshall was almost killed."

"That ass is one of them too."

Samantha remembered her conversation with the sergeant on the way home. Talking to Fulton would be first. The two of them would need to apologize and tell Tyson what they were after. They were on the same team.

CHAPTER 73

The morning sun peeked through Tina's room window. She turned in her bed and smiled. The other side of the bed was empty, but she could smell the food, puzzled, she thought she smelled coffee. She heard Damien's voice and realized he was on the phone. Her phone buzzed, an alarm she hated, she had to change the tone. Blake set it for a Will Downing tune, and she deleted it when she told herself Blake wasn't her type. Now the simplistic buzz was annoying, but not as annoying as dealing with "fake Blake." It was the nickname that Marcie gave him. Tina laughed whenever she called him that, but it was true, he was a fake.

Tina couldn't say why, or how she fell for his temporary actions, or false promises. He became more annoying shortly after she was assigned to the Moorestown area. Blake seemed to be jealous whenever she stayed home or spoke about her assignments. Once he found out she'd be dealing with an investigation of the precinct where she once worked, he started calling whenever she wasn't in the main office. If he came to visit it was an interrogation before his so-called romantic visit. Always with flowers and dinner on Friday, movies or an outing on Saturday, and the argument he'd start on Sunday, then his departure. As the relationship was coming to an end, Tina decided to have the departure speech and reasoning prepared on that last Friday.

Her phone buzzed again, and she tapped it to stop the alarm. Her phone rang and she frowned at the time that read 6:45 a.m." Hello?" she answered, sitting up to have what should have been an after eight o'clock conversation.

"Hey, I was wondering if you were reporting to the office next week. I mean this week is over and we don't have your weekly report from last week and now…"

"Phillip, I know you didn't call me about a report this early in the morning. You know me. Why would you call me? I just saw Banks yesterday; he didn't mention my report. That's who gets it!!" She sighed deeply to emphasize her agitation.

"Banks doesn't get it until it's reviewed."

"Reviewed by who? This is not a regular report Philip. Who has been requesting it?"

"Blake, he said he needed to see exactly what work you were doing with the precinct."

"Did he say why? That wasn't ordered by the governor, was it?"

"Don't know. He didn't start asking for it until this week."

"Okay, I'll check with Banks. Seems weird. Blake doesn't work with my projects."

"He wanted paperwork from Sharice too. She said the same thing."

"What? Never mind. I'll call Sharice. Hold Blake at bay. We'll get back to you."

Tina put the phone down, slipped into her robe and slippers. She made her way into the kitchen. Damien turned from refrigerator and smiled. When she didn't return his smile, he paused before moving to the island.

"What's up?"

"That damn Blake. He's requesting my report for this week. He's not my boss nor does he work… never mind. Good morning, I guess."

"Yes, good morning. Your breakfast is ready and as requested I made tea for you. The coffee is for me. We'll stop at your favorite spot for your coffee, it you'd like. It's Friday, it will be a good day. I declare it."

"Okay, so you're in a good mood. What's on the agenda if I may ask?"

"Tina, I don't know to be truthful. Everything seems to lead to a dead end. We can't tip off the 'untouchables' by asking too many questions, you know? If we follow the leads we have, the questions are inevitable. I was hoping Sharice would get Marshall moved and we'd have one solid witness for Fulton."

"They didn't move him, why?"

"Something about his stability. The doctors promised he'd be ready to move early this morning. I'm still waiting for the call that the move is complete."

"I've got to call Sharice. I'll find out."

After breakfast, phones rang call after call. Damien first, then Tina. As they packed their satchels with paperwork, they yelled between the bedrooms about the calls.

"The move is complete, no problems. What did Sharice tell you about Blake?"

"She didn't know what I was talking about. Blake called her, but it wasn't about the reports."

"You okay?"

"No, he's got some damn nerve. He's checking on me. What I'm doing and of course, he wants to know why I accepted the assignment. Hell, it wasn't like I could tell the governor no. It's his insecurity and he wants Sharice to calm his nervous energy."

The two met in the living room. Damien reached for her to walk closer to him. As they met in the middle of the room, they kissed. Tina backed away smiling. She was glad he didn't ask any questions. They gathered their things and walked to the front door. Tina opened the door as Officer Boone was walking up the stairs. Shocked Tina slammed the door.

"What's wrong?"

"It's Boone. He's at the door. Where's the detail?"

"I had to cut the hours. I'm here so it's okay. Calm down, I'll answer the door."

Damien waited until Tina took a seat on the couch. He was sure Boone saw her and he was waiting patiently for the door to re-open. Damien opened the door to find the officer sitting on the porch in one of the wicker chairs.

"Morning Sir, I hope I didn't startle Ms. Justlin. I wanted to talk with her without… well you should know them, they're watching. You probably had that figured out. Talking somewhere they wouldn't expect is why I'm here. Can you ask her if she'd talk to me here or a place of her choice, where we won't be seen or watched?"

Damien held up his finger and Boone returned to the chair where he was found. While dialing Stands on his phone Damien walked into the living room. Tina was sitting patiently and stood when he held the same finger up for her.

"Stands, man I need you and Wilson here. Now. Don't go to the office come to Tina's house. Boone is here and I don't know what he'll be telling us."

"Shit, he's that bold? Got some balls, really?"

"Man, I don't know about that, but I do know he's here and understands they may be watching his moves."

"Why, ain't he one of them?"

"He had an interview with Tina. He didn't talk then but wants to talk now."

"Okay, on our way."

Damien put the phone in his pocket. He picked up his bag and took out his shoulder holster with his gun and put it on.

"What the hell is going on Damien?" Tina stood looking from him to the door.

"He wants to talk with you. Tina he may be what can break this case."

"So why didn't he just call and meet me or us somewhere else? Why at my home Damien?"

"Look, we'll leave here and talk somewhere else. But he's here let's go."

The two walked out on the porch. Boone was not there. Damien looked at the car parked down the street.

"Maybe that's him. He didn't want to bring attention to the meeting. Stay here."

Tyson walked around the house and walked to the parked car on the corner of the street. As he predicted Boone was in the car on the phone. He rolled the window down and put the phone on speaker.

"Where are you? I thought you would meet us early?"

"Had to make a run for my wife. Something her and her mother needed. Yeah, even after birth, they still need stuff. I'll be in after I pick up what's needed and drop it off."

The voice on the other end replied, and Tyson knew it was Sheers.

"You better be here in the next two hours. That's all I'm giving you, two hours, or questions will be asked and not by me. You know how they are. Sergeant Braize is the desk sergeant today; he's waiting for us."

Boone hung up the phone and turned toward Tyson. "It's better if you follow me."

Appalachian Park wasn't far. Tyson and Justlin followed Boone and parked not far from the entry. Tyson sent a text of the location to Stands, Wilson and Porter. Stands responded and told Porter he and Wilson would be there in fifteen minutes.

Boone was sure to park further into the park where his car wouldn't be seen. The three got out of the cars and approached each other on a path leading from the entrance. There were various trail signs for hikers and a sheltered picnic table where the three decided they would sit.

"Good morning Ms. Justlin. I guess Detective Tyson explained my concerns and reason for meeting you outside of the offices." Boone paused waiting for Justlin to respond. She remained silent and he continued. "You both already have information regarding the 'untouchables' and what they've been involved in. I decided along with the Chief and Lieutenant Marshall, I would get out. I didn't know how or when, but I knew I would be separating myself from them. As I explained to Simmons, this shit is short-lived. You get what you need for the moment, but each thing you think is a step up, you pay for it. He explained his problem, his wife, a new home, and family, it is complicated for him. It's been complicated for me, so I understand. After talking with the chief and the lieutenant, they warned me. I've been dodging Sheers and the others since the murders. Sergeant Braize is with us, as is Mancy we lost Marshall, they won't accept him back even if he wanted to continue. Someone will be promoted without cause as his replacement. That will be done by Mancy. They usually promote within and recruit to fill in, although I could be wrong. Mancy doesn't know many in line for lieutenant he can trust, so he might bring someone in."

"So, who is above the chief that's a part of this operation."

"I don't know. Sheers does all the inside work. I make sure orders, or the jobs are completed as assigned."

Justlin was still quiet. Tyson waited for her to interject with a question. When she didn't, he continued.

"So, you sent Longo to the house."

"Yes sir, as ordered to do so. I didn't know he went there to kill the chief. He was to talk with him. They, Sheers and others, visited the chief in his home often, as a group and individually. I never went there. I'd go on the outings but never in his home."

"We've got evidence that says that's a lie."

"Tyson, I'd like to see that man, because I swear to you, as I'm sitting here—"

A shot was heard, and Boone slumped over. More gunfire was heard near the entrance of the path. Tyson grabbed Justlin and ran to the car for cover. Once they reached the car Tyson instructed her to get in the car and lay across the back seat. He then returned to the path walking carefully. The gunfire from the main road ceased. He could see Stands at the entrance of the park.

"What the hell? You invite us to a shootout?" Stands shook Tyson's hand and pointed to the officer lying in the road. An unmarked vehicle sat in the road.

"Who is he?"

"Some new joker; his uniform still smells new."

"Okay, you or Wilson call it in. Solid reports from both of you. Who shot him?"

"C'mon Damien, you know damn well she did. I saw him but she had the better shot. Why were you guys here?"

"Boone thought this would be better than Justlin's home. He wanted out of the group. Do we know this guy's name? He followed Boone here. The same way they tracked the Marshall's transport. He knew he was in danger."

"Knew? Where is he?" Wilson questioned Damien as she approached the two looking down the road.

"Listen, can you walk to my car. Justlin is in the car. Stay with her. Boone is just past the car, but I'm certain with a shot to the head, he's dead." Tyson turned to Stands. "As I said Boone is dead. Head shot, I'm assuming from your boy here."

"Yeah, he used a scope, so I'm sure it was his shot. There's got to be another officer. Although I can't confirm it. I saw personal items in the passenger seat of the car. I locked the car, here's the keys. So, if he comes back to the car, he can't get in." Wilson smiled, pleased with her work.

"He's in the same shape as Boone and this puppet. We'll be here when the ambulance and other units arrive. So that's three dead before nine. Good work, detective, you saved our lives…"

"Stands, really. Call this mess in. You and Wilson wait for it to be cleaned up. Don't tell the responding unit we were here. You rolled up on a meeting if questioned by anyone other than…"

"I know. I got you." Stands smiled. The two shook hands.

"Thanks, man."

CHAPTER 74

Tyson walked pass his car to check on Boone's slumped body. Boone had been sitting opposite Tyson and Justlin. The thought of the shot hitting Justlin brought on unexpected emotions. A tear fell from his eyes. He couldn't explain it, but he didn't want to think about the reality. The "untouchables" were dangerous and uncaring of who or what it would take to accomplish their goals. Tyson checked for a pulse knowing Boone was dead after the bullet pierced his head. He was careful not to move or turn the body. Forensics and the team would need to trace where the shot came from. Wilson was sure she shot the shooter but there were other bullets aiming in their direction. Tyson felt there were more than two shooters, definitely more, than one. As he approached his car Wilson got out of the car on the driver's side. Justlin was sitting upright in the passenger's seat.

"Did he say anything that would help?" Wilson turned her body to cover the driver side window.

"Nothing we didn't know. He did confirm that desk sergeant, Braize and Mancy are a part of their operation. He didn't know who covered them from the top. It's a lead, I mean we knew about Mancy."

"Braize, wasn't he a transfer?" Wilson asked and turned to the tapping on the window.

Justlin opened the window and gave her phone to Wilson. The information on the phone answered Wilson's question. Braize was a transfer and had only been in the Moorestown Precinct three years.

"Can we find out who approved his transfer and if there was an underlying reason? According to Boone there was always a reason to move them around."

Tyson was surprised. Justlin didn't seem upset or disturbed after being close to being shot. He wondered if she understood, she could have been the target.

"Okay, Stands has the orders for you guys. We'll check out Braize and any other leads once we get back. I'll check with Worthy about the possibilities of others. I'll send Knowles and Miller to stay with the forensic team. If you need more coverage or have a problem…"

"We got you."

Tyson smiled and got in the car. He looked over to Justlin for a comment.

"Do they ever say they have a problem?"

"Who? What do you mean?"

"I got you seems to be the unit's signature line." Justlin smiled and shook her head. "I guess it's just something between you and your team."

"Never thought about it. We've been saying it so long, it's just understood. Whatever needs to be done, they'll handle it and report it later. If there's a problem along the way, they'll call. It works. I can move onto the next issue knowing they've got me."

"I wish. Our office is… well it's the governor's place, so everyone walks on their toes."

Justlin's response was interrupted by her phone ringing. Tyson turned the car to exit the park. He waved at Stands and Wilson as he exited the path.

"What? How do you know that?" Justlin looked at Tyson and mouthed "Blake." She pressed the speaker.

"There was a relay coming from that precinct and I tuned in."

"Why? Did it have my name on it or about it? Blake first you bother Phillip about reports and pretend you want Sharice's as well. Now you're tracking relay calls from the Moorestown Precinct. Why?"

"Can't I be worried about you? Listen, you're in a bad spot. You and I both know there's a group within that precinct that doesn't want the dirt that's there, uncovered."

"Oh, what dirt do you know about? Maybe you can answer a few questions regarding the report you want to review. Listen, I don't need any help with this investigation. I definitely don't need you tracking my whereabouts or my moves."

"I disagree. You shouldn't be riding with a detective into situations that involve this group. Stay out of it Justlin. They obviously think you're tied into Tyson's unit. They're out to take him down and you as well, if necessary."

"Blake, why does that sound like a threat?"

"It's just a warning baby."

"I'm warning you and them, stay the fuck away from me and my home. Any information you have, I'm going to let Banks know you'll be reporting to him."

"I'm not a part of any investigation."

"Well then keep your fake ass in your office and do what you're assigned to do. I don't need you tracking me."

"So, let me ask you one last question."

Tina sighed. "What is it?"

"Does he ever go home?"

Before she could render her answer, the phone disconnected.

"Tina, he's got ties with them or…"

"He's one of them. I wondered about him for months, you know, the closer he got. Damien, I've got to wonder about Banks. Could he be one of the higher-ups we're trying to find?"

"Yeah, and now we need to talk with Fulton. I'm sure he can tell us who he thinks may be in the courts, or their offices to help move records, files, and evidence."

"Did they follow Marshall again? I wonder if Sharice…never mind I'll call her."

Tyson nodded in agreement. Justlin began texting her questions and responses to Sharice. There was no reason for Tyson to ask how she felt. Tina Justlin looked and spoke as though she hadn't left her position as Lieutenant. He smiled, enjoying the lack of nagging, and complaining he would have got from any other woman he was intimate with. He didn't often compare his relationships, but if he and Justlin could avoid the gossip, they could make it.

Justlin put her phone down. "Sharice said she put someone on Blake this morning. After his call, and no call from me this morning, she thought his questions sounded suspicious. He asked about Marshall and where his transfer was, of course he wanted to know why it was done outside of our department. It caused her to wonder. She contacted Banks and he didn't want to know where the transfer was or any of the questions Blake asked. I guess Banks is not with them. I'd keep an eye on him though."

"I understand and agree. Listen, I don't want to ask but…" He paused giving her a concerned look.

"I'm okay. I haven't been involved in a shooting, God it's been years, but He's still watching over me."

"Us baby us. God didn't start this relationship to have someone take you from me."

He turned into the precinct parking lot and tapped her hand. "Let's go, I got you."

"Hmm… I got you too."

CHAPTER 75

There wasn't much foot traffic in the rotunda. The stillness gave way to the conversations between the officers coming in and out. They nodded to Justlin and Tyson as they passed the office door. Porter met him at the entrance of the conference room.

"Hey, have Justlin sit in your office a moment," whispered Porter.

"What? Who's in the conference room?" Tyson's question was answered when he opened the door.

"Hey, I've been waiting long enough. You don't stay at home, you don't come in early, are you changing your ways? Impossible, old habits die hard. Isn't that what they say? How are you?"

Porter and Justlin walked through the room to Tyson's office. Tyson took a deep breath and avoided answering his ex-wife's questions. He had questions of his own but chose not to delve into her reasons for meeting him at his job.

"I called your home, went by there too. I asked the girls had they spoke with you. You know how they are. They told me they usually reach you here when you're not answering their calls. I called your parents too. How is it that you don't stay in touch with them on a regular basis?"

"Sonya, what is it you want or need? I've got work to do here." Tyson asked with all the patience he could muster. He knew money was included in any request, but he agreed the girls could be with her over the summer. "If you've come to ask me about the summer arrangement, I agreed so how much will it cost me."

"I didn't ask for money, and they can't stay with me this summer. I came to say I'll be in Europe."

Sonya waited for his reaction. She expected him to reason with her, tell her how the girls needed to spend time with her more often than they had. Tyson was sure she spoke with his parents about arrangements. He hadn't been home other than to pack clothes for a few days. He didn't have any messages from his parents or his girls.

"You could have called. You didn't need to come here. Unless, what else is this about?"

"Hey Tyson, the captain is calling for you and Justlin. He said he's waiting in his office, something about where you were this morning?" Montez interrupted as he nodded to Sonya with a smile.

"Okay, let her know. I'll be there in a minute."

Montez walked through the conference room to alert Justlin to the message. She packed her satchel and left it on Tyson's desk and followed Montez through the conference room.

"Sorry, to interrupt." Justlin smiled as she spoke. "Damien, I'll meet you upstairs." Justlin knew as soon as she said the detective's name who the woman was.

"Hmm, no handle on his name. Who is she Detective Tyson? Someone who needs to be introduced to your wife I would say. Hello Ms?"

"I really didn't mean to disturb your conversation, detective," Justlin stated, her attention totally on Tyson's response.

"No problem. I got you. Sonya, this is Principal Investigator Tina Justlin. She's a co-worker and the lady I am in a relationship with. Tina, this is the mother of my children. I'll meet you upstairs, please let Worthy know. Thanks."

Tina turned to leave the room. Sonya stood, as though the investigator needed to see her full body. She straightened out her skirt and blouse bringing attention to her larger breast. Tina shook her head and reached to open the door.

"Don't leave on my accord. He failed to mention we were married. You'll find a dead end with him. He's not fond of a woman who seek to advance themselves. You have to remain an underling to keep his attention. Wow, a Principal Investigator how far behind detective is that, Damien?"

"Not behind at all, is it Sonya? We've had a rough morning so excuse me ignoring your need this morning. I don't know why you're here pretending you need special treatment or respect. If I was to be a part of the ranks here, my next promotion would be Captain. I've known Damien for quite a while now and I can say, he's been my target for a few years. Off the job of course, but sometimes the departments do work together. How lucky am I to have him all day and… Damien, the captain is waiting for us, don't be long. Nice meeting you, sorry I couldn't get to compare notes. That is what you wanted to do, right?"

Justlin stood at the door waiting for Sonya to answer. When she said nothing and took her seat, Justlin left closing the door behind her.

"Well, I'd say she has her hands full. I'll wait until her first disappointment with you and then we'll talk again."

"What do you want Sonya? As you have heard I have a meeting to attend."

"Busy? Why don't I stop by tonight? Your place at what, eight is late enough. That's your time to wind down as you always say."

"I won't be home. As you said you couldn't reach me there. I'm sure after a call or two, you stopped by. I can call you later. You don't have to see me to tell me what it is you want. Why not just tell me now?"

"What if I said I've been thinking about moving closer to the girls and you, maybe home."

"Home? Whose home? The girls stay with my parents and visit their home. You left home, it's no longer your home. Your family is not here so what home?"

"That's what I want to talk about. I can work from home and do what I do now. Just what you wanted. No more fashion runways. I can design and make whatever from home. I do that in California between shows. It would only require me to travel now and then."

"Why are you telling me this? You can't come in and out of our lives and expect us to accept you as though you went on vacation. No, I'm done. We're divorced and I've learned to live with that. I'm into a relationship and I think it will work out for me."

"So, has she met the girls? I mean, what the hell are you thinking? The girls don't need someone replacing me as their mother!"

"Sonya, their grandparents have been parents, my mother and father raised them. I was there more than you, but I can admit I have not been a parent and you…"

"And me what Damien? Blame me for wanting more? Blame me for leaving and achieving? What Damien?"

"Stay gone or at least stay away from me. I don't want to rekindle anything. I barely want to talk about you or us. What we had produced two beautiful girls, other than that, Sonya it was time wasted."

Sonya grabbed her purse and stormed pass Damien out the door. He shrugged his shoulders and hoped Tina would understand. Sonya noticed Tina standing at the elevator. Her attention wasn't on the unexpected visit nor Sonya's approach.

"So how long have you been in a relationship with him? He's thinking you're it. Fulfilling the dream, he had when he married me. I assume you asked questions about me, what did he say?"

Tina turned to face who she thought regretted her choices. It was too late. As Damien explained, it had been years. His daughters were teenagers and their mother left when they were in grade school. He struggled as a single parent with the help of his parents. Tina could only imagine his working as an officer and raising two children without their mother.

"He's over you. As for what he told me, that's it. He's been in and out of a few dating disasters, his words not mine, but he's giving love a chance with me. I don't hold any gripes about his past relationships. That's not my style. So, we've gotten to know each other over the years. I knew about you, where you went, and when you left. If it's your intention to come back and be the mother your girls may need, hey their yours. If your intention was to come and re-kindle what you had with your husband, hey he's mine. I'm sure he'll make that clear."

Sonya rolled her eyes and although Tina's words sank in, she wanted to stand her ground.

"I am their mother and his wife. Our separation doesn't change the facts. Hmm… you would know that if you had your own."

"Not that you need to know, I'm a widow. I was married and just like you, I lost the man I loved. Damien, is my renewal and I'm looking forward to us. Oh, and separation doesn't change the facts sweetie you did. You're divorced. You don't lose the children you lose the spouse." The elevator doors opened. Tina held the door as Sonya remained standing in what Tina would describe as shock. "Oh, and when you want to ask questions about me, I prefer them to be direct. I don't do well with chasing answers. It's okay. I'm not going anywhere. My house, his house, at work, I can be found. Have a good day. I'm sure we'll talk again."

The elevator door closed, and Tina shook her head and sighed. Sonya remained at the elevator for a moment. She didn't know how she'd come back into Damien's life, but she knew Tina Justlin would be a challenge.

CHAPTER 76

Tyson walked into the captain's office and took a seat. Worthy was on the phone and Justlin was typing a text on her phone. Tyson's phone alerted him causing him to smile. It was from Justlin.

> Take a breath babe, we're good.

He smiled and as their eyes met, he winked at her.

"Okay, before this phone rings again, continue Tina." The captain was becoming agitated with the interruptions.

"That was basically it. Boone wanted to clear up as much as he could. I think he expected them to follow him, trace his calls, and possibly make him pay for whatever he did against them."

"Cap, he knew," Tyson's irritation was revealed. "He knew more. He didn't get a chance to tell it all. Most of it we know, but Boone was willing to tell more."

"They're running in circles. I was telling Tina about Banks' people. There's a few in his ranks that need to be challenged. The good thing is he didn't appoint them. I'm waiting for his call. Blake is one, I'm sure his secretary is with them, and Sharice has a few others she's watching. So that's up the chain. I need your people to check higher, the courts. Someone is there as well." Worthy waited for Tyson or Justlin to comment before he continued. "I don't know that Banks doesn't know or see what's going on. He wants to walk quietly and get out unharmed." The captain pushed a folder across the desk to Tyson. "These are the names we have here in the precinct, on the task force, special ops, and the State Office. It's a couple of pages. Have your people do what they do with this. You'll get two officers tomorrow per your request. They're to work on the files and ongoing complaints. I'm not trusting Braize, or anyone he sends our way."

"So that gives us one in the field, Miller. Sssh…" Tyson shook his head.

"What? You've got that boy Knight, right?"

"I don't know, Cap. Do we? He was assigned to us, but that damn Sheers had him yesterday afternoon."

Justlin looked at the two men. She could see the stress mounting. "Hey, we want him close Tyson. In the office is fine, I'll be there as will Montez. Don't turn him away, he may have information he's now willing to tell."

"Where's he assigned today?" Worthy looked to Tyson for an answer.

"I haven't seen him."

The captain pressed the button on his phone. "Yes," replied the sergeant at the front desk.

"Find out where Officer Gary Knight is assigned today."

It only took a minute for the information to be found and confirmed. "He's not in today, sir. It's recorded as a call-in sick, sir."

"Thanks. Tell Fabian to step into my office."

As he hung up the phone, the door opened, and Fabian entered. "What's up, Captain?"

"Wellness check on an officer. Take one with you and be careful. Get the address from the roster."

"Tyson, I pray this boy is at home and not dead somewhere. I don't need this shit."

"Let's see what turns up. I'll let you know who was sent as a filler. Tina, anything else we need from our great leader." Tyson teased hoping it would change the mood in the room.

"Oh yeah, Tina leave him here with me a minute if you don't mind."

"Not at all Captain. I'll wait for you just in case now that I know we're being stalked."

Tina left smiling at the questionable face the captain had.

"What's going on Damien?"

"Sonya, after a morning shooting doesn't sit well to a Principal Investigator, I guess."

"You think? Did you say, you think? But you know what son, you're ahead of Sonya's game. The shooting comes with your line of work. Although this killing stuff is extreme Justlin can understand it. Sonya is a different thing."

"Yeah, a beast. She had the nerve to say she was thinking about moving back…"

"I thought she would eventually."

"Back in my house, no, you didn't really think I would allow that."

"Didn't know if you would or wouldn't but if Justlin wasn't in the picture, what would you have done?"

"Not let that psycho back in my home or my life. I only deal with her because of the girls."

"Well, you need to talk to Tina and make certain she understands your feelings."

"Sonya is crazy. She was supposed to have the girls with her this summer; then she said she'd be in Europe. When I didn't respond, she talked about moving back home. She can do anything and everything except live in my house."

"Listen women like Sonya don't give up or let go. Be careful, now that she knows you're dating someone else she'll be around just to make things miserable."

Tyson stood from his chair and offered a handshake. "Thanks, Captain. I'll call you when I think I have something to tell."

He stopped at the sergeant's desk on his way out. "Sarge, did we find Knight?"

"Tyson, he called out sick, but the entry was strange. Look." The sergeant pulled up the sick and vacation calls on her computer. "Sick calls are assigned a number, as you well know. Knight's call wasn't given a number. Usually that happens when whoever picked up the call doesn't have a sign on. It says he called at five thirty this morning, another flag. Everyone who worked third shift has a sign on, meaning the number should have been noted here." The sergeant pointed to the screen. Tyson looked at the other entries and noticed there were no initials to indicate who entered the call.

"So, humor me. The call was entered later, maybe this morning?"

"That would be another report with the time and sign on information of all that used the computers last night or…"

"This morning and the morning shift sign-ons is more than we want to delve in."

"Yes, that's what you guys do in your office, cold cases."

They both laughed, avoiding the reality of her answers.

"Thanks, I'll call later. Maybe we'll have more information."

The sergeant smiled and watched as Tyson left the office. He passed the other officers standing in the hall waiting for their assignments. Tyson thought about the easy, yet hectic schedule they were assigned to handle. He didn't miss those days. He was sure Sergeant Smith didn't mind the eye candy hanging around. The small group entered the office greeting Smith with smiles. Tyson remembered those days of "who would be able to date her" as each officer smiled as they entered to take a seat before the captain pulled them in his office.

Returning to his office, the captain's words crossed his mind. He needed to talk with Justlin. Sonya would be a problem if they fed into her antics. The divorce was signed and finalized more than eight years prior. They continued to live together in separate rooms for another year. Sonya used the excuse she hadn't found a place that would satisfy their daughter's needs. Moving to California was another ploy, an attempt to get Tyson to extend her stay at the home he bought for their "family." He wanted Justlin to understand he was serious when he said Sonya was no longer a part of his life.

As he entered the unit, he noticed the new officers talking with Miller and Montez. He nodded to Montez, not to disturb the conversation. Kai met him at the conference door with paperwork.

"Hey, have you had a moment to grasp all of this?" She asked as they stood at the conference door watching Montez and Miller explaining the unit's functions.

"Not really. I'm sorry I meant to call you about the officers coming this morning. It wouldn't have helped, now that I think about it, I had no names."

Kai nodded her head. "Malik Spears and Colette Myers. They both have five years in. Transferred from patrol. A problem for Montez not you…"

Tyson interrupted her update. "Why would they be a problem?"

"You know, they don't understand this unit. I get it. Being on patrol they don't pay much attention to following the written rules. You know, following the rules for court, lawyers, admin, it can be confusing if you want to do your job. On the street, you don't worry about that stuff and you're on your own."

"Okay, and you transferred from the street patrol to this?"

"Tyson, no. You know I only wanted this transfer because I'm secretly in love with you."

It was a rumor that spread quickly when she signed on to the unit. Tyson trained her and Montez, but the rumors were about him and the "new boot" from patrol.

"Okay, you're right. Have Miller come and see me. I'll talk to the add-ons at some point. Did you see Porter or Stands?"

"They got a call from Inspector Tully. They left to meet her."

"Okay, thanks. When Montez is done, tell him to see me as well."

Tyson glanced at his watch. It read eleven o'clock. The morning was gone, and he hadn't started any planned work. Justlin was sitting at the table with papers surrounding her. Tyson put his hand on her shoulder.

"Looks like you've got a lot here. Any luck connecting the dots."

"Yeah, I think so. We're going to have to speak with Fulton and Sayers. They know more than missing files and information. I think they know who they are dealing with. We've got to get in the loop. I think they're waiting for the players of this game to be exposed."

"Hmmm… you may have a point. So, do you want us to call them for the meeting or wait for the call?"

"Wait. Stands and Porter got a call from Sharice. That sergeant, Braize called her wanting to know where Lieutenant Marshall was being transported. It was a good thing that she was at the meeting and recognized the name. She called and they left.

She's not at the hospital, Marshall was moved but I think they want him in a safe house now."

"Damn, we need something, you know something to keep them at bay. They really want this guy killed."

"I don't think Braize is top dog. That's what we need to know. Who oversees the 'untouchables'?"

"Can you get answers from your boy, Blake?"

"We talked about that as well. I think he knows something, what, I don't know. Anyway, Phillip is on it. I'm waiting to call Banks."

Tyson pulled out the chair next to her and took a seat. He reached for her hand and held it under the table. "Do we need to talk about this morning? I mean things have been moving so fast, I want you to be okay."

"I'm good. You may have to check your ex. I know I'll be checking mine. I'm good, I gotcha."

"She's going to be a thorn in my side. I don't know what she thought she'd get from me, but I'm sure now, she won't go away easily."

"Well, those divorce papers bring clarity. You pay her alimony, you've got custody of the children, and whatever else was agreed upon on that day… is what she'll have today. I explained that to her at the elevator."

"At the elevator? Okay, if you're good, I don't want to know what was said."

"She'll try again. I'm not a young chick trying to interfere in one's marriage. She'll learn that lesson or be upset as I teach her."

"Well Justice…"

"Hush, this has nothing to do with justice."

"Say what you want baby, it's justice for me."

CHAPTER 77

The day ended with no answer to the lingering questions presented over the last week. A meeting for Monday morning was set up for Sergeant Braize, Captain Worthy, and Detective Tyson. The email Tyson received was sent close to the end of the day. He didn't have any questions. If he had a choice, he'd watch Braize closely as well as Sheers without a meeting. He was sure Worthy knew how he felt.

He waited in the front office while Justlin packed her satchel in the conference room. The two agreed to stop at his home on the way to her home. It was the first weekend for the "security" assignment. Tyson dialed Porter's number and waited for him to pick up the line. Montez and the others waved one by one as they left the office. It was then that he realized he hadn't spoken to the new staff that were now assigned to the unit. He left a message for Porter when he didn't answer after a few rings.

"Hey, Montez wait a minute." Montez turned at the door with a raised brow.

"Just for a minute man, why the look?"

"I thought something came up. You had that look man and, on the phone, hey it's Friday. You know."

"Man, ain't nothing you can't handle, I'm sure. Did you tell them I wanted to talk with them or what?"

"Yes, and you've been busy all afternoon. They'll be here early Monday, 'cause I told them you'd want to talk to them before they start any assignments. Damien, you know we've got this. Handle the other mess, no need to worry about the new boots."

"Okay, well… okay. Look man I wasn't trying to say you didn't know how to handle it. That's why you're in that position."

"Alright sir, goodnight. Have a good weekend. Take it down, seriously. Relax."

Justlin came out of the conference room smiling. "Montez, we're all taking it down. You as well. It's been a ride this week for sure."

"Ms. Justlin, I'm gonna take it down. Starting with a drink or two. Y'all be safe. Oh, a man by the name of Blake, uh… damn I can't remember his last name."

"Blake Franks, yes, he reached me. I don't know why he called here." Justlin rolled her eyes as she handed her satchel to Tyson. "Shall we go, sir?"

"Sure, good night, man. Have a great weekend."

They parted ways at the door leaving the precinct.

"Tina, I need to pick up more clothes than I thought, so it will take a little longer. Change of plans for the week. I'll need at least two suits. I guess I could pick them up the night before though…"

"Whatever you want to do Damien, but let's change the plans. Since the shooting I've felt funny about being at my house at all. I mean I've spent more time there than usual. You can cancel the weekend security coverage."

"Oh, so I'm fired now?" He teased, smiling as she shook her head.

"No, what if I stayed with you at your home or Marcie's. You can take me to my home, and I'll pack a few things. Wilson and Stands can take the weekend off. I'll feel safer after the week we've had."

"So, you want to go pack now?"

"If you're agreeing I can ride with Marcie and meet you at your place later."

"Okay, if you're okay with that, it's fine."

Marcie smiled as she came out of the precinct. "Hey, y'all. You good?"

"Yes, the sweet detective agrees, right baby?" She asked with a raised brow.

"Yeah, just call when you leave your home. I'll release the security unit then. Will you be driving to my place or is Marcie dropping you off?"

"I don't know yet. Maybe leaving the car there will be a target for them, you know?"

"No, it won't. The captain and I are meeting with Braize Monday morning. They won't try anything over the weekend."

"I think he's got a point Tina. We'll call before we pull off. It will be fine." Marcie said waiting at her car door.

"It'll be fine babe, whatever you choose. Call and let me know." Tyson leaned in giving her a passionate kiss. The two separated with a smile and touch of their hands. Tyson waved at Marcie and watched as they pulled off. He didn't want to sound pushy but with all that was going on he could use the weekend to rest and regroup.

He dialed Porter's number again and once again left a message. He thought twice about calling Stands, but his phone rang before he could finish dialing his number.

"Hey Tyson, sorry for calling you before reporting to Inspector Justlin's place, but did you switch Stands for the evening? I called him and he said he was with Porter and Inspector Tully, no details, but I haven't heard from him since then. That was about two this afternoon. I called Knowles to see if he'd been asked to cover. He said *"no,"* now I'm wondering will he meet me there or what."

"Call Knowles tell him to meet you. I'll reach out to Inspector Tully and see what's going on. Listen, you're only there until Justlin leaves. You won't be needed for the weekend. She won't be home."

"Oh, okay. Hey, let me know what you find out. It's not like Stands not to return my calls."

"Yes ma'am. I'll reach out now."

The decision to call Sharice, Porter, or Stands hadn't been sorted out as he drove to his home. Ten minutes into his drive his phone rang.

"Yeah, what's up? You guys change departments?"

"Tyson, man, it's been hectic just trying to keep tempers and shit level."

Tyson could tell Porter was upset. He shook his head and listened as Porter explained the reason Sharice asked for them to report.

"That damn Braize is worse than Sheers. Long story short, they wanted to know where Lt. Marshall was and demanded that the officers who were with Sharice be replaced. That's why we went, as replacements. It was the quickest replacement within our department she could get. Once Braize raised nothing more than her eyebrow, he and that jackass Sheers and some other rookie left. Lt. Marshall had to be moved again. That spot was compromised so we waited for the order from Worthy to take him to an unknown location. It's' under the Feds."

"Damn, so you're just leaving there. I just spoke with Wilson. Tell Stands to call her, she was upset she couldn't reach him. Listen man, Tina is with her girl. I'm sure they'll hang together this weekend. I need to talk to you."

"C'mon man, can we deal with this Monday?"

"It ain't about this shit, it's personal and I need to talk to you."

"Oh, okay when. You need advice already about your new lady?"

"What the hell can you tell me about her? Man, naw, you ain't got it like that. It's Sonya and her shit. I just need to down a few and talk. The weekend is open Tina won't be at her house."

"Oh, so I'll call you when we get near you."

"Where the hell did you have to go?"

"Maryland man, a few of Worthy's boys showed up. I recognized them. Special Ops. Unit with the Feds or something. This ain't no kiddie game no more."

"Yeah, it got real when they killed their own."

CHAPTER 78

Tyson noticed the car parked in front of his house. It piqued his interest, no one parked on that side of the street. There was a male sitting in the driver's seat. Tyson tapped the window to get the man's attention.

"Yeah, what's up?" Tyson sighed hoping he wouldn't have a problem.

"My question exactly. No sitting or parking here my man. It's my property."

"I'm waiting for my lady friend to let me know she's good or still needs my service." The driver was in his twenties. Tyson couldn't believe he was dumb enough to drop off someone and just sit.

"Well, you can wait on the other side. Not here."

The window shut and he started the engine. Tyson approached his front door and heard her voice. She rose from the seat on the extended porch.

"Why are you here?" Tyson took a deep breath while thanking God Tina wasn't with him. Sonya smiled as she approached him. She waved to the driver who then pulled off. "You got his number, I hope. You're not staying here."

"Eight o'clock Damien, remember, I said meet me at eight. I thought why wait that late. I thought, since it was Friday, you may have plans for later, so I stopped by earlier."

"Hmm. You thought, you thought? No, you didn't think. That would mean you thought about your drop-in visit to my office. You've had time to process what I told you. We're done Sonya. The girls aren't here so you have no reason for being here."

"We need to talk. Things have changed for me. I need you and our children in my life."

"Not my problem. We've been divorced for years, are you understanding that the divorce is not a temporary situation. You have the right to see and visit the children."

"And where am I supposed to stay while I visit? Damien, those provisions weren't discussed at all!"

"Not here, the kids aren't here, and I live an hour away from where they are. I visit them there, or they come here. You haven't been visiting them and staying here."

"Damien, can we go inside to talk. I've been waiting for you to get here. May I use your bathroom and we can straighten this out. After that, I promise, I'll leave."

Damien opened the door. He felt like there was more to what she was saying. He closed the den and bedroom doors when she went to the bathroom. The bedrooms were upstairs, but he knew she wouldn't dare try to climb the stairs. He knew the routine from the earlier years. She'd look for new items throughout the house and complain she hadn't bought anything over the years. Once she moved all her belongings out, with the few he mailed to her family's home, he changed the locks and painted the entire interior.

After her first visit, he promised the girls she wouldn't be there to stay again. The weekend visit became a nightmare for them. Being young they didn't understand the separation, their mother breaking promises, and the babysitter changes over the years. Damien and his parents agreed to living arrangements that would agree with their stability. Sonya came out of the bathroom and met him in the kitchen. Noticing the doors to the extending rooms were closed her facial expression changed.

"Really! Were you scared I was going to take or break something. You're too much of nothing. As usual that job makes you feel everyone is suspect."

"Call for your ride. You're not staying and I'm not taking you anywhere."

"Hmm… where's your lady friend. On a Friday? She didn't come home with you, or is that your evening delight?"

"Sonya, why are you here? What do you want? I don't want to have to take measures against you."

"What? Damien, I'm trying here. I made a mistake. It didn't work. I don't understand you and this attitude like I cheated or something. That would be a reason for me not to be able to return to my home. There is no other man."

"Sonya, it's been years. Close to ten years. I don't need to rehash the times I tried to rekindle just a friendship with you. I gave up. I gave in. I had to let go and for years I prayed that I was doing the right thing. I gave you the freedom to be you. You said that you couldn't live with your family and be you. So now, you want me to change my mind about what? The children have two more years and they both will be in college. You missed their childhood."

"You did too. Your parents, you said it, your parents raised them. You weren't the fabulous father you predicted you would be."

"No, I wasn't but I watched them grow. I was there for recitals, after school events, plays, and holidays. I didn't flaunt my loves in their face or pretend there were other people more important than them. As I said, make that damn call before you'll be standing outside wondering why?"

"I know why! That damn inspector, investigator, principal whatever she is, has found a home and you're waiting for her to get here. I see your tension rising, scared you'll be caught with your ex. I told her my kids, my husband, my family."

"Make the call Sonya or I'll make it for you."

"Why did you close the doors to the other rooms?"

"You don't need to be in them." Tyson made a call. "Hey, send a car to my home. He's cool. Okay, thanks."

"What the hell? Damien, I know you didn't send for a police car!"

"Sure did. I made my call now make yours, or they'll be here to pick you up."

Sonya shook her head slowly and rolled her eyes. She dialed what Damien knew wasn't for a ride.

"Yeah, this asshole is putting me out again. I thought I was welcomed to visit." She paused to see his reaction. "Sitting here. Waiting hold on. Never mind he went in the other room. Call him and talk to him. I'm trying to see the girls, that's all."

Damien was standing in the grand room looking out the window. Sonya walked behind him and reached to embrace him around his waist.

"This is why you can't stay. You don't know or respect boundaries. I'm a grown man, and I can't be your toy. You got a ride coming? If they're not here by the time the squad car comes, I'll file charges."

A moment of silence passed between them. Damien remained in the grand room and Sonya waited, seated at the island. She hoped after what seemed like more than fifteen minutes, he'd join her.

"Damn! It's like that?!"

"I don't need your games. We're done. You want to see the girls; you know where they are. Stop looking for a family reunion."

"All right, I'll leave, and this is not over. I'll file for custody and then we'll see how you handle the rules."

Damien walked to the door and opened it. The officers smiled as they paused before ringing the bell. Damien waved them in.

"Sonya, you can leave with them on your own or I can get them to take you out of my house. Officers I'll file the report from here."

"Oh, oh, I see. You didn't want me reporting anything happening here. Damien, really, she's got you twisted like that? Where's your pups, Porter, Stands and that stud Wilson? These boys look like regulars."

"Is that it, Sir?"

"Yes, thanks for coming out. You can drop her off at the precinct. The report will be waiting."

It was close to an hour before Porter arrived. Damien spoke to Tina and ended the conversation by telling her to have a good time. He didn't mention Sonya's antics. His report would reflect his reason for calling the unit. He knew she would eventually get angry and turn the table. Her claim to a domestic violence situation would cause eyebrows to rise at the precinct and problems with Tina. He'd talk about other alternatives later. He fixed a few things for his friend to nibble on. He was sure Porter wouldn't stop on his way to eat. Knowles and Wilson called to say they were off duty, and the final check of Tina's home was made once she and Marcie left. Tina decided to leave her car. The doorbell rang and Tyson wondered why Porter didn't use his key.

"Hey man, you, okay?"

"Yeah, what's up? I thought you and Porter parted at the precinct."

Stands stepped inside and handed his friend the twelve pack of beer.

"C'mon in, I was just cooking some wings. You know your boy will get here, sit a minute and then want to order for us only to wait another hour or more to eat."

"You got enough? Need me to make a run?"

"No man, there's enough, unless you're expecting someone." The two laughed and the door opened. Porter walked in with a twelve pack of beer.

"Hey, hey now. I thought it was just me. I saw your car and thought to myself, does Wilson know we're back?"

"Man, you know the answer to that. His alarm went off as soon as he hit the state line." Porter pointed to Stands who could only shake his head accepting the tease.

The three men laughed and walked into the kitchen where Damien was preparing the wings.

"Okay, okay, I see we got things in the works. Hey why are the room doors closed. What you doing boss, something new?"

"No, that damn Sonya was here when I got here. I told Porter I needed to talk about this. My thought was you'd be with your lady tonight."

"She went out with Marcie and your lady. Hell, she should have been here to deal with your visitor."

"Man, it would have been ugly. But let me tell you how she ruined the entire day."

CHAPTER 79

"Girl, no she didn't! What did you say to Detective Tyson about is ex-beast."

"Ex-beast?" Tina couldn't help but laugh. She noticed Marcie and Wilson were closer than she thought. She struggled for the first hour with calling her by her first name. Leana Wilson didn't go out much, but when she did, she let Tina know Marcie was her choice of company.

"Listen, I was being nice. She really got close to pushing me to…"

"I'm surprised you didn't get there after the morning you had. Leana is just as bad. The two of you."

"Us??" The women replied in unison. The three laughed as the waiter approached their table with another round of drinks. They ordered their food and told the waitress to keep their glasses full.

"And? I ask again, what did Damien say? Tina she is a trip! Marcie, you know some of her antics. How does one leave their home and want to control it when they snap out of their daze?"

"Well if she thinks she needs to be slapped, I mean needs help to snap out of it…"

The ladies laughed again. "What did he say?" Marcie raised her eyebrow and pointed to the basket of bread.

"You know the man better than me. What do you think he said?" Tina teased as Leana was more than willing to share what she knew.

"Girl, you don't have a worry when it comes to her. She made her decision, hell, about ten years ago. He tried over and over again to fix their marriage. I mean, she even lived there after the divorce for a year. Who allows that shit?! It was nasty and he was a mess after she left. Jeff and Amir, sorry Tina, Porter and Stands kept a close watch on our boy. He didn't date much and he's careful who he deals with. Damien's a good guy."

"Yep, so if you need us to kick ass, no problem." Marcie looked over the brim of her glass and nodded. "Wow, so much going on in the unit across the hall."

"Stop comparing. You've got those dead beats in your unit." Tina tapped Leana's glass in agreement.

"So, what are they going to do about all of this? I mean, Sheers and Braize refuse to follow procedures. Whenever Sheers shows up, Braize jumps. Whatever they're up to, they seem to be stuck. You know in a permanent bend over position."

"Wow, they must have been doing this for years, huh, and where did the newly assigned officers come from?"

"Patrol. They weren't officers that were in their pool of choices. The lieutenant on duty assigned them randomly. I don't think he gave any thought to it, other than it being a temporary reassignment he'd complain about. It doesn't balance assignments. He got his orders from Worthy not to include Braize about the assignment. Everyone is under a spotlight. What's up with your ex?"

"Who?" Tina looked at Leana thinking the question was meant for her.

"You, Blake called the office twice. He was looking for Braize."

"Girl don't ruin my weekend. No, he didn't call there. What does he have to do with…"

Her voice faded as thoughts crossed her mind. She didn't know how much Leana knew.

"Okay, I wanted to come out and release some of this tension. Blake is tension on the next level. I'll call Sharice tomorrow and see what she knows."

Tina refused to talk about it further. She needed the weekend break.

It was close to ten and Jeff and Amir were trying to give Damien reasons to file charges against Sonya.

"Listen man, your report may get lost in the mix but a charge, man she'll leave you alone for sure."

"What charge? That's what I keep asking the two of you. What am I charging her with? I opened the door and let her in. I gave her a warning, told her to call for a ride. She didn't, I called for her to have one. My report will be why I needed the car, that's it. I'll use it if I have to file a restraining order. I really don't want to do that because of the girls."

"Understandable, but she won't hesitate to file one on you."

"Amir, you know I know about how they'll do. I'm still in court with that crazy broad. I can't stop her no matter what."

"Man, ain't nobody listening to your nonsense Jeff. You can't get rid of the girl you sleeping with whenever you call her."

"Stop man, I didn't call her. She called me."

Damien and Amir laughed. Jeff sat back and drank his beer.

"I've got the girls to worry about. I just hope she caught the hint. I mean she met Tina and…"

"Hold up." Amir put his hand out signaling Damien to stop talking. "She met Tina, Investigator Justlin?"

"Keep up man. He said she was in the conference room waiting for him."

"Oh wow, I forgot you said that. Well, what is left for her to believe? You've got a new woman; the house is off limits. Damn, you closed all the room doors, and you had a police car come get her. What else does she need?"

"Amir, you know she wants him to lay her down. One more time…" Jeff laughed and winked at Damien.

"Man, that's why you have the trouble you have. She won't be laying down here and I won't be laying with her anywhere. I'm good."

"I'd be too. Ms. Justlin, yeah, I understand you, man. Has she been here?"

"What? Uh, no. Why?"

Amir walked to the island. "You guys good?" He asked raising two bottles of beer. "Listen, have the sexy investigator, I say that respectfully man, have her leave a few of her things here. That's what Sonya is looking for. You know that. She notices all the changes and what's laying around. It doesn't have to be a wardrobe but just a few things in the bathroom or in the kitchen. She'll back up for sure."

"How the hell do you know that? You and Leana been together for what four or five years, you're still engaged right?"

"Jeff, man it's what they do. That's how you stay in trouble. You know damn well I'm engaged. I still remember my past endeavors."

"You may be right. Listen changing the subject. I've got a meeting Monday morning with Braize and Worthy. Anything you guys observed about this guy?"

Jeff answered without giving it any thought. "He's an ass, just like the rest of those 'untouchables.' He tried to sway Sharice's decisions. She didn't budge. He even tried to soften the atmosphere by calling her by her first name."

"Yeah, she cut him quickly. She told him she was Inspector Tully, and they weren't on first name basis. You could tell he was shook." Porter pointed to Stands and they both nodded in agreement.

"Man, me and Amir agree, she's tough. He tried everything including calling a lieutenant. She shut him down by saying, *'I'll call the governor'.*"

"Damn, so you guys just waited for the escorts?"

"Damien, when we got the call, they were there. I think Sharice called us so Sheers and Braize could be seen by us. If anyone questions it, they can't say they weren't there." Stands walked back to his seat as he listened to Porter explain the scene at the hospital when they arrived. "We were told to turn in our reports on Monday. I bet there won't be a report written by them."

"I'll have Worthy ask for one. They shouldn't have been there. I'm sure there wasn't a call for them to go there at all."

"Damien, you know there wasn't. Sharice had a team with her already and then they were joined by Special Ops officers. Why would they need our officers at all? Not only that, the move was to be done without being disclosed to anyone other than those assigned. We were talking about it earlier. The 'untouchables' are aware of what's going on with the lieutenant."

"Jeff, it's just a matter of time. We just need a few more pieces to the puzzle. I told Tina, I don't think we'll get them all. One thing is for sure, those we get have to be an example to others. I'm hoping we hit the main players. The others may go and hide then."

"Damien, we need to expose them like they would do if it was us."

"You're right, man, they did everything they could to get rid of us. They forgot; we've been fighting…"

The three men laughed and said in unison," We've been fighting all our lives."

CHAPTER 80

"I'll call after the service. I thought it was a great gesture for Leana to invite us. She asked if you would like to join us. I have the address of the church; do you want me to send it to you?"

Sharice looked at her phone. She nor Tina seldom went to church. Sunday was usually her day of rest. She wondered what happened that changed her friend's attitude about those who praised on Sunday and sinned again on Monday.

"Tell me what's really going on. I mean, you, me, we, and church, oh happy day, what's up?" Leana is Wilson, right? I don't think I met her. You're really fitting in with the unit huh?

"No, I still work and have an office next to the governor, for now. Yes, she's Wilson and we all were invited by her to come to her church. I'm extending the invitation to you, with her approval. So..."

"Send the address, I'll meet you there."

Tina smiled; happy Sharice accepted the invitation. They would attend church and she'd spend some time with her friends. Leana didn't say anything about Amir joining her, so she didn't invite Damien. They spoke briefly before they said goodnight. They both spent Saturday relaxing and agreed to meet on Sunday evening for dinner. Tina spent the night alone in her home. She knew if she was to get over her fears, she needed to be home alone, without security. She went to her closet and chose a dress that would keep her temperature stable. The first dress and jacket she pulled from her closet was her favorite pick for dinners and special outings. She put the ensemble back in the closet and stood pondering what would be suitable for church and dinner. She was sure she wouldn't have time for a wardrobe change. She sighed and decided to shower first.

It was close to eleven when the ladies met at the church. There was a small crowd at the entrance. Leana smiled and waved when she spotted Tina and Marcie. Sharice crossed the street and approached the trio at the same time. Sharice was introduced to the other ladies and immediately felt welcomed. The service was an hour long and the ladies accepted the invitation extended to all to meet in the banquet hall for greetings and refreshments. The church members began to separate. Those who stayed said their parting farewells to those who were leaving. They talked as they enjoyed the light refreshments. The nods and smiles of the members was welcoming. Thirty minutes passed before Sharice made mention of the time.

"So, what's on the agenda for the rest of the day. I've got a request from my family for dinner."

"I think we all have the afternoon booked. I have a dinner date. What about you two?" Tina directed her question to Marcie and Leana.

"Home, that's it for me. I'm looking forward to an afternoon of movies and relaxing."

"Marcie, you got it, me as well. Amir will probably stop by since I haven't been home all weekend."

The ladies exited the church. There were police cars surrounding Tina's car. She tapped Sharice and Leana. Marcie pulled out her phone and began taking photos.

"What the hell?" Tina asked as the four ladies approached the car.

"Hold on ladies. This is a police matter." The officer stated as he turned to face them.

"A matter that damn well better be worth you and your boys peering in my car. What's the problem?"

Leana, Sharice, and Marcie walked around the car looking for any problems. The other officers stood by making no attempt to stop them.

"Well, if you're Ms. Justlin, we got a call that you needed assistance."

"Bullshit. What's your name and why aren't you in uniform like your partners here?"

"We got a call, ma'am." The officer on the opposite side of the car repeated.

"I didn't get a notification. There was no call about my car, my home, or me. So, what were you looking for?"

"Justlin, it doesn't matter what they wanted. I just alerted a team; they can explain it to them." Sharice responded without pausing as she and Marcie continued around the car.

"What team?" The man who seemed to be in charge questioned. The other officers joined him mumbling they didn't want any trouble. "Hush. Just wait a minute. She's bluffing, I know she is."

"What you don't know who it is you just fucked with. Who sent you, Sheers or Braize?"

Marcie and Leana instructed the crowd to move on. As they spoke, they showed their badges as reinforcement. Within minutes the area was clear of spectators and the four ladies stood with the men who claimed they received a call.

"Let me see some ID since you're responding to a call. I'm the owner of the vehicle, who are you? What was supposed to be the emergency concerning my car?"

"You say you alerted a team. Your team has ten minutes, or we finish what we came to do."

Tina turned to the man who spoke. She didn't recognize him from the files they had reviewed. Marcie didn't give any indication she knew them. Again, she asked for their identification.

"So, you're not going to identify yourselves. You know refusing state and city officials is a problem."

"Do I seem worried about your problems. If your team don't get here, these officers here are going to search your car, with your permission or not."

Sharice took pictures of the officers and their vehicles and who appeared to be their supervisor without their knowledge. She sent the photos to the operations team. They would alert Captain Worthy and the governor. A phone buzzed and Sharice noticed the smaller framed officer peering at his phone. He walked over to the large-framed man who was barking all the orders.

"You ladies have a blessed day. We've got another call, a little more urgent. I'm sure our paths will cross again. Y'all be careful and call your local police if you should need assistance."

The men didn't hesitate. They immediately retreated to their vehicles, one unmarked car and two police vehicles.

Leana watched as they left noticing who drove each car. "Those cars aren't from our precinct. I can call the tags in to see who they are."

"No need, we've got a bigger problem." The women listened as Sharice spoke. "I sent the picture to the special ops team, Worthy and the governor's line. The officer who spoke about getting the call, his phone buzzed a few minutes later. He told their supervisor, and they left. There's more than one leak. It's either the ops team, or the governor's office. Get away from the car. We need a team to get anything they can. Leana call your boys, they may have been to her home."

Marcie grabbed Tina just before she screamed in anger. Pulling her friend to her chest she could feel the vibration of her sobs. "What do they want with me? Marcie, it's that damn Blake, I know it! I've got to call Damien. This is, this is bull-shit. That's what it is Marcie. I can't deal with this."

"You were built for this shit, girl. Blake? What he's got connects now? Blake the fake? If he's involved, we'll get him. Leana call the guys, Damien too. We'll just wait for them. Don't touch the car." Sharice's phone buzzed and she stepped away from the others.

CHAPTER 81

Thirty minutes passed before the captain and his ops team arrived. Fabian instructed them to check the car thoroughly. The van of men nodded as they passed the angered females standing on the sidewalk. Marcie bid her farewells, but was told by the captain she would have to turn in a report once she reported to work.

"Captain, maybe it would be better if no one in my department knew I was here. I can send the photos taken to Justlin if needed. I'd rather watch the schedule changes and odd calls without them being alerted I'm watching."

"I think they know you and Justlin are friends. They are careless because they feel they can't be touched. I won't ask formally for the report, nor will I ask you to perform any task outside of your daily duties. However, yes, we need you to be our eyes and ears without being noticed. It would help uncover some of the internal problems this group causes. Do send the photos as well."

"Understood Captain Worthy. Whatever I can do to assist, I will." She waved and yelled to the ladies. "We'll talk soon."

Fabian stood with Worthy as Stands, Porter and Tyson double parked in the street. Porter reported to the captain as Stands and Tyson checked on Wilson and Justlin.

"We're okay. This is getting a bit uncomfortable. I stayed at home last night praying I'd be safe without security, now this. I don't know if they were at my house before coming here." Tina's frustration was evident.

"We'll get the house checked now. I'll send Miller and Knowles along with two of the Ops officers. They'll wait for us to get there before leaving."

"Damien, this is way out of my norm. I don't live like this. Has the governor returned any calls, Sharice?"

"No, just an acknowledgment that it had been received."

"This is what I'm talking about. I know Blake answered the call and handled this mess by sending a message to the officers asking them to leave. I want to know why they were here? Did Blake send them or are we now on the governor's radar too?"

"Justlin, did I hear you correctly? Banks didn't call you? He called me stating he had the office answering his calls. He didn't say he sent anyone. Is Blake the one who assigns staff, I mean, doesn't he need approval for dispatching officers. You said there was a patrol car and one supervisor?"

Sharice answered slowly. "I sent photos of the officers and the plates on their vehicles. I didn't recognize what precinct they were from, but it wasn't yours. I called for the governor or you to answer. He never called back."

"He got the message. He called me and I told him I had dispatched officers and ops. He didn't ask questions just a softened 'thank you'."

The forensic officer walked over to the group, who were intently waiting for them to finish.

"If you're sure no one was in your vehicle, I'm done with what I found on the outside. I'll have the results in a day or two. There's a lot of prints on the car. I'm sure we can narrow it down, but it will take some time."

Worthy looked at Tyson for him to respond. "That's good, man. Thanks. If we can, we'll have a few names to compare. It probably will take us a day or two as well. Thanks, man."

Tyson shook his head. "Listen, it's Sunday. Tomorrow carries its own problems. We really need a break from this sshh…, you know? Hey, Porter man, call me later. Stands you and Wilson have a better evening. Sharice, can you make it to the office tomorrow or are you with Lieutenant Marshall?"

"No, I was going to check a few things in the office. Blake's ass for one. Unless you need me earlier?"

"Okay, after you do what you do, stop by the office. We're trying to connect the dots and I think your input would be helpful. Captain, if that's alright with you?"

"Damien, whatever can put out this fire they're creating, yes let's make it happen."

The group began to separate. "C'mon, babe, give me your keys."

"Damien, did they check the car for a tracker?"

"I'm sure they did. Let me check with Porter."

Damien returned after he, Stands and Porter checked the car over again. They shook hands and walked away.

"It's good. Let's get to your house."

Tina was silent most of the way to her home. Her thoughts drifted between what was old and new. She kept dissecting incidents since being assigned to check the reports of the Cold Case Unit. It was more than what the reports revealed. The "untouchables" sprinkled their poison throughout the community. She couldn't believe it was rooted in the Moorestown Precinct. The reports, investigation, and charges would affect a few, but the dangers touched the innocent. They would have to tread lightly if they couldn't get those who sat at the top.

"Damien, do you think we still need to talk with Fulton and Sayers?"

"Hmm, I almost forgot about meeting with them. Let's wait until later in the week to contact them. They may reach out before then. They still need information from us. Tina, this meeting with Braize may answer a few questions. So, I prefer to wait."

"This Braize, is he someone who you've worked with in the past?"

"No, and from the part he's played, I just want to know how deep he's in. There's so much more to this. I don't understand how they've been getting away with it over the years. Well…"

"Damien, you know damn well how. Everyone is out for self. No one says anything. Either they turn a blind eye or they're getting paid. Blake, this Braize guy, I believe it goes higher. Hell, Blake is in the governor's office. What about the others, I know, getting paid."

"Not all of them. A lot of them, I think, are on an ego trip. Gloating about what they do to the lower class, invading people's livelihood, damaging their future; Tina it's in their makeup. It's who they are. No application, hiring process, or training can change that."

They rode in silence. Each in their own thoughts of what could or should be done. The afternoon was blending into the evening light and air. As they traveled Tina let her thoughts drift to what could be next. She realized it would be difficult to go back to her office and be silent. The truth was hard to overcome when those who took an oath were the culprits of murders.

"Damien, if Blake is a part of this…" She paused knowing the answer." How much time can he get? I know this is not as simple as a fine, right?"

"Depends on what part he played in what the court deems as illegal. Did he know they were going to kill the Chief or the Lieutenant? What else did he know or do?"

Tina sighed," I don't know. I was just thinking how stupid could he be to get tied up with these…"

"I know babe, but let's not get ahead of this. If he's involved, let's see how. It could answer a few questions. Maybe there's others in the office. Did Sharice find out anything?"

"She didn't mention it. I think we all were trying to enjoy the weekend."

"Hmm, I agree with that. Let's check your home. Go to dinner, and try to enjoy…"

Tina smiled as he pulled into her driveway. "I believe we can do more than try."

CHAPTER 82

Miller approached them in the driveway. They could see Knowles standing at the end of the drive near the black sedan. The couple walked toward her and stopped noticing she held her hand out to stop them from approaching. They stood where they could see just past the end of the home to the adjacent street.

"That's Blake's car," whispered Tina. "Why is he here?"

Miller spoke quietly. "Ma'am, he said he had a dinner date with you. I told him you weren't home. He wanted to know who we were and who assigned us. Of course, I showed him my badge. Knowles stayed near the car. He returned to his car and has been waiting for about an hour."

"Thanks Miller. You and Knowles have a good night. I'll see you in the morning. Oh, and no report about him waiting here." Damien nodded to Knowles as Miller said good night and returned to their car. "Tina, we don't see him. We're going in the house and let him ring the bell."

"I don't want him ringing the bell!"

"I don't want him following them or tracking them down either. If he thinks she didn't tell us about him, he'll have to come to the door. I'm sure he's put in a word with their license plate number attached. Let him be the jealous man watching you with someone else."

"Damien, I'm sure he has seen you or a photo of you."

"He hasn't seen me with you," Damien smiled as he leaned in to kiss her softly before they ascended the front stairs. Neither looked in Blake's direction. Tina caught on quickly and hit Damien teasingly on the shoulder as he unlocked the door. They walked into the grand room and waited, knowing the doorbell would ring shortly.

"I'm not going to stand around waiting. What are we doing for dinner. I need to change my shoes, too long in these heels." Tina laughed and went into her bedroom.

"I put my suits in your car. I forgot to get them out. That will pique his curiosity, I'm sure."

"Go get them. Unless we're going out for dinner. We could call the restaurant and have it delivered."

"Tina, stay in the bedroom."

"What's going on?"

Damien was looking out the window through the Levolor blinds. "Another car has pulled up. Blake is talking with the driver." Walking to the other side of the house he looked through the blinds again. "Doesn't look like any other cars. I'll wait and see if this one leaves."

"We don't get much traffic, especially on Sunday. Why would he be talking to just anyone in a passing car? I should have stayed at your place."

"It wouldn't matter. If Blake is looking to talk with you, he would have come there too. Let's just wait before we assume too much."

Minutes passed, what Tina thought was too long for Blake to cross the street and get the heart to ring the bell. "Do you want me to call him? I can simply state the car outside looks like his."

"No. The other car left, and he went back to his car. He'll ring the bell. Trust me baby, he's waiting to see if I'm staying. So, I'm going to the car and get my things."

"Damien, take your gun."

Damien stepped out onto the porch and continued to the car. He heard the car door slam across the street and smiled. He knew then that Blake would approach the front door thinking he wouldn't have to deal with a man coming to Tina's defense. He grabbed his bag and suits, locked the car, and proceeded back to the front door.

"Hey man, how are you? You looking for someone?" Damien asked as he turned the doorknob to enter.

"Oh, I'm sorry who are you?" Blake replied. His question showed a bit of irritation. Damien ignored his attitude and invited him in.

"Hun, are you expecting someone? He was at the door, I guess you were right. Have a seat, we just got here. Well, you know that don't you. Give her a minute."

Before Blake could respond, Damien took his clothes into the guest room. He stayed in the room, deliberately allowing Tina to have time to address her guest.

"Blake. Hmm why are you here? I don't think I missed your call saying you were coming here."

Blake shook his head before he spoke. "So, this is what you're doing now? I can remember I asked could I stay with you. I was attempting to be with you more on weekends, after work, holidays, and you said that wasn't something that you did. You changed your mind. You said you didn't want a relationship that would conflict with your job. You couldn't work with me all day and be with me all night. So, what is this?"

"Actually, it's none of your business. I'm not in a relationship with you, so I owe you no explanation. What brings you this way? This is not your way home or to the job."

"Okay, okay, you're right you don't owe me an explanation. But this is a violation of ethics within the department." He stated emphasizing his displeasure.

"You're full of it, Blake. What do you want?"

"Well, your friend need not be the extra person here. We need to clear up a few things."

"My friend is my guest for the evening and there's no violation of anything here. My questions about you and I have been clear for months. I told you I was done, and I meant it. You didn't have to come here to verify that. If you're here for that so-called report. I sent it to Banks; you can speak to him about it. Hmmm. I don't think there's anything else between us. Oh, I am being rude though. Damien, honey can you come here please?"

Damien entered the room smiling. Blake sighed deeply.

"Fucking games Tina. Do you think I'm here to play your games?"

"No, why are you here? I did ask you that."

Damien interjected hoping to relieve the tension that was building. "Hey, can I get you a beer, man, a drink? Tina, babe, do you want a glass of that wine we have some left?"

"Yes, Blake you like that wine, do you want that or a beer?"

Blake's face showed his anger. He couldn't disguise his emotions. "No, I'm good."

"C'mon man, water, a beer, I mean you look like you got a lot to say."

"No, he can't have a lot to say because if he was the man he claimed to be, he would have called. Called so I could tell him unless you've got information I can use, I don't want to talk. There is no us, there is no reason for you to be here. So, what is this, Blake?"

Damien offered the seat across from where he and Tina sat.

"You may be in danger. You need to come back to the home office and let go of this hunt you and your friend here have started. These people are dangerous, and they don't care who they hurt."

"Okay, let's put some names to these people and how do you know? What's your connection to them?"

"I've got my ways." Blake sat back in the chair. Damien noticed there was a shift in his attitude.

"What do you know that we don't know, Blake? Why haven't you reported it to those in charge?"

"Tina, you know damn well why."

Tina's face asked her question. Blake looked at Damien. "Hey, maybe a beer man, please?"

Damien stood and Tina grabbed his pant leg stopping him from moving.

"Say why you haven't told anyone? You could have told Sharice, Banks, or me. Hell, you could have called Captain Worthy. I think you need to leave Blake. Get the fuck out of my house. Damien call the unit. He's setting us up."

Blake jumped up with his gun drawn. His actions were met with Damien's draw of his weapon from his holster. Tina drew her weapon from the seat of the couch. Two guns on Blake, he holstered his weapon.

"It's not over. They'll get what they want, and your reports won't stop them."

"Turn around and give me your damn hands." Damien shook his head as he placed Blake in handcuffs. "Have a seat again. You want to talk here or at the precinct."

"You ain't no hero Tina, and your boy ain't one either."

"I always wondered why you were so … damn corny. You want to share information or should we just tell them to come and get your sorry ass."

"Tina, I'm trying to save you. The trouble you and your sidekick or maybe you're his sidekick are causing ain't worth it."

"How much do they pay you Blake? What have you sold your all for?"

Blake shook his head. Handcuffed and seated he waited for the Special Ops officers to arrive. Damien called the captain. He arrived followed by two unmarked cars. The officers placed Blake in the car and informed the captain they'd call once he was secured in holding.

"So, what was he thinking?"

"Captain, he drew his weapon on us, he's compromised. Who else from that office? We need to know." Damien looked to the older man for answers.

"If he calls Banks we'll know. I pray the governor is not in on this. What was he thinking Tina?"

"It was something about him. Captain, I just don't know. We dated for about nine months, but he was always unsettled. Now that I think about it, he never settled into our relationship. He always seemed distant and disappointed that I wouldn't tell him about my assignments at your precinct. Now I know why. I don't know what Sharice found out about him."

"Give her a call. Make her aware of the situation. I hate to have to deal with this today, but as you well know, it's a part of a bigger problem."

Damien stood on the porch deep in thought. The captain told them he'd be at the precinct writing up the paperwork. He'd be waiting for the call once Tina reached Sharice. The couple watched the cars pull away.

"Damien, we didn't mention the other vehicle. Suppose that was one belonging to the 'untouchables.'"

"I don't want to leave your house unguarded. They may want to see if you've got reports here and come into your home. We'll stay here tonight and put a plan in place if you still feel unsafe here."

"I've never felt like this before, even when I was in uniform. This is my home. This is some shit."

CHAPTER 83

"Tina, wait, I got a message from Phillip. I was going to wait until the morning to call him. Hold on, let me pull up this message. I went straight to my family's house once I left you at the church. Let's see…"

Tina and Damien sat waiting for her to thumb through her messages. They made the call to the diner for dinner to be delivered and took the time to eat and relax before Sharice returned the call.

"Here it is. He sent it about six tonight. He says, got information about Blake. Something seems wrong. He's got a few correspondences and notes on his desk about the Moorestown Precinct. He didn't say what they were. He also said there was a few calls on Friday from Fulton. Hey, that's the lawyer you told me about right?"

"Yea, that's him. What would they have to talk about?"

"Well listen, Phillip looked at his calendar. He's in Moorestown all this week. Tina, Banks would have to know that Blake was going to be out of the office for a week. No one told me."

"Did you speak to Banks? I don't know why I'm asking, what did he say?"

"He didn't know anything about Blake taking off a week. Maybe Blake goes in each morning before he leaves to come to the precinct. Maybe, he's intent on seeing you and Fulton."

"Well, we just told you what he did. He's a total ass, total. He's too dumb to be checking out the mess this group is in. When has he ever done any investigative work?"

"He's got the credentials."

"What? Sharice, what credentials?"

"Military, I forgot the title but that's his extensive background. Oh, Investigations Specialist."

"So, that's how he got the position with the governor. Maybe he is investigating the 'untouchables' for the governor."

Damien nodded his head in agreement. "I'll call the captain, but I'd think Banks would have forewarned you ladies or the captain about him."

"Damien, maybe that's why he's been mad about my assignment. I mean if he was an Investigator in the Military, this operation as specialists working with us. Aren't the men assigned by the captain special forces from the military?"

"Yes, let me make this call. Excuse me Sharice." Damien went into the guestroom to make the call.

"Sharice, a specialist? Blake? Hard to believe girl."

"Hey, Damien is your first real bad-boy? Those educated nerds you—"

"Girl, let's not go there."

"No, I'm going there. You live a hidden nerd life after dark and you been seeing a secret agent and didn't know it." Sharice laughed as Tina gave serious thought to those she dated over the years.

"Stop laughing. I'm trying to deny it." They both laughed. "I'll see you in the morning girl. This just keeps getting deeper and deeper."

"Tina, are you going to stay at your house. Maybe you need to stay with Marcie or that fine man of yours for a few days."

"I gave it a quick thought. Marcie wouldn't mind, but…"

"I know. See you tomorrow. Be careful and don't talk to Blake until you find out what's going on."

"You're right. I wonder if Banks, nah, he's keeping quiet."

"It may not be his choice. It may be the demand he got."

"Girl, goodnight. I won't be able to sleep if I keep speculating about this mess."

Damien met Tina at the window looking over her yard.

"You want to sit on the deck for a while. It was a nice breeze when we ate dinner. I can pour you a glass of wine. It may relax you."

"This is crazy! How could Blake have a secret agent life. How could he hide that?"

"Tina, it's okay. You know that's why they call it 'secret'."

She smiled and followed him to the deck. The night air wasn't cold enough for a coat or sweater, but the breeze made her ask Damien to bring the blanket from the couch. He nodded his head smiling. He and Sonya enjoyed sitting on his deck with the cover over their lap. It was when they could talk about anything, and the children were in bed. He brought the glasses of wine and sat them on the table. He decided they had had enough of the 'job' for the evening. He needed to tell her about Sonya and her drop-in visit. He explained his decision to call for a car. He wasn't sure if he would file formal paperwork.

"Would the paperwork jeopardize her rights to visit the girls.?"

"I don't think so. I mean, they don't live with me. I don't want her showing up at my home whenever she gets the urge. I would think she wouldn't want to jeopardize that, but she always pictures the fairy-tale about us being a family again. Tina, I'm a family man, truly I am. If I'm going to get into that type of living again it won't be with her."

Tina took a deep breath. She thought he was going to say he wanted a family life with her. She was pleased with the dating and getting to know him phase. She hoped it wouldn't have been as intense, but it showed her a side of the detective she was sure many hadn't seen.

"It's going to take time. She's not used to you being in a committed relationship."

"Hmmm…"

"Well has she met other women you've dated?"

"No, I can't say I went out of my way to even tell her I was dating."

"Okay, so, she may not believe you're in that type of relationship."

"You may have a point, but it doesn't matter. Her relationship is with her daughters. Listen, those girls barely want to make time for me. So, she'll be working to get their attention. I'm not trying to intervene or be as concerned as I was years ago. The girls are fine, my parents are enjoying their lives with them, and I no longer feel guilty about any of it. I understand what she wants, she just can't have me."

He smiled and winked. They leaned into each other to kiss, and the phone rang.

"Damn, you're popular Ms. Justice."

"That's your phone Tyson."

"Tyson, Banks hasn't answered. His team is at his home. His wife said he went for a walk and hadn't returned."

"Captain, where's his security. He goes for a walk, and no one knows… see if you had been in his shoes…"

"Tyson, it's a problem. I'm on my way there with my team."

"Call me back, sir."

CHAPTER 84

The phone rang at six. Both Tina and Damien were up eating breakfast and preparing for what they knew would be a grueling day. Tina recognized the number and answered shaking her head slowly. Damien left her to deal with another call from Blake.

"Hello?"

"Good morning. Tina, if you had allowed me to explain, I could have told you what I was doing. Orders from authorities I can't name. You know how that is."

"Blake you've been lying to me from the start. I don't want to know what your involvement is. I'll read the reports. I assume you're not locked up or locked down. Why are you calling me?"

"We had a relationship. I want to know why? Why couldn't we, why didn't you try, I mean you could have asked questions if you were wondering about my actions."

"Blake, there's no need to rehash us. You did what you thought was best and your methods turned me off. You chose them. What's your involvement in this case? I still have to make sense of all of this."

"I'm working with Fulton, per Banks. He had some major concerns about some of the higher ups. Hey, you know, you go where you're told. Once I found out how dangerous these guys were, I wanted you out of the main frame. I mean, they're after those in the Cold Case Unit. From what I understand, your friends, they've ruffled a few feathers before becoming a part of the unit. So, I was checking the cases that Fulton brought to our attention, and it led me to them, as it did you. I was searching to find out who they used to make the changes in these cases. Illegal, I may add. Listen, you've got some heavy meetings today. I'll be looking into Forensics and the court documents. Can we meet at the end of the day to, say, compare notes?"

"No, there's no need. If you're giving your information to Banks, that's where my information is going. Do you think he may be deeper in this mess than what he's showing? Or, for that matter what about you? Why or when did you start working with Fulton? Listen, on second thought, I'll call you during the day and then we'll meet you."

"We? Oh, you and him?"

"Stop it! You sound like there's a problem. Seriously Blake, you can't… never mind. I'll call you."

Tina hung up the phone and plopped back on the couch letting out a frustrated breath. "Damien, can we get out of here. Oh, I need to talk with you before we leave."

Damien smiled as he nodded, taking a seat next to her. "Yes, ma'am. What's up?"

Tina told Damien her concerns and asked for his regarding her conversation with Blake." I don't understand what he wants me to say. Our relationship was crippled before this assignment."

"Maybe he thought he could work through it. I mean trying to keep his position secret could have had him thinking he'd ruin one or the other."

"One or the other? As far as I'm concerned, he was crippling the job and the relationship. Damien, I don't believe him. Working with Fulton because Banks ordered him to? No, something is not right."

"I reached out to Captain Worthy. Banks is still missing. It's still quietly kept. They haven't had any reason to think there's a problem, but his team, or at least those at the office, don't know where he is."

"And Blake claimed Banks gave him the go ahead to work with Fulton, I wonder when? If he's working with the 'untouchables,' maybe they got to Banks to fix things from the top down. Blake is their cover?"

"Well, there's a way to find out. You told him we would meet with him, but in the meantime, we'll reach out to Fulton."

Arriving at the precinct, Porter met the couple in the parking garage. He was on his phone as he passed them waving and pointing to the phone. Tina and Damien laughed at his gesture but understood, it probably was his family. They walked into Monday morning chaos. Miller and Knowles were standing at the door.

"Good morning, detectives, investigator," Miller spoke for the two of them.

"Good morning, Miller, Knowles. What's going on?"

"Sir, Captain Worthy told us to monitor the hall and the door. No one other than those working on this unit are to enter. Well, other than Mr. Fulton, he's here. We turned away Sergeant Braize, telling him they would meet at ten."

Tyson raised his brow and allowed Justlin and Porter to enter before him. "Miller, anything from Knight?"

"He's in the hospital sir. In a coma, no one knows anything other than the call received this morning. Montez and one of the officers assigned by the captain went to the hospital."

"And how are you this morning Knowles?"

"Sir," he answered smiling," I'm here for you."

"It's 'I've got you,' Knowles. Glad you're here."

Tyson shook his hand understanding the two were beginning to settle in. His phone rang as he entered the office. Worthy, hearing it ring stood from his seat in the conference room and waved, while shaking his head no. Tyson let the call go to his voice mail. Justlin and Tyson gave each other a concerned look and went into the conference area. Fulton was making himself a cup of coffee as Kai entered with paperwork for the group to discuss. Wilson and Stands entered greeting the others and taking a seat. The last to enter was Fabian who took a seat away from the conference table, near the captain's seat. Captain Worthy stood at the head of the table and looked at each of the staff members seated before him. He planned the meeting at the last minute deliberately, so no one had an opportunity to inform others. Each were attentively waiting to hear what the captain had to say.

"Good morning, good people. Seems like we've got more than what I thought would be put to rest by now. I invited two people you know but aren't usually included in many of our meetings. You all know Mr. Fulton and the head of the Special Operations Unit that's been working with us, Fabian Younger. I've spoken with those we were scheduled to meet with this morning and those meetings have been rescheduled to follow our meeting here. First let's address the elephants, or the missing pieces, to what's gone on these past few weeks. As you all know, Mr. Fulton has cases that have been brought to light. It appears that there's been tampering with evidence and cases within this unit. We've been trying to keep the investigation findings and information from each office until now. It's time to put the pieces together.

I want to clear up a few loose ends before we tie things together. Detective Knight has been severely injured. It is the thought of the medical staff that he wouldn't have lived much longer if they hadn't received the 9-1-1 call when they did. He was found in his vehicle and until Tuesday past, they had no identification or way of knowing who he was. He will be on close watch with two officers as long as needed. Prayerfully, he will pull through.

Blake Franks, the governor's assistant has been arrested and released. We have reasons to believe he will be arrested again, but I don't want to get ahead of myself. We have to be careful going forward and that's why I called this meeting this morning. Mr. Fulton was called this morning to meet with us since Blake contended that he was to work with him as ordered by Governor Banks. Governor Banks has denied such an order. It is my belief that Mr. Fulton may be in danger since his appeal may spark a reason for revenge with this group. Mr. Fulton has agreed to cooperate with this internal investigation as it may be valuable to his pending appeals."

The captain nodded to Fulton for his input as they had discussed.

"As you know, I've put in an appeal for three of my clients. I've pushed the Foster case forward awaiting the court's response, however my team has informed me that there are similar problems. After receiving information from the Cold Case Unit, Forensics, and reading my files from the court documents, there's been tampering in the files. I don't want to go to the media but…"

"Yeah, we don't need the threat if you're willing to work with us. Or is it you need protection because you fear they may do you in like they've done others."

Fulton started his response to Porter's obvious discomfort with him being in the room, he was interrupted by Tyson.

"Hold on man. We've known about the problem with reports, paperwork, and all else. You've brought reporters in and out of this office. So, before you cry out your explanation understand, we had reason to believe you were or are playing both sides. You had no intention on working with us so closely before, why now?"

Tyson calmed the storm temporarily but after the meeting that took more than an hour the team still wasn't comfortable with the captain's decision. The captain continued hoping to add a peaceful solution.

"We've openly shared all we know. It may not be much, but we've got, or I've got, a better understanding of what needs to be done. Fulton, man, I understand your dilemma, but until we get a handle on these murders, and what appears to be this assault, we can't allow you to join in this investigation. We do, however, need you to report any conversations, meetings, or new information you receive on your cases. We will continue to provide you with any information you need to move forward with your appeals. If you think you need protection, contact us immediately. Fulton, seriously, any direct contact from them, contact us. I want to thank you for being as patient as you have."

At that, Fulton stood and thanked the captain for inviting him to the meeting. He told Tyson he'd stay in touch throughout the week. Porter showed his disgust as he opened the door, a direct invitation for the lawyer to exit the room.

"Captain, you and Tyson may trust that dude, but it's something about him that ain't right."

"Porter, he's a lawyer. One who has been trying to discredit us for how long? Not one of us here has a reason to trust him but if he's got information about these guys or can get information, we need to be able to talk to him." Stands changed the direction of the conversation. "Captain, what's next? I mean with this Blake guy, who's on him?"

Justlin sent a text to Sharice hoping she would have responded before the meeting began. Phillip hadn't returned her call and she was in the dark about Banks.

"We've got eyes on him. We didn't want to alert him that we were on to his lie. So, for now he believes he's in the clear. If that leads him to Braize we'll know. Banks should be here by noon."

"Captain, I don't mean to question you, but why isn't Banks answering my calls and have you heard from Sharice?"

"They're together. Sharice thought there was a problem, as you did, with Blake. She's on the security team covering Banks."

"Well, who is with the Lieutenant?" Justlin's questions caused Fabian's eyebrows to rise.

"Captain, if I may." Justlin turned her attention to Fabian. She hadn't paid much attention to the captain's chosen security team. The man that stood before them looked as though he was a well-trained fighter. She could tell he was a confident, no nonsense, officer. She allowed her doubts to settle.

"As most of you know the lieutenant was moved to a military site out of state. There he is being seen by medical and secured by the staff on the base. It's impossible for anyone to get to him or near him. Pulley and her team were relieved and sent to be with the governor. As the captain said, they'll be here at noon. We think it better that all security of this nature be officers that the 'untouchables' don't know or recognize. They'll be in touch with me, Tyson, or the captain if there any problems."

Fabian took his seat and a moment of silence fell in the room.

"Okay, well if there are no other questions. The day, as abnormal as it may be, must go on without sending an alert to any other units. Tyson, Porter, we have a meeting with Braize. I told him we'd meet at ten in my office. So that gives you about an hour. I'm out of your way for now. Thank you all for indulging me and my tactics in this matter."

Fabian and the captain left the room leaving the officers to their thoughts.

"Hell, indulge in his tactics? He's in charge, what are we supposed to do? I mean really do any of you like dealing with these outside units?"

Justlin looked at Porter and gave him a smirk.

"Oh, not you Justice. I was talking about your boy Blake and that fake-ass lawyer. He'll be bringing Sayers back in here with her nosey—"

"Porter!! Can it, man. We get it. We all have feelings about this and none of us are overjoyed with dealing with these others. It's a must and we've got to stay together with this. Call Miller and Knowles in here. This needs to be dealt with now." Tyson shook his head and prepared to give the remaining staff an update.

CHAPTER 85

Justlin was the last to leave the office for the meeting with Worthy. She gathered the paperwork she thought would be a part of the discussion, reports Braize should have had. As she waited for the elevator, she noticed Fulton talking with Marcie in the hall. It seemed strange but the smile on Marcie's face gave her a brief moment of relief. She made a mental note to call Marcie after her meeting. She watched the traffic passing the two as they talked. Fulton seemed to be a bit nervous, turning his head and moving ever so slightly, not to be noticed, or so Justlin summarized. Just as the elevator's bell rang and the door opened, Marcie noticed Justlin. She nodded her head slowly, a signal she'd be waiting for the call. Justlin wondered what Fulton wanted. She was sure it was more than information in the files.

The special operation officers were few with regular assignments throughout the precinct. Fabian was working with Sergeant Sanders. The paperwork Justlin was sure she had submitted regarding the weekend chaos was now a part of the packet they were reviewing.

"Morning ma'am. You can go right in. They're still waiting for Braize."

"Thank you, and good morning." Justlin did as she was directed and walked into Captain Worthy's office. She was surprised Porter was not in attendance. "Hey, will Porter be joining us."

The men responded in unison. "No."

Justlin was taken aback a bit, but she took her seat without question. Sergeant Braize entered the office followed by Sheers and Simmons. Captain Worthy stood, trying not to show his surprise or rising anger. Tyson followed the gesture standing as well. The two waited for the explanation of the additional personnel.

"Captain, Tyson, this is…"

"We know who they are. The question is why are they here? This meeting is not being held for front line personnel. I'm sorry guys you can wait for your Sergeant in his office or wherever, not here."

The captain waited as they made no motion toward the door.

"Captain, we need to clear up a few things before we move forward. I'm sure you're aware of the under currents that are making problems for all of us. So, these officers can answer any questions and we can move on as one unit. I'm sure that's what this meeting is about, working together as one, right?"

Worthy looked at Tyson who took his seat. The captain caught on, he too sat and offered seats to the men. Braize looked at Justlin and smiled. She had no forethought to who the man would be. His appearance was sharp. She could tell from his demeanor he had military experience. That was what he wanted everyone to believe and Justlin knew he worked hard at it. He was a puppet to the "untouchables" and the officers being with him supported her assumption.

Sheers spoke up before the Captain could begin. "Sir, I'm sure you're aware of the tension the staff has been under since the death of the Chief and all else that has followed."

"Where's your union rep? I think a good bit of what you want to discuss should be presented to him."

"Can it Worthy. You and I know that's not the route we intend on taking. Things have gotten out of hand and there are people we all have to answer to. They're not looking to tidy things up before moving on with their plans. So, since you have your people in place for whatever it is you think we're about to do, this meeting is to openly tell you how things will be carried out going forward."

Justlin stood. "I don't think this conversation involves me, or the reports I've been sent here to review. Captain Worthy, I'll wait for your call to discuss these reports which I hope will put to rest my investigation and involvement in your precinct."

Sheers clapped his hands. "Your choice, sweetie, but I'm sure if the captain has problems with our proposal your office will be disheveled, and you'll be a part of it."

Justlin left without replying. Braize tapped his pen on the table in front of him. Tyson noticed immediately; the sergeant was nervous. Worthy followed their eyes and nodded in agreement.

"Well, let's get started. Captain how many years before you'll be retiring sir? Here or will you and your family relocate?"

Worthy folded his hands in front of him on the desk. "Braize, it doesn't matter. As you well know, this job has its own perimeters. As they change so does one's decisions. When are they replacing me is the better question? We've really been in limbo since the chief's murder, the attempted murder of the lieutenant, you know, I know you do.

Your group, or their group need not worry about me. I don't have any desire to push for what I know I deserve. I'm done with this."

"Captain, I think you'll be doing the city and the department a disservice if you leave."

"Sheers, this is not a conversation I'll be having with you at all. Once they appoint a chief and a lieutenant, I'm out."

Braize interjected before Sheers could answer. "That's not the plan Sir. Everyone has seen how you've handled this. Your discretion, the people you've chosen to work with as well as those you've kept at bay is notable. Those higher up the chain appreciate your work, your type of diplomacy."

"Who are they? Seems to me that as this unravels people are being exposed. I have no desire to cover for wrongdoings, especially murder."

"You want protection, I'm sure. For those who you've chosen as your team, your family, yourself."

Tyson couldn't keep quiet. "What the fuck is that Sheers, a threat? Are you serious? These scare tactics won't work."

"Well, we don't want to have to continue proving what we're willing to do. Listen, we all joined this organization to collect a salary, provide for our families, and retire to good living. This can be beneficial for everyone involved. We can't offer it to everyone, of course but on each level, we've been able to progress our agenda."

"What's the agenda Sheers? Obviously, you know we don't answer to you and your asshole buddies."

"Tyson, but you do. We've been steering things along for years. You, and your boss, your unit of flunkies, the captain here… do you really think we couldn't have stopped some of this shit along the way. Now, I'll admit, a few of us have made mistakes. We fixed what we wanted to fix and we're here to explain the conditions going forward."

"I'm still in charge. I'm not negotiating terms to be a puppet in the seat. Tell your people, they can have this shit, today. I'll walk away and won't look back, but what I won't do is sell my soul to be puppet for an agenda I don't agree with."

"Hmmm, and you?" Sheers looked at Tyson. "You've got a lot longer to be in this career than your guardian angel here. How will you be able to function when he's gone?"

"According to the governing rules. No different than we do now. As you said, we've got years left. When your boys fuck up, I won't be co-signing or covering for them. You keep them at bay, and I don't have a problem, none of my unit does. We won't be going to court, lying on documents, or backing up any criminal activity."

"I know you love to stand on your soap box…."

"Sheers, fuck you, and your racist team of assholes. Stay out of my way, but if we should bump heads, you'll be like others wondering where I came from and how I got to you."

"Now who is making the threats? Listen, we're showing our hand. We're trying to keep the wall of blue united in any way possible. I'll admit what most won't say. This type of employment wasn't meant for some people and we're just making sure the wrong folks don't try to take over. You know? We can't have some folks thinking they can move up the ranks and put their people in charge of us."

"Who is us? What the hell does that mean? Man, this ain't the place for that type of bull, not if we're trying to protect and serve."

"Tyson, you don't believe that shit, do you? Now I don't know what you guys and Braize have to discuss unless you're willing to tell us everything that's going on in the investigation. Captain, that would include the lieutenant's location."

"Braize, I see clearly now, you're just filling a spot. I'm sure we can talk about this shit at another time. Soon, you'll be moved as well. Sheers as I said, as soon as whoever appoints the new asshole for chief and lieutenant, I'm done. I don't care who it is. You've given me enough to leave the rest up to your people, whoever they are. I'm only concerned that those who sit on or protect my wall are okay. As far as I'm concerned, the meeting is over. Oh, and if you want to know about the lieutenant's location, contact the governor's office."

"Your special ops boys, captain?" Braize questioned as they stood to leave.

"Direct all your questions to the governor's office Braize. I follow what they tell me to do. If you don't mind, this is still my office, and we no longer have business to discuss."

The captain stood and waited for the three men to leave the office before he spoke again. He came from behind his desk and started pacing the length of the conference table.

"What was that, Cap?"

"Tyson call Justlin. I want background checks on all of them. They're deeper than just the average cop. I want to know what her office may have on them." He hit the button on his desk phone. "Sarge, send in Fabian please."

"I know you're going to think I'm crazy, but we may need Fulton after all."

Tyson could only shake his head in agreement. The "untouchables" had shown their hand.

CHAPTER 86

Tyson asked everyone to report to the conference room upon his return to the office. His phone rang again, it was then he remembered Samantha had called. He excused himself, answering the phone and hoping she wasn't calling just to be nosey.

"Is it afternoon yet? I guess, good afternoon, lady. How's your day going?"

"Rough morning, I'm just saying, listen when can we talk?"

"We do need to meet, and it is important. You and Fulton, uh nowhere near here. See if Fulton is free this evening. We need to meet as soon as possible; I'll text you the location."

"Wow, I was calling to see how the investigation was going. Okay, I'll call him. I thought you met with him this morning."

"I'll explain, just tell him we've got to make moves quickly. Listen, I've got to meet with my staff, but I'll text you before I leave this afternoon. Oh, the time doesn't matter."

Miller and Montez were the last to enter the conference area and the buzzing conversations ended when Tyson entered the room. The meeting lasted fifteen minutes. Tyson was direct, he answered most of their questions before they asked.

"So, we're fast pacing this folder thing?" Montez braced himself for the answer.

"Yeah, I guess you could say that. Listen, these people, and I'm sure we would be shocked who they've got in their pockets, they've made a mess. The only way they can clean it up is to openly say, hey, even if you know who we are, it won't matter. They think the repercussions they'll face in the department aren't serious enough to matter. They think this will all blow over. Whatever Fulton or Sayers need, provide it. I'll be meeting with them later. Pressure from the public is the only way to stop them. The media, lawsuits, and exposure will stop them or at least slow them down. We need to know as many of the players, so let's investigate any information we can find on the players that have exposed themselves. Montez, I'll need you to stay close to Knight. He may have information that we won't find in any reports. As usual family, this is an in-house matter. We do things differently for a reason. I don't need to tell you these people are dangerous. If we can weed them out, let's clean house."

Justlin took a deep breath as she left the office. Once again, stress was building. She wanted to scream, but decided a minute with Marcie would calm her nerves. She grabbed her cell phone, still waiting for Sharice to return her call, she sent a text with explanation points. Marcie met her outside the building where most stepped out to take a smoke break. There weren't many smokers, and no one occupied the bench closer to the parking lot.

"Wow, afternoon break, are you okay?" Marcie's question caused her friend to sigh deeply. She lifted her eyes to Marcie and her tears fell slowly. "Tina, you okay? What's up?"

"Marcie, we're working with… dangerous people. I didn't begin this career to lose my life trying to simply do my job. We've got to be careful simply because they want to be in charge. I thought, you know, it would be just a few bad cops. Marcie, there's a few in every department. I didn't call you, but Blake is one of them or he's working with them. His punk ass is probably thinking it will elevate his dumb ass in some way."

"Wait, Blake? Oh, hell no. They're definitely using him. Fulton stopped by to say he thanked me for helping him. He's got more than enough to cause a question or two about them in court. Maybe that will keep them at bay."

"Girl, long enough for us to retire and collect our pension? We need to be away from this mess. It's going to get ugly if they're not stopped."

"So, what's the plan? I'm sure your boys aren't taking a back seat to what's been found."

"What did Fulton find out?"

"He's got names, dates, and it's attached to his cases. He can take down enough to cause a stir."

"Sheers and how many others?"

"Tina, even the chief's name was mentioned in some of those cases. He signed off on a few of the reports and complaints. If Fulton discloses his findings, they could do serious jail time. Witness tampering, documents filed and then removed, there's some serious charges that can be brought up. Officers, supervisors, court employees, he's right Tina, they've sent some people to jail who were innocent.

"Stay away from Blake. Don't extend your help beyond your duties. Be aware of your surroundings and pay attention to Braize and those who he works with closely. Knight is in the hospital, they found him. Damn near dead, but they found him.

They have no problem killing to cover their agenda. There's got to be money, drugs, or something they're getting out of all of this. Whatever it is, it's dangerous."

The friends talked for another ten minutes and returned to their offices. Tina decided she was ready to leave, go home, go anywhere. She needed fresh air. There were times when she was an officer when she felt that way, needing to escape the chaos. Once she took the offer to work in the governor's office, she felt instant relief. No one knew or understood the pressure that was lifted. Although she was assigned to work with law enforcement, she could detach herself. She'd be dealing with paperwork and not people. She didn't need to know them to make determinations or recommend actions against them. This case, the staff she got to know, and Tyson were growing on her. She was too close to the people she had to review. She dialed Tyson's number as she remained in the hall. She couldn't go back to the office.

"Hey babe, where are you calling me from?"

"I'm in the hall. I need to get away from here, it's too much."

"Okay, give me a minute. I'll meet you at the car."

She disconnected the call without giving a response. Tyson looked at his watch and decided leaving would be a plus. He'd be meeting with Sayers and Fulton early in the evening. Whatever Tina needed he'd handle it so it wouldn't affect the arrangements. He dialed Worthy's number.

"Cap, I'm leaving early. Tina seems out of sorts so she's leaving early as well. Anything you need?"

"No man. I'm about to leave as well. What is it… three, yeah, I've done enough today. We need to get together, maybe tomorrow sometime to figure this mess out. It's, as I said, enough for today."

"Cap, I'm meeting with Fulton and Sayers. I think that's our out. We can expose them through the media and the court cases he's appealing. If what I think will work, we can cause a rumble."

"That's a thought. Fabian mentioned digging deeper into the evidence and backgrounds of those attached to what we've found. I've got some guys checking it."

"Hey, can we talk with Marshall? I mean he can expose all of them in exchange for his charge, right?"

"He hasn't asked for a lawyer. I guess he's just waiting to be charged."

"I wonder if Fulton would…" The men had the same thought.

"Damien, even if Fulton won't take his case, he knows what to ask. I can arrange for Fabian to take him to Marshall.

"I'll send you the time and place. Tell Fabian to meet with us tonight."

CHAPTER 87

"They'll help this mess how? Damien, I can't keep this up. They're dangerous. If you tip their hand, you may put everyone connected in danger, us, you may put us in danger. It's too much."

Silence fell between them.

"Tina, do you want to go home or to my house? I'm meeting with Fulton and Sayers tonight. It may be better if you stay where you're comfortable."

"Damien, I don't know… I need to clear my mind. I told Blake I'd meet him, or we would. I'll ask Sharice to meet us. He thought it would be you, she'll be a shock for him." Tina laughed before she continued her thoughts. "I just need a moment to breathe through this. Us, the job, the 'untouchables,' Blake, and the list goes on. I guess I just need to put everything into some sort of order, or… I don't know, Damien."

"Babe, whatever you need. I want us to be okay. I want us to be safe and our jobs to remain secure. I think I may be able to stop this circus or quell the performers. Honestly, I don't think it will stop completely. You and I both know what the root of all of this is. I can only do so much, and reports and court cases will always be unbalanced. We can only stop those we catch. It's like the criminals; the reason we have cold cases, we can only move forward with prosecuting the cases. We go where the evidence points. Tina, we can't go with what we know, they've got that covered. This mess started with the mistakes they made. The cases that Fulton has and is appealing is the answer. If he pursues them in court, according to his investigations and findings, the court will charge them. Lieutenant Marshall's testimony, the attempt on his life will add credence to Fulton's complaint. We won't get them all, but the media coverage will put the public's eye on to them and those like them."

"Damien, how do we protect us? What protection will we have if we're a part of Fulton's attack on the department and those we work with? They'll know we were a part of him dismantling the so-called 'untouchables.'" Tina's voice showed more than her anger, she was visibly scared.

"Babe let's not worry about how. All we are obligated to do is give the information as requested by the attorney. We don't have to add admissible evidence but if asked by anyone's lawyer we must comply with what we have. Fulton needs to tell us what he needs, and we'll provide what we have. Now the difference in this will be if we don't have it… we'll look for it. No one need to be wiser. If it removes a few of them, so be it. We won't catch them all, but Sheers and his asshole partners have to go. They threatened Worthy Tina. I guess if he said he wanted to go for the open position or move up in the ranks, who knows how far they would take it. Hell, we need to keep our eyes open for him."

The radio could be heard faintly in the background as their ride to Damien's home came to an end. The conversation faded into their feelings as he pulled into his driveway and noticed Sonya standing on the porch.

"No, I ain't in for this shit today." He didn't wait for Tina to notice the woman who was facing the opposite direction. She didn't rush to join Damien who was closer to the front of the house. She could hear Damien as she got closer and walked toward them on the front porch.

"Oh, I see why you're upset. I interrupted what? A hook-up date?"

"Sonya, why are you here? I know I told you don't come back here."

"You and I need to talk, seriously. We need a better plan if I'm going to be in our daughters' lives."

"What?"

It was then that Tina walked past Damien and put her hand out. He placed the keys in her hand, and she proceeded to the front door.

"Damien don't stand out here talking. Invite her in and discuss whatever is needed. Your front porch isn't the proper setting."

Damien stepped back making way for Sonya to follow Tina through the front door. Tina put her things down and went upstairs.

"Humph. So, she has access to everything, huh?"

"What plans don't work for you Sonya? You set up the arrangements for the girls or don't you remember that. If you need to change things talk to the girls and my parents. I'll go to court with you to change whatever documents are necessary. I won't go back and forth with you and no negotiations will be held here. I'll talk to the lawyer tomorrow to start the paperwork."

"What paperwork Damien? There's really no need for that. You and I can just agree, but it needs to be easier. I can't get to your parent's home for visitation."

"And that's my problem how? They can come to where you live, stay with you for the weekend visits, or meet you for outings. Those arrangements are to be made and agreed between you and them. My parents know to work with you whenever they can. If things can't work out, then and only then will I intervene. So, what's the problem?"

"I don't have a place to live, that's the problem. Damn, you're not making this easy."

Damien couldn't make it any clearer. Sonya wouldn't give up and he knew it would have to be another day in court. He looked at her leaning on the kitchen counter. She smiled and tilted her head to the side. He saw his daughters in her appearance. It was one of the reasons he hadn't fought harder about guidelines and restrictions for her visits. His parents didn't object to any arrangements, but the girls were older, and their schedules demanded more of their time.

"I don't know what to tell you. What are you expecting me or my parents to do? You wanted visits and you can't expect the visits to be here. You can visit at my parents' home, and that's easier because that's where they live."

"So, you're refusing to help me or assist me in finding a place to live?"

"That's not my responsibility."

"Damien, I'm not working. I can't afford the places near your parents' home or here."

"Sonya, I can't help you. Call a car, we're done here."

"No, the car is waiting. We're nowhere near done. Don't change your number."

Damien frowned and shook his head as he escorted her to the front door. He watched as she crossed the street and got into the silver Honda waiting. He slammed the door and decided he needed a drink.

"Damien, does she understand the agreement you made. I think she's looking for you to still be a part of her life."

Damien stopped pouring his drink. "You want one? You need one, if you think that's going to happen. Look she's tried less in the past. She's beginning to understand I've moved on and she's trying any and everything to get me to pay attention to her and her fake needs."

"I was just wondering how your daughters feel about her not having a place to live and what you're doing about it."

"Baby, they're teens. The girls haven't had a decent visit with her since they were in grammar school. She ruined the relationship with them years ago. They've been to family therapy with me and my parents. We deal with her because the court order demands it. She has family and friends, they'll help her. She has money too. Listen, it's over, just like you and Blake. It's us now. I'm not rushing things with any of us. I'd love for you to meet the girls once this mess is over."

"Listen, I'm going to shower and take a nap. Sharice won't be able to meet with me until six, we're meeting Blake at seven. What time are you meeting with the lawyer and the mouthpiece?"

"Hey, c'mon Justice, baby that ain't you."

"It's gonna have to be to get through all of this shit. Oh, and yeah, I'd love to meet the girls as soon as possible. Maybe Sonya will realize she has to get her shit together too."

Damien watched as she walked to the stairs. She smiled teasingly, but he deliberately ignored the hint. He had calls to make.

CHAPTER 88

It was close to six and although Sharice didn't seem worried about Blake meeting her and Tina, Tina was watching her phone for the time. She chose a restaurant close to the downtown area where there would be people. The interviews with officers and supervisors, the reports and missing evidence, the words that weren't spoken between co-workers, told a story that she and Sharice agreed needed to be told. The ladies agreed with Damien. The "untouchables" would have to be picked apart.

"You think he backed out? I mean, maybe Braize and Sheers told him to lay low. I know Banks didn't know he was in as deep as he is. You know those calls Phillip mentioned to Fulton? They were just calls; no conversation. He reached out to Fulton but there was no connection, unless they made one later."

"No, Fulton denied speaking with him. Here he is." Tina spoke silencing Sharice's response.

Blake was making his way through the crowded restaurant.

"You picked this spot. Not what I thought it was from the outside. Is it always this crowded?"

"Blake, have a seat. We're not here for the crowd." Tina couldn't contain her annoyance.

"Humph, good to see you didn't bring your man, like you needed protection. Sharice, how are you?"

"This ain't no reacquaintance meeting Blake. What are you doing? No, why are you doing this?" Tina questioned trying to remain calm.

"What, you ladies have it all wrong. I'm trying to keep you out of it. I mean, at least you Tina. Sharice has been assigned to be in this, but you have a choice."

"And you? Blake your background says one thing and…"

"And I'm doing what I'm trained to do. Your boy and his handpicked crew has to go. No, I don't agree with the methods Sheers and the boys use, but hey, it works."

"What works! Blake they're harming more than the precinct. They're dangerous for the community. They're dangerous for all of us."

"You don't understand. Once we put the right people in position, its going to be alright."

"Blake! You don't believe that these people are about to give you, me, or anyone like us the ability to uphold the law. I know you don't believe that."

"Wait, Tina. Blake, what have they promised you?" Sharice waited for him to answer.

"Look, Tina, you've got to stop this investigation. The numbers, the evidence Fulton is claiming he has, will hurt the precinct and the community more."

"Tina, they've brainwashed him. What do they have on you? What have they promised you?"

"Sharice, I just want Tina out of this. I've talked to Banks…"

"Blake, like you did with Fulton? You're full of shit. What did they promise you?"

Damien waived for the waiter to come to the table. The waiter took the drink orders from the trio and asked would they be having dessert.

"Go ahead, Samantha. I know you want the chocolate cake."

"Stop, Damien! Don't you ever stop?" They laughed despite the debate they ended minutes earlier.

"So, do you think we really can pull this off?" Samantha asked the men; her doubt was diminishing.

"Yeah, we have most of what we need. I mean it's the evidence I was using in the appeal process. They can't get away with what's presented in court with the media staying on top of it. Usually, one fades and the guilty parties escape punishment. Damien is right. We won't get all of them, but with the three cases causing a stir, they'll back up a bit or be exposed. The ones in the precinct will get paid to do the time, but those who sit higher don't want to be touched with proceedings and the possibility of losing what they've built over the years."

"So where is Banks in all of this? We know Blake is caught up, who else in that office?"

"Man, we've been seeing bits and pieces coming from his office, but I think it's all been steered by Blake. Now that we know Blake is involved, I can have my office check on it closer."

"So, when does it hit the paper? I mean, do I mention what we know now?

"No. I haven't gotten the dates for the appeal. As soon as the court grants them, it's a go. We can't show our hand yet and even when we're waiting to appear only bits and pieces can be leaked."

"Samantha you can talk about Lieutenant Marshall and Detective Knight. Link them in an indirect way with the chief's murder. Ask those questions and see what it stirs up."

"Okay, umm." She looked at Damien and smiled.

"Umm what?"

"Do I get the protection you promised Fulton?" She asked teasingly.

Fulton raised his eyebrow and leaned his ear toward Tyson.

"Samantha! You got this man here thinking he's not going to keep a close eye on you." Damien teased.

Fulton shook his head and looked to her for the response. She picked up her glass and took a sip of her wine.

"We've got you. It won't be one of the regulars though. All Ops officers for this. Officers that they can't identify."

"Oh, okay. So, when do we start?" Fulton and Sayers were anxious to hear the response.

"Listen, don't change your norm. Get together and come to the office. Once you come in, we'll assign officers to you both."

Banks began to pace the length of the conference table while Worthy uttered his disgust about the impromptu meeting with Sheers.

"Man, he's got more than balls. I'm telling you; he's pushing things too far. The meeting wasn't called for the 'untouchables.' Braize didn't even say anything. Nothing, Sheers is close to whoever is at the top."

"Listen, there's not much I can say Dennis until we name the players. We've got to get those at the top to tear them down."

"Who told you to switch your security teams? Can we start there? Someone knows something."

"It was Marshall. He sent a message, Sharice delivered it. We switched teams once he was on base. It didn't alert anyone since Sharice and Fabian arranged coverage for him. Those officers and Sharice came and got me from the office yesterday. No one was notified until today about the coverage."

"What was the message?"

"Dennis, it was simple. They know."

"They know what?"

"They knew he wasn't dying and that I wasn't buying their story about him being in the driver's seat. I guess if they attempted to see him in the hospital, well… We started an investigation into Marshall and the 'untouchables' before Michaels was murdered. We thought Marshall was running things. Michaels kept my unit at bay. We knew he had been compromised. We didn't suspect Blake and he kept pushing Marshall and Michaels. The standstill came with the murder and the attempt on Marshall. I like this plan you've come up with. Let's put it to work and see what snakes come out."

"I don't like it Banks. My family, hell, your family, and our staff… this is a risk."

"Our careers, it all has always been a risk. You know that. Dennis if we're going to slow them down, they've got to be exposed."

"Who's the judge?"

"I'll work on it. Fulton put in the appeals, let me see who's on the calendar."

"Alright, now what about Blake?"

"Let him chase his tail. He was exposed before he really got started. Sharice and Tina will lock him down, I'm sure. Sheers and Braize will keep him at bay. He likes playing both sides and everyone knows this about him. Listen, let's stay in touch. My family is leaving tonight. I'm glad this is near the end of the school year. It's nothing for them to go to my wife's family in Florida."

"I hear you." Worthy thought about his family staying longer at their location than he initially expected.

The captain stood and the two men shook hands and walked to the office door. Met by the ops officers they said their farewells again. Worthy felt better talking with Banks, but he wondered if Banks understood what they were facing.

CHAPTER 89

"Listen man, I know I can be an ass at times…"

"Porter, we need to work with these people regardless. Now you can work through this or work in the office and I'll pull Stands. I can't have you going off on the man because you can't trust him. Hell, we don't really know who to trust, but we need him and Sayers to pull this off. It's a wild shot, I know, but if we can get those who are rearing their heads, let's cut them off at their necks."

"Shit, we both know a quick and precise way to get rid of them."

"Now, Detective Porter, you're an officer of the law. What are you implying?"

"You cute. What does your girl think about this?"

"Man, Sonya has been here; Blake came to her home; you know about Boone being shot and all else. She's still hanging with me."

"Yeah, and she ain't the criminal. You're moving forward. Who is the Blake guy? What's his story?"

"Not sure what his story is yet. Sharice and Tina are meeting with him. He was dating Tina."

"Damien?? Nah, shit man, I thought you'd be in the clear. Is she tangled in the mess in some way?"

"You know what man, you really are off the hook. No! She's pissed about his involvement and that was before they went to meet with him."

Tina called to say she would be with Sharice and return to her home later. She wanted to stay at home for the evening. Damien didn't agree but he didn't want her to know, he too was worried about the possibility of trouble.

"Sonya? She needs a man in her life. I mean other than you. She needs to move on."

"Glad you see that. I am not seeking to be the man in her life. The girls are old enough to decide whether they want to spend time with her."

"You know where she wants to spend her time. Now that your dating, may be serious, she's wilding out."

"Man, she had the nerve to say she needed me to help her find a place to stay. Man, I can't deal with her and her shit. If you remember I offered her an apartment after the divorce."

"I remember. I remember you allowed her to stay with you for a year. She probably thought you'd offer your home again."

"Listen man. I'm no longer dazed about losing my marriage or my wife. I'm not even in that fog that invited me to her bed every now and then. I'm done with her and her antics. Like I said, she's about to be upset with her girls. They've got teenage schedules and my parents, and I have adjusted to them not needing us to hold their hands."

"I hear you. Listen, that's my doorbell. I'll see you in the morning. You know I'm down with whatever. I guess that will include that fake-ass…"

"Goodnight, man. See you in the morning."

Damien hung up the phone and returned to his den where music was playing low. Turning up the volume he rocked his head to the sound of Boney James, one of his favorite jazz artists. He hadn't had the time to sit and relax with a book or good music for weeks. It was then he realized Tina was right. They needed a moment to breathe. Taking in cases hadn't been a worry for the past four years. His cases seemed easier to solve in the early years of him becoming a detective. Once he began naming cases, teasingly of course, it seemed those were the ones chosen to break him or his team. Most in the department would attest that it was those broken moments that gave him the position in the Cold Case Unit. He took on the challenge rather than the transfer, an option he knew came from the under currents caused by the "untouchables."

Damien was the senior to his team as well as those who he knew were connected to Sheers and his boys. He couldn't remember when problems with the group surfaced, but Sheers had initiated an argument with him when they were both officers on the beat.

It was years before he made rank, but he was given special assignments and coupled with many of the political personnel early in his career. Sheers argued with the union and supervisors about rotating the jobs and they passed his complaints over calling them "officer tears." Once Tyson's connections got promotions, they saw to it to give opportunities to him and those he worked with over the years. When Tyson became Lieutenant, then Detective he did as his mentors had in the past. Porter, Stands, and Wilson moved with him up the ranks and within the departments.

Sheers took no backseat to addressing each special unit, assignment, arrangement made for Tyson to shine. As his cronies grew in number so did his anger. It took only one threat to stop him. Tyson told him he'd speak with the mayor and the council regarding his interference in the cases assigned to him. Although Sheers would bark every now and then, the negative reports and nudging stopped. Now that the detective was able to sit and allow himself to sink in deep thought, he decided to dial a number he hadn't dialed in years.

"Good evening your honor. How are you?"

"Tyson, well wouldn't you know it. I just told the wife that I had to get down to the precinct to see you boys. How the hell are you?"

"Doing well, sir. Always thinking of you and your family. How's retirement treating you?"

"It's good. You know we stayed here because of the school system. The youngest graduates this year. I'm hoping we've seen enough winters. I want to go south. Do some traveling first and then pick a spot where I can build and fish."

"Build? What you building…another town?"

There was a hearty laugh shared between them. Mayor Thomas Allen was the mayor for three terms. His wife Audrey was a councilwoman for most of his time in office. Their staff, city officials, and the citizens loved them.

"No, son. Those days are over. How's Worthy? I bet he's ready to get out of there with all that mess going on. Hey, did y'all get rid of those crazy boys? What was that kid's name? Sheers, that's it. Did he and his crew leave or get fired? I remember everyone having a time with them. I told Audrey he was a ticking time bomb. Just couldn't get enough on him."

"Your Honor, I need your opinion. I think we finally got enough."

CHAPTER 90

Two weeks passed before Fulton and Sayers asked to meet with Tyson regarding the appeal for the Foster case. The precinct had been "quiet" which worried Worthy more than Tyson, Justlin or Banks. Justlin returned to the governor's office where she avoided Blake daily. Investigator Pulley and her team remained assigned to the Governor. Lt. Marshall was slowly working through therapy and was still being monitored by the Special Operations Unit. It hadn't been determined how they would handle his case, but it was confirmed he'd be a witness against Sheers and his merry band of men.

Detective Knight was moved temporarily to another hospital and was under close watch as he continued to heal. No longer in a coma, he was recovering slowly. There was no other information shared regarding his condition and he too was under the eye of the Special Operations Unit. Fulton was seeking to win his three appeals while building his case against the precinct. Marshall and Knight stepping forward as witnesses would connect the "untouchables" to the murder of Chief Walter Michaels, the attempted murder of Lieutenant Maurice Marshall, and the rape of Tammilyn Watson. Although each of those cases would have to be heard in separate courts. The reports would establish a pattern, the basis and reason for the release of Julian Foster, and his other clients. He'd be seeking reparations for all.

Montez entered the conference room to let the lawyer and the reporter know Tyson would be with them shortly. They nodded they understood, not in a rush they continued their conversation.

"We've got a little more than a month. Samantha, I can't say I'm totally confident. Tyson said he had good news, that's why we're here."

"So, continue the reporting as we have?"

"Yes, definitely. Get a response from Tammilyn and Ms. Foster, Julian's aunt. What's their reaction to finally having a court appearance? Let them rehash what happened, you know the angle. Also, see if you can talk with forensics. They were very helpful with my office investigations. Oh, I hear Tina Justlin is back at her office. We'll have to reach her for a comment as well."

Tyson walked in the room and shook Fulton's hand. He gave Sayers a teasing wink.

"Good mid-morning folks. How's it going, we're getting close huh?"

"Yeah, really thanks. I didn't expect to get a date for at least a few more months." Fulton's relief was evident.

"I wasn't sure you got the news. I wanted to let you know I did. My contacts called late Monday, so I figured you needed to get ready if they hadn't informed you."

"That's what usually happens when it involves misconduct. You know politics, anything that will cause them discomfort, they attempt to get rid of. Man, you don't know how hard this has been. Years of this. It's not just the Foster case, it's all that has been the rumble under the case."

Sayers leaned in and interrupted Fulton's thought. "Murder, rape, how far will they go before someone stops them?"

"I hear you. Let's hope this causes some closed ears and eyes to open. I can't tell you how, but I can say that if we can help, we will. Montez and Miller are here for you. We've pulled the files for the cases you asked about. We can't produce what's not found in the files, but they've been instructed to lead you where the information may be. You know, a little more than when you started questioning this unit. We've got things in better order now. I've got a copy of the final report filed in the governor's office. That should be a start."

"I appreciate it man. I don't think there's much more needed. The main connections other than the reports are the witnesses. Do you think I'll be able to talk with Knight or Marshall?"

"Fulton, I'm going to be honest with you. I know Marshall could care less about representation. I don't know about Knight. My concern is who they'll send as a representative. He's still not really in any condition to talk for a long period of time. Depending on how long the case is or when he would be needed, I'd talk with Worthy and see what his thought is about it."

"Hey, maybe getting an angle from the union would be good for reporting. I'll talk to the union rep and see if they want to comment on any of this." Samantha's smile made Tyson laugh. "What, that's not good? What?"

"No, just the way you said it, that's all. Go for it. I don't know that they would answer any questions."

"He's right Samantha. They usually take a back seat to speaking up about the actions of officers, good or bad."

"I know someone who will. We'll see." She smiled again writing on her pad. "How do I reach Investigator Justlin?"

Tyson knew the question was leading into sarcasm, but he decided to get it in the open.

"I'll get Kai to give you her card. It has her direct line on it. Anyone else?"

Sayers rolled her eyes and smiled. She knew he ducked the question professionally. She wanted to know if they were still connecting after hours. Now that Justlin was back in her office was she still sexing the handsome detective? Tyson stood, an indication the meeting was over.

"If you need anything else don't hesitate to call. Man, best of luck. I hope this starts a snowball effect."

"It will. I've got two other cases following the Foster Case. The antics are the same, bad cops, bad reports, missing information, unlawful arrests, and false imprisonment. Someone's got to speak up. Thanks man, this really helps. Hey, don't you want to tell me how you got this case moved up?"

"Nope. Don't know about that. How would I have a voice in those circles?"

Damien could only smile. Fulton extended his hand. He and Damien said goodbye.

"Hey, Damien can we talk later?" Sayers whispered as they exited the conference room.

"We can talk now if you like. Don't know what the rest of today or later will be like."

"Hmmm, should I ask?"

Tyson smiled. She was beautiful but had always been too forward for him. He thought she'd be a better fit for Porter. He liked pushy females.

"No, you don't have to ask. Yes, we're still together."

"Oh, okay. She doesn't understand you. You know that, right?"

"I know. I ain't easy. That's what turns you on, right?"

"Huh?"

"Samantha, it's not hard to understand. You and I are friends, nothing more. It's okay, we'll probably always be just friends. You know how that goes right? Let me know how you make out with the union rep."

The days in the Cold Case Unit were finally operating with a focus on incoming cases and those with active leads. Forensics sent regular reports and it was becoming easier to assign the staff to cases and get timely results and closer. Porter, Stands, and Wilson felt instant relief. The Monday morning meetings were no longer a lecture or a chaotic debate. Miller and Knowles were fitting in, a part of the team, although they were still considered "new boots." Everyone had become comfortable with their assignments. Tyson didn't anticipate the email that came across his desk shortly after

Fulton and Sayers left the office. He picked up the phone and dialed Worthy's number for an explanation.

"Hey, Sarge. Is he in the office?"

"He's on the phone with the mayor's office. Excuse the expression but it sounds like the shit finally hit the big fan. Everyone is getting it. I think it's the mayor's way of cleaning house before this court case, if you know what I mean. All promotions, temporary assignments, special operations coverage, have been put on hold. Yeah, his office must approve it. You want to call him back, come up to the office, or do you want me to give him a message."

"Damn, what did the mayor find out?"

"Whatever it is, he's on it. Maybe he got a call or two. Tyson, it's about time. How long have we been asking for someone to step in?"

"You're right, step in or step on them."

Tyson hung up the phone as Porter entered his office. He stood in silence.

"Say it man. I don't know what's going on."

"You know what's going on. Ole' boy called in a few favors to move that case to a court where it could be trusted. Once he told them what was going on, man… there's those that don't want their neck in that noose. You know how it was. Mayor Allen ran this place. It didn't matter who it was, they all fell in line when he spoke. Program and community leaders, all the precincts, and the courts too. Politicians as well as the governor's office backed that man. He called some folks, I bet. Now if some of those seats owe him, like our new mayor, or anyone he has moved in place, whew bro, payback time. Fulton will have a field day but before then, heads are rolling. So, how's our captain?"

"Don't know. I just tried to call. I was going to call Tina; maybe she got wind of something."

Porter pulled the chair across from Tyson's desk closer and looked toward the phone.

"Man, you'll never change, will you?"

"No. Hurry up before Stands and Wilson catch on that I'm in here."

By the end of the conversation with Justlin, Tyson's office was full. It looked like another morning meeting. He hung up the phone and sighed.

"We got 'em, at least it seems that way. Stand by for some drastic, drastic changes. Until these investigations are over, there will be some internal moves made. A few officers and other personnel will be moved around or put on leave. If their names are sited in the case, they may be on suspension. The union reps have been notified and are meeting with the mayor's office. This is based on the case Lt. Marshall has opened on those who attempted to kill him. He's been joined in a second case opened by Detective Knight. These coupled with Fulton's case has come to the attention of the mayor and he's trying to quell the attention of the media."

"Sayers didn't get wind of this? That's hard to believe." Wilson stated, shaking her head.

"You know she's right there in the midst of it all, her and that backstabbing street lawyer."

In unison the group shouted," Porter!"

...AND

Tina set the table. She was looking forward to the candlelit dinner and night after a week of surprises. Damien agreed he didn't want to share his Friday any other way. Their time together changed when she went back to her regular assignments. She spent most of her week preparing other investigations. She promised herself there would be no other investigations that would interrupt her livelihood. Although she would admit, she loved the relationships that developed. She put the wine bottle in the center of the ice bucket and heard the oven bell indicate the lasagna was ready. Celebrating Damien's birthday was a planned gathering for the next day, but Tina wanted to add to his weekend. The phone rang, just as she was about to turn on the music she had selected for the evening.

"Hello, Tina? Can I call you that, or should we keep it formal? I really don't know, but since you've been with my children's father and don't seem to be one of his flings—"

"Sonya, what can I do for you?" Tina answered wondering how she got her number. She shook loose the thoughts of what to say and then remembered she was a public figure with a business card. Her cell number was on her cards.

"Hmmm…" Sonya was taken off guard not expecting Tina to be so pleasant. "Uh, as you well know, it's Damien's birthday this weekend. I don't think the girls appreciate not being with their father to celebrate his day. I was going to speak with him about it, but you'd understand better. Maybe you need to persuade him to spend the day with them."

Tina laughed, it was keeping her from losing her temper. Her doorbell rang and she laughed again knowing it was Damien at the door. "Hold on, please." She muted the call.

"Hey, you're in a good mood. How was your day?" Damien leaned in and gave her a kiss. Tina unmuted the call.

"I'm sorry Sonya, now you said it would help if I persuaded him to spend the day with the girls?"

Damien stopped in the middle of the floor. He shook his head no with a questioning look.

"Yea, family time. You do know that it matters right?"

"I do indeed. Did the girls tell you they wouldn't be seeing him this weekend?"

"Listen, I don't know what he's told you, have you met the girls?"

"Well…"

"You can tell the truth. I know his sorry ass is keeping you in the dark. We've been battling the thought of getting back together, but he's been blaming it on the girls. I knew you hadn't met them. Listen, I don't want him to hurt you in this process."

"Oh, you don't have to worry about me. I'm good, believe me. Sonya, why did you really call?"

"Huh? I just told you."

"Oh, I heard you. It's not what you said, it's what you didn't say. You didn't say that you tried to stop the girls from coming to Damien's celebration tomorrow. You did know they are a part of that celebration, right? They mentioned it to you right? I believe it was when you told them they needed to press their father about me being their second mom. Dirty trick lady. Anyway, hold on Damien is here. You should speak with him about arrangements."

"Damien? Damien? Wait, you can't… Damien?"

"Sonya, why are you calling her with this mess? Why are you calling her at all?"

"Damien, you've got to put a stop to this. The girls…"

"The girls are fine, you know that. I believe you spoke with them this week, right? That's all you need to know. I don't worry about your relationship with them, don't worry about mine. We're good, they're good, and they're good with Tina. Move on Sonya, you deserve to get yourself together."

"Or?"

"What do you mean or…"

"You always give off a damn threat, Damien. Or what?"

Damien shook his head and disconnected the call.

"Babe, I am so sorry. She shouldn't call you with this mess; she shouldn't call your number at all. Why does she have it?"

"My business card, I guess. It's okay, I can block her number. Did you talk to Worthy? Hey, let's eat and talk, then we can truly have the evening to ourselves."

Tina prepared their plates and Damien could only smile each time she brought another dish to the table. They held hands and prayed. It wasn't prearranged but moved by the spirit and releasing more than a month's worth of anxiety, they both said, "Amen."

"So, what did Worthy say? Banks was a bit hushed by all the goings on. He did say Blake would lose his position and be moved immediately."

"Temporarily reassigned?"

"He didn't say. Just that we would be hiring for his position. Who's been temporarily reassigned?"

"A few of the names that the investigation turned up and Worthy."

"Worthy? Where are they sending him?"

"He's the interim until another chief and lieutenant is assigned to the offices."

"Do you think they'll appoint him chief?"

"Hey, above the clouds, I don't doubt anything these days."

"Above the clouds? What does that mean?" Tina laughed at the thought. "Is that another Porter saying?"

"See, you know him better than you thought you did. Yes, his analogy of those who work in the upper room offices. Sorry, another saying of his."

They shared a laugh. "So, how long will Worthy work with them before he takes heed to his wife's warning."

"Worthy loves his job. She knows it. They'll be fine, but if they move him under what he thinks is a thumbprint of the past, he'll retire. The mayor won't let that happen unless their positions are secure. It's like a building. If the foundation is weak…"

"Sssh…eat." Tina could only smile knowing he meant more than the job.

...THEN

The small group of men listened as the agitated voice spewed anger and frustration. The meeting was called as a reminder of what could and would be done if things weren't handled accordingly. Sheers turned up the volume on the computer for himself and Simmons. The zoom conference call would not be recorded or, as the voice stated, repeated. It was crucial that there be a hold on all business throughout the township until further notice. The call ended without questions. The group would be notified individually as to their next meeting or assignment.

"It's bull man. That damn lawyer ain't got shit on the group. Why stop the norm? We can't have others running the street pickups."

"Simmons, did you hear him say wait for the assignments? We can't have business as normal. Eyes are on us, hell it's a spotlight. I knew Lugo going to the chief's house started this…"

"Shit! Man, I can't go down with…"

"With what? Just be cool, ride it out. Keep your mouth closed and this will be over before it gets started."

"Man, they didn't transfer you. I'm sitting on my ass assigned to phones all day. Dispatch? What the hell is that?"

"It's safe. That's what it is. You're out of sight."

The phone rang before Sheers could give any other words of encouragement. He walked to his desk, hoping he didn't have any further instructions to follow. He listened as his orders were clear. There was a pause. He answered slowly, trying not to sound confused.

"Yeah… Uh, no. I was told to report to the sergeant Monday morning. I usually go to his office anyway… No, what is it about?"

Simmons could tell the change in his partner's demeanor. Sheers disconnected the call and threw his phone against the wall.

"What? What now?"

Sheers turned his back trying to calm his mounting anger as he holstered his loaded weapon.

"I'm suspended pending further investigation. I'm to report to the union representative for the Foster case."

"What? Why? Hell, you weren't there or involved in any of those reports. I made sure of that."

"Someone talked. That's the only way man. I watched the streets in that area for years. Someone talked. That night everything was done like clockwork. I sent them into that girls place to be roughed up a bit. What they did, how they did it, didn't matter. There was no money or drugs, just shut her up, you know? I didn't give the go ahead for her to be raped. Someone talked."

"What did they say? What could they say? Everyone knows the orders come from the office, not us."

"Did you talk with that investigator, Justlin again? I remember you and Boone had to meet with her."

"No. After the initial meeting we never met again. Then you know Boone was taken out. So, I guess her questions held no lead."

Simmons remembered the conversation he had with Fulton during the weeks that followed. The lawyer met with him and explained he would keep him on his list of witnesses. If Simmons thought he needed to go into witness protection all he had to do was call. It was time to make that call… but first he needed to convince Sheers to let him leave.

Sheers was mumbling to himself as he turned to face Simmons. Anger and fear reshaped his face into a frightening stare. Boone being killed was a clear indication that Sheers followed orders. Sheers explained how his friend, Boone, was killed to protect the group. Sheers pointed the loaded weapon as Simmons squeezed his cell phone and prayed silently. He asked Sheers why. He never got an answer.

Other Novels by Nanette M. Buchanan

Family Secrets Lies and Alibi's
A Different Kind of Love
Bruised Love
Skeletons Behind The Closed Door
Gossip Line
Bonded Betrayal
Scattered Pieces
The Stranger Within
The Perfect Side Piece
The Hustler's Touch
Duplicity
The Corner Pew

Non-Fiction
Managing Your Madness – A Lifestyle of Deliberate Redirection

Children's Books
Marquis The Great
Heaven Sent Kisses

Purchase Your Copies Today at

www.NanetteMBuchanan.com

Books are also available in Kindle, Nook and other ebook formats

Made in the USA
Middletown, DE
23 September 2024